THE DARK ROAD

A JONMARC VAHANIAN COLLECTION: VOL II

GAIL Z. MARTIN

CONTENTS

The Dark Road	v
Introduction	ix
Bad Blood	1
Haunts	33
Cursed	63
Brigands	91
Bleak Harvest	121
Hard Choices	145
Dead Reckoning	175
Desperate Flight	201
Death Match	223
Guardian	325
Smuggler	429
BONUS	525
About the Author	573
Other books by Gail Z. Martin	575

THE DARK ROAD

A JONMARC VAHANIAN COLLECTION:
VOL II

By Gail Z. Martin

SOL

ebook ISBN: 978-1-939704-76-4
Print ISBN: 978-1-939704-77-1

The Dark Road: Copyright © 2018 by Gail Z. Martin. Bad Blood © 2014, Haunts © 2014, Cursed © 2014, Death Plot © 2015, Brigands © 2015, Bleak Harvest © 2015, Hard Choices © 2015, Dead Reckoning © 2015, Desperate Flight © 2015, Death Match © 2017, Guardian © 2017, Smuggler © 2017, The Long Mile © 2016, The Summoner © 2007

The right of the author to be identified as the author of this work has been asserted in accordance with the Copyright, Designs and Patents Act 1988.

No part of this book may be reproduced in any form or by any electronic or mechanical means, including information storage and retrieval systems, without written permission from the author, except for the use of brief quotations in a book review.

This is a work of fiction. Any resemblance to actual persons (living or dead), locales, and incidents are either coincidental or used fictitiously. Any trademarks used belong to their owners. No infringement is intended.

Cover art by Lou Harper
SOL Publishing is an imprint of DreamSpinner Communications, LLC

To fans and family, for believing.

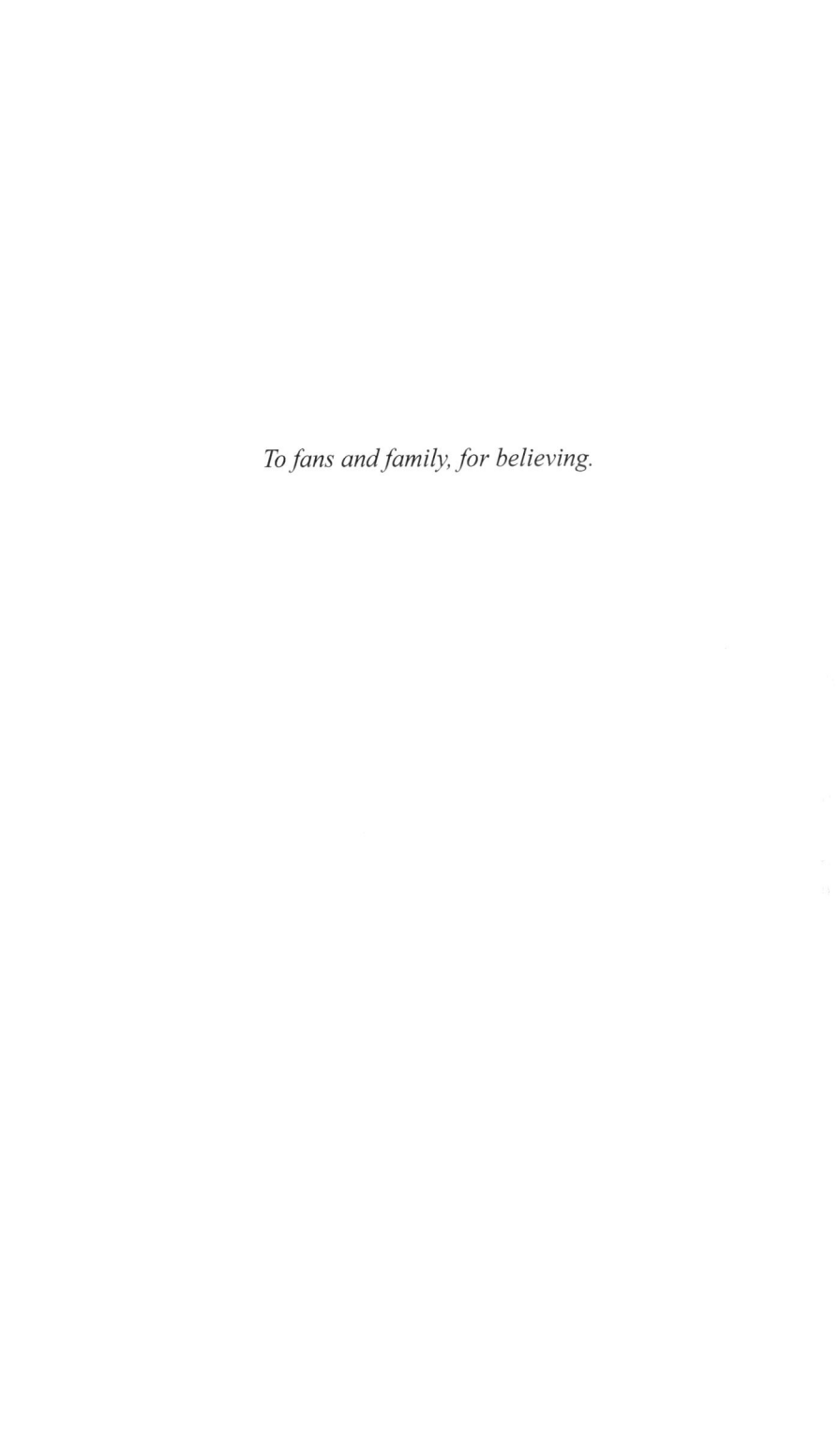

INTRODUCTION

WE FIRST MEET Jonmarc Vahanian in *The Summoner*, the first book in the Chronicles of the Necromancer series. Jonmarc is the experienced, bitter mercenary who reluctantly agrees to guide an exiled prince and his companions to safety. Over the course of the four books in the Chronicles series and the two books in the Fallen Kings Cycle, Jonmarc grows into a very significant character, second only to Tris Drayke, the series' protagonist. Along the way, readers see glimpses of his past and get hints about his background, but never his whole story.

Jonmarc turned out to be a favorite character for readers, who wanted to know how he became the man we meet in *The Summoner*. I decided to write a series of sequential short stories—ultimately serialized novels—that tell Jonmarc's backstory. This anthology is the second set of those short stories and novellas that reveal another phase of Jonmarc's growth from a blacksmith's son to becoming one of the greatest warriors in the history of the Winter Kingdoms.

If you haven't read the novels, you'll want to start with *The Shadowed Path*, a collection of the first ten short stories, plus a bonus story only available in the collection. *The Dark*

INTRODUCTION

Road picks up where *The Shadowed Path* ends and continues Jonmarc's journey. You'll see a lot of people and places again in the books, usually from a different perspective. Consider these stories to be a prequel to *The Summoner*.

Readers of the Chronicles series and the Fallen Kings books will recognize a number of familiar characters, met here ten years or more before we encounter them in *The Summoner*. Many things that were hinted at in the novels are fleshed out in these stories. Readers who paid close attention in the novels will recognize watershed moments in Jonmarc's life, and may have a sense of fate or déjà vu as he moves, step by step, along the Dark Road that takes him to his destiny.

Soldier. Fight slave. Smuggler. Warrior. Brigand lord. If you've met Jonmarc Vahanian in the Chronicles of the Necromancer and Fallen Kings Cycle books, you don't really know him until you walk in his footsteps.

BAD BLOOD

BAD BLOOD

"SOMEHOW, WHEN I SIGNED UP TO BE A MERCENARY, THIS wasn't what I had in mind." Jonmarc Vahanian nudged his horse to keep up with the rest of the traveling group.

Tov Harrtuck, his companion, chuckled. "Did you expect never-ending battles and armies on the march?"

Jonmarc shrugged. "I didn't think I'd be playing nanny-nursemaid to a bunch of traveling musicians," he grumbled. "Could have stayed where I was and done that."

"You joined up in the slow season," Harrtuck replied. "Coming on toward winter. Anyone who was going to field an army did so a few months ago, expecting to be done before the snow flies. This far north, no one goes to war in the coldest months without a death wish. But we still need to eat, so we pick up what work comes our way."

Jonmarc mumbled assent. At eighteen, he was a head taller than Harrtuck, even though his companion was a decade older. Jonmarc's dark chestnut hair was tied back, and out of long habit, his brown eyes scanned the horizon for attackers. The upturned collar of his long coat hid the scar that ran from one ear down to his shoulder, a hint that he was not new to fighting. "At least the food's good," he replied.

Tov Harrtuck's head came up to Jonmarc's shoulder, and where Jonmarc was trim and built like an athlete, Harrtuck's barrel chest and stout legs gave him the stalwart look of a grouchy ox. "If you want to know the truth of it, these kinds of jobs are the best of paid soldiering. Good pay, good food, and little risk you'll lose your head over it. Can't say the same for being on a battlefield."

Jonmarc had spent the last year as a blacksmith, and a guard with Maynard Linton's traveling caravan of wonders as the itinerant group of performers and artisans made their way across the Kingdom of Margolan. Along the way, there had been plenty of chances to hone his skill as a swordsman and in hand-to-hand fights, defending the caravan from the dangers of the open road. A caravan friend had introduced him to Harrtuck, who in turn had put in a good word with Captain Valjan of the War Dogs, and a month later, here he was, guarding another caravan as it made its way from one noble's manor to another noble's manor across the byways of Principality.

"Can't help wondering, if they're such bloody good musicians, why they haven't played anything since we've been on the road?" Jonmarc muttered, keeping his voice low.

"Maybe the cold weather doesn't agree with their instruments," Harrtuck said, watching the riders and wagons ahead of them with bored detachment. "Musicians are a fickle lot."

"Maybe," Jonmarc replied. "But the ones with Maynard's caravan played day-in and day-out, and even under an awning on rainy days. Didn't seem any worse for the wear."

He eyed the small group of travelers he and a handful of the War Dogs had been hired to protect. Lord Eston wished to honor Lord Nemic with the gift of a troupe of performers as a peace offering after a heated squabble over the rights to water from a river that flowed through both men's lands. So here they were, freezing their backsides off, riding through the middle of Principality to escort a bunch of pampered musicians to patch up hard feelings.

Jonmarc sighed. Harrtuck was right: the job was easy and safe, compared to the kind of work mercenaries often did. And Jonmarc had seen enough of fighting to know that skill and practice could be bested by overwhelming numbers and sheer bad luck. Escort duty, however boring, was decidedly less likely to kill him. Yet as they pushed on through the cold, Jonmarc could not shake the feeling that something about this easy job was wrong.

"WE'LL CAMP HERE," Vos Peters, the leader of Lord Eston's musicians, announced when he had brought the group to a stand-still. "There's a flat area to make camp, a well by the road not far back, and room to circle our wagons for the night." Peters's voice had a raspy quality to it that was unmistakable, but it made Jonmarc wonder what the man's singing voice sounded like.

"Beggin' your pardon," Harrtuck replied, with as much diplomacy as he could muster, "but I'd rather see us camp a little less close to the forest. For safety's sake."

Peters regarded Harrtuck stonily, and Jonmarc could see in the tilt of Peters's chin, and the glint in his eye at the musician was going to be trouble. "That's why Lord Eston is paying you. For safety's sake."

Harrtuck's expression was utterly neutral, but he did not back down. "And when we took the job, we promised his lordship that we would see you safely from Lammergeier

House to Hastenmoor," he replied evenly. "I take that promise seriously. That means we need to make sure that wherever we camp is defensible. The closer we are to the forest edge, the easier it is for brigands or wild creatures to attack."

For that matter, Jonmarc thought, *we could have stayed at the inn about a mile back. Would have been a damn sight warmer.*

Peters shrugged. "My colleagues find the site inspiring. This is where we'll camp. See to your men, Captain."

Only the glint in Harrtuck's eyes revealed to Jonmarc how angry he was over Peters's refusal. "Yes, sir," Harrtuck replied, and turned his horse, starting to shout orders to his men in preparation to make camp.

Jonmarc lashed his horse to a sapling and fell into the familiar routine of setting up camp. As the youngest member of the merc guards, he was not surprised to be sent to bring back water for the cooks, and he trudged off toward the roadside well not far from the clearing. Behind him, he could hear the creak of wagons being maneuvered into position, the quiet snuffling of horses looking for something to eat beneath the light dusting of snow, the voices giving orders.

The trek back to the well was cold, as the wind grew harsh and the evening sky darkened with clouds. Not many travelers were on the road, and as Jonmarc filled the buckets, he watched a man ride by, no doubt heading toward the warmth and welcome of the inn. The traveler wore a dark cloak that had seen hard use, his battered hat was pulled low to shield his face from the wind, and his horse was mud-spattered. Jonmarc wondered idly what brought the lone rider out on such a miserable evening. He was just about to look away, back to the well, when something caught his eye. The stranger's boots were the finest Jonmarc had ever seen.

Now there's an interesting question, Jonmarc thought. *There's nothing special about his cloak or his horse. Did he steal the boots or win them in a card game?* He did not debate the matter for long since it was none of his business and the buckets were full. Shouldering the yoke once more that enabled him to carry back four buckets of ice cold water, Jonmarc put the rider out of his mind as he watched the hedgerow warily, unwilling to be jumped by a brigand on his way back.

When he returned, the simple camp was well-along. Peters and the musicians had unhitched their horses and drawn their small, boxy wagons into a circle around a roaring campfire. Jonmarc delivered the buckets and then helped two of the other War Dogs make sure that the horses were fed and brushed down, before heading over to the more modest base the mercenaries had pitched for themselves. Five canvas tents, each big enough for two men and their bedrolls, dotted the trampled ground. Harrtuck and several of the other mercs stood near the fire, warming themselves as the burning logs sent embers into the night sky.

"Glad you're back," Harrtuck said, moving to the side so that Jonmarc could step closer to the fire. "Grab some food while you can. I've got another job for you."

Jonmarc walked away from the fire and immediately felt the bite of the wind. He took a slab of hard bread, a hunk of dried meat, a chunk of cheese, and an apple from Geb, the merc in charge of rations. It was hardly a feast, but Jonmarc was too tired and hungry to care. He had been among the War Dogs long enough to know that they made sure their men ate well and that their rations were worth eating. The same could not be said, he had heard, about many of the other mercenary groups that made Principality their winter camp.

When he returned, Geb's helper, Anselm, had put a kettle

7

on the coals to boil to make *kerif*, the bitter black drink that kept soldiers on their feet. Jonmarc accepted a cup of *kerif* gratefully when it had brewed, and hung back, sipping his drink and watching his new-found comrades in arms. Geb, the cook, was as stout as Harrtuck, but he was surprisingly fast on his feet and particularly good with a quarterstaff. Anselm was tall and bony, and despite his job as assistant trail cook, looked as if he missed more meals than he ate. His long reach made him wicked with a broadsword. Gif and Hanry were brothers, pale and blond-haired, and they had the best aim with a knife or a rock of anyone in the War Dogs. Lygart preferred a war axe in combat, and Jonmarc had seen him throw an axe with frightening accuracy. Milo was a bear of a man who often preferred to wade into battle with a mace and his steel-clad fists, clearing a path for the others to follow. Odger was a short, quiet fellow who could shoot a bow with deadly accuracy while standing in his saddle and riding at full gallop. Higg was the last of the War Dogs' contingent, a dark-haired man with piercing blue eyes who was a competent fighter when sober and an unstoppable force when drunk. Except for Milo and Gif, who were on patrol, the other War Dogs stood close to the fire, laughing and talking.

"You're quiet," Harrtuck said, jostling Jonmarc from his thoughts.

Jonmarc shrugged. "I can't shake the feeling that this job isn't going to be as easy as it looks. It's probably nothing."

Harrtuck frowned. "I've learned over the years to pay attention when my gut is telling me something—at least until I've checked it out and know what's going on. Anything, in particular, bothering you?"

Jonmarc thought about the stranger with the expensive boots, but that seemed too odd to mention. "Just something about the musicians that doesn't seem quite right," he said with a nod toward the circle of wagons. "Back at Linton's caravan, the musicians were always playing after dinner, either around the fire or in their wagons. Sometimes it was practice, or to entertain the rest of us, and oft times just because they liked to play."

Harrtuck nodded. "Aye, seems strange. Then again, these aren't musicians who go begging for their meals from inn to inn, or playing for a crowd to earn a few coppers. As Peters has reminded me a number of times, they're 'minstrels,'" he added, with an emphasis on the last word that made clear his opinion of Peters's high-handed opinions. "They only play for noble houses."

"That just means they beg at a better type of inn," Odger said, overhearing. "Kind of like the difference between a trollop and a courtesan."

Jonmarc and Harrtuck chuckled, then grew serious as Odger moved away. "Have you even seen their instruments?" Jonmarc asked.

Harrtuck looked over toward the wagons. "We loaded several fancy boxes into that blue wagon, and Peters pitched a fit over how gently we carried them because they were 'finely tuned instruments.'" Harrtuck replied drily. He looked over to Jonmarc. "What are you suggesting?"

Jonmarc shook his head and spread his hands palms up. "Nothing. Just that they don't act like the musicians I've traveled with, and it's odd with them keeping to themselves like that."

Harrtuck clapped him on the shoulder. "You're not in Margolan anymore, Jonmarc. Principality draws people from all over the Winter Kingdoms, and they bring their own ways with them. Peters is hardly the strangest thing I've seen in these parts."

Principality was indeed a trade crossroads and a place where merchants and travelers from most of the seven neighboring kingdoms felt safe to mingle and conduct business. The region's gem mines made it wealthy despite its small size, and a long-ago king had ensured Principality's security by welcoming mercenary groups to set up their headquarters and their winter bases in return for an oath of protection. No Principality-based merc outfit would ever sell their swords against the region's king, and protecting the kingdom's borders kept their own base camps secure as well. King Staden ruled over a prosperous kingdom at peace with its three neighbors: Margolan, Eastmark, and Dhasson.

"It's probably nothing," Jonmarc said, chagrined he had mentioned his reservations.

Harrtuck chuckled. "You know, the night is still young. If you're game to take a horse down to the inn we passed and bring back jugs of ale, we'll all be a bit warmer." He pressed a pouch with coins into Jonmarc's hand. "Just make sure you take your swords. No telling who's on the road at this time."

Jonmarc took the coins and headed for where his horse was tethered. Out of habit, he counted the horses, came up one short and counted again. He frowned, walking over to where Peters's horse had been tied. Hoof prints marked the ground and what remained of the snow, as well as a man's boot prints. It was clear the horse had not run off. Jonmarc glanced back toward the War Dogs, and past them, to the circle of wagons. This late, there was only one place Peters was likely to have gone, and it was the same place Jonmarc was heading. One way or the other, he might get an answer to his questions.

The ride to the inn went much faster than walking with the water buckets, for which Jonmarc was grateful. Even so, he was cold enough to linger for a moment at the bonfire behind the inn where the servants warmed themselves before he went to the kitchen door and knocked.

"Four jugs of ale," he said, and handed over the coins.

The serving girl who answered the door smiled at him. "Come on in for a moment," she offered, with a glance over her shoulder. Jonmarc brushed the snow from his cloak and stepped into the warmth. "You're out late," she observed and favored him with a smile. "Stand by the fire and get warm," she offered. "I'm Cara."

"Thanks… Cara. I got sent back for the ale," Jonmarc replied, feeling suddenly awkward. It had only been a little over a year since Shanna had died, and the memory was too vivid and the grief too fresh to allow for even casual interest.

"Stay by the fire. I'll be back shortly," she said. "Bring the jugs back when you're done with them, and the owner will give you a few coppers."

Jonmarc waited until Cara had left the kitchen, then dared to move closer to the doorway for a look into the inn's common room. Thanks to the snow and cold, the room was busy. Men leaned at the bar drinking or sat around the tables eating, talking, and wagering. Jonmarc strained for a better view, wondering if Peters and the man with the boots were there, but he could not see either of them.

He barely got back to the fireplace before Cara came back with his four jugs of ale. "Hope it's not all for you!" she said with a grin.

"This is going to make some friends of mine very happy," Jonmarc replied. He paused, then launched into the questions that had been on his mind. "What do you hear in these parts about Lord Nemic?"

Cara frowned. "Bits and pieces. Just what men say out in the common room. There's been bad blood between Lord Nemic and our Lord Eston for a while—don't know what about, but it must be something big. One trader said Lord Eston would rather drink a pitcher of spit than have anything to do with Lord Nemic." She visibly shuddered. "Heard some of the traders complaining because their feud makes it harder to go back and forth across the border." She shrugged as if wondering why anyone would care.

"What about the road between here and the border?" Jonmarc asked. "Is it good road? Safe from highwaymen?"

For the first time, Cara noticed the swords Jonmarc wore beneath his cloak. "You're pretty well armed for an errand boy."

Jonmarc managed a half-smile that he hoped looked non-threatening. "You never know when there might be wolves about. Better to be safe than sorry."

Cara shrugged again. "I guess. You'd better get going before the innkeeper finds you in here."

"Thanks," Jonmarc said, slipping her a few extra coppers for her trouble. He managed to close the door behind him while hugging the jugs of ale in his arms and made it to his horse without dropping anything. As he was securing the jugs in his saddlebags, he saw two figures emerging from the inn's barn. In the moonlight, he recognized Peters, who was talking with "Boots."

Jonmarc stepped into the shadows, hoping the men did not look up as they passed.

"Then it's arranged," Peters said to the man with the expensive boots.

"Aye. Before dawn at the border. We'll be there," Boots replied. "You have what you need."

Peters patted his coat as if to reassure himself there was something in one of the pockets. "It had better work."

"It'll work," Boots said sharply. "Just don't get any on yourself, or you'll be dead, too."

They passed out of earshot. Jonmarc could see the men by the light of the inn's windows. They spoke briefly as they untethered their horses from the hitching post, then both Peters and Boots mounted up and headed off in different directions.

Cold as he was, Jonmarc knew he dared not ride for the camp until he had given Peters time to return. There was nowhere else for Jonmarc to have been at this hour except the inn, and he did not want to give Peters cause to wonder whether or not his meeting had been observed.

The ale jugs clinked against each other in his saddlebags as Jonmarc rode back to camp. It was later than he had planned to return, and he was nearly frozen, but by the time he headed back, Peters was not in sight. Jonmarc kept one hand on his sword the entire ride, as his thoughts raced trying to make sense of Peters's rendezvous.

"Did you ride the whole way to Principality City?" Harrtuck asked when Jonmarc returned. Most of the War Dogs were still gathered around the fire since the night was cold enough that no one was in a hurry to go to their tents.

"Something's going on," Jonmarc said in a whisper as he passed off the jugs to Harrtuck.

Harrtuck gave him a questioning glance. "You've said that."

Jonmarc shook his head. "There's more. Peters slipped out and met a man at the inn. Something's been arranged for the night we cross the border, and it didn't sound like a delivery."

Harrtuck clapped him on the shoulder. "Probably nothing to do with us, but we'll keep extra sharp, just in case. Come over to the fire and drink some of that ale."

Jonmarc joined the crew around the fire, but his attention strayed from their ribald banter. He saw Higg and Odger return from patrol and heard Harrtuck question them more thoroughly than usual, onto to find that neither man had noticed Peters departure or return, nor anything else amiss. Harrtuck walked over to where the horses were tethered and returned a few minutes later shaking his head.

"Aye," he said to Jonmarc in a low voice. "Peters's horse was moved, and there are footprints in the snow to prove it, even if the patrols didn't see him," Harrtuck reported. "Question is, why did he try so hard not to be noticed? And who was the fellow who met with him? From what you saw, it makes me wonder if they hadn't planned to meet in advance."

"Which means that camping here wasn't for inspiration," Jonmarc finished.

Harrtuck met his gaze and nodded. "Peters is lying about something. Question is, does it concern us? Maybe he's going to try to smuggle something across the border."

"He wouldn't need poison for that," Jonmarc pointed out.

Harrtuck grimaced as he thought. "We don't know that he's got poison," he replied. "Lots of cures can make you sick. Maybe one of his musicians has the clap." He shook his head. "Sweet Chenne! If it was mercury Peters got from that stranger, he'd be better off with the disease than with the cure."

"I'll keep my ears open, see if I can hear anything tomorrow," Jonmarc promised, glad that Harrtuck at least took his warning seriously.

Harrtuck looked toward the circled wagons and their banked fire. "I'll put Lygart and Hanry on night watch. Maybe have them take Gif with them, just in case. But if you heard right, whatever's going to happen will be tomorrow. We're likely to be near the border by nightfall, too far away from Lord Nemic's manor to make it the rest of the way in one day."

"I wonder if the rest of the musicians know, or if it's just Peters's scheme?" Jonmarc mused.

Harrtuck shrugged. "No idea. But we'll watch and wait. We made Lord Eston a promise, and we'll get Peters's skinny ass to Hastenmoor if I have to tie him up and haul him behind my horse to do it."

THE NEXT DAY dawned cold and overcast, with leaden clouds threatening snow. Jonmarc and the War Dogs were ready to go at dawn, but Peters and his musicians lingered at the fire as if they were in no hurry to get on the road.

By the time they started toward Hastenmoor, the wind had picked up. Jonmarc pulled his heavy cloak around him and tried to remember the warmth of the blacksmith's forge. Peters and the musicians took turns riding in their enclosed wagons, a much more pleasant way to travel than exposed to the wind on horseback. By midday, snow was falling in large, wet flakes, making a miserable ride even worse.

Principality was a small country, longer than it was wide, and the distance they had already traveled placed them in the center of the kingdom. Here the land was hilly, with steep rises and sharp descents made the more treacherous with ice. Jonmarc and the other War Dogs staggered their riding positions, changing places every few hours in teams of two.

By afternoon, Jonmarc found himself paired with Lygart, the axe-fighter. Lygart's full beard was speckled with gray, and Jonmarc guessed the seasoned mercenary was half a decade older than Harrtuck. A scar crossed from Lygart's right eyebrow to his ear, which was missing its tip. Lygart did not seem to mind the cold, although his face was red from the wind and snow.

"You've been with the mercs in Principality for a while, haven't you?" Jonmarc asked after they had ridden in silence for more than a candlemark.

"Ay-yah," Lygart drawled. "Been back and forth and all around more than once."

"Ever been to Hastenmoor?"

Lygart regarded him and nodded. "Once. Hadn't planned to go back."

"Why?"

"Didn't seem like a healthy idea. Lord Nemic lets his suspicions get the best of him."

It's what Lygart isn't saying aloud that's important, Jonmarc thought. *Suspicious men love their spies and private soldiers. Pretty soon, everyone is watching their backs for good reason.*

"Of course, there are worse places," Lygart continued laconically. "Wouldn't set foot in Dark Haven, not for all the gems in Principality."

"Why not?"

Lygart looked at him as if Jonmarc had somehow revealed his utter lack of experience. "Whole place is full of biters," he said, referring to the undead *vayash moru*. "That's the truth."

"What about Lord Eston? I don't know much about the man who hired us," Jonmarc asked, as much to pass the time as to grill his riding partner.

Lygart gave a snort that startled his horse. "Not much different from Nemic, least that's what I've heard. Hard-nosed gent, drives a cold bargain, doesn't forgive a slight. Or that's what they say."

"Delivering the musicians is supposed to patch up a feud," Jonmarc said. "So what started the fight?" If even the serving girl at the inn knew that there was bad blood between the neighboring nobles, he figured the story was both dramatic and well-known.

"Depends on who you ask," Lygart replied. "Folks on Eston's side say Nemic interfered with the trade routes that ran through his lands, charged a high tax for safe passage." He shrugged. "Wouldn't be the first lord to think of that. They say it came to a head when Nemic had his men arrest a group of wealthy merchants from Lord Eston's lands who were in Hastenmoor to trade gems. Charged them with being spies. Hanged them for treason, and kept their gems—which they had been trading on behalf of Lord Eston."

"And what do the people on Nemic's side say about Eston?" Jonmarc asked, beginning to get an idea of just what a hornet's nest they had stumbled into.

Another shrug. "Oh, Nemic and Eston are cut from the same cloth when it comes to squeezing bribes from merchants and travelers. But word has it that Eston's been trying to take Nemic's lands one way or the other for a long time." He gave another snort. "Might explain why Nemic looks over his shoulder all the time, eh? You're not crazy to sleep with a knife under your pillow if people really are trying to kill you."

After that, Jonmarc and Lygart rode in silence until it was time to change riding order again. Jonmarc was just as glad that Gif was quiet because his own thoughts jangled so loudly in his mind that he imagined others might hear them. *Two lords, each with good reason to distrust the other, each nursing grudges with cause. Now Eston, the one who sounds like he would be least likely to back down, sends a peace offering. Why?*

Sure enough, Peters insisted that the small caravan camp for the night on a field just inside the border of Lord Nemic's lands.

"It's still early," Harrtuck argued. "We could travel another hour, be that much closer to the manor, and arrive before noon."

"It will do no good for us to arrive exhausted," Peters sniffed. "We are performers. We must be sufficiently rested. Lord Eston's orders were clear. We are to provide an excellent performance for Lord Nemic, as befits a gift of this magnitude. We will not drag in like peddlers, half-asleep and unable to give our best showing."

"We were hired to defend you," Harrtuck snapped. "And as your guards, I need to warn you that this position is once again too close to the trees and difficult to defend."

"Deal with it," Peters replied, eyes narrowing. "We are camping here."

This time, Harrtuck did not attempt to hide his muttered curses as he stalked away. "Either that man is incredibly stupid, or he wants to be attacked," he mumbled to Jonmarc when he had returned to where the rest of the War Dogs waited with their horses.

Jonmarc raised an eyebrow. "I'm not questioning his stupidity, but maybe he does want to be attacked—there's something about this whole thing we don't know, a piece we're missing."

Harrtuck nodded. "Aye. But I can't figure out what it is." He looked at the rest of the mercs. "You know what Jonmarc heard at the inn. Something's afoot, and whatever the game is, we're in the thick of it. Set up your tents, walk your patrol, and expect action sometime tonight." He paused. "We've got to protect those bloody sons-of-bitches," he said with a glance toward Peters and his minstrels, "but we don't have to trust them."

THE ATTACK CAME that night just after bells in the distant tower struck twelve times.

"Get up! We're under attack!" Jonmarc heard the sentry's shouts and scrambled free of his blankets. It was cold enough that he had slept in his clothing, so boots and sword belt were all that he needed before heading out of his tent, weapon already in hand.

Jonmarc heard a footstep to his left, and instinct made him duck to the right, barely missing the sweep of a saber that sliced down through the canvas tent he had just exited. For a second, the attacker's blade was caught in the canvas, and Jonmarc wheeled in a high kick, catching the man in the chest and knocking him flat on his ass. Before the brigand could scramble to his feet, Jonmarc dodged forward, sinking his blade into his opponent's chest.

"Behind you!" Harrtuck shouted. Jonmarc dove to the side and a blade whooshed past him closed enough to cut a slice in his coat sleeve. Jonmarc had a sword in each hand now, and he blocked the man's next swing with one blade as he slashed down with the other, opening the attacker's belly and sending a steaming cascade of entrails down onto the screaming man's shoes. Harrtuck lopped off the dying man's head before the wounded attacker had made it to his knees.

"Who in the name of the Crone are we fighting?" Jonmarc asked, catching his breath and straining to get his bearings.

"No idea," Harrtuck replied. "They just showed up a moment before the sentries yelled, and we caught them heading for the minstrels' wagons.

Moonlight bathed the clearing in a blue glow. Jonmarc could make out the shadows of dueling pairs across the open space, and from what he could see, it looked as if the attackers outnumbered the War Dogs.

"You think someone wanted to disrupt Eston's gift?" Jonmarc asked as he and Harrtuck ran toward where Gif and Hanry were fighting three attackers. He saw panic on one of the brigand's faces when the man realized the odds had turned against him, but the four War Dogs positioned themselves so that their opponents could not easily flee. Gif had a sword in one hand and a knife in the other, and he dodged and feinted, intentionally frustrating his attacker to draw the man into making a mistake.

Hanry countered his enemy's powerful sword-strikes, staying at the edge of his attacker's range, dancing back and forth to keep the man on edge, looking for an opening. A bloody gash on Hanry's shoulder suggested that his attacker was good enough to land a blow, although the brigand was bleeding from several slashes to the shoulder and forearm.

Jonmarc and Harrtuck went for the third brigand, easily trapping him between them. "Who sent you?" Harrtuck growled and laid open a slice on the brigand's right arm to show that he was impatient for an answer.

"What do you care? You'll be dead soon enough." The rogue was good enough to keep Jonmarc and Harrtuck from boxing him in. Everything about him, from the smashed nose to the scarred face to his practiced footwork told Jonmarc the man was not a common thief.

"Let's just say I'm curious," Jonmarc replied drily. He had practiced enough with Harrtuck to have a sense of the other man's moves, and he worked with Harrtuck to maneuver so that the older mercenary would be in position to get inside their attacker's guard.

"We were just told to take out the escort," the brigand replied.

"Why?" Harrtuck grated.

The brigand's laugh was sharp. "I don't ask 'why,' mate. I take the money where I get it and go on."

Jonmarc came at the attacker in a rush, and it was clear from the man's expression he had not expected either Jonmarc's skill or his ferocity. For a moment, the brigand's full attention focused on Jonmarc, as Harrtuck took a step to the side, giving him a clear strike at the attacker's unprotected back.

"Not for long, you don't." Harrtuck brought his blade down hard, slicing through the attacker's shoulder, taking off his sword-arm and sending a spray of blood into the cold night air. With a scream, the man collapsed, and Jonmarc kicked the knife from the man's left hand, bringing the point of his sword to bear over the man's heart.

"Tell us what we want to know, and you can die easy," Jonmarc said quietly. "You've got nothing left to lose."

The brigand's face was pale with fear and shock. "Ain't much to tell I haven't told you. We got hired in Lammergeier, and paid half up front to find you and attack you on the road to Hastenmoor."

"Who hired you?" Harrtuck stood watch as Jonmarc interrogated their dying prisoner.

"I don't know."

Jonmarc sighed. "Bleeding out takes a while," he said. "The wolves could get you before then. Or the foxes. Tell us everything, and we'll send you to the Lady fast and easy."

The downed man swallowed hard and licked his dry lips. "It's all I know, I swear it by the Crone," he said, breath coming shallowly with the pain. "A fellow showed up and wanted us to track a bunch of musicians in wagons with guards. The deal was, we kill the guards and leave the musicians alone."

"Why?"

"I don't know!" Panic and terror shone from the man's eyes, which were round and white in the moonlight. "He just said we couldn't strike until you were at the border, and that none of the minstrels were to be hurt." The brigand's body shook with pain.

"That's all. I swear by the Crone. That's all I know."

"It's enough," Harrtuck said. He swung his sword and cut off the dying man's head in one clean blow.

Gif and Hanry had finished their opponents and returned to the fight. In the distance, Jonmarc could see Milo, unmistakable for his size and lumbering gate, smashing his way through his enemy's defenses with his mace and the raw power of his steel-clad fist. Lygart's axe left a trail of bloodied bodies.

To one side, Anselm was fighting off attackers twohanded, and it looked to Jonmarc as if he was doing his best to keep the fighters from getting to someone on the ground behind him.

"Anselm's in trouble!" Jonmarc shouted, already beginning to sprint in the lanky cook's direction. Harrtuck was heading the opposite way, barreling toward one of the brigands who was fighting with Higg.

Out of the corner of his eye, Jonmarc could see Milo and his enemy lurching close to the circled wagons of the minstrels. None of the musicians had peeked from the safety of their carriages, he thought sourly, though given the ferocity with which the brigands fought, that might be for the best.

Wood splintered with a crash as Milo's mace went wide, slamming into one of the boxes of supplies on a wagon near the edge of the circle. The brigand lunged with his sword, and Milo brought the mace back across with a deadly sweep so that it connected with the brigand's skull with a crack and a wet thud.

By the time Jonmarc reached Anselm, the thin man was tiring, keeping his opponent at bay, but only just. Anselm held his position as his attacker tried to draw him forward, and as Jonmarc neared the fight, he saw Geb lying behind Anselm on the ground.

With a roar, Jonmarc ran to Anselm's aid. Up close, he could see that Anselm was bleeding from a dozen gashes, and his features were drawn and pale. At Jonmarc's cry, the brigand moved as if to prepare for Jonmarc to attack, then lunged toward Anselm, driving his blade through Anselm's chest.

"You bastard!" Jonmarc shouted, attacking with a strength born of anger. Anselm clutched his chest and sank to his knees. The brigand looked as if he might make a smart reply, but one glance at Jonmarc's face sobered the man to the business of staying alive.

The brigand's sword was wet with Anselm's blood. If the hireling had expected Jonmarc to be an easy kill because of his age, he was quickly informed otherwise. Jonmarc's anger found release in his sword, and years working in the forge had made him strong enough to pound his opponent back onto his heels with a series of brutal strikes.

We were set up. We were betrayed. Our men are dying. Someone is going to pay. Jonmarc no longer felt the cold night wind or the pain of the gashes he had taken on his arms and shoulders. All of his rage narrowed his focus to the face of the man he was going to kill. It wouldn't be payment enough, but it would be a start.

The wind had picked up, whipping a dusting of snow around them. Behind him, Jonmarc heard shouts and the clang of steel, but he could not afford to let his attention stray. Every sword strike reverberated up his arm, jarring his bones. His fingers were numb from cold, cramping from their grip on his swords. But the adrenaline that coursed through his blood did not let him feel either pain or fear, just simple, raw fury. That was enough.

The attacker lunged. Jonmarc parried, and his blade skidded against the other's sword, pushing the weapon out of his way so he could strike with the sword in his left hand.

The brigand countered with a short sword, barely deflecting Jonmarc's blow, and taking a gash across his fingers that made the attacker drop his knife, nearly severing the fingers. Desperate, the brigand slashed down with a powerful blow, going for Jonmarc's sword arm. Jonmarc blocked the strike, and this time, his second sword's tip caught the brigand in the throat, driving its point upward through the soft flesh of the bottom jaw, and into the skull.

For a moment, the brigand went rigid, and his body convulsed, awareness dimming in his eyes until Jonmarc shook the body free of his sword and wiped his blades clean on the dead man's cloak.

Geb's groan drew him to the mercenary's side. Geb's hands were pressed against his abdomen, where coils of slick, gray entrails had already bulged out of the deep slash through his belly. Even in the moonlight, Jonmarc could see Geb's face was deathly pale, and his breathing was labored.

"My fault," Geb whispered. "I was slow."

"Sooner or later, we all are," Jonmarc said, laying a hand on Geb's shoulder. He looked around, but the fight was over. In the distance, Jonmarc could hear Harrtuck shouting orders, and the War Dogs still on their feet began the sober task of gathering the dead.

"Don't let the wolves get me," Geb murmured. "Swear it."

"I swear," Jonmarc said, clasping Geb's cold hand. For a second, Geb's fingers closed around Jonmarc's palm, then slowly went slack as one last, wheezing breath escaped in a faint cloud of mist.

Jonmarc sighed and released Geb's hand. He went to Anselm, but the lanky man was already dead. Footsteps sounded nearby, and Jonmarc was on his feet with his sword drawn before he realized that it was Lygert who strode toward him.

"Both dead," Jonmarc reported, lowering his sword.

"Fighting's done," Lygert replied. "Come on. They'll need a cairn. It won't wait until morning."

As much as his wounds ached, Jonmarc knew they could wait a while longer. He sheathed his sword and followed Lygert to the edge of the clearing where some past farmer had dumped the large rocks he had removed from the field. Wordlessly, Gif and Hanry joined them, and then Higg and Milo. By the time they had the cairn finished, Harrtuck and the others were there as well.

Eight standing, two dead. And at least fifteen attackers dead as well. A bloody night's work. Jonmarc glanced at his companions, noting that each had taken some damage, though, like him, not enough to put them out of the fight.

Harrtuck cleared his throat. "We will not forget Geb and Anselm, and we will not forgive those who took them from us." Then he began the passage prayer; one Jonmarc had already learned at the graveside of friends who had died protecting Linton's caravan.

"Let the sword be sheathed, and the helm shuttered. Prepare a feast in the hall of your fallen heroes. Geb and Anselm died with valor. Make their passage swift and their journey easy, until their souls rest in the arms of the Lady."

One by one, they had all joined into the prayer, their voices carrying on the cold night air. Then with a nod, Harrtuck turned to walk back toward the camp and the others, when they had added whatever good-bye the needed to make, followed.

From Harrtuck's stride, Jonmarc knew trouble was not over for the night. "Who were they?" he asked, catching up with Harrtuck.

"I don't know, but I aim to find out," Harrtuck said through clenched teeth. "Especially since their leader carried a letter of safe passage from Lord Eston."

"Peters and his crew never showed their faces," Jonmarc said, still too angry to let his wounds slow him down.

"No, they didn't," Harrtuck replied. "And I think I know why."

By now, all the rest of the War Dogs had fallen in behind them as Harrtuck marched across the trampled snow and headed straight for Peters's wagon. He reached the brightly painted door of the traveling carriage and hammered on the wood with his fist.

"Come out before I come in after you!" Harrtuck shouted.

"Captain Harrtuck! Return to your tent. I shall report your conduct to Lord Eston!" Peters's aggrieved voice carried through the wood.

"Milo?" Harrtuck said and stepped aside.

With a crash, Milo's mace ripped the handle off of the wagon door and tore a hole through the painted wood. In the next moment, Harrtuck flung the door open so hard that it cracked against the side of the carriage, reached in and grabbed Peters by the throat. He dragged the minstrel out of his carriage and slammed him up against the side of the coach.

"Let go of me, you lout!"

Harrtuck tightened his grip. Jonmarc heard the slip of steel on leather, telling him the War Dogs had drawn their swords, and he did the same, too angry to worry about the consequences.

"You set us up," Harrtuck grated.

"I did nothing of the kind!"

Harrtuck's thumb dug into Peters' throat, and the minstrel's voice ended in a choked gargle. "That 'instrument' box Milo smashed into was full of weapons," Harrtuck said coldly. "Jonmarc saw you at the inn last night. What he overheard didn't make sense then, but it does now. You arranged the ambush, didn't you?" he charged, his voice as cold as the Formless One.

"You are insane."

Harrtuck gave Peters a shake, silencing him. "One of those 'brigands' had a letter of safe passage signed by Lord Eston himself," he continued in a voice any reasonable man would know augured his death. "We weren't supposed to live long enough to find that out, were we?"

Jonmarc watched the change in Peters's face as the minstrel dropped the façade. Gone was self-absorbed performer. In its place was a man as cold and hard as Harrtuck. "No. You're supposed to be dead."

"Tell them," Harrtuck commanded, giving Peters another violent shake. It would be a toss-up as to whether Harrtuck snapped the man's spine or crushed his throat, Jonmarc thought.

"Your deaths—" Peters began, strangling on the chokehold Harrtuck had on his neck. Harrtuck lessened the pressure just enough to allow Peters to suck in a desperate breath.

"Your deaths," Peters repeated, "would have bought us legitimacy. Lord Nemic would have believed we were a sincere peace offering."

"And then you would have poisoned him," Jonmarc finished.

Peters gave him a murderous look but said nothing.

"You're assassins," Harrtuck took up the story. "In the employ of Lord Eston, who's been out for Lord Nemic's blood for some time. Of course, Eston was willing to throw your lives away, too, since you would never have made it out of Hastenmoor alive."

"It is a privilege to die for a worthy cause," Peters replied.

"Surviving is a worthy cause," Harrtuck snapped.

By now, the other minstrels had emerged from their wagons, and to no one's surprise, they were as lethally armed as the War Dogs.

"Let me make something clear to you," Harrtuck said in a low, deadly voice. "We. Are. Not. Expendable."

An unpleasant smile touched Peters's face. "Oh, you are. You just don't know it. This is much bigger than a handful of sellswords."

Harrtuck brought his sword up to rest beneath Peters' chin. "I believe you've violated the terms of our contract."

"Put down your weapons." The voice echoed from the darkness, everywhere at once. "War Dogs. Step aside. This is not your fight."

"The hell it's not," Harrtuck muttered, jabbing Peters's beneath his chin hard enough to draw blood. "Two of my men are dead tonight because of your betrayal."

"War Dogs. This is your last warning. Our quarrel is not with you. Step aside."

Only then did Harrtuck look up. Jonmarc followed his gaze. In the moonlight, he could make out the shapes of men surrounding the minstrels' camp. By Jonmarc's count, they were far out-numbered. Perhaps, in daylight and in peak condition, the War Dogs might have taken the newcomers, despite the odds. Wounded, cold, exhausted from the fight, the best the mercenaries could hope for was a noble death.

Jonmarc could almost see the debate in Harrtuck's mind. *Kill Peters and be avenged, even if I die for it, or step away.*

With a curse, Harrtuck lowered his sword, pushing Peters away with enough force to throw the erstwhile minstrel on his ass in the snow. "You're not worth dying for," Harrtuck said. "Crone take your soul."

"Do we fight them?" Milo spoke for all of the War Dogs.

"Sheath your swords, men. We stand down."

Shadows rushed toward them, and as they neared enough to make out their features in the moonlight, Jonmarc realized that the newcomers wore the uniforms of a noble house. Some of the minstrels tried to flee, while others turned on the incoming force with curses and raised swords. The War Dogs stood back, watching their leader questioningly, waiting for the strangers to turn on them.

"I'm sorry to tell you this, but you've been used." The speaker was a man a little older than Harrtuck, with a heavy Eastern Principality accent.

"We'd figured that out," Harrtuck said, with a murderous look in Peters's direction.

"Sorry we didn't arrive sooner," the man said in a perfunctory manner that made it impossible to know whether the sentiment was true or not. "We've ridden through the night. Lord Nemic received intelligence of an assassination plot. We're here to take the plotters into custody."

"Technically, we're contracted to Lord Eston to protect his entourage until they reach Hastenmoor," Harrtuck replied. He turned a scathing glare toward Peters. "Although, I'd be willing to turn my back while you run this bastard through."

Lord Nemic's commander gave a cold chuckle. "I'm sure you would," he agreed. "And the War Dogs's reputation is legendary. You've done service in the past for Lord Nemic, which is why he is willing to, shall we say, overlook this lapse in judgment?"

"We had no part in any plot," Harrtuck said, drawing himself up to his full height. "It was supposed to be a peace-gift."

The captain nodded. "Clever, sending minstrels as assassins. Word only reached Lord Nemic of the plot yesterday."

Harrtuck scowled. "So Eston betrayed us."

"Afraid so."

Harrtuck met the captain's eyes. "My men and I believed that our contract was legitimate. If there's to be punishment, let it fall on me as their commander, but let them go. We've already lost two men tonight."

The captain's expression darkened, and he nodded in acknowledgment. "Lord Nemic has no quarrel with the War Dogs. All we ask is that you turn these assassins over to us, and you're free to go on your way."

Harrtuck looked to Peters in silence for a moment. Jonmarc could guess the struggle going on in Harrtuck's mind. *Even though Peters betrayed us, safeguarding them was our contract. The War Dogs gave their word.*

"We had a contract," Peters said desperately, his arrogance replaced by panic. "You have to protect us."

"You served us up like lambs to wolves," Harrtuck replied, his voice pitiless. He turned to Nemic's captain. "They're all yours," he said.

Harrtuck turned his back and began walking, though Peters alternately screamed curses and begged for protection. The War Dogs looked to Harrtuck for direction, and he silenced any questions with a glare. They drew back to the perimeter of the minstrels' camp, where Harrtuck turned and stood, hands clasped in front of him, a silent witness as Nemic's troops rousted the false minstrels from their wagons and bound them with shackles. Soldiers fastened the minstrels' horses to their wagons, while the captain herded the prisoners into the open storage cart, where they would be lucky not to be dead of cold by the time they reached Hastenmoor. The wagons rolled across the bloodied clearing and onto the northern road as the sun rose.

"Well, that's done." Harrtuck's voice was resolute.

"Captain?" Milo asked. "What now? How can we go back?"

Harrtuck's eyes were cold, and he gave a short, sharp mirthless laugh. "Eston broke faith with the War Dogs. Nemic's people will see to it that the story spreads far and wide. We did ourselves proud tonight, killing off Eston's assassins. That's to our credit. And when the other mercs learn that Eston betrayed us, there won't be a mercenary troop in Principality that will lift a finger to defend him." A vengeful smile touched his lips. "I suspect Eston will be dead within the month."

They watched the wagons disappear over a rise as the sun splashed the sky with bloody streaks of light. Harrtuck sighed. "Gather your things, men. We're going home."

HAUNTS

HAUNTS

"Do you believe in ghosts?" Tov Harrtuck and Jonmarc Vahanian walked through the crowded streets of Linbourne, jostled by the crowd of drunken revelers celebrating the Feast of the Departed, better known by most as simply "Haunts."

"Maybe," Jonmarc replied. "I mean, it's Haunts. The one night of the year when even people without magic can see spirits. So if you mean, can we see whatever stray ghosts are hanging around, then yes. But the people we really want to see?" He shook his head. "Doesn't seem like they're easy to find."

Linbourne was the third largest city in Principality, and tonight its streets were packed with pilgrims and revelers who had traveled to celebrate one of the Winter Kingdoms' most popular holidays. The smell of roasting meat from the street vendors mingled with the scent of the incense that wafted from censers that burned on every corner, and the perfume worn by the whores who waited on the side of the street, calling out to the passers-by.

Of the eight faces of the Sacred Lady, Principality was

most devoted to that of Athira, the Whore. That devotion colored Principality's approach to celebrating the feast day. Simultaneously a remembrance of death and a celebration of life, Haunts provided an excuse for revelers to push Principality's already permissive standards toward overload and excess.

"Judging from the number of whores, business must be good this year," Harrtuck mused, noting the trollops who beckoned to them as they passed by. "I wonder if the Sacred Vessels are seeing a jump in visitors to the temple." The Vessels were oracles and priestesses. Their followers believed that carnal union with the Vessels equated to being one with the goddess, and so the Vessels made themselves available for that service for a handsome fee. Those who did not have the money found their union elsewhere or merely took advantage of a pious excuse for harder than usual drinking and wenching. In a kingdom where mercenary groups were encouraged to spend their winter months, Haunts celebrations were not a place for those with fragile sensibilities.

"Judging from the amount of ale being drunk, I'd say most of Linbourne will be penniless by the end of the feast," Jonmarc replied.

"The captain said he'd make sure he saved us some ale, for after our shift," Harrtuck said with a chuckle. "In case we were worried that it would all be gone."

"I'm more worried about Captain Valjan guarding our ale," Jonmarc retorted.

Colorful banners fluttered from windows and flagpoles throughout the city. Peddlers hawked charms, beads, and trinkets while musicians played in the plazas and on the steps of buildings. Many of the festival-goers had costumed themselves as one of the eight Aspects of the Lady: Mother, Childe, Warrior, Lover, Whore, Dark Lady, Crone, and Formless One. Those who were not costumed wore strands of cheap beads in the colors sacred to one or more of the Aspects. Not surprisingly, most of the beads he spotted were either yellow for the Lover, Principality's patron Aspect, or Red for the Whore, always popular with soldiers, mercenaries, and criminals, those whose lives might be foreshortened and therefore were dedicated to living life to its fullest.

"Did your village back in Margolan celebrate Haunts?" Harrtuck asked, watching a particularly pretty, and nearly naked, young woman walk past, clothed in almost nothing other than strands of red beads.

"Not like this," Jonmarc replied.

Harrtuck chuckled. He was older than Jonmarc, already a seasoned soldier and an experienced mercenary. Average height, barrel-chested, and strong, Harrtuck was faster than he looked and wicked with a sword. Jonmarc had only just signed on to their mercenary group, the War Dogs, a month before. He had seen some skirmishes and vicious but small-scale fighting helping to protect a traveling caravan, but nothing on the order of a full battle.

And if our duties as mercenaries continue being guarding groups of travelers and patrolling a nobleman's city during a festival, I might as well have stayed with the caravan, Jonmarc thought sourly.

"For someone in the middle of a festival surrounded by beer, nearly naked women, and more whores than you can count, you don't look very happy," Harrtuck observed.

Jonmarc shrugged. "It's been a long year."

Harrtuck nodded. "Aye. You've had a bad go of it. Not sure why you thought signing on with a bunch of mercs would improve your luck, though."

Jonmarc watched a parade of life-sized puppets of the eight Aspects make its way down the street. These puppets were maneuvered by long poles held by the black-clad puppeteers, giving the puppets a life-like but unsettling appearance. Giant straw effigies towered over the crowd near some of the city's more important buildings, and bonfires burned in the wide spaces of the plazas, sending the prayers of the faithful to the goddess along with the smoke.

"I think I've seen more puppets during this feast than I've ever seen in my life," Jonmarc said, intentionally changing the subject. So far, they had spotted giant puppets manipulated by people hidden on the inside, doll-sized marionettes, and large effigies rolled on carts.

Harrtuck's sidelong glance made it clear that he recognized the diversion for what it was. "It's the way Principality has always celebrated Haunts," he said with a shrug. "Go to Dhasson or Isencroft or Eastmark; they do it differently."

"Lord Eriston knows how to throw a party," Jonmarc said, taking in the trappings of the festival around them. Eriston's battle pennants flew alongside the banners and streamers in the eight sacred colors, bright red, blood red, yellow, black, orange, green, blue, and white. Musicians and street performers wore clothing in those colors, and some of them had dyed their hair and painted their skin to better match a favored Aspect. Since the feast day was considered a lucky time to gamble, games of chance with dice and cards crowded every open space. Captain Valjan had been particularly testy about warning his men off the rigged games.

"Yeah," Harrtuck agreed. "It keeps the people happy. But they won't stay that way if he and Lord Fallmount can't come to some kind of truce."

This was the second time in little more than a month that the War Dogs had been retained by one noble for protection against a neighboring noble's possible treachery. Principality was a small, wealthy kingdom that had remained secure from outside invaders during the reign of King Staden. Gem mines made it prosperous, as did brisk trade with the neighboring kingdoms in goods that were difficult, if not illegal, to purchase from other sources. Smuggling was Principality's well-known but hotly denied second-largest business, and in each of Principality's cities, there were rumored to be successful smugglers who had set themselves up nearly as well as lords.

"What's it this time? Access to the river? Trade routes?" Jonmarc replied, thinking about reasons for the nobles to wage an undeclared, but nasty silent war on each other.

"Oh, probably," Harrtuck said absently, looking hungrily at the sausages a nearby street vendor offered for sale. "It's amazing how people who already have a lot always want a little more."

Most revelers who were still sober avoided Jonmarc and Harrtuck, who were conspicuously armed with their battle swords and daggers. But the War Dogs had been hired as more than patrols to keep the drunken crowds in line. Lord Eriston had been sure that his rival would attempt to disrupt the festival, and the War Dogs were on guard to assure a peaceful and successful feast.

So far, their duties had been more like those of a constable, and less like soldiering. Since morning, Jonmarc and Harrtuck had dragged half a dozen drunks out of the main roadways before they were trampled under horse carts, and they had run down two cutpurses. And while most revelers came into the city at Haunts to have a good time, too much ale and whiskey made for more than the usual number of fist fights over card cheats, women, or often, nothing at all.

"Tell your fortune, soldier?" The woman sat cross-legged on the ground next to an overturned wooden box. Jalbet cards and ivory rune stones lay across the faded cloth that covered the box. A canny look gleamed in the fortune-teller's eyes.

"Be off with you," Harrtuck said. "Nothing but made-up rubbish."

The woman gave a raspy laugh. "True for some, not for me. She flipped over one illustrated card and then another. "Chenne smiles on you," she said, naming the warrior aspect of the goddess. "Success in battle will be yours," she promised and turned another card. Her smile faded. "You will be hunted," she said, giving Harrtuck a warning glance, "and powerful hands will turn against you." One more card turned up. "Great favor awaits you."

Harrtuck snorted. "Great favor? I'll be happy for a tankard of ale and a warm trollop in my bed tonight," he said, but he tossed a coin to the seer who caught it in her bony hands.

"How about you?" she said, giving Jonmarc a look as if she could see down to his bones. He took a step back and started to protest, but she was already flipping over cards.

The fortune-teller took a sharp breath. "You have been marked by fire and darkness," she said. "So much loss for one so young." She turned another card. "You will have great success in battle, and your skill will earn many coins." Another card made her pause. "But it is the Dark Lady, not Chenne, who watches over you. Her hand is on you, but she is not a gentle mistress." A final card turned at an angle showed a hangman, and the color drained from the seer's face.

"A warning," she breathed. "Do not go to Dhasson." She looked at him with piercingly blue eyes. "Rarely have I seen so strong a warning. Great danger awaits if you travel southward."

"I'm not going to Dhasson," Jonmarc muttered, frightened by the woman's intensity, and unsettled by her words. It was customary to give alms to the beggars and performers on a feast day, so he dug in his pocket for a couple of coppers and tossed them her way. "What you saw there, you're wrong," he said.

The woman gathered the coins and tucked them in her purse. "Not wrong. Cards and the spirits don't lie. Stay away from Dhasson."

"Come on," Harrtuck said, steering Jonmarc back into the stream of pedestrians. "Let it go. Nothing but a crazy old woman." He nudged Jonmarc good-naturedly. "I mean, did you hear what she said about me? Great success in battle, but I'll still be hunted, and I'll end up with great favor?" He shook his head, grinning. "Sounds like I'll win a bar fight, get chased down by an angry husband, and still end up with a trollop and a full bottle of whiskey."

Fire and darkness, the seer had said. Her words had rattled Jonmarc more than he wanted to let on, and anger won over fear. "I've got no plans to go to Dhasson," he repeated.

"See? Proof she's just making things up," Harrtuck said. "The War Dogs haven't had a contract in Dhasson for ten years, and the only place south of Dhasson is Nargi, which no sane person has cause to go to." He clucked his tongue. "Utter nonsense."

Jonmarc tried to shake off the woman's warning, but his mood had soured. It was hard enough to avoid thinking about Shanna, his late wife, when autumn days grew cold and short near the anniversary of the raid that had killed her and the rest of their village. As the afternoon shadows lengthened and the light dimmed, he caught glimpses of women in the crowd who had her blonde hair, her walk, her laugh, and for an instant, his heart leaped with foolish hope, only to plummet a breath later.

"You can't mourn the dead forever, m'boy," Harrtuck remarked without looking at him as if he guessed Jonmarc's thoughts. "You're not even twenty summers old."

Jonmarc shrugged moodily. "It's only been a year." A year in which he had left his small village and traveled the width of Margolan to get away from those memories, then crossed into a foreign land and signed on with a group of desperate men in a profession not known for longevity. Learning to fight had been the only respite. His training lessons with former soldiers back in the caravan had been almost joyful as his body learned the routines quickly and his movements showed innate skill. Fighting eased the pain, anger crowded out the guilt, and whiskey dulled the nightmares. That had been enough to get him this far.

As twilight fell, the spirits became more noticeable. "Back home, we didn't have this many ghosts," Jonmarc muttered.

"Back home, you probably weren't in a place that's been a battleground for hundreds of years," Harrtuck retorted. A waifish girl with short dark hair and large, sad eyes reached out to them as they passed, gesturing for them to give her coins, but her fingers slipped through them with a chill, and her image disappeared as soon as they moved on.

"Why don't they cross the Gray Sea?" Jonmarc asked. He nearly moved to go around a vagrant lying sprawled on the side of the road, only to have the man vanish though he had seemed nearly solid a moment before.

"Can't," Harrtuck replied. "Or so they say. Who knows?" he added with a shrug. "Maybe they don't know they're dead. Maybe they've got something left to do. Or maybe they can't find their way."

A shiver ran down Jonmarc's back despite his warm cloak. He skirted the gray, insubstantial form of a woman who lay against the side of a building, head lolling at an unnatural angle, throat cut from ear to ear. The darker it got, the more ghostly figures joined the throngs of revelers who crowded the streets and jammed the walkways. Yet the dead seemed to take no notice of the festival, despite it being the reason more than mages could see their spirits.

It's like two different crowds, in the same space, paying no attention to each other, he thought. The revelers sang and cat-called, weaving an inebriated path through the city, joining behind the parades and the puppet masters. The dead were a silent, despondent wave, passing through and around the living but utterly, eternally separate.

"Are there mages who can call for the dead?" Jonmarc asked.

Harrtuck shook his head. "You mean a summoner? A mage who can command the spirits, maybe even raise the dead? Just the sorceress, Bava K'aa. She's the mother of Queen Serae in Margolan. No other summoner but her in the whole of the Winter Kingdoms, or so they say."

"What about the mediums?" Jonmarc pressed. He had tried and failed, over the last year to reach Shanna's spirit for one last apology, one last good-bye. No one in the caravan had real power to speak to the dead. But perhaps here, in the midst of a festival to commemorate the dead, he might be able to find someone who could actually make that connection.

Harrtuck gave another shrug. "Maybe someone like that could call to them, and hear something back. But they say ghosts can't travel from where they were buried, least not on their own, unless you've taken their skull, breastbone, and right hand and burned them to powder and brought them with you." He snorted. "Or so I've heard."

They left the street with the fortune-teller behind them,

and the road widened into a large plaza. A bonfire blazed in front of a stone statue of the Sacred Lady in her Aspect of Athira the Whore. Revelers sang and chanted, filling the plaza, which was bounded by buildings on all four sides and four different roads. A large fountain stood in the back corner, and a line of women with pitchers filed up to draw their water, watching the drunken celebration warily.

Pilgrims and party-goers jostled together in the crowded plaza. Along one side of the square, a line of devout worshippers wore white robes and strands of red beads. They stood in a silent line, each holding a lit candle, observing the feast of the Lady. More common were the throngs of half-dressed men and women who were well into their ale, pairing up or fighting over partners as food vendors hawked their wares and peddlers pushed through the crowd selling beads and amulets.

"It's going to be a long night," Harrtuck sighed.

Jonmarc gave him a sidelong glance. "It's going to be a long week," he replied.

Haunts revelry would run for eight days and nights, one for each of the Aspects. But on the first and last nights, Lord Eriston made an appearance to present an offering to the goddess. And it was on these nights especially that the War Dogs had been warned to make sure there was no trouble, and no danger to the Lord.

"Get your hands off my girl!" A blond man dressed in costume as the Crone Aspect of the goddess shoved the man next to him, a dark-haired fellow who wore a dozen strands of red beads on his shirtless chest and was otherwise clad only in a loincloth. The woman in question, a jaded-looking trollop, watched the men with boredom.

"She's only yours for an hour," the man in the loincloth shot back. "And your time is up. I paid for my turn."

"I'm enjoying her company," the first man slurred, making it obvious that he had also enjoyed more than his share of ale.

"Not anymore." The dark-haired man took the woman by her arm and began to move away through the crowd. It was clear that she did not care which of the men she accompanied. But the first man grabbed his rival by the shoulder, swinging him around and landing a punch so hard it made the interloper stagger.

"Time to go to work," Harrtuck muttered. He and Jonmarc shouldered their way through the crowd. Though the two men were only a few feet in front of them, maneuvering through the crowd was difficult if they didn't want to start a slew more fights.

The two men were exchanging blows, and the crowd had stepped back to watch the show. Meanwhile, the trollop slipped off into the throng without a backward glance.

Across the plaza, servants bustled to ready the area around the bonfire for Lord Eriston's arrival, and twenty of the War Dogs rallied to form an honor guard along a path leading to the fire. Jonmarc was too busy dodging the Crone-costumed man's fists to worry about joining the other guards. Harrtuck was trying to dissuade the interloper without resorting to his sword, but the man was too drunk to appreciate the courtesy.

The blond man swung his heavy tankard at Jonmarc's head. Jonmarc ducked, taking a glancing blow on the shoulder, and pivoted, getting close enough to land a punch to his opponent's gut, then as the man doubled over, a solid fist to the jaw finished him off. With a wheeze, the drunk sank to his knees and then fell face-forward onto the paving stones.

The second man was not so drunk, making him a more agile opponent. Harrtuck's grin told Jonmarc that his friend was mentally a few steps ahead of the man he was fighting, waiting for his adversary to maneuver himself into a corner. Jonmarc sighed, rolled his eyes, and grabbed the heavy tankard his opponent had dropped, then swung hard and clipped the dark-haired man behind the ear. He fell like a bag of rocks.

"What did you go and do that for?" Harrtuck demanded.

"Why waste energy fighting when there's an easier way?" Jonmarc replied. He suspected that Harrtuck mostly minded not getting to see his mental choreography for the fight play out, but Jonmarc was equally certain that there would be many more fights to come, and plenty of time to test Harrtuck's battle plans.

"Besides, we're needed over there," Jonmarc said, pointing to where the Lord would arrive very soon. The War Dogs made an impressive corridor, two rows with their backs to each other, facing outward to guard against any threat. Mercenaries normally eschewed regular uniforms, leaving them for the conscripts and volunteers of the small regular army, but they did wear either a black armband or a surcoat for battle emblazoned with the head of a large, snarling dog. Given the formality of the occasion and the prominence of their patron, all the War Dogs wore black surcoats, and a line of them, looking well-armed and dour, made an impressive honor guard. Captain Valjan planned to personally escort Lord Eriston to make his offering, and back again.

Jonmarc and Harrtuck maneuvered through the crowd to join the line. But as Jonmarc took his place, he glanced to one side and spotted a tall man wearing a black surcoat who was hanging back in the shadows, close to where the offering would be made. It was hard in the crowd and smoke to make out the man's face. Jonmarc turned to ask Harrtuck if he knew the soldier, but Harrtuck had taken a position on the other side, and the man next to Jonmarc was muttering under his breath to the next soldier in line.

Jonmarc fidgeted. His gut told him that there was something wrong about the soldier in the shadows, but the trumpets were already blaring to signal the lord's approach, and he dared not move out of position. He scanned the crowd, but the tall man was gone, and Jonmarc wondered if he had mistaken a dark tunic for one of the War Dog's surcoats. He glanced down the line. Valjan had put twenty of his men on duty tonight, and twenty stood in the lines for Lord Eriston's bodyguards. Which meant that the man Jonmarc had spotted couldn't be a War Dog.

There's no law against wearing a black tunic, he thought. *And I didn't get a look at the front of it. I've been too many fights today; I'm getting jumpy.* It was a rational explanation, but it did not quell the feeling in the pit of his stomach that something was amiss.

Fanfare echoed from the buildings that enclosed the plaza, and the crowd milled more quietly. Some in the throng were even sober enough to turn toward the trumpeters with puzzled expressions or stand on their toes to see what was going on. Jonmarc suspected that the feast-goers were really wondering whether the trumpets heralded the arrival of more food and drink, and sure enough, most turned away muttering when they realized nothing of the sort was forthcoming.

Jonmarc faced outward so he could not see Captain Valjan and Lord Eriston making their way up the soldier-lined corridor. But out of the corner of his eye, he caught a glimpse of motion near the altar that had been set up in front of the bonfire. Hanging back from the edge of the crowd, Jonmarc glimpsed the top of the tall man's head, and a nagging sense of familiarity tugged at his memory once more. His hand fell to the pommel of his sword, and he found himself mentally gauging how many steps it might take to reach the altar if things went awry.

The trumpets kept up their fanfare, and Jonmarc heard the boot steps behind him marking Captain Valjan's approach with Lord Eriston. The most dangerous part of the ceremony would be when Valjan and Eriston emerged from the guarded corridor and crossed a ten-foot-wide expanse of open pavement that had been cleared by Eriston's retainers shooing festival-goers out of the way. Eriston had flatly turned down Valjan's objections to the unguarded space and refused the idea of having extra guards extend the corridor.

He wants to be seen making his offering, Jonmarc thought. *After all, what good is a public spectacle if no one can see you?*

Jonmarc scanned the crowd, but the man he had spotted had moved once again. Valjan was forced to walk on Eriston's left so as not to block the crowd's view of their lord. Three of the Sacred Vessels oracles stepped out from behind the statue of the goddess to accept the offering. The crowd shifted, just a bit, as the more sober participants moved for a better vantage point.

Valjan stopped at the inside corner of the cleared space. It was obvious from his expression that he was chafing at not being closer or being between his patron and the crowd. Valjan's dark, wary eyes flickered over the revelers, watching.

Lord Eriston moved away from Valjan, toward the stone altar in front of the bonfire. The dancing flames cast the plaza in a pulsing orange glow and wavering shadows. Eriston carried a large flat basket with the ceremonial gifts required of a lord to his goddess at this feast day: a freshly slaughtered rabbit, turnips, cabbages, and parsnips, and a generous bundle of autumn flowers clipped from the manor garden along with a freshly baked loaf of bread and a flagon of wine.

Jonmarc nearly stepped out of ranks as he spotted the tall stranger's head in the crowd at the midpoint of the path Eriston would have to take to the altar. The priestesses were out of the way flanking the altar and the bonfire. Valjan had been told to remain behind and to the left to allow Eriston center stage. And heavily laden with his offering, Eriston would have no opportunity to reach for his weapon.

The fanfare blared. Wind whipped the bonfire into a high flare. A flicker of firelight on silver glinted there and gone, and Lord Eriston stopped in his tracks. It took half a heartbeat for the lord and the crowd to realize that the hilt of a knife protruded from the Lord's chest. And it took that same heartbeat for Jonmarc to finally realize why the tall stranger looked familiar.

He'd seen that man before. Tarren. A bounty hunter who often worked with Vakkis, someone who was near the top of the list of people Jonmarc someday hoped to kill.

Valjan shouted orders for the War Dogs to circle the fallen lord. "I saw who did it," Jonmarc said as he ran past Harrtuck. "I'm going after him."

Jonmarc was already crossing the open space, keeping Tarren in his sights. The onlookers close enough and sober enough to see what was going on drew back. Jonmarc plunged into the crowd, jockeying his way through the press of bodies and the staggering drunks to keep Tarren in view. Whether or not Tarren knew he was being followed, he kept a brisk pace without resorting to an open run, and Jonmarc bet that the bounty hunter was counting on the unruly crowd to hide his exit even as the ale blurred their memories of anything they had seen.

At the end of the plaza, Jonmarc glimpsed Tarren turning

left, away from the main festivities. Jonmarc swore under his breath. He alone of the War Dogs had seen the would-be killer, and a glimpse behind him confirmed that he was the only one to go after the assassin. But Harrtuck had been the one who knew the streets of Linbourne, and on his own, Jonmarc knew he could easily get lost in the winding alleys and meandering ginnels, or lose sight of his quarry.

He turned the corner and spotted Tarren up ahead. Either the bounty hunter was impossibly cool about the attempted assassination, or he did not realize he was being followed. There were enough festival-goers in the street who had not bothered to attend the ceremony in the plaza that Jonmarc could weave through the pedestrians, keeping a screen of bodies between him and Tarren. As he strode after Tarren, Jonmarc found himself spoiling for a fight.

All day, Jonmarc had felt restless and out of sorts. He had chalked it up to the memories of Shanna's death and the uncertainty of his new situation with the War Dogs. Yet he had already learned that anger was easier to channel than grief, and sometimes more productive. And he had an old score to settle with Tarren and the two other bounty hunters with whom he could usually be found, Vakkis and Chessis. Venting his frustration sounded appealing, though Jonmarc knew Tarren would not be an easy opponent to best. He had survived as a bounty hunter by being wily and ruthless, and even if he believed that no one had witnessed his treachery, Tarren was not the kind to take chances.

Jonmarc was glad for the cuirass he wore beneath his War Dogs surcoat. He pulled his cloak across his chest with his left hand, hiding the mercenary emblem, knowing that it would be all too recognizable should Tarren glance behind him.

After a quarter of a candlemark's walk, the streets grew

more deserted, save for drunks who lolled along the building walls and strumpets who lingered in the doorways. They were a distance from the center of the city, far enough away that the smells of food from the vendors' carts had been replaced by the tang of unwashed bodies and stale urine, and the music of the minstrels was drowned out by the snoring of drunks.

But there were plenty of ghosts. Spectral women dressed in ragged clothing watched from upstairs windows, still marked by the wounds of the beatings that killed them. Ghostly drunks lay where they had fallen when their last batch of liquor overwhelmed their failing hearts. From the alleyways, Jonmarc could hear the rustle of spirits killed by cutpurses or done in by faithless lovers. And he felt sure that their anger matched or exceeded his own.

These streets were no place for a man to walk alone, even armed with a sword. Jonmarc was aware of the glances he drew from those he passed, but he kept his head down, hoping to shield his face from view should Tarren look back.

"Fancy a little warmth tonight?" the strumpet asked, leaning against the doorframe in what she might have thought was a suggestive pose. She looked twice Jonmarc's age, her teeth stained from tobacco, her clothing reeking of dreamweed. But at just that moment, Tarren paused before going into a doorway, and Jonmarc pivoted, moving so that his back was to Tarren, and flashed a smile to the strumpet.

"I think you're just what I need," he murmured, grabbing her into a clinch with his right arm while his left hand came across his body to grab her wrists should she be inclined to use a dagger on him.

"Hey now, you've got pay for that!" she sputtered as he released her a moment later. Jonmarc pulled a few coppers out of the purse on his belt.

"I'll pay you more if you can tell me anything about that

man, the tall one who went into that building," Jonmarc said, knowing that the handful of coins would be enough to get the woman both a decent meal and enough ale to drink the night away. If she could see the baleful ghost of a dead trollop in the next doorway, the woman did not seem to care.

The strumpet gave Jonmarc a mistrustful look. "I stay out of Tarren's business," she said. "You will too if you want to stay alive."

"Whose house is it?" he asked, keeping the coins out of reach. He glanced at the bottle that sat on the step near the woman's feet. It was almost empty. She'd be wanting another before too long, he wagered.

The woman hesitated, torn between fear of Tarren and desire for the coins and what they would buy. Hunger won out. "It ain't Tarren's, that's for sure," she said with a raspy laugh. "He comes and goes. They all do. Mostly, Big Sid holds court in there."

"Sid?"

She gave him a look like he was mad. "Big Sid, the smuggler. He's got a fine place away from here, but this is his meeting place."

Jonmarc toyed with the coins, knowing that she was watching his every move. "What's Sid got against Lord Eriston?"

This time, the strumpet hesitated for longer. "Couple of coppers ain't worth my life," she said. "Maybe you'd better move along."

Jonmarc dug into his purse and pulled out a small silver coin. It was a quarter of his wages for the week, and it might mean that he skipped a few meals, but if he was going to corner Tarren, he needed information and this woman was his best bet for getting it.

The strumpet caught her breath as the coin flashed in his

hand. "I don't have much time," Jonmarc said. "Talk fast, and this is yours with the coppers. Otherwise—"

"Sid controls everything that crosses this territory," she said, never taking her eyes off his fist as if she expected the coins to vanish into thin air. "Eriston's been taking a bigger percentage, and his fight with Lord Fallmount is making it harder to get goods in and out." She shrugged and spat to one side. "At least, that's what I hear."

"So Sid does business with Fallmount?"

She nodded and gave a nervous glance toward the rundown building where Tarren had entered. "Yeah. And Fallmount makes it worth his while. I hear Fallmount makes it easier to do business than Eriston does."

"And Tarren works for Sid?"

"Gimme the coins!" the strumpet said urgently. "If Tarren sees me talking to you, I won't need no money because I won't be alive to drink the ale."

"Just answer the question. Tarren works for Sid?"

She nodded desperately. "Yeah. Now pay up and get out of here."

Jonmarc handed over the coins. He flashed a second silver coin. "Keep your mouth shut about talking to me, and I'll circle back and give this to you. That's more than Tarren will give for information."

Her eyes went wide, and he saw a flash of guilt telling him that she had been thinking of selling him out. "All right. But you'd better come back," she hissed.

I will, if I survive the fight, he thought, which was not a sure proposition. If Harrtuck or any other of the War Dogs had managed to follow him, Jonmarc would have felt much more confident. His skill with a sword was above average, despite his age. He had faced vicious skirmishing and fought supernatural creatures. But Tarren was an experienced assassin and bounty hunter, ruthless and clever. Jonmarc had no illusions about how he might fare in a straight fight.

Which means I'll have to cheat.

The whole exchange with the strumpet had taken only minutes, yet Jonmarc felt the delay made him too visible. He glanced up and down the street, and began to walk briskly past the building where Taren had entered, continuing on as if it were of no interest. A man with an empty jug lay passed out against the building steps, but Jonmarc knew it was easy for a guard to pretend to be asleep. A couple of men loitered on the steps of a partly burned building on the other side of the street from the strumpet, and in the next block, he passed two men smoking dreamweed and another tawdry trollop. After he had gone just far enough to have momentarily passed out of sight of Sid's house, Jonmarc crossed the street and peered down an alleyway, wondering if he could double back on another street.

He never knew Tarren was behind him until he felt the knife plunge into his side.

"Looking for me?" Tarren's voice was as raw as Jonmarc remembered it. "This is a long way to come when the festival's back there." He chuckled. "War Dogs don't usually slip the leash."

Jonmarc could feel warm blood starting down his skin. He focused on his anger and kicked backward with his boot, catching Tarren in the balls, then wheeled and kicked the knife from Tarren's wrist with a perfect Eastmark kick. The pain of movement made Jonmarc gasp and stumble, but Tarren was on the ground. Jonmarc ran as fast as he could down the darkened alley, gritting his teeth against the pain.

Tarren was down, but not out. Jonmarc was certain of that. And when Tarren got back up, he would be twice as vengeful. The quick death Tarren had meted out in the square would be a mercy Jonmarc could not expect. Jonmarc was sure that Tarren also knew how to make a man's last candlemarks last exquisitely, excruciatingly long.

What a damn-fool errand this was, chasing him on my own, Jonmarc berated himself, but it was too late for second thoughts. He careened down the alley, stumbling over trash and bodies, trying to put as much distance as he could between himself and Tarren. He turned down a corner, hoping that he would eventually double back toward the festival plaza. This alley proved even darker than the last. Jonmarc stumbled again and leaned against the wall to catch his breath. He drew his hand away from where it clutched his side, and his fingers were covered in blood.

I can't run far enough, he thought. *I don't know where I'm going. I'll never make it back to warn the others.*

"You lost, mate?" The voice took him by surprise. Jonmarc looked up to see a young man with a hat jammed down over his forehead dressed in ragged clothing. "You got Tarren in the nuts. That was worth watching." Only then did Jonmarc realize he could see through the ghostly image.

"I can hear you," Jonmarc replied. "But you're dead."

The young man shrugged. "Probably because you don't have long yourself." He nodded toward Jonmarc's bloody side. "But maybe I can help."

"How?"

"I know a way out that Tarren doesn't," the young man said. "He's not from here."

"Will it get me back to Goddess Plaza?"

The ghost nodded. "It will if you can make it."

"Show me." Jonmarc knew he was taking a crazy chance. The ghost could easily be leading him into a trap, maybe even delivering him into Tarren's hands, and in his current condition, Jonmarc would not be able to fight his way free. But he was certain he heard running steps heading their way, and he also knew that outrunning Tarren was impossible.

"My name's Mim," the ghost said, though Jonmarc hadn't asked. "This way."

"Why help me?" Jonmarc questioned, still standing where he was.

Mim turned halfway around to look at him. "Because Tarren killed me over a two-skrivven debt, and sold my wife to the trollop-master. I'd like to see him sent to the Crone."

Jonmarc was desperate enough to follow Mim into a ginnel so narrow they had to turn sideways to keep their shoulders from brushing against the walls. Halfway down the stinking, narrow passage, Mim gestured to a doorway that gaped into the side of an old brick wall. "In there," he said.

"What is it?" Jonmarc asked.

"Tunnels. Old ones. Go just about everywhere. Mind the rats," Mim said.

Jonmarc heard the running steps growing closer. *If I'm going to die, might as well cheat Tarren of the pleasure.*

The doorway led into a dank cellar. Jonmarc reached into a pouch at his belt and took out a candle, flint, and steel. "You may be able to see in the dark, but I can't," he said.

Mim watched the flame with an expression of longing. "Keep it shaded," he cautioned. "Don't know what else is down here." In the dark tunnels, Mim's figure glowed with a faint, greenish inner light.

Jonmarc kept one hand in front of the flame, dampening its light. It was too cramped a space to draw his sword, and he was losing enough blood he doubted he could fight for more than a minute or two without collapsing. He tried not to think about the blood that was running down his side, down his leg and dripping onto the floor, leaving a trail for any predator that could scent him.

"This way," Mim said, choosing a winding path across the debris-strewn cellar until a hole gaped in front of them. "Down there," he said, pointing.

"How?" Jonmarc said, peering into the darkness. It could have been a drop of a few feet, or a fall into oblivion.

"Ladder," Mim replied. "It's the entrance to the tunnels."

Trying to make it back through the streets was suicide. Going below on nothing more than the word of a ghost wasn't much better, but it presented a slightly greater chance of success. Jonmarc eased himself down the hole, trying to hold onto his candle as he navigated the rungs. Mim waited at the bottom.

"Sid never found these tunnels," Mim said, starting on ahead of Jonmarc. "They're real old. Might have been from the first city, the one that drowned in the flood. They say people built over it, forgot it."

"Why can I hear you so clearly?" Jonmarc asked. He hadn't heard anything at all from the ghosts he had passed that day in the city, or the ones in the streets as he followed Tarren. Even mediums claimed to only get a few words from those on the other side.

Mim looked at him as if he had asked an obvious question. "I told you. Because you're dying. You're almost one of us."

It took all of Jonmarc's strength to stumble down the twisting passageways, following Mim's luminous image. Rats scurried around his feet, and Jonmarc's boots kicked aside soft, solid things that felt like remains of creatures that had unwisely wandered down into the dark. From somewhere behind them, he heard a *skritch-skritch* noise that reminded him of claws on pavement, but he did not let his mind dwell on it. Anything was better than boot steps. Besides, it was taking all his concentration to stay on his feet.

The tunnels were cool, but Jonmarc knew the growing coldness he felt had more to do with the warm blood leaking from his side than from the temperature. Mim kept a steady pace, and sheer willpower drove Jonmarc on. *If I die down here, no one will find me, and the rats will eat me. Valjan will think I've deserted. No one will bury my bones.*

The darkness was total, except for the wavering flicker of his candle and Mim's faint glowing outline. It seemed like they traveled for miles when Jonmarc knew the festival plaza was only blocks away from where he had tracked Tarren. He was listing like a drunkard, trying to keep his feet, using the rough stone walls to hold himself up despite the slick, dark slime that covered them.

"How much farther?" he panted, fighting the vertigo that threatened to topple him. *If I go down, I won't get up.*

The farther into the tunnels they went, the more the ghosts crowded around them. Men, women, and children, dressed in the ragged fashions of times current and long passed. They, too, had come down here to die. When Jonmarc had passed the ghosts earlier in the day, they were insubstantial, wisps of mist that parted with a breath. Now, they pulled at his cloak and sleeves, and he felt as if he were hemmed in by the press of them, as he had been in the festival plaza.

It can't be a good thing that they're becoming more solid. It must mean that I'm fading.

His candle was guttering, and the hot wax burned his fingers, but Jonmarc dared not let go. "Nearly there now," Mim said, but his voice had a bleak quality to it, and Jonmarc wondered whether they were nearing the end of the tunnel or the end of his life.

The ground was rising beneath Jonmarc's boots, climbing from the depths of the tunnels. In the distance, he caught a whiff of roasting meat and incense. Voices carried in the night, and faint strains of music. He stumbled again and crashed down on one knee, cutting the skin on the rough stone.

"Go on!" Mim said urgently. "Get up. If you don't tell them what you saw, I don't get my vengeance. Now get up!"

Jonmarc's head was spinning, and the world slanted and tilted in strange directions. The candle had fallen from his hands when he stumbled, and he could see nothing in the darkness except for the ghosts. Those behind him pulled at his cloak, tugging at him to come into the darkness. Mim stood in front of him, and beyond Mim's glowing figure, the darkness seemed less absolute.

"Go on!" Mim urged, and grabbed Jonmarc by the wrist with a solid grip. He half-dragged, half-threw Jonmarc out of a hole in the wall and into the night. The torches that ringed the festival plaza were so bright Jonmarc blinked, blinded.

"Get my vengeance," Mim begged. "Don't let me have died for nothing." His voice trailed off as Jonmarc staggered toward the light.

He was approaching the plaza from one of the side streets, but despite Tarren's strike, the celebration continued. Jonmarc felt like a shade of himself, cold and weakened by the blood that continued to drip through his fingers. After the passage in the darkness, the voices sounded too loud, the music seemed shrill, and the smell of food and incense were so strong they were almost nauseating. The torches wavered in his vision, ringed by a nimbus of light.

As he stumbled out into the plaza, a woman gasped. Someone screamed. Men shouted. Jonmarc dropped to his knees, and this time, he knew he could not rise on his own. He fell forward onto the cold stone, too spent to try to move. *I'm back among the living, at least. For now.*

He looked out toward the crowd and saw a blonde woman

standing a few feet away. "Shanna?" he murmured in a whisper.

She turned, just slightly, enough for him to know her profile. Then as quickly as the figure appeared, she vanished, and Jonmarc sank back against the pavement, resigned to what was to come.

"Are you always this hard to kill?"

Jonmarc heard the man's voice close at hand, but he struggled for a moment before he could place it as belonging to Harrtuck. Another moment passed before he realized he was on a cot, not lying on the stone of the festival plaza, and that he was warm, covered with blankets. He shifted position, and his side twinged uncomfortably, but it did not immobilize him with pain.

"So I'm alive?"

Harrtuck chuckled. "Apparently so, or the other side of the Gray Sea looks a lot like the War Dogs camp. Which would be a bloody awful turn of events. Especially if the food isn't better."

Jonmarc started to rise. "Tarren. Sid. The house—"

Harrtuck pushed him back. "Relax. You already told us who and where to find them—almost with your last breath. Good thing Valjan had a healer with us in the square. You very nearly didn't make it."

Jonmarc was silent for a moment. "Valjan had a healer because he expected an attack. It was a set-up?"

Harrtuck nodded. "Eriston was wearing mail beneath his clothing. He wanted to present an 'easy' target so he could flush his enemies from cover. They took the bait."

"Did they get caught? Tarren and Sid."

Harrtuck sighed. "Not exactly. Tarren slipped the noose. He was nowhere to be found, more's the pity. Valjan and the rest of us raided Sid's house, gathered up a lot of his underlings and his contraband, but Sid was nowhere to be found. Seems he's also left his fancy house to go traveling as well," he added.

"Tarren was wearing a black surcoat," Jonmarc said. "Like he wanted the War Dogs to get the blame."

Harrtuck nodded. "Probably. When we got to the house, we found ledgers linking Sid's smuggling operation to Lord Fallmount. Eriston figured as much, but now he has proof, which puts pressure on Fallmount." He grimaced. "It's always politics," he added, leaning back in his chair. "Otherwise, all we found was a dead whore."

"Where?" Jonmarc asked.

Harrtuck frowned. "Don't know why you'd care, but she was propped up in a doorway near Sid's headquarters. Throat slit, tongue cut out. Couple of coins shoved in her mouth. Why?"

Jonmarc lay back and swallowed hard, trying not to throw up. "She spoke to me. Tarren killed her because she spoke to me. That's where I got the information."

Harrtuck regarded him silently for a moment. "It goes like that sometimes," he said finally. "We're in a rough business. People die. Today, it wasn't you. That's a good thing."

"What now?" Jonmarc asked, hoping Harrtuck couldn't hear the guilt and anger in his voice.

"Valjan says there's going to be fighting between Eriston and Fallmount. No declared war, nothing official, but a lot of sniping and raiding." Harrtuck shrugged. "Eriston's willing to pay well, so off we go." He paused. "Oh, and Valjan says if you ever run off without back-up again, he will personally run you through." Harrtuck shot Jonmarc a grin. "That means he thinks you did well today."

"How would I know if he didn't think I did well?"

Harrtuck met his gaze. "He'd just run you through without saying anything at all." He clapped Jonmarc on the shoulder. "The healer said to let you rest. Do it while you can. We break camp day after tomorrow." With that, Harrtuck walked out of the tent, leaving Jonmarc alone with his thoughts.

A tangle of emotions blurred his thinking. Amazement that he was actually alive. Rage that Tarren had gotten away. Guilt for his role in the whore's death. And underneath the anger, worry that perhaps the fortune-teller had actually been right.

The Dark Lady's hand is one you, but she is not a gentle mistress.

CURSED

CURSED

Jonmarc Vahanian had been in plenty of fights before. But this was the first time he had been to war.

"All this, over smuggling percentages?" Jonmarc asked, ducking back under cover as arrows rained down on their position.

"Nobles don't have anything better to do except whore, eat, and count their money—and have pissing contests over power," Tov Harrtuck replied. "And we get to be the game pieces on the board."

"It would be easier to just hand them both swords and have at it," Jonmarc muttered.

"That's true of all wars, m'boy. But it doesn't work like that."

Principality, under King Staden, gave its nobles wide leeway to rule their territories as they saw best. That included making war on each other, so long as they kept the conflict restricted to their own territories and did not challenge the sovereignty of the king. Those rules left a lot of room for interpretation, as did accords on everything from water access to right-of-way. And from what Jonmarc could see, no quibble was too small to avoid a military solution.

Some other time, the wide-open meadows and pastures might have been serene with changing leaves and herds of contented cows. But not this year. Now, the rolling hills were pock-marked with holes where catapulted rocks had flung up showers of wet dirt, and dozens of the trees along the forest's edge were broken or scarred. A nearby barn was now a ruin, with its roof caved in and its stone walls battered and fallen. Wooden fences had been snapped or knocked down, and the tall grasses ridden over and churned by horses' hooves.

Behind them snaked the Jorn River on its way to join the flow of the mighty Nu River. By comparison, the Jorn was a swollen stream, but it was deep enough for flat-bottomed boats to carry cargo, and its banks hid enough coves and hidden inlets to be a favorite of smugglers. From the Jorn, boats could slip past the harbor sentries and bring goods in from Margolan or Dhasson, or carry out gems and other luxuries from Principality to the rest of the Winter Kingdoms. The potential for profit was enormous, and the disputed river ran through portions of each noble's lands so that both men believed themselves to be entitled to free access to the length of the waterway.

A hail of rocks came clattering down from the enemy catapult. Jonmarc held his shield over his head and huddled against what remained of a stacked stone fence, cursing under his breath as the rocks pelted him.

"Be glad it's not a full-size catapult," Harrtuck shouted from where he crouched. "Send rocks at you that would squash you flat."

Tov Harrtuck had seen real warfare in his five years with the War Dogs mercenaries. He was a few years older than Jonmarc, which put him in his mid-twenties. Short and barrel-chested, with a deep laugh and a seemingly endless appetite for ale, Harrtuck was a career soldier and proud of it. And as a favor to a mutual friend, he had agreed to watch out for the new guy.

Jonmarc found himself in the uncomfortable role of being that newcomer. Nearly nineteen years old, he had spent the last year and a half outrunning a painful past that left him with dangerous enemies, bad nightmares and a long scar running from one ear down below his collar.

"What in the name of the Crone is that?" Jonmarc swore, wide-eyed, as he looked out over the no man's land. Men were running toward the line the War Dogs had established, but something about their movements did not seem quite right.

"*Ashtenerath*," Harrtuck muttered, making the word a curse. "Just the kind of trick I'd expect from the Night Wolves."

"What are they and how do we fight them?" Jonmarc asked, gripping his sword.

"They're men broken by drugs and magic. And you don't. Leave this to the old-timers," Harrtuck said, rising to his feet.

"Not going to happen," Jonmarc snapped, rising as well.

Harrtuck glowered at him, but there was no time to argue. The *ashtenerath* were already on them.

Jonmarc's attacker stared at him wild-eyed, his eyes glazed, his mouth twisted in a feral cry. The attacker's movements were jerky and unpredictable, but fast and unexpectedly strong. Jonmarc was hard-pressed to parry, let alone go on the offense. Every strike vibrated down his arms with bone-crushing intensity. It took Jonmarc's full concentration to fight the madman, an opponent utterly without regard for his own survival, an enemy focused only on killing.

Jonmarc was fast, but the *ashtenerath* was faster. The

wild man opened a slash on Jonmarc's left arm before Jonmarc could beat him back. Madness glimmered in the attacker's eyes, and spittle dripped from his slack mouth. Jonmarc had little time to appraise his attacker, but he noted that the man was dressed in rags and seemed heedless of the festering wounds on his arms and hands. His fingernails looked as if he had clawed his way out of the grave, and his face was flushed with homicidal zeal.

Jonmarc parried, doing his best to block the sword-strikes that came nearly too fast to see. He was operating on pure instinct, trusting to the native talent that had earned him the regard of his training partners, hoping it would be enough and doubting that he could hold out long.

For all his experience, Harrtuck was struggling against an opponent of his own. Winded and red in the face, Harrtuck managed to beat back his attacker only to yield the same ground as the madman went on the offensive once again.

"How do we beat them?" Jonmarc shouted. Down the War Dogs line, he saw his fellow mercenaries straining to hold the foe at bay. Even Captain Valjan was hard-pressed, though he swung at the *ashtenerath* with two swords and his full strength.

"Burn them out," Harrtuck puffed. "They can't last long."

Jonmarc danced backward, enticing his attacker to follow. He dodged right and left, parrying only when he could not get out of the way. The *ashtenerath's* sword whistled near his ear, and on the next swing, it opened a painful slice on Jonmarc's shoulder. Still, he was leading his enemy on a merry chase, forcing the *ashtenerath* to come after him, intentionally choosing uneven footing and jumping from flat ground to the top of the ruined wall and back again.

The *ashtenerath* swung again with enough strength to part Jonmarc's head from his shoulders. Jonmarc parried. The blow smashed the sword from his numb fingers. The *ashtenerath* looked at him with eyes alight, slashing one way and then the next with his long, sharp sword.

Jonmarc scrambled to get out of the way. His sword had fallen out of reach, and he couldn't pull his second sword without opening himself to the *ashtenerath*. He had no doubt that his enemy meant to kill him and then hack his body into tiny pieces. He was backing toward the edge of the forest, and he grabbed a fallen tree branch. It was too long and unwieldy, but it caught the worst of two of the *ashtenerath's* strikes before it cracked uselessly. Even then, the branch caught the attacker's blade just long enough to buy Jonmarc precious seconds as he dropped the limb, drew his second sword and ran.

The *ashtenerath* had changed the battle. All afternoon, the War Dogs had made steady advances across the battlefield, using their small catapults and longbow archers to drive the opposing side back to the road. Casualties for the Night Wolves had been heavy. Despite the fact that both sides were paid soldiers and neither army fought for home or hearth, the action had been particularly vicious. *Old rivalries*, Harrtuck said, Jonmarc recalled. *Nothing matters more to a merc than pride.*

The Night Wolves seemed content to allow their drugged and magicked proxies to do the fighting for them, staying off the field and letting the madmen press their advantage. *Ashtenerath* howled and screamed in voices more animal than human. War Dogs shouted curses or battle cries. The *ashtenerath* seemed incapable of anything except blood rage.

Jonmarc managed to circle around the attacker and leaped the wall to retrieve his weapon and slung his shield to protect his back. Now armed with both, he scythed his swords, going high with the sword in his right hand and low with the sword in his left. He opened up a deep gash in the *ashtenerath's* thigh, enough to lame a normal man. But the crazed opponent never slowed, heedless of the blood that flowed from the wound.

No pain. No fear. They're killing machines, Jonmarc thought. By now, he was bleeding from a dozen gashes, though none were life-threatening. The light was fading, but he could see Harrtuck nearby, swinging a war hammer and a sword, covered in blood. How much of it was his own, Jonmarc could not tell.

Can we wear them down before they cut their way through our line? he wondered.

"Run for it, boys! Whatever it takes to live to fight. Don't let your pride get you killed!" Valjan's voice rang out over the battle.

Jonmarc had already decided that surviving was the ultimate victory. *If I'm still alive, my pride can nurse itself back to health,* he thought, running for a few lengths and then turning to fight, leading his opponent this way and that, sometimes in circles as it became increasingly apparent that the *ashtenerath* fixed on an enemy but brought few thinking skills to the battle. The *ashtenerath* was slowing, his movements becoming more erratic. Even so, his swings were powerful enough to sever a limb, and Jonmarc was tiring as well.

Question is, which of us makes a mistake first.

The battlefield had turned into a free-for-all, and in the waning light, Jonmarc dodged into the forest's edge, using the trees to screen him from the *ashtenerath's* sight. Tall ash and rowan trees loomed over them, and beneath their feet, monkshood bloomed its last before the winter.

If they're addled with magic and potions, maybe it won't

take too much to confuse him. Dark Lady take my soul! I can't keep this up much longer!

Run. Parry. Dodge. Hide. Moments seemed to last forever. The *ashtenerath* had grown unnaturally pale, wheezing for breath, his eyes wide and pupils dilated. He was covered in blood, dripping with sweat despite the cool autumn evening, heedless to his wounds, which should have stopped even a seasoned fighter.

Just the look of the *ashtenerath* fueled Jonmarc with rage. *What in the name of the Formless One have the Night Wolves done? He used to be a man. Now he's nothing but a monster. By the Crone's tits! They deserve to die for this, even if we weren't paid to fight them.*

It had not escaped his notice that he was bleeding from several nasty gashes himself. Harrtuck had also taken the battle into the woods, playing with the waning light and lengthening shadows to attack before the *ashtenerath* could orient himself and then dodge back into the shelter of the trees. The noise of battle sounded all around them. Catapults thudded, sending sprays of dirt high into the air. Arrows twanged through the air. Men shouted and screamed, cursing their enemies or begging for mercy.

With a savage cry, the *ashtenerath* sprang at Jonmarc from behind one of the tall trees. He had moved a few feet to one side, not where Jonmarc had expected, and it gave him an advantage. Jonmarc dove out of the way, but the *ashtenerath's* sword caught him deep on his left arm, and he cried out despite himself. A killing gleam came into the *ashtenerath's* eyes.

Jonmarc hung onto his swords. They were the last, precious, work of his father, a master blacksmith. But his left arm was nearly useless. He blocked and parried with all his strength with this right arm as the *ashtenerath* came at him in a burst of fury, moving nearly too quickly to be seen. Jonmarc stumbled, falling backward, barely bringing his sword up to block a swing that would have taken his head from his shoulders.

He hit the ground and rolled, and the *ashtenerath's* sword missed his ear, slicing a lock of hair from his head. Jonmarc dropped the sword in his weakened left hand, swung with all his might to block the next blow, and grabbed at a handful of leaves, dirt, and debris with his left. He flung the dirt into the *ashtenerath's* face, and scythed his legs, taking the *ashtenerath* down at the knees.

The wild man screamed and flailed, but Jonmarc dove at him, giving his rage full vent, allowing it to take him past pain and exhaustion. He slammed the *ashtenerath's* wrist down over and over again on the hard, raised root of a nearby tree, ignoring the shrieks of pain, until the bone snapped beneath his grip and the sword fell from the useless hand. He was heavier than the *ashtenerath*, but madness more than made up for the difference in bulk. It took all of Jonmarc's waning strength to pin the crazed fighter, straddling his twisting body and using his full weight to wrestle the man to the ground.

Once, the *ashtenerath* had been human. Now, he was bent and broken, a tool of his captors. *Slave or prisoner of war?* Jonmarc wondered. It did not matter. No one, mage or not, should have the right to turn a man into such a beast. A fresh surge of rage gave Jonmarc the energy he needed to snatch a knife from his belt and raise it for the deathblow.

For just a second, he saw comprehension in the eyes of the *ashtenerath*. "Please." The word was slurred, hard to hear, as if forced from lips that had forgotten how to do more than howl and shriek. The *ashtenerath* seemed to struggle with an inner battle, and then the instant came when the crazed pawn managed to lay still, surrendered to his fate.

Jonmarc brought the knife down two-handed, with all his waning strength, right into the *ashtenerath's* heart.

The body bucked and jerked. Blood started from the man's lips. The *ashtenerath* twitched, gave a gasp, and fell still. Just in case, Jonmarc slashed his bloody blade across the cursed man's neck, slicing clean through to the spine.

Rest in peace, he thought, realizing that he was shaking.

Just then, he heard the howl of wolves, nearby.

"Oh, it just gets better," he muttered. He took a deep breath to steady himself, taking a mental inventory of his injuries. He ripped off strips of his shirt to bind the wounds that were bleeding the hardest, then wiped his knife on the dead *ashtenerath's* pants, and looked about in the scant moonlight for his swords. His left arm hurt to move, and his grip with that hand was too weak to wield a sword. Jonmarc sheathed one of his swords and his knife, holding his other sword in his right hand.

A moan in the darkness put him on defense. Wolves howled again, closer now. He glanced toward the tree line. In the fight, he had moved farther into the forest than he had intended. He could make out the light of torches, and hear the thud of catapults and the shouts of the War Dogs and Night Wolves.

The moan came again, and Jonmarc moved forward cautiously. Harrtuck lay sprawled on the ground, bleeding from a deep belly wound. Near him lay a dead *ashtenerath*.

"Hang on," Jonmarc murmured. He was exhausted and hungry, light-headed from his loss of blood. But there was no chance that he was leaving Harrtuck behind. None at all. He tore at Harrtuck's shirt until he had strips of cloth sufficient to bind the belly wound closed. It was no substitute for a healer, but it might keep his innards inside, and slow the loss of blood. And it made it possible for him to move Harrtuck. *If the wolves catch us, we're dead men.*

"Sweet Chenne, you're heavy!" Jonmarc grunted as he got Harrtuck up on his feet. His friend was conscious enough to move his feet now that Jonmarc was under one arm, holding him up. That left Jonmarc's right hand free to fight.

"Forget me carrying you," Jonmarc muttered. "That's not going to happen."

Another howl, even closer. Jonmarc had heard tell of large wolves in these forests, unafraid of man or fire. But another possibility, even more fearsome, presented itself. He had also heard of men forced by dark magic to change into beasts and fight for their masters. *If Lord Fallmount and the Night Wolves aren't above using* ashtenerath, *could they not make men into wolves to do their bidding?*

When he had been with Maynard Linton's caravan, Jonmarc had known *vyrkin*, shapeshifters who could transform themselves into wolves. They had been decent, ordinary folks, friends. Only the fears of others had forced the *vyrkin* to fight.

Those were men who knew the wolf inside, who claimed it and owned the change. What would it be to have it forced upon you, to have the predator dragged to the forefront, robbed of will and mind? He had seen the madness in the eyes of the *ashtenerath*. Jonmarc was afraid he knew the answer to that question.

Harrtuck moaned. "Not too much farther, though I think it will be a while before either of us get to see our cots," Jonmarc whispered. If there were wolves after them, magicked or not, the beasts could certainly smell their blood. Perhaps that was why the forest seemed suddenly, unnaturally silent, as if the creatures were holding their breath, hoping the predators would choose another victim.

A small clearing just inside the tree line separated them from the main battle. Jonmarc could see the flickering of the torches, hear the cries and screams of men on the main field. He and Harrtuck had left their *ashtenerath* behind them, dead, but from the sounds of the fight ahead of them, the Night Wolves had more where that came from, maybe even *vyrkin* allies Captain Valjan had not expected.

Harrtuck leaned heavily on Jonmarc, one staggering step after another. Neither of them were going to be much use in battle until they healed, and if the fight went on too long without a healer, Jonmarc doubted either of them would make it to morning. He was light-headed, chilled from the loss of blood, and he was certain Harrtuck was even worse off.

"Not much farther," Jonmarc murmured. He had heard no howls from the wolves for a few moments, but the night seemed to watch them, and Jonmarc was certain there were predators in the darkness, waiting for an opportunity to strike.

I am not going to be eaten by wolves, vyrkin *or not*, he vowed silently. His boot hit a small raised stone sunk deep into the ground. The clearing's footing was uneven, with an odd rise and fall to the land. Jonmarc sidestepped and hit another stone. A third made him stumble, just a step over.

"We're in a bloody graveyard," he muttered.

He took a step, and Harrtuck shifted his weight, throwing Jonmarc off balance. Jonmarc staggered, and his foot sank deep into the soft ground.

The next thing he knew, the ground was falling away beneath him, and he and Harrtuck were tumbling amid a shower of dirt, leaves, branches, and plants. They landed hard on old wood that splintered and broke beneath their weight

Jonmarc threw an arm behind him to catch himself and felt his hand close on bones and ragged cloth.

"By the Whore! We're in a tomb."

A low growl made him look up. Six violet-eyed wolves ringed the edge of the hole, looking down at them with teeth bared.

Jonmarc cursed under his breath. The tomb was cold, even colder than the autumn night aboveground. It smelled of damp earth and rotted linen, trampled plants and old death. Jonmarc shifted his weight, and the coffin gave a little more, making him wonder if they had not fallen atop the last in a long series of dead buried in a deep shaft.

Wonderful. If everything collapses under our weight, we could end up in an even deeper hole, with no way out and no one to come looking for us. Jonmarc sighed. *Then again, it won't be a long wait. Either we bleed to death, or the wolves decide to come down here and get us.*

Harrtuck had fallen badly, twisting his leg under him in a way Jonmarc was certain had broken a bone. "Where are we?" he groaned.

"In a hole," Jonmarc replied. "Wolves above, no way out that I can see."

"Not wolves," Harrtuck said groggily. "*Vyrkin*. Makes a difference."

Not when it's got its teeth on your throat, Jonmarc thought, but there was no reason to speak his thoughts aloud.

"I've got flint and steel in my pouch," Harrtuck said. "Take it. Blighters don't like fire." He might have said something more, but his voice trailed off, and his eyes rolled back in his head as he lost consciousness.

Jonmarc found the items and put them in his own pouch, then took stock of what he had to work with. The shrouds of the dead would provide plenty of tinder, and he would be willing to sacrifice his tattered shirt to make a torch. That would help to fend off the *vyrkin*, and it might even catch the attention of someone on the War Dogs' side if anyone had noticed yet that he and Harrtuck had gone missing.

A large, dark wolf snarled. His violet eyes were a sure sign that he was a shapeshifter, a man or woman who could become a wolf. Jonmarc wondered how much the *vyrkin* were acting on their own, and how much of their menace was directed by the same dark mage who had created *ashtenerath* for the Night Wolves offense.

Jonmarc winced as he moved, favoring his injured arm and leg. He dug around in the wreckage beneath him, forcing the thought out of his mind that he was shuffling amid the bones of a long-ago burial. *Rummaging around in burial caves got you into this mess*, he thought. *No time to get squeamish now.*

The shrouds were tattered, tinder dry, but Jonmarc wound them around the longest staff of wood that had fallen into the tomb with them. One of the wolves was pawing at the edge of the hole as if testing his nerve to jump in. If that happened, Jonmarc knew that he and Harrtuck were dead men. He struck the flint to steel and said a prayer or the Dark Lady.

A spark flickered and went out. The wolf tested the ground, and an uncanny intelligence seemed to be measuring the distance down. *Not just wolves. Wolves with the intelligence of men.*

Jonmarc struck the flint again. This time, the spark caught in the friable old winding sheets, bursting into flame. Jonmarc hefted the wooden branch and poked the burning rags at the wolves. They yipped and backed up, but Jonmarc knew that wolves were patient, and *vyrkin* more so. The man-wolves knew that flames die out. When they did, the contest would begin anew.

Harrtuck moaned but showed no signs of coming around. Jonmarc cursed under his breath. The rags were already burning down. Embers dropped from the makeshift torch, burning his hand. As the flames grew dimmer, the wolves came closer. Jonmarc poked the torch at the wolves again, and in response heard a snarl.

The flames went out.

Jonmarc ripped strips from his shirt, knowing that this torch would also burn down too quickly. He lit the cloth, and again the wolves backed up. Perhaps it was his imagination, but Jonmarc thought he caught a glimpse of dark humor in the lead wolf's eyes. *All right, mortal. We'll play your game*; the glowing eyes seemed to say. *We both know how it ends.*

Two more times, Jonmarc managed to find enough rags to light the torch. But as the last torch sputtered out, Jonmarc had no more easy tinder. He watched as the flames faded and flickered, then went dark. At the top of the hole, the wolves drew closer, and Jonmarc heard a growl that sounded almost triumphant.

Angry, bleeding, and frightened, he grabbed a rock and lobbed it at the nearest wolf with all his might. The rock hit the wolf squarely between the eyes, making it stagger and fall back. Another wolf moved forward, and Jonmarc jabbed the wooden branch that had been his torch at the animal. It drew away, even before he could make contact. A growl from the other side of the pit drew Jonmarc's attention there, and he thrust the branch at another wolf, only to have it also draw back.

Puzzled, he looked more closely at the branch, and then shook his head. *I've been a fool*, he thought. *Rowan wood. Monkshood—also called wolfsbane. Let's see if these* vyrkin *are real wolves, with real wolves' weaknesses.*

Shanna, Jonmarc's late wife, had been the daughter of a

powerful hedge witch, a woman who knew the lore of plants and herbs to curse and cure. Many a time, Jonmarc had helped Shanna and her mother gather leaves, roots, and berries to be dried, steeped, mashed, or ground to a paste. He knew first-hand the power such plants possessed, both for curing mortal sickness and warding off danger and supernatural predators.

Rowan wood had magical qualities, or so the hedge witches claimed. It could protect against supernatural threats, especially werewolves. It was dark in the hole, so Jonmarc struck the flint again and managed a small fire in some twigs and dry grass, enough for him to see what he had to work with. Harrtuck lay still and pale. It would be lucky if he survived, if either of them made it to morning. A number of staff-sized pieces of wood and a sizeable branch had tumbled into the hole with them. Jonmarc inched his way over to where Harrtuck lay, keeping an eye on the wolves as he moved. He poked his branch at them if they snarled, and saw the reproach in their eyes as they backed away.

Grimacing at the pain in his injured leg, Jonmarc managed to collect the larger rowan branches and make a lean-to of sorts over Harrtuck. As he moved, he crushed some of the plants beneath his hand, and a familiar odor made him scratch through the dirt for more of the damaged flowers and leaves. *Monkshood. Wolfsbane. I can't kill them, but I can keep them back, at least for a while.*

The strips of cloth he had used to bind up his wounds were soaked through with blood. He tried to ignore that fact, as well as the pain, since there was nothing to be done about it. *It'll work out, one way or another, soon enough*, he thought. He gathered as much of the monkshood as he could find, picking it out of the loose dirt. First, Jonmarc took a handful of the leaves and flowers and crushed them in his hand, rubbing them over the end of the rowan staff he had fashioned as a torch. Then, he placed the mashed plants onto an edge of his cloak and drew the flat of his swords through them, tainting the blades with their poison. Finally, he did the same for his knives and the knives he could take from Harrtuck's belt.

His left arm felt like it was on fire. The sleeve of his shirt was wet with blood, and the wound had been deep enough that any motion of his arm or hand hurt enough to make him stifle a cry. The gash in his leg was nearly as bad, and Jonmarc knew that he had lost a lot of blood. It had been a long time since he had eaten, and his wineskin was empty.

When he was finished, Jonmarc sat back, surrounded by his poisoned weapons, rowan staff in his right hand, and glared at the ring of *vyrkin* watching from the lip of the grave.

"Listen up," he growled. "I know you can understand me. I am not going down without a fight. I will take as many of you with me as I can. Do yourself a favor, and leave now."

"Whoever's controlling you, fight it," Jonmarc urged the snarling *vyrkin*. He knew he dared not show weakness, although his wounds were fast getting the better of him. "You're men. You have minds. You don't have to be used against your will."

Then again, he was gambling that the *vyrkin* had not enlisted to Lord Fallmount's side willingly. In Margolan, the *vyrkin* generally stayed away from mortal politics. Perhaps things were different here.

He had no energy left to argue, and the *vyrkin* did not move away. Harrtuck did not move, and Jonmarc wondered if his friend was already dead. Maybe the tomb would have two new residents before morning. This was not the way he had hoped things would turn out.

You're fading. All the lovely blood. So warm. Give it to us. We are so cold.

At first, Jonmarc thought he had imagined the voices. He was light-headed and cold from blood loss, shaking from exposure and pain, and his heart was thudding in terror of the predators that ringed the top of the hole, waiting for an opening.

Let us in. Beneath your skin. Just for a little while. To feel a heartbeat once more. Let us feel life again before it fades.

Mist rose around Jonmarc, coming not from the forest floor above, but from the ruined tomb all around him. The wisps grew more solid, still vapor, but luminous. Faces shifted and changed in the fog. Human faces, once upon a time, long ago. Now, the faces of the long dead were something less than living, more than memory. Above him, the *vyrkin* gave deep-throated warning growls that for once Jonmarc did not think were intended for him.

"Go to the Crone," Jonmarc muttered. "You can't have either of us. Not until we're dead, at least."

Not long to wait. The voices crooned. *You'll stay warm for a while. Better if the blood still flows.*

"Not if I can help it," Jonmarc growled. He dug into his pouch for a small bag of salt, part of the rations of every War Dog, a necessity when meals on the road were made from whatever was cheap and handy. Keeping one eye on the *vyrkin*, Jonmarc loosened the drawstring on the bag and crawled slowly in a circle that surrounded Harrtuck and himself, leaving behind a trail of salt and monkshood. It was not as thick a line of salt as the hedge witches would have preferred, but it was a single, unbroken line, and Jonmarc bared his teeth as the ghosts drew back. Salt was power, especially here in the land of the dead.

What a small prison you've made for yourself, the ghosts

murmured. *We can't get in. You can't get out. The salt will last until morning. But will you?*

That was a good question, and Jonmarc was pretty sure he knew the answer, at least for Harrtuck. His own wounds had gone from sharp pain to something dull and deep, not a good thing. Pain goes with life. When pain recedes, life dims.

At the rim of the hole, the *vyrkin* still waited. Jonmarc laid out his poisoned weapons within arm's reach, knowing that the best he could hope for would be to take his attacker with him in death.

We cannot reach you within the circle, the ghosts said, many voices speaking at once. *But we can show you what awaits.*

The fog swirled and the shapes dissipated into a scrim of fog. Images began to appear in the mist, like looking out a window onto a distant scene. Jonmarc could see through the fog to the *vyrkin*, but whether or not the wolves could see the images, he did not know.

They were real enough for him. He saw a peddler on the road, beset by thieves, beaten and stripped of clothes and coin, stabbed and left for dead. He had crawled into these woods on his own to die. The scavengers had not waited for him to be fully gone before they came to feast.

The next image showed an old man, gaunt and sick. Even without sound accompanying the pictures, Jonmarc could imagine the man's hacking cough from the way the movement bent the man's body and distorted his features. The old man's eyes were sunken, and his skin was yellow. No one came into his room, and the fear of those in the house was clear from their furtive glances. His housemates, maybe even family, were waiting for him to die, hoping he would go soon enough that none of them would catch what ailed him.

Scavengers of another sort, they did not wait. Jonmarc

saw through the eyes of the old ghost as the man was bundled roughly into blankets, hauled from his bed and loaded into a wagon, then dumped just inside the trees to let the cold finish what the sickness had begun.

That image dimmed, and another took its place. A woman, large with child, struggling alone on the road. That spoke volumes about her situation. No husband or lover, father or friend accompanied her, and this meadow was far from towns or farms. Outcast, dispossessed and unwanted, she staggered along the road, pausing as spasms made her double over. She fell to her knees, and it took effort to rise.

Jonmarc saw the woman make her way to the field at the side of the road, saw her ease her awkward body down onto the plowed ground and wrap herself in her cloak. Exhausted and alone, she could go no farther. And when the child forced itself from her body, it did so awash in her warm blood. Far too much blood, soaking into the dirt, calling to the animals in the nearby forest, draining both their lives.

See how we came to this place of forgetting, the ghosts said. *You will also be forgotten, soon enough. Who will mourn you? Who will notice?*

Jonmarc kept his face impassive, although the questions stung. His family was dead, killed by raiders. That he had killed more than a few of the raiders in return was cold comfort. His wife, their child, her family, and village, killed by monsters he had unwittingly called to them. His friends with the caravan, good mates when he was with them but used to people coming and going from their company. The War Dogs, too new to care, except perhaps for Harrtuck, who was ahead of him on Death's road.

Jonmarc heard a thud, the scrabble of claws, and the mist with its images vanished. In its place was a chunk of the grave wall that had collapsed. And climbing from the damp ground was a *vyrkin* easily the same size and weight as Jonmarc himself.

The wolf gets the meat. We get the blood and the memories. You will not leave this place alive.

The ghosts' taunt lingered after their presence faded, leaving Jonmarc facing the *vyrkin*. The huge wolf casually shook the dirt out of his fur and stared at Jonmarc with violet eyes far too knowing for an animal.

A low growl reverberated from the tomb walls. The *vyrkin* advanced toward the circle then drew back at the smell of wolfsbane.

"Standoff," Jonmarc said, trying not to let his pain show in his voice.

The *vyrkin* leaped the circle.

A wolf the size of a grown man landed in front of Jonmarc, who scrambled backward to avoid having a muzzle full of sharp teeth right in his face. Jonmarc grabbed his rowan staff in his left hand and his sword in his right. He did not wait for the *vyrkin* to strike. Instead, he swung the staff as hard as his injured arm would allow, enough to crack against the wolf's shoulder with a satisfying thud. Pain and monkshood made the wolf recoil, and Jonmarc lunged forward, sinking his sword with its poisoned blade into the *vyrkin's* other shoulder.

I'm not a mage. So the circle had no more power than the salt itself. The ghosts are weak. They couldn't cross. For the vyrkin, *so long as he didn't touch the wolfsbane, it was no more than a line in the dirt.*

The *vyrkin* howled in pain, and Jonmarc bit back a cry of his own as the staff's strike reverberated up his damaged arm. His hand went numb, but he held onto the staff, bracing it across him like a shield. He made a point to drag his sword's point through the wolfsbane and hold the blade up like a warning.

"I intend to make this expensive," he said. Interestingly, the *vyrkin* paid no heed to Harrtuck beneath his improvised shelter of rowan boughs. Maybe it was the rowan. Or perhaps Harrtuck was already dead. The *vyrkin's* violet eyes fixed Jonmarc with uncanny intelligence and very human anger.

The ghosts swept back with a fury.

Without the salt circle to hold them at bay, the ghosts surged back into the tomb like a storm wind. But to Jonmarc's surprise, they buffeted the *vyrkin* as well, driving both man and wolf to the ground.

Shapeshifter or not, the vyrkin *is a man, not a real wolf. And the ghosts can feed from him as well as me.*

Jonmarc fought to remain on his knees as the ghosts buffeted him. He dared not let himself be forced against the walls of the tomb, lest the *vyrkin* snatch at him from above. And he feared that if he fell he would not rise again, prey either of the ghosts or the *vyrkin*.

The ghosts swirled around him like a vortex, sliding against his warm skin like icy fingertips, hovering in the warmth of his breath, slipping through his clothing to steal what remained of his body heat, straining against his skin to get inside and bask in the faltering consciousness. It felt as if they tore his memories from his thoughts, riffling through them, rummaging among his secrets.

Cursed... this one is cursed... flames and death...

The *vyrkin* fared no better, though it snarled and snapped at its ghostly tormentors. For an instant, the *vyrkin* turned to bite at the spirits that tortured it, and Jonmarc swung as hard as the narrow tomb would allow, opening a deep gash along the *vyrkin's* ribs.

The wolf lunged at him, howling in pain and fear, and his

teeth grazed Jonmarc's forearm. The sword fell from his hand, and while he thumped at the *vyrkin* with the rowan staff and beat it back, his injured left arm was so weak that he knew he could not fend off another attack.

The ground beneath Jonmarc's feet shifted with the additional weight of the *vyrkin*, dropping by another inch. Jonmarc fell backward, and once more his hand plunged down through the loose dirt, closing around splintered bones. The *vyrkin*, mad with pain and fear and the torment of the ghosts lunged again, was going for Jonmarc's throat.

Sheer instinct took over. Jonmarc brought his right fist out of the ground, gripping whatever he could grab and thrust the bone out in front of him. The *vyrkin* had no chance to adjust its course, and the splintered leg bone plunged deep into the wolf's chest. Hot blood flowed down over the old bone, over Jonmarc's hand, into the wolf's fur. The ghosts swarmed toward them, massing around the dying wolf.

There was desperation in the violet eyes, and as Jonmarc watched in horror, the *vyrkin's* shape began to waver. Its entire silhouette shimmied and shifted, and the powerful wolf let out a despairing howl. And then, the wolf's whole body trembled and shuddered, and when Jonmarc could see him clearly through the fog of ghosts, the wolf was gone. In his place lay a bloody, naked man who looked to be Jonmarc's own age, possibly younger. The *vyrkin* gave a long, wet breath, and then lay still.

At the edge of the grave, the other *vyrkin* howled and barked, growling at the swarm of ghosts that swooped in to leech heat from the corpse and power from the blood. But none of them leaped into the grave to avenge their pack member. *Just as well*, Jonmarc thought. *It's crowded enough in here.*

As the ghosts dodged and massed around the dead *vyrkin*,

their misty shapes became more solid. Shadowy images became the gray forms of men and women, more substantial and detailed than they had been before. Jonmarc could spot the unlucky peddler and the outcast woman and her stillborn child, as well as the sick old man whose eyes burned with unspent fury.

The air in the tomb grew cold enough that frost began to form on the rowan wood boughs that protected Harrtuck's body. Jonmarc was shivering so hard that his teeth clattered, growing numb from blood loss and exposure. He was drifting in and out of clarity, "battle shock" he had heard some of the War Dogs call it, nature's last mercy for the dying. He brandished the blood-soaked bone, holding it between himself and the ghosts, knowing that the strength the spirits had gained from the *vyrkin's* blood made them more than capable of battering down his fading defenses.

"Go on," Jonmarc dared the ghosts. "Do your damnedest. What are you waiting for?"

He steeled himself as the ghosts swirled in anticipation, and their thoughts jabbered at his mind. *Dying... such delicious blood... keep him here with us...* The ghosts gathered into a cloud of grasping hands and open mouths, and swept toward him like a storm gust.

Lightning or something like it crackled down into the tomb between Jonmarc and the ghosts. Fresh dirt flew in all directions. Jonmarc was thrown back against the far wall of the tomb. Overhead, the *vyrkin* scattered, barking and yelping in fear.

Perhaps it was because of how close he was to unconsciousness, or maybe the lightning scrambled his thoughts, but Jonmarc swore he saw lightning crackling *sideways* like long, slender whips of light, snapping and buzzing as they drove off the howling wolves.

I'm seeing things, Jonmarc thought, too exhausted and weak to move. *At least I haven't been eaten. Yet.*

"Are they alive?" The voice was distant but familiar, and Jonmarc figured it to be part of his hallucination.

"One of them is. I think the other one is, too, but he's fading fast."

"Let's get them out of here."

One man climbed down into the tomb, and the ground dropped again. "Sweet Chenne!" he swore under his breath. "What in the name of the Crone happened down here?"

"Nothing good." Two more men remained outside the tomb, just shadowed figures. Jonmarc's vision was blurry, but he could still recognize Captain Valjan as he moved toward where Jonmarc lay.

"Put down your weapon, soldier. I'm here to take you back to camp."

"Get Harrtuck," Jonmarc slurred. "Over there."

Valjan looked at him for a moment, then nodded. He stepped over the dead *vyrkin* and began to dismantle the grid of rowan branches Jonmarc had used to protect Harrtuck from the scavengers.

"Rowan. Salt. Wolfsbane. Pretty clever," Valjan said as he hefted Harrtuck into his arms and passed the body out of the grave to the other two men.

"Not much choice," Jonmarc murmured. He had stopped shivering. That was probably a bad thing. Instead, his battered body just wanted to lay where it was on the soft, fresh ground, and go to sleep.

"War Dogs don't die easy," Valjan grunted, getting Jonmarc over his shoulder in a rescue carry. He made it seem easy, although Jonmarc was tall and strong for his age. Jonmarc groaned as Valjan pushed him up over the lip of the tomb and two men dragged him onto the flat ground. The forest was quiet. No thudding catapults or clanging steel, no battle cries or screams.

"My swords," Jonmarc murmured. "Please—my swords." Valjan looked around and retrieved the two weapons.

"We won—barely," Valjan said as he lifted Jonmarc again once they were both out of the tomb. Henders, one of Valjan's top captains, picked up Harrtuck as if the stocky soldier were a sleeping child. Only then did Jonmarc finally place the third man. Muko, the War Dogs' battle mage. Muko was walking beside Henders, one hand on Harrtuck's limp form, chanting under his breath.

"Fallmount broke the agreement. There was to be no magic. He had his mages out on the front almost from the beginning." Valjan's voice was thick with anger. "Cost us a dozen good men. Thought you two were among them, for a while."

"*Vyrkin*?" Jonmarc managed.

"Fallmount doesn't play fair," Valjan replied. "The *vyrkin* were prisoners forced to shift and fight. They didn't want to be here, but they didn't have a choice. Fortunately, once Fallmount showed his hand, we brought in our mages, too. It got even nastier after that. But by then, you and Harrtuck had gone missing. Be grateful. It was bad."

"Not too easy here, either." Jonmarc's voice was a coarse whisper. Still, his comment made Valjan chuckle.

"Looks like you put up quite a fight. The Dark Lady's hand must have been with you. Never saw a man fight his way out of an open grave before. Guess there's a first time for everything."

"Over?" Jonmarc managed.

"For today," Valjan replied. "The battle isn't over until one of the lords gives in. But now we know what kind of man

Fallmount is, we'll be ready. If that's the way they want it, we can play just as rough. Now, it's personal."

Jonmarc had other questions, but no energy left to form the words. Muko murmured something to Henders, then drifted back to walk in step with Valjan. "Interesting," the mage said quietly.

"What?" Valjan asked.

"Even with as bad shape as he's in, he's got natural shields on his mind. Strong as steel. Well, dented steel at the moment, but unusual, to say the least."

"Huh," Valjan replied. "Save your curiosity for another day. Can you help him?"

"Yeah," the mage replied. "Sleep."

The command was like hot soup and a warm, soft blanket, safe and irresistible. And yet, even as Jonmarc drifted off, he could still hear the ghosts in his mind.

Cursed… This one is cursed…

BRIGANDS

BRIGANDS

Jonmarc Vahanian swung his sword, and steel ground against steel as his blade slid past his opponent's weapon to find its target. Blood sprayed as his sword pierced flesh, slipped between rib bones, and sank deep into the brigand's heart.

The highwayman's body jerked and bucked, and the defeated fighter dropped his sword as his whole form spasmed, going rigid with pain and shock, before slumping heavily against Jonmarc's blade.

"Leave one of them alive!" Jonmarc shouted to his unit as they fought their way through the robbers' forest hiding place. "The general wants one left to interrogate!"

The thick forest made visibility difficult even in broad daylight. That was why it was a favored hiding place for thieves, vagrants, and squatters. Located near a major route into town, the forest had been a perfect hideout for the band of brigands accused of waylaying travelers, murdering them, and stealing their goods.

Now, as Jonmarc and his soldiers fought against the rag-tag robber band, he wondered if some of those reports had been exaggerated. At nineteen, he suspected he was older than many of the "brigands." Even the eldest of the bunch, who looked like he might be in his mid-twenties, hardly fought like an experienced swordsman. If they were the terror of the highway, the travelers they accosted must have been pitifully unprepared to defend themselves. Had it been left to Jonmarc's discretion, as the unit leader, he would have frightened them off, given them a few scars to learn from, and chased them to the border of the next kingdom.

But General Alcion, his commander, had not given him that discretion. Their orders had been clear: to wipe out the brigands, kill all but one, destroy their camp, and bring back any of their ill-gotten gains. And as a Principality mercenary on loan to the Eastmark army, it was Jonmarc's sworn duty to do as he had been commanded.

Grimly, he set about his task. The thieves tried to flee, after seeing their fellow brigands handily defeated, but the soldiers had made a second cordon around the camp, easily running them down. Some of the brigands begged for their lives or offered to pay all they had in exchange for their escape. But Jonmarc's orders were clear, and he followed them. Even if he hated himself for doing so.

When the fighting was done, one wretched highwayman was left, a man only a few years older than Jonmarc. He was wounded and terrified, and he had soiled himself. He lay, bound hand and foot, in the middle of a battleground. The robbers' meager camp of lean-tos and shabby tents had been destroyed in the fighting. If they were thieves, then by the look of it, they were not good at their trade, since they seemed to have little of value aside from their horses, a few bottles of whiskey, and some battered cookware.

"We've searched the camp, sir." One of Jonmarc's soldiers walked toward him with a small wooden chest in his hands. "Other than clothing and liquor, and the weapons they have on them, this was the only thing of value we found." He held out the box for Jonmarc to take.

A sharp blow to the lock easily opened the chest. Inside were a few handfuls of copper coins, not enough to buy the whole bunch of brigands a meal at a cheap tavern. The soldier was watching Jonmarc, waiting for his response. "Bring it," Jonmarc snapped, thrusting the box back at the solider.

He raised his voice. "Throw the bodies over their horses, including the prisoner. We've got what we came for. Let's go." Jonmarc forced down his revulsion and turned away, wiping his blade clean on one of the dead men's cloaks.

Unlike with other campaigns, there was no rowdy rejoicing among the soldiers on the way back to their camp outside the city. Jonmarc kept his face impassive, hoping he was unreadable. A few of his men talked quietly among themselves, but most were silent, a bellwether of their mood.

It had been six months since Jonmarc had left the War Dogs mercenaries in Principality at the personal request of General Alcion and traveled to Eastmark. As his friend Tov Harrtuck had predicted, Jonmarc had been placed with a troop of other soldiers who were also not native to Eastmark. Jonmarc's natural skill as a fighter and his aptitude for the complex footwork of the Eastmark style of fighting earned him several promotions, most recently, command of his own small team of men.

Like the other non-native soldiers, Jonmarc's team assignments were usually routine. They collected King Radomar's taxes from local villages, escorted local dignitaries in need of extra protection, patrolled the roads, broke up bar fights, and ran down the occasional miscreant or two. Not much different from what he would have been doing much of the time when the War Dogs were not under contract to fight on behalf of a patron. At least, until today.

The other soldiers moved out of their way as Jonmarc's unit rode back into camp. The Eastmark-born men barely spared them a glance, but the other foreign-born soldiers watched them with an expression Jonmarc could not clearly read. Veiled derision, perhaps, or shared pity. *We're the general's clean-up crew,* Jonmarc thought, holding his back straight and his chin up. *I get it now. We do the jobs that his Eastmark soldiers consider to be beneath them.*

Someone must have alerted General Alcion to their arrival, because when Jonmarc's soldiers reached the parade ground in the center of the camp, the General was waiting for them on horseback, next to the hanging tree. Jonmarc felt his gut clench, and their prisoner saw enough to begin pleading for his life.

General Alcion was the brother of Eastmark's King Radomar. A series of complex black tattoos made his royal status clear, standing out even on his ebony skin. Tall and strong, Alcion was an excellent fighter, and the tavern bards sang stories celebrating his many victories. Jonmarc had been instrumental in saving the general's life when the War Dogs had been assigned to escort him in Principality, and in return, Alcion had requested Jonmarc on loan from the mercenaries for a year.

"I see you were successful." Alcion spoke Common to his outlander forces, though after six months, Jonmarc had picked up enough Markian to understand most of the conversations around him.

"Yes, sir," Jonmarc replied. "Brought the bodies back as you requested, routed the camp. Not much to show for it," he said, offering up the small wooden chest. "And a captive, as you requested."

"Bring him to me," Alcion ordered.

Two of Jonmarc's soldiers pulled the surviving brigand from across his horse, where he had been tossed like a sack of flour. Alcion looked the man up and down. The highwaymen was Eastmark-born, and when the ruffian saw the tattoos on Alcion's face, he threw himself to the ground.

"Your Highness! Mercy! I beg of you—we were just trying to keep from starving. Mercy, please!" the man sobbed.

Alcion was impassive. "Cut the bonds on his ankles," he ordered. "Sit him on his horse, and bring him to the tree."

A fresh sob tore from the thief's throat as Jonmarc's soldiers did as they were bid. The tree was old, with a broad trunk and many strong branches. A noose hung from a sturdy limb, ready for a victim.

"Slip the noose over his head," Alcion ordered. The prisoner looked as if he might pass out as the rough rope settled around his neck.

"What is the law of Eastmark, regarding thievery?" Alcion demanded. "Speak!"

It took the prisoner two tries to find his voice, which came out like a terrified squeak. "Thievery is forbidden, m'lord."

"And the penalty for thieving?" Alcion questioned.

"A brand or a hand, or your neck for a peck," the man stuttered, repeating the cautionary rhyme Jonmarc had heard oft repeated.

"You were caught among thieves. Do you deny it?" Alcion asked.

"No, Your Highness," the prisoner replied, barely able to form the words he was so frightened.

"You preyed on travelers on the royal road. That's more than a 'peck' of goods stolen, wouldn't you say?"

Once more, the prisoner looked as if he might swoon. "Yes, Your Highness."

Alcion hesitated, drawing out the suspense. "I would be entirely right to hang you," he observed after a moment. "You've more than earned it." Still, he did not make the gesture that would have signaled to the soldier standing behind the prisoner's horse to slap the animal on its hindquarters and send the man dangling.

"Remove the noose," he said after another long pause. "Untie his hands." The soldiers did as they were told, while the prisoner stared at Alcion in stupefaction.

"Go back to your village," Alcion ordered. "Tell them what you did and what was done to you. Tell them General Alcion is stern and merciful."

"Yes, Your Highness," the thief babbled, clutching his reins white-knuckled as if he might fall from his horse.

"Go!" Alcion ordered and gave the signal. A slap sent the horse bolting from its place, running from the camp as the thief spurred it on with his heels, no doubt desperate to escape before the General changed his mind.

For a moment, Jonmarc wondered if the pardon was some kind of awful sport and whether soldiers would be dispatched to ride down the robber just as the man believed himself to be free. But to his relief, no one blocked the man's way, though the Eastmark soldiers jeered and shouted as the horse and its panicked rider ran for their lives. Few if any of the outlander troops joined in the catcalls.

"Well done, Lieutenant," General Alcion said, looking at Jonmarc. "Commendable work. Give your men my thanks." With that, the general abruptly turned his horse and rode away.

Jonmarc let the routine of taking care of his horse keep his mind occupied after he left the parade grounds. Though the outland troops were equally well provisioned with equipment, barracks, tents, and horses as the Eastmark soldiers, and though their rations and pay were equivalent, the outland troops had their own enclave to one side of the large permanent army camp. The two groups shared a mess tent, but they rarely fraternized, even among men of similar rank.

Unwilling to engage in conversation, even with his own men, Jonmarc took the roundabout way back to his quarters. *They say every army camp looks alike,* he thought. *But I'd know I wasn't in Margolan or Principality, even with my eyes shut.*

Some of that lay in the spices favored by Markian troops, combinations and flavors uncommon in Margolan or Principality. It had taken Jonmarc a while to adjust to the heavily seasoned, unfamiliar foods, though he had eventually found some he not only tolerated but actually liked. The beer and spirits in Eastmark also had a unique taste, reminding him with every swallow that he was far from home. Even the music was different, though the bards and minstrels in the taverns often played songs from across the Winter Kingdoms. At least Eastmark's terrain and landscape were not alien, though there were more mountains and the weather was colder than where Jonmarc had grown up.

Even though I understand what they're saying now, everything still feels strange. I wonder how the long time outlanders do it, staying on for years. Do they really make a place for themselves, or is anything better for them than going back to where they came from?

A large road ran down the middle of the village-within-a-city that was the camp. Most of the main functions of the camp—the parade ground, the mess tent, infirmary, and armory, among others—were set up on this main road. Officers' quarters were on the end of camp farthest from the latrines and stables, and with his promotion in rank, Jonmarc had gained better quarters and an increase in pay. If he was lucky, he might make captain by the end of his year of duty, though Eastmark was notorious for not promoting outlanders higher than colonel. *I'm not planning to stay that long,* Jonmarc thought. *Captain would be plenty high enough for me.*

Twenty thousand soldiers were based at the Caldon camp, outside the city of Talonia, the third largest in Eastmark. Talonia was a royal city, a place where the King of Eastmark had a residence, and where the king himself was considered to directly rule the city when he was present. Jonmarc had no idea how often King Radomar visited Talonia, though he had seen the flags flying once that indicated the king was present. He had heard that Alcion availed himself of the royal residence whenever the army was going to be in camp for any length of time.

Alcion might not be the heir, but he certainly enjoys the benefits of being in the royal family, Jonmarc thought. *Radomar has quite a reputation as hard-nosed enough to try to kidnap his own daughter back when she eloped with an outland king. I wonder how Alcion gets along with his big brother? Did he always want to be a general, or was it the role offered to him?* If anyone knew for certain, they were hardly likely to share such news with an outland mercenary.

Jonmarc had never ventured far from the gates of the army camp, even when he had leave time since he was acutely aware of not speaking Markian well and of being unfamiliar with Eastmark's social customs. Just outside the camp perimeter were several taverns, shops, and brothels that catered to soldiers. Losing Shanna was still recent enough a wound that Jonmarc had no interest in the brothels, but he and some of his fellow outlander friends sometimes went drinking together at the taverns. Aside from that, he had not explored Talonia. Off the base, it would be painfully obvious that he was not of Eastmark. Inside the camp, while foreigners did not have equivalent promotion opportunities as Eastmark-born soldiers, the outlanders were treated with respect and did not fear for their safety. He was not confident the same would be true should he venture by himself into Talonia.

Not far from the parade grounds was the shrine, a place General Alcion made a personal stop to present offerings before every campaign. Yet again, it was a reminder that Jonmarc was no longer in familiar territory. The lands of the Winter Kingdoms worshiped the Eight Faces, or aspects, of the Sacred Lady, a single goddess with eight very different representations: Mother, Childe, Warrior, Lover, Whore, Crone, the Dark Lady, and the Formless One. Margolan venerated the Mother and Childe, while Principality honored the Whore. Eastmark worshipped the Lover, and her Sacred Consort, the *Stawar* God.

Tonight, there was one of the many religious festivals that commemorated the Lady and the *Stawar* God. Musicians played, singers sang, and a procession of orange-robed Hojun priests, their bald heads tattooed with patterns that spoke to their vocation, brought armloads of offerings to lay before the shrine.

Fresh flowers and baskets of vegetables, pitchers of wine and water, fresh loaves of bread, a freshly-slaughtered pig, and a chicken were part of the gifts paid in tribute to the god and goddess. The Eastmark troops were not required to attend the festivals, but many did, either because of piety or perhaps to curry favor by being seen. Outlanders were exempted but not unwelcome, and so Jonmarc hung back, watching from a distance.

"Good festival to you all," General Alcion greeted the troops, presenting his gift of bread and wine with a bow to each of the figures before leaving the Hojun priests to their songs and prayers and incense. Once the general was gone, most of the soldiers dispersed, giving credence to Jonmarc's suspicion that it was ambition, more than devotion that encouraged attendance.

Jonmarc stopped to ponder the statue for a moment. The Lover Aspect of the Sacred Lady was a beautiful woman, carved from polished onyx, just a bit darker in hue than the complexions of the Eastmark soldiers who worshipped her. Complex, swirling inlays of jet marked her face and arms, and since Alcion's tattoos conveyed his royal stature, Jonmarc guessed that the statues' markings attested to her deity. But it was the *Stawar* God that caught Jonmarc's attention.

Nowhere else had he heard of the Lady taking a Consort. He had been in Eastmark long enough to know the legend. *Stawars* were big predatory cats with midnight-black pelts and luminous yellow eyes that stalked the thick forest. They were rare elsewhere in the Winter Kingdoms and said to be native to Eastmark alone. The Hojun Priests held that a divine being that could shift like a *vyrkin* from man to *stawar* had wed the Lover and created the Eastmark people in the Southlands, then led them on a dangerous trek to their present kingdom.

The *Stawar* God story explained a lot about the Markians, Jonmarc thought. They took great pride in being fierce warriors, and in the dark skin that made them uncommon among the other nations of the Winter Kingdoms, both resemblances of the great cat whose likeness the *Stawar* God embodied. And like the predator cat, Markians seemed to keep their distance from those around them, at least from what Jonmarc had witnessed. The weight of their solitary dignity seemed to be a burden each carried with heroic stoicism. *Maybe it looks different if you're one of them,* he thought. *But it sure looks that way from the outside.*

Far from home and in a strange land, Jonmarc felt the events of the day keenly. *Captain Valjan would never have ordered us to kill those brigands,* Jonmarc thought, remembering his War Dogs commander. *Not when they posed so little of a threat and begged for their lives. What game is Alcion playing?* But the general's words to the departing brigand gave him a chilling suspicion. "*Tell them that General Alcion is stern and merciful,*" he said, Jonmarc thought. *Not "the king" or "King Radomar." Generals, from what I've heard, aren't supposed to be courting public opinion. Unless they don't plan on remaining "mere" generals.*

Too restless to return to his tent and not feeling very hungry, Jonmarc wandered the camp, hoping a walk would clear his head and lift his mood. He paused for a while to watch soldiers sparring with each other on the parade grounds. *If anything good has come of this tour, it's been perfecting my Eastmark kick,* Jonmarc thought cynically.

Few outlanders tried to learn the complicated footwork and stances of the traditional Eastmark way of fighting, but Jonmarc had a talent for it, and the moves came naturally to him. He had surprised Alcion with his ability, and held his own sparring with some of the best fighters, though he was still young enough and lacked the mature strength and bulk that would really let him hold his own. Still, it was a good beginning, and it had won him grudging respect from some of the other Eastmark commanders, and acceptance from some of his Eastmark peers.

He listened to the soldiers talking as he walked around camp. It was useful to be able to understand Markian, even if his ability to speak the language was hampered by his own Borderlands accent and lack of practice. Even more useful was the fact that most of the Eastmark soldiers took it for granted that none of the recent outlander recruits spoke Markian, though the long-time mercs were fluent. That meant that the soldiers did not censor their comments as Jonmarc passed by, letting him listen in on news that did not always reach the "foreigner" side of camp.

Most of the conversations were the stuff of soldiering: complaints about the food, accusations of ale being watered down, exaggerated exploits told and retold from the most recent trip to the brothel. But amidst the gossip and bellyaching, Jonmarc heard a few whispers that gave him pause.

Another feather in the general's cap… probably would have gone easier on them if they'd given him the cut he wanted… Alcion the magnanimous, just before it's time to collect more taxes… Haven't heard tell of the king in weeks…

Without intending to, Jonmarc arrived at the gate that separated the Caldon army enclave from Talonia. The guard gave him a nod as he passed through the checkpoint into the bustling street. It was suppertime, and the food smells that wafted from the taverns and street vendors made Jonmarc hungry in spite of his worries.

Pollune Street catered to soldiers from Caldon camp. Few if any regular Talonia residents had reason to frequent the area, and Jonmarc assumed that there were other—probably better—shops, taverns, and brothels for the city dwellers elsewhere. Like the seedier areas of Principality City that stayed in business by separating soldiers from their pay, the establishments on Pollune were hard-used and not for the faint of heart.

Cheers and shouts drew Jonmarc's attention to the street in front of one of the taverns, where two Markian soldiers pummeled each other. Curse words were among the first Markian Jonmarc had learned, but the phrases the fighting soldiers traded tested the limits of Jonmarc's ability to translate, and from the shouts of the crowd, he guessed the two men were being particularly creative in their vulgarity.

He stepped around the fight and its audience, as bets were being taken in the crowd, both on the identity of the winner and the injuries sustained by the loser. Strumpets watched with middling interest from the Jolly Maiden brothel across the street, and they beckoned to Jonmarc as he passed, jeering when he paid them no heed. The Pollune Street whores were all outlanders, since Eastmark took a dim view of sharing its women, casually or in marriage, with men who were not of Eastmark blood.

It had been a long time since he had reason to see the homes and shops of regular people, Jonmarc thought. His travels with Maynard Linton's caravan of wonders had meant that visits to the villages and towns they passed were brief, usually limited to markets for supplies and taverns for sustenance. In Principality, mercs had no reason to be near the quarters of the city where decent people made their homes. For the first time in a long while, Jonmarc felt a stab of homesickness he could not quell.

His wandering led him to the Ewe & Sow, a tavern that not only welcomed soldiers but had been claimed by outlanders for their own. Just walking into the tavern and smelling food he could identify lifted Jonmarc's spirits, just a bit. He ordered a whiskey and a meat pie and found a table where he could sit with his back against the wall. For a little while, he dug into his pie, enjoying a familiar favorite made in the Margolan way. The whiskey was from Principality, smoky and strong, without the odd aftertaste of Eastmark spirits. All around him, soldiers spoke Common with accents that reminded him of Principality and Margolan, conversations on which he could eavesdrop without expending the effort to translate. Jonmarc accepted the comfort without wanting to delve too deeply into what left him so bereft. For now, whiskey was enough.

"You look like you could use another one." Jonmarc looked up at the blond man who stood on the other side of the table. Jod Keller stood with a grin, holding up two full glasses of amber liquid. "Mind if I sit down?" Over on the other side of the bar, musicians were setting up to play, and two of the men near where Jonmarc sat got up to fetch themselves more ale before the entertainment started.

Jonmarc kicked under the table to push out the chair he had been using as a footstool. "Sure, if you're buying."

Keller chuckled. "At least for this round," he replied, sliding one of the glasses over to replace the nearly empty one in front of Jonmarc. Jonmarc tossed off the remainder of his drink and nodded his thanks.

"What brings you out?" Jonmarc asked.

Keller shrugged. "Felt like taking a walk. Thought I might run into you here." Like Jonmarc, Keller was from Margolan. He was older than Jonmarc by a decade, and his flattened nose and the scar that marred one cheek were testimony to a career soldiering. They often reminisced about the things they missed about their homeland: food, songs, festivals, and the weather. By unspoken agreement, no one mentioned family. Jonmarc had no idea whether or not Keller had loved ones back home, or what circumstances sent him to far-away Eastmark, and he doubted he would ever find out. Since he had no desire to share his own story, that was fine with him.

"Not one of my best days," Jonmarc said, taking a sip of the whiskey.

"Heard your men brought in the brigands from the forest

road," Keller said. "Saw a bit of it when I passed by the parade grounds earlier."

Jonmarc shrugged moodily. "Hard to imagine they posed much of a threat," he replied. "Didn't feel much like soldiering, cutting them down."

Keller said nothing for a moment, but the look in his eyes told Jonmarc that the other man not only understood his comment but had already guessed that was at least partly behind Jonmarc's presence at the Ewe & Sow. "Happens like that, sometimes," Keller allowed after a while.

"Valjan wouldn't have done it like that," Jonmarc said. Keller knew of Jonmarc's old commander by reputation and had crossed paths with him on prior campaigns. Everyone seemed to know of Valjan, and what was remarkable for a mercenary commander, most people thought well of him.

"The general isn't Valjan."

Jonmarc sighed. "Yeah."

Keller glanced around them as he took another sip of his drink. It was never wise to be overheard talking about one's commander in a place like this. There was always someone willing to carry a tale to curry favor, or just for the enjoyment of making trouble. Tonight, three traveling musicians played in the far corner of the tavern, reeling through familiar ballads and bar songs the patrons knew by heart. It was difficult to hear yourself think over the clamor as the drunken soldiers sang along, and just as hard to overhear anyone else. "These days, the general isn't always the general he used to be," Keller observed quietly.

Jonmarc's eyebrow quirked upward. "Oh?"

"You know about Alcion's reputation as a war hero," Keller said.

Jonmarc nodded. "Yeah. Fought off pirates on the coast, won some victories against the raiders on the eastern border, cracked down on the river pirates. He's put a lot of miles on his boots, and won more battles than he lost." Eastmark took its history seriously. New outlander recruits were regaled from their first day with stories and lengthy ballads recounting the glories of Eastmark's army. General Alcion's victories and daring exploits were a particular source of pride, and while Jonmarc suspected that some of the tales had been exaggerated, he was equally sure that the majority of the stories were true.

Keller took another drink of whiskey. "Heard much about the king?"

Jonmarc gave Keller an uncertain glance. "If you mean the story about how he almost started a war when his daughter ran off with the heir to the Isencroft throne, then yes."

"That story is true, by the way," Keller replied. "We've got King Bricen of Margolan to thank for keeping the mess from plunging the Winter Kingdoms into a disaster." Bricen had put his substantial influence—and sizeable military—on the Isencroft side, giving Eastmark no alternative but to back down. "And I hear there's bad blood between the kings to this day."

Not surprising, Jonmarc thought. *Though normal people would have settled it with a fistfight instead of a war.*

"I meant, have you heard much lately," Keller asked.

Jonmarc frowned. "Only that no one has heard anything," he replied, wondering now if there was more to the gossip he had overheard than he originally thought.

Keller nodded. "Yep. Has people worried. Plenty of speculation about why especially when the king wasn't seen at the palace for the festival last week."

"People get sick. They travel. They get busy doing important king-stuff," Jonmarc replied. "Could be nothing."

Keller shrugged. "Maybe. But kings like to be seen at festivals, and showing up at religious ceremonies is pretty much of an obligation. Keeps people happy, keeps the priests happy, and reminds people who's in charge."

"You think anyone's likely to forget?"

Another shrug. "Maybe not. But people worry when a king gets older. Eastmark's succession hasn't always gone smoothly."

"Isn't there a prince or two, waiting on the sidelines?" Jonmarc asked. He had learned a little about Eastmark's royal family, besides the story of the old scandal. There were enough statues around that it would take effort not to pick up bits and pieces of the history.

"Two sons, in good health," Keller replied. "The eldest, Doran, is in line for the throne. Until he's crowned, he's the king's foremost ambassador. The second son, Kalcen, oversees foreign trade."

Jonmarc resisted a snort that would have sent whiskey up his nose. Keller was being careful with his phrasing in case anyone was listening, but from what Jonmarc heard, the eldest prince was widely regarded as a wastrel and a cad. If he was sent anywhere with the title of "ambassador," it was likely to get him out of the way. "So there's an heir and a spare," he replied.

"Yes. But as I said, Eastmark's history hasn't always seen succession follow the traditional path," Keller said with a meaningful look.

Tell them General Alcion is stern and merciful. The general's words took on a whole new, ominous tone in light of Keller's implication, and Jonmarc shivered despite how warm it was in the tavern common room.

"I see," he replied. Their conversation was on dangerous ground. Spies for the king would not be pleased at suggestions that succession was even a concern for years to come, and spies for the general would hardly like any questionable ambitions widely discussed.

He was spared thinking of what to say next when two more men jostled their way to the table. "Jonmarc! Jod! The two of you together is trouble waiting to happen." Two Eastmark lieutenants, Ronn and Tamm stood behind Jod, each holding two full tankards of ale and grinning broadly. "Mind if we join you?"

"Always room for more," Jonmarc said, moving down the bench to let the two men squeeze into seats. Ronn and Tamm were two of the friendliest Eastmark soldiers he had met and were his frequent sparring partners at the salle.

"What brings you to the outlander bar?" Keller asked. "Or did you miss Principality cooking?"

Ronn's grin widened. "I miss Margolan cooking and Principality whiskey."

"I just miss Principality women," Tamm said with a sigh. "And the whiskey, too."

Both Ronn and Tamm had served for several years with mercenary groups in Principality before returning to the Eastmark army. Their Common was excellent, and they understood outlander ways better than their comrades who had never spent time outside the kingdom. "We were just getting started," Keller said, indicating the four glasses, two full and two empty, in front him and Jonmarc.

"By the Whore!" Tamm said as the musicians swung into a rousing tavern song. "I haven't heard that song since I came back to Eastmark." He hummed along but spared them his singing.

Ronn was too busy eating his stew and sopping up the gravy with his bread to sing. He tucked into his food with such gusto that Jonmarc chuckled despite himself. When

BRIGANDS

Ronn finally looked up, he had gravy on his chin, and his eyes had a sleepy glaze. "Now that's good eating!" he declared, washing the meal down with most of one tankard of ale.

"Go easy on that stuff, or I'll kick your ass tomorrow in the salle," Jonmarc warned jokingly.

Ronn burped loudly. "No chance of that. You're good, but I'm better—even fat and drunk." It was a friendly competition, and Jonmarc took no offense. Unlike most of the Eastmark soldiers who were polite but aloof, Ronn and Tamm seemed to enjoy spending time among the outlanders. They had been Jonmarc's mentors in everything from pronunciation to fighting tactics, and he valued their friendship.

"Heard the general had some good words for you today," Tamm said as the musicians started up another tune and he returned his attention to the table.

Jonmarc nodded. "Yeah. Mopped up some brigands. Didn't seem like a big deal." As much as he liked Ronn and Tamm, he did not want to voice his concerns to them.

"The general's seen you fight," Ronn said. "He appreciates anyone with talent for the traditional fighting style." He leaned over the table and whispered conspiratorially. "In case you hadn't noticed, just being Markian doesn't make a person coordinated, if you know what I mean."

Jonmarc did, but he just gave a polite chuckle. The complicated footwork and traditional sequence of movements came easily to him, but he had seen Eastmark-born soldiers struggling. He figured that his natural talent with the fighting style had probably not endeared him to some of the soldiers, though others, like Ronn and Tamm, did not seem to mind, and cheered for him in sparring rounds. His abilities had won him a small circle of Eastmark friends, which was somewhat unusual in a camp where the two sides generally stuck to their own.

"It's always been the general's way to use outlanders to crack down on Markian troublemakers, and use Markian troops when he's fighting outlanders," Tamm remarked. "Political, but true. Cuts down on the friction between the army and the locals if the outlanders are the ones to keep the ruffians in line."

While breeding mistrust of outlanders with the residents, and saving the Markian troops for the kind of fighting that warrants a parade when you win, Jonmarc thought. *Alcion has a penchant for making himself look good.*

"Has it always been like that?" Jonmarc asked, figuring that as a newcomer he could get away with questions.

Tamm shook his head, though, with a mouthful of food, it took a moment for him to reply. "No. Just the last year or so, since Alcion was promoted to general and took charge of the Talonia camp. That's when he boosted the number of outlanders and changed the duties around. Before, everyone did everything." Jonmarc glanced at Keller, who nodded, but whose expression was guarded.

"Don't the locals mind?" Jonmarc took a sip of his beer and tried to be nonchalant. "I mean, being policed by soldiers who aren't from here? I would have thought he'd use you guys to take care of the local stuff and throw us at the big bad threats from beyond the borders." He leaned back and finished most of his ale, hoping he gave the appearance that the answer was of no consequence.

Ronn shrugged. "Yeah, you'd think, wouldn't you?" he said. "That's how it used to work, and everyone seemed to be happy with it. Now, I guess it's a little safer for the outlanders, not going up against the big threats, but there's been some stir in the villages, or so I've heard." He tossed off the rest of his drink. "Then again, no matter what we do, some of the people in the villages are upset. Can't rightly win for trying."

"I figure it's the doing of that new advisor he's got," Tamm said, and glanced left and right, dropping his voice. "Don't like the look of him, hanging back all spooky-like. Only saw him once, and couldn't see his face, but something about him set my teeth on edge."

"New advisor?" Keller asked, eyes narrowing with interest.

Tamm finished his last bite and pushed the bowl away with a satisfied sigh. "Yeah. Don't know anything about him, except that he's only been around for a year or so. About the time the general started to do things differently. Figured that was why." He took a deep gulp of his ale. "Maybe the king sent the advisor. Big brothers like to keep an eye on things, you know."

Ronn shook his head, although he looked uncomfortable with the topic. "I'll grant you that I didn't like the look of him either, the time he came to see the troops with the general. But I heard Alcion found his own advisor. I imagine the king has better things to do."

Or maybe the king wasn't told, Jonmarc thought. *Curious —and dangerous.*

The door opened, and an old woman entered. Jonmarc recognized her. Nonna, the hedge witch, was a regular on Pollune Street. Sometimes she sold her powders and potions from a pushcart along the street. When the weather was bad, she made the rounds of the taverns, offering her cures and spells for a few coins, the price of dinner, or a drink. He had often wondered if she visited the brothels as well, and decided that it was likely since their strumpets might well want to avail themselves of her cures and curses.

Nonna was bent with age, and her face was deeply furrowed. Though the night was fairly warm, she clutched a shawl around her bony shoulders. Her clothing was worn but not ragged. As Jonmarc watched, she moved from table to table, offering a charm or a bag of healing herbs.

"Got anything for the clap?" the barkeeper yelled, and the patrons guffawed and elbowed their friends.

"Aye, same stuff I sold you last week!" Nonna bantered back, leading to louder laughter. She did a brisk business, working her way around the room. From what Jonmarc had seen before, Nonna sold a lot of protective amulets, as well as powders and remedies for all kinds of ailments, from foot rot to stomach problems, the kinds of things the army healers were too busy to bother with.

Shanna's mother had been a hedge witch, and Jonmarc had often helped her gather the plants she needed for her cures. As Nonna dispensed her wares in small cloth bags, Jonmarc could hazard a good guess as to what her mixtures probably included, especially from the scent of the more potent herbs.

Nonna finally made her way to their table. "Fix what ails you?" she asked, with a grin that revealed crooked, mottled teeth.

"Got anything to make me irresistible to the ladies?" Ronn asked, patting his full belly.

"I'm a hedge witch, not a mage," Nonna bantered back. "And I don't work miracles."

Tamm elbowed Ronn as the others laughed. "I could use something for my stomach," Keller said, passing a few coins to Nonna. "Cook's food isn't nearly as good as this."

Nonna took his coins and gave him a small cloth bundle tied with twine. "Add it to tea, not *kerif*, and drink it morning and night for three days. That should help."

"You got any of that foot blister salve?" Tamm asked. "Nothing's as bad as marching with sore feet."

Nonna took a little clay pot from the bag at her belt. "I've got it—you have coins for me?"

Tamm handed over payment and took the pot as if it were gold. "My feet thank you."

Nonna sniffed derisively. "If your feet are talking, you've got bigger problems than my salve can fix." She leveled her gaze at Ronn. "How about you?"

He held up a hand. "I've still got the powder you gave me last time," he said, though his cheeks colored as he spoke.

"What kind of powder, Ronn?" Tamm asked.

Ronn mumbled his reply. "What was that? I couldn't hear you?" Tamm prodded.

"It's not my fault if my pants chafe," he shot back, as Tamm doubled with laughter at his expense.

Nonna sobered as she looked at Jonmarc. She was quiet for a moment, and he shifted uncomfortably beneath her gaze. "Well now. I've got no powders that can help you," she said, focused on Jonmarc as if the rest of the room had vanished. "Just a warning. Stay away from the south. I see fire and death in that direction. If you lose your way, there will be darkness, and the Dark Lady will take your soul."

The others at the table had fallen silent, glancing nervously from Nonna to Jonmarc. Nonna seemed to come back to herself with a shudder. She tilted her head and looked at Jonmarc. "I don't usually get visions like that, young man. When I do, I'm never wrong. Best you heed what I say." With that, she brushed past them and headed out the door.

Jonmarc felt the pressure of his friends' stares. "I have no idea what that was about," he lied.

"I've never seen her do that," Keller said, giving Jonmarc

a measured look as if he doubted Jonmarc was telling the whole truth.

"Me neither," agreed Tamm.

"Probably wanted to make some extra coins," Jonmarc grumbled, ducking his head and finishing his ale.

They spent the rest of the evening gossiping about mutual acquaintances, speculating about the weather and the next maneuvers, and playing some friendly rounds of dice and darts. The foreboding Jonmarc felt did not leave him, but his companions made it easy for him to squelch his worries, at least for a while.

They headed back to camp together, trading ribald stories and joking insults. As they passed the guard at the gate, the soldier stopped Jonmarc. "Lieutenant Vahanian. Message from the General. He wants to see you."

Jonmarc frowned. "It's past tenth bells," he said.

The gate guard shrugged. "Just got the word half a candlemark ago. Better stop by, just in case."

Nonna's warning had unsettled Jonmarc more than he cared to let on, especially since it echoed the warnings he had received, unbidden, from other seers who had singled him out. Drawing the general's attention, even on the heels of a commendation, made him even more nervous.

"Hey, maybe you'll get another promotion," Ronn said. "You've come up pretty fast since you've been here. Wouldn't doubt you'll make captain before too long."

"Probably a new assignment, maybe something that came up suddenly," Keller said, in a tone that was carefully neutral. Jonmarc took that to mean that his friend was uncertain as to whether the general's summons was a good thing or not.

"Yeah, probably," Jonmarc muttered. They parted ways not far into the camp, leaving Jonmarc to head toward the general's quarters alone.

When he approached the building that Alcion lived in when he stayed in the camp, light shone through the windows, indicating that the general was still awake. Clamping down on his fear, Jonmarc stood tall, lifted his head, and approached the two guards at the door. It was obvious that they were expecting him.

"General said to let you in, Lieutenant Vahanian," the guard on the right said, and his counterpart nodded assent.

Jonmarc hoped he looked confident as he walked inside. Alcion's quarters were not opulent on the outside, but inside they were well-appointed, as befitted royalty. Noorish carpets covered the floor, and beautifully finished furniture with rich inlay graced the rooms. Paintings and statuary adorned tables that looked as if they belonged in a palace. It was a jarring departure from the ascetic accommodations Valjan had kept with the War Dogs.

"Lieutenant." Alcion summoned Jonmarc into his study. Alcion sat behind an inlaid wooden desk covered with scrolls and maps. He looked Jonmarc over from head to toe as if he guessed where Jonmarc had been. "You'll be leading your team on assignment tomorrow," he said. "The annual taxes are due, and your unit will be one of several dispatched to collect payment," he added.

"You'll have ten villages to visit in three days, south to Ayerby, then over to Chauvrenne and back here with the taxes along the western road," Alcion continued. "Leave in the morning. Make sure the villages understand that you come in the name of King Radomar the Unforgiving." He looked back down at his maps. "That is all. You're dismissed."

Jonmarc gave a stiff nod, then turned and left without a word. His heart was thudding as he headed into the cool night air. *South to Ayerby*, he thought. *Nonna warned me about heading south. But I'm unlikely to lose my way—it's a day's journey to Ayerby, another day along the road to Chauvrenne, and then back up a third day, hitting the villages as we go. Nothing to warrant a seer's warning.* His attempts to reassure himself did nothing to quell the icy tingle down his spine.

There was no use going back to his quarters. He would not be able to sleep, not yet. Instead, Jonmarc headed for the salle, which was open for practice all day and night. Alcion prized training and initiative and encouraged his soldiers to practice whenever they had the time. At this hour, the salle was empty, lit by a single torch that had nearly burned out. He eyed the burning brand and figured there was enough light left to let him work off his mood.

Jonmarc ran at the quintain, swinging into a solid Eastmark kick that reverberated up his leg. *Radomar the Unforgiving,* he thought. *Quite a difference from Alcion, the stern and merciful.*

Thwack. He shifted position, kicking from the other side. *Outlander troops to enforce the most unpopular of the kings' laws. Engineered to make the villagers resent their taxes more than usual.*

Wham. Another strike, hard enough that if the quintain had been a living opponent, the man would have been on the ground and groggy. *While the real army is kept aside for high profile, hero jobs.*

Whack. He might be sore on his ride tomorrow, but tonight, working up a sweat helped Jonmarc clear his head. *Meaning that Alcion ducks any of the resentment, and Radomar gets all the blame.*

Crack. This time, Jonmarc's kick splintered the target board. *Just what someone might do if he were thinking about trying to unseat the king and take his place,* Jonmarc thought. *Dark Lady take my soul! Alcion and his advisor are plotting a coup, and the outlanders are right in the middle of it.* He had no option except to obey. His term of duty with Alcion did not expire for six more months, and the penalty for desertion was hanging.

Nonna was right. Trouble's coming. And there's not a thing I can do about it.

BLEAK HARVEST

BLEAK HARVEST

"They say no one likes death or taxes, but I've heard people beg for death. Never heard someone beg for taxes." Jonmarc Vahanian, mercenary and newly promoted captain rode down the dusty road with a troop of eleven soldiers. Outlander mercenaries under contract to the Eastmark army, they were headed to collect taxes for King Radomar.

It was a thankless task given to hired soldiers to protect the popularity of General Alcion's Markian soldiers. The politics of the mission rankled Jonmarc, and although he had said nothing aloud, he was sure his men both understood and resented the situation.

"You know, that's a good point," Circan replied. He was Jonmarc's second-in-command, a fellow mercenary who was also from Margolan, and over the last few months, the two had become good friends. "Although I imagine it depends on whether or not the taxes get used for improving the road or going into someone's pocket."

Jonmarc shrugged. "Well, that's always the question, isn't it?" Growing up in a small village in Margolan's Borderlands, things like politics and kings had seemed distant matters, far removed from the daily lives of blacksmiths, fishermen, and other "regular" people. After his family was murdered, he had traveled across Margolan with a caravan, and the transient life made such matters even less of interest.

Now, as an outlander in a strange kingdom serving for pay instead of loyalty, he felt even less attachment to political maneuvering, except where it threatened his men. His intuition prickled with warning that somehow, a real threat loomed from what should have been a simple errand.

"These villages aren't much different from the ones back home," Circan went on. "No one liked paying coin when tax time came, but they always wanted plenty of king's guards around when problems arose." He shrugged. "Can't have one without the other, I guess."

Jonmarc mumbled an agreement, but he knew there was more at stake. Alcion, brother to King Radomar, made a habit of using mercenary troops to enforce unfavorable decrees. Having foreign soldiers force compliance with unpopular laws increased anger against the king and stirred unrest. Jonmarc feared that Alcion was setting himself up as a challenger for the throne, and the outland soldiers could find themselves caught in the crossfire.

Three days had passed since Jonmarc and his men had set out on a circuit of ten villages to collect the king's taxes. Ayerby, the first village, was a prosperous trading town. Merchants grumbled as they handed over pouches full of silver to pay their due, but the amount gathered matched what was expected. Bennerton, the next village, paid the tax collection scant attention as if its farmers and tradesmen could not be bothered to fuss about something as inevitable as sunup and sundown. In the third town, Kespermoor, the initial collection was short, but the village elders pressed the holdouts to make good on their obligation, and the soldiers departed without incident.

Now, heading toward the fourth stop, Ettenheld, Jonmarc could not shake a feeling of foreboding. His soldiers seemed restless as if they sensed something was wrong but could not pin down the cause. As outlanders, they were painfully obvious, since all of Jonmarc's soldiers hailed from Margolan or Dhasson, with light skin, while Eastmark prided itself on the ebony coloring of its native sons and daughters, bloodlines that were jealously guarded. There was no hope that his soldiers would be overlooked, or that passers-by could mistake them for anything other than what they were: foreigners sent to enforce the king's law

The road thus far took them south, though it would turn west after Ettenheld. That suited Jonmarc just fine, since two seers had given him dire warnings against traveling south, cautions that haunted his dreams. He tried to dismiss the predictions as superstition or the sham prophecies of dishonest fortune-tellers, but he could not ignore the caution so easily. Deep in his heart, he feared the warnings were true, though he had no idea of what shape the danger would take.

"Looks like a pretty quiet place, Cap'n," Lieutenant Markelson said, as Ettenheld came into sight. Markelson was one of the newest soldiers under Jonmarc's command. At nineteen, Jonmarc was younger than several of his soldiers, but Markelson struck Jonmarc as barely old enough to enlist, though the lieutenant vigorously denied lying about his age.

"Let's hope so," Jonmarc replied as they rode for town.

Ettenheld was a market town, the place all of the farmers whose fields lay to either side of the road brought their produce and livestock to sell, and where they came to purchase what they could not produce themselves. A windmill on a hill turned the grain from nearby farms into flour.

Jonmarc was willing to bet that the main street offered a blacksmith-farrier, an inn that doubled as a tavern, a cooper, cobbler, and chandler, as well as a few other shops. It was largely self-sufficient, as were many of the villages, this far from any major city or the main thoroughfares leading to the palace.

Yet before Jonmarc and his soldiers could get beyond the outskirts of town, they found a hastily-built barricade made of wood and stones blocking their entrance.

"Go back where you came from," a man shouted from behind the barricade. "We get none of the king's protection when we need it, so he'll get none of our coin now."

Jonmarc sighed and moved to the front of his contingent of troops. He did not draw his sword—yet—but he let his hand fall to the pommel in a gesture he was certain would not be overlooked. "If you've got a grievance, take it to the tribunal. All Eastmark citizens are bound by law to pay the taxes decreed by King Radomar. We're here at the king's command to do just that."

"What does the king do for us?" the man demanded. "We never see patrols unless they come to collect the tax money. When someone was stealing our sheep, there wasn't a guardsman to be found. We had to hunt the blighter down and hang him ourselves." The man stood with his hands on his hips, and more of the townspeople had gathered behind him, though Jonmarc noticed that they were not armed.

"What did the king ever do for us?" a woman demanded. "Did he send us any help when that big storm flattened all those trees and knocked down two barns? No. We had to clean it up and rebuild all by ourselves—and pay as much tax as if we hadn't lost what was in the barns."

The arguments were familiar ones. Jonmarc had heard the adults of his own village back in Margolan make the same comments when he was growing up. Margolan and Eastmark were large kingdoms. It would be impossible to have enough soldiers to meet the kinds of needs the townsfolk wanted.

"Have you been invaded lately by raiders from across the Northern Sea?" Jonmarc asked.

The man who spoke first looked taken aback. "Raiders? In Eastmark?"

"How about the nomads from the East?" Jonmarc said. "Have they burned any villages or kidnapped your women and children?"

The villagers looked at one another, then shook their heads.

"Do you know why?" Jonmarc continued. "The sea raiders and the Eastern nomads haven't come riding through your fields, burning your barns and taking your sheep and women because General Alcion's troops fought them at the shoreline and at the border and drove them back. That's what the king's troops have been doing, instead of clearing your trees and building your barns."

"I'm tired of paying coin to the king and seeing nothing in return." This time, it was an older woman who spoke.

"If the king allowed the raiders and nomads past the border and fought them in the middle of your village, would it please you more?" Jonmarc argued. He did not want the altercation to turn violent, and he understood the villagers' point of view, yet he had orders to carry out. "That way you'd see what you get for your money."

The villagers spoke in low tones to one another, but they did not attack. "Tell me," Jonmarc added. "Does your village flood as often now, since the dam was built?" They shook their heads. "Do you know who built that dam? King Radomar's soldiers. Do you know what he paid them with? Your tax coin and the coin of all the other villages downriver that don't wash away every spring the way they used to."

Some of the villagers were nodding in agreement. Several had left the crowd and gone back to their shops and businesses. The blustering man had grown red in the face, and he seemed ready to let loose another tirade until two older men pushed through the crowd.

"Morton! What in the name of the Dark Lady are you doing?" The taller of the two older men strode up to the angry protester until they stood nearly belly to belly. "Did you block the road? Crone's tits, Morton! These are royal soldiers. You've been drinking again, haven't you?" He grabbed Morton by the collar, lifted him up onto his tiptoes, and gave him a shake.

"Get out of here now before I kick your ass." He gave Morton a shove and then looked at the barricade, shaking his head. "Now we've got to clean this up," he muttered.

The other newcomer looked embarrassed by the display but retained his dignity. "My good men," he said with a slight bow. "I apologize. Morton hasn't been right in the head for a long time. I assure you, we knew nothing of this."

Jonmarc doubted that Morton had made the barricade all by himself, but since none of the rest of the villagers seemed inclined to defend him and the other speakers had vanished, he accepted the older man's apology. "Things happen," Jonmarc replied with a shrug. "May we enter peacefully? We still have a job to do."

"Of course, of course," the man said, and motioned to several of the other townsmen to clear the road so the soldiers could ride in. Most of the villagers had gone back to whatever they had been doing, but a few lingered to watch as the soldiers rode to the town square.

In the other towns, Jonmarc made the gathering of tax

monies as friendly as he could, dismounting and shaking hands with the village leaders. Here, he stayed on his horse as did the other soldiers, with a gut feeling that the sooner they put Ettenheld behind them, the better.

"Good sir," the first older man said when he and a small group of villagers gathered in the square. "We've gathered the tax money as decreed. You can check—it's all there." He gave a nervous smile that was more like a twitch. "Since that's the case, I'm sure you'll agree there's no need to mention any of the... unpleasantness... to your commanding officer."

Jonmarc accepted the bag of coins and counted through them. The amount was indeed correct. He put the bag in a pouch beside his saddle. "Thank you, on behalf of King Radomar."

By unspoken agreement, the soldiers fell into battle formation as they rode away from the town. *Apparently, I'm not the only one who got a bad feeling about that place,* Jonmarc thought, though he was just as glad the incident ended peacefully.

"Do you think they were all in on it?" Circan asked after they had put the village behind them.

Jonmarc shrugged. "Maybe not all of them. More than Morton, that's certain. It took them some time to drag all that junk into the road, and it's hard to believe everyone didn't see them doing it."

Circan nodded. "I thought the same thing. I'm from a town that size. Everyone always knows what everyone else is doing." He paused. "Did they really think we'd just ride away without their money?"

"Maybe. Fools like Morton don't think, they bluster. It was probably easier for everyone to go along with him than to try to argue him out of it."

Circan raised an eyebrow. "They're lucky you're the officer in charge. I can think of a few who wouldn't have minded the chance to bust a few heads together and flex their muscles on behalf of the king."

Jonmarc grimaced. He knew exactly which soldiers Circan was talking about, and shared his opinion. "I'm thinking that since we got their money, it's best if no one mentions the barricade," he said. "I'm not sure the General is of a mind to take those kinds of affronts in stride."

"I think you're right," Circan agreed.

In the few months since Jonmarc had been promoted to a small command of his own, he had spent most of the time patrolling the Eastmark countryside. Most villagers were wary of them because they were outlanders as much as because they wore the livery of King Radomar. Much of what Jonmarc and his men did was unremarkable: chasing down highwaymen, settling disputes, and checking traveling peddlers and merchants to make sure their wares carried the king's revenue stamp. Hardly the stuff of legend. And while the actions they took worked in the best interest of the villagers, Jonmarc knew that a level of distrust and resentment still lingered among the country folks when it came to the long arm of the king.

By the time the light faded, they were a candlemark's ride beyond Ettenheld. Unwilling to risk laming a horse in the dark, Jonmarc called a halt for the night. They found a level meadow near a stream, affording the horses both grass and water, and pitched their tents.

Soldiering was still relatively new to Jonmarc. He had been fifteen when his family was killed by raiders, seventeen when his wife and unborn child died along with the rest of their village when monsters attacked. For a year, he had traveled with Maynard Linton's caravan of wonders from one side of Margolan to the other, and his natural ability with a sword landed him in with the caravan's defenders. That meant he had seen a lot of action and real fighting, even before he had joined up with the War Dog mercenaries in Principality a year ago. His accidental involvement foiling a plot to kill General Alcion had earned him the general's personal request that Jonmarc join his outlander army for at least a year. One did not refuse such a request from a prince of Eastmark.

So here he was, serving in Eastmark, and rising quickly through the ranks. Field promotions tended to come because of casualties, and Jonmarc was mindful of the fate of those whose positions he had inherited. Now, with half a year left before he was free to rejoin the War Dogs, his goal was to keep the peace, avoid trouble, and return to Principality at the first opportunity.

"Wish we could swap these trail rations for some nice, fresh venison," Markelson said as the troop gathered around a small fire that evening. Two men walked on patrol around the camp, while the others ate the provisions that had been packed for their mission.

"I've had worse," Jonmarc replied, tearing into a tough piece of dried meat. Sausage, cheese, and hard bread were the food that kept an army in the field moving without the need to stop and hunt, steal livestock or spend time looking for merchants to trade with. If they were lucky, the army cooks might have thrown in some dried berries and fruit. If not, such luxuries were easy to forage on the move. Usually, everyone was satisfied so long as no one forgot the wine.

"I've got four months until I muster out," Soster, one of the older soldiers, said, and took a bite of his hard biscuit. "Sent my pay back to my wife in Margolan. She bought a piece of land for us to do some farming. I'll be glad if I never have to shoot at anything besides a deer or a fox again."

Circan grunted in agreement. "I hear that after you spent a few years with the Principality mercs—and the Eastmark troops—it's almost a sure thing you can get a good spot with the Margolan army. I don't mind soldiering, but I'd like to see my parents again before they cross the Gray Shore."

In the few months the group had been together, Jonmarc had learned quite a bit about his men. Hendin, a dark-haired man with a quick temper, came to Principality because of some kind of problem with the law back in Margolan. Whatever the issue had been, Hendin's conduct had been acceptable if not exemplary since then, and he was as fast with his sword as he was to take umbrage with an insult.

Ost, a red-head who was one of the best hunters in the troop, was a quiet man who preferred whittling to talking, could carve just about any animal out of a stick of wood. He usually presented his treasures to children they met along the road. Kester left Principality due to some unpaid gambling debts, but that had not taught him to stay out of dubious card games. Penn juggled when he had free time and was as good as many of the performers Jonmarc had known with the caravan. Good enough that Jonmarc doubted Penn's denials about having been an entertainer, though his frequent scrapes with the husbands and boyfriends of the ladies he wooed gave Jonmarc an idea of why Penn ended up in Eastmark.

Tor was a good hedge witch and a decent soldier. He whiled away their travel time watching the ditches and hedgerows for the plants and bark to make the powders and potions he used to treat their injuries and sicknesses since he was the group's erstwhile healer. Rodd played the pennywhistle and told fantastical stories about legendary fighters of yore. Bann seemed to live for the soldiering life, pestering the others for sparring matches or archery competitions and saying little else about where he had come from or what he wanted to do. Quan was a wiry fellow in his early twenties who looked like he would be more at home in a library or as a merchant. He had taken up soldiering since he could expect no inheritance as the youngest of five sons and hoped to take his wages and open a tavern when he mustered out.

Tonight, Quan, and Tor were on guard duty for two more candlemarks before they returned for their dinner and others took their place. Rodd played his pennywhistle and Ost had found a stick to carve. Bann had finished his dinner quickly and gone to have a few rounds of friendly sword sparring with Penn in the fringe of the firelight. Jonmarc listened to the rest of them talk about the weather and the things they had seen on the road that day, stories of girlfriends wooed and lost, and a few ribald jokes. Most nights when they were out on a mission, he was surprisingly content to enjoy the fire and the companionship of his men. Tonight, he could not shake a gut feeling that something was amiss.

"I want three-man shifts on two-candlemark watches tonight," Jonmarc said as he stood. "One man stays with the horses, and the other two patrol the camp perimeter."

"Expecting trouble, Cap'n?" Tor asked.

Jonmarc shrugged, not feeling inclined to explain a hunch. "Word's out we're collecting taxes," he said. "That means we've got plenty of coin. Might give someone ideas."

Usually, the fact that they rode in the uniform of Alcion's Outlander Guard was enough to make brigands go out of their way to avoid them. Those highwaymen who had not avoided the troop had been routed, and Jonmarc was certain news of their victories had spread through the taverns from other travelers. Most robbers would choose a less well-armed and professionally-trained target, like a peddler or traveling merchant.

I don't think Morton was the kind to take "no" for an answer, Jonmarc thought, but he had nothing but intuition to vouch for his concerns. *I would have liked to have put a lot more road between us and Ettenheld. A long ride on a dark road would make most hotheads think twice.* But it had been late enough in the day that traveling farther presented its own risks, and so here they were. The sooner they were gone, the better.

"We're going to get off right after sunrise," he added, anticipating the groans of his men. "Lots to do, and the sooner we're back to camp, the sooner we get some good ale instead of piss-poor wine."

That brought a chuckle of agreement, and Jonmarc headed toward where the horses were tied to pass the word to the two men on sentry. Walking kept him from fidgeting, and he wanted to see for himself that the night thus far held no looming threats. He found the horses safely with food and water, and the sentries reported no cause for alarm. Jonmarc headed back to his tent and bedroll, momentarily satisfied but not wholly convinced. For once, morning would not come soon enough to please him.

THE ATTACK CAME JUST after third bells. A shout came from Rodd, who was guarding the horses, and the panicked whinnies and stomping of hooves corroborated Rodd's cry of alarm. Penn and Ost were walking the perimeter, and they shouted a warning just a few minutes later.

By the time the third guard called out, the rest of the camp was already on their feet and ready for a fight. Morton had indeed come looking to finish the argument and brought with him a dozen of his own supporters, young men armed with knives, staves, and scythes.

"We came to get our coin back from that thieving excuse for a king," Morton said as the two sides squared off.

"Go home now," Jonmarc ordered. "We won't spare you if you fight us. Nothing good can come of your deaths, and if you draw blood from my men, you strike at the law of King Radomar, and he will avenge harm done."

Morton's response was a full-throated battle cry as he lifted a long harvesting knife and came at Jonmarc in a fury. The other men with Morton ran toward the soldiers, swinging their weapons as they came.

Jonmarc had a sword in both hands, and he blocked Morton's press with one blade as he nicked Morton's thigh with the other, a warning to stand down that he doubted Morton was wise enough to take. Morton cursed as the sword's tip slashed his skin, but he did not pause in his attack.

Jonmarc parried and blocked, fighting defensively in the hope outright slaughter could be averted. Morton had the skills and instincts of a brawler, but no formal training and his blows were clumsy, more of a threat from sheer force than from any skill.

"We're tired of seeing our hard-earned coin go to the palace," Morton snarled. "We do just fine out here on our own. Leave us alone, and we'll leave you alone."

"Too late for that now," Jonmarc muttered, returning Morton's blows and launching a press of his own that forced Morton to retreat, barely moving fast enough to avert the worst of his strikes. Morton was bleeding from several gashes on his forearms and a deep cut to his left shoulder. Yet the glint in his eyes told Jonmarc the villager was not yet ready to yield.

Quan, Circan, and Markelson had gone to help Rodd protect the horses. Half of Morton's fighters waded into combat on that side of the meadow, and Jonmarc wondered if they weren't more intent on stealing good horses than they were on getting back their tax money. That left six of the attackers focused on the soldiers who remained near the camp with Jonmarc.

Morton remained intent on Jonmarc, looking for a way to vent his spleen over the taxes and the king's control. Hendin's quick temper served him as he went on the offensive against a man half again his size, attacking with speed and skill that enabled him to dodge the powerful strikes of his angry but untrained opponent.

Penn's dexterity and sleight of hand gave him an advantage as he took on a man with the strong arms and shoulders of a farm hand. Penn had a dagger in his left hand, using it to distract his opponent, who obviously had never fought in anything except a barroom tussle. Every time Penn made threatening slashes with the dagger, his attacker forgot to keep his eye on Penn's sword, and in three strokes, Penn had the man on the ground and bleeding badly from a gash deep enough to cost the man his leg.

Tor had his hedge witch magic to help him, though he was quite able to hold his own with a sword. His attacker was a man in his middle years with huge, calloused hands and the thick neck of a laborer. Jonmarc knew for a fact that Tor routinely tainted his blades with a potent plant mixture designed to cause nausea and hallucinations. He had already scored half a dozen cuts on his attacker, while the villager had only managed to bloody Tor's forearm with a shallow slice that was easily healed. The attacker staggered on his next thrust and had gone ashen in the face, a sure sign that the poison was already at work. The man's next strike went wild, and from his shout, it was clear that he was battling monsters only he could see, overtaken by hallucinations. Tor disliked killing, and he had perfected a number of moves to disarm an opponent without too much blood. Raving and thrashing, the big man went down, losing his staff in the process and fell still from a solid thump on the head.

Bann seemed to be enjoying the fight, having found a willing opponent against whom to test his skill. Though the villager swung a scythe with potentially lethal force, Bann took it as a challenge, bobbing and weaving until he had scored a dozen gashes, and only then did the angry farmer realized he was being toyed with by someone with far more skill at fighting. Once Bann finally pressed his advantage, the farmer fell back and looked like he might have made a run for it had there been anywhere to go.

Kester was a gambler through and through. Jonmarc had admonished him more than once for taking crazy chances, knowing that Kester's fondness for risk usually got the better of him. Despite his weakness for a bet, Kester was good with a sword and smarter than average. Both helped his odds in a fight. Now, Kester tempted fate, purposely giving his attacker chance after chance to land a blow, counting on his skill and speed to avoid disaster. While Kester thought it a great game, it was clear that his opponent was intent on causing harm.

"Be done with it, Kester!" Jonmarc shouted. Kester was not in the mood to heed a warning, recklessly dodging in and out of his attacker's reach as if it were all a grand joke.

Ost, the hunter, circled his opponent like prey. Most men in these parts—and a lot of the women—were skilled woodsmen, and hunting or poaching kept body and soul together when harvests were bad. Ost had often told stories about his most successful hunts, bringing down a deer or elk in foul weather, after a long and arduous trek. He had the quiet patience to wait in a blind until his prey came into sight, and the skill to make a shot on the first try. As he moved warily around his attacker, Ost let the man betray his strengths and weaknesses before committing himself to the fight. Within a few moves, it was clear that Ost had a longer reach, and that his opponent seemed to have poor vision on one side. Too late, the villager realized he was being stalked, and reacted with a flailing sequence of moves that left himself open to attack. Ost's strike was graceful and merciless, opening the farmer from gut to groin with a single, swift strike that was over before the doomed man realized he was dying.

Bann finished off his attacker, and two of the villagers that had gone after the horses lay on the ground. That meant six of the twelve attackers were already down, and out of the corner of his eye, Jonmarc saw Quan run another of the men through when the villager moved to slash one of the horses. Five against twelve were much better odds, and Jonmarc gave a feral grin, showing his teeth.

"I came for my coins, and I'll have them!" Morton growled, springing at Jonmarc with a ferocity that required his full focus to avoid being killed. Morton might not be a trained swordsman, but he had been in enough knife fights to be a skilled opponent, and Jonmarc did not discount the edge that rage and fanaticism lent to Morton's strength.

He and Morton were both bleeding from too many cuts and gashes to count. Blood ran down Jonmarc's arms and started down his thigh where Morton had managed to score. Jonmarc had been in enough fights to know that luck and will could triumph over ability unless a swordsman was very careful.

"A dead Markian is still worth more than a live outlander," Morton goaded. "No one will mourn you. We'll give you to the crows."

Jonmarc did not doubt that no one at the Eastmark palace would particularly note their deaths on their own merit should he and his men fall in the fight. But Morton was missing the main point. "We're not important," Jonmarc replied, falling into the thrust, block, parry sequence he had practiced countless times. "But we are the king's law, and King Radomar will not allow a challenge to his rule."

Morton snorted derisively. "We're nobodies in the middle of nowhere. The king doesn't give a damn about the likes of us."

As Jonmarc turned to deflect another of Morton's wild swings, he saw Kester's eyes open wide with horror and surprise as his opponent sank his blade deep into Kester's side. Fury overtook reason, and Jonmarc went on the offensive, beating Morton back with a sudden sequence of powerful blows. One of his strikes ripped Morton's sword from his hand, and Jonmarc wheeled into a perfect Eastmark kick, planting the sole of his boot hard against Morton's chest and sending him to the ground. In the next second, Bann wheeled and caught Kester's attacker by surprise, getting inside his guard and slitting his belly wide open with the tip of his blade, while his other sword opened the man's throat.

Morton scrambled to his feet, but Jonmarc was done with patience. Scything his blades as his mentors had taught him, Jonmarc went for the kill. Only then did it seem to dawn on Morton that this was not a game. He came at Jonmarc hard and fast, as if having made up his mind to die putting up a good fight. Jonmarc's first blow took off Morton's right hand at the wrist. His second strike cleaved the village agitator from shoulder to hip, sending a spray of hot blood into the night air. Morton collapsed to the ground in a heap and did not move again.

Tor was already kneeling next to Kester, while Ost and

Bann covered him. Circan and Markelson each battled attackers, while Soster and Penn gave chase to two of the villagers who had decided to make a run for it. In a few more moments, the battle was over, and all twelve of the attackers lay dead on the bloody meadow grass.

"How is he?" Jonmarc asked, kneeling on the other side of Kester's body from Tor.

"Not good," Tor said grimly. "At least he didn't get run through. I don't think the blade hit any vital organs, but he's losing blood, and the wound could go bad." He looked up at Jonmarc.

"I'm a hedge witch, not a full battle healer. I can keep him alive, slow the bleeding, use some powders to keep the wound from going bad right away. But come morning, we need to get him to someone who's got more power than I do if you want him to make it back to the city."

"What about them?" Circan stood a few paces away and motioned toward the fallen villagers with a bloodied sword.

Jonmarc stood and looked out over the campground that had become a battlefield. No matter what course of action he envisioned, there were reprisals and ramifications. "We collected the full taxes due from the village," he said, working out a solution aloud. Circan nodded.

"The village elders disavowed Morton and told us he was mad," Jonmarc continued. "They welcomed us and treated us with respect, as due the emissaries of the king," he added.

"If we report that villagers attacked us, the king—or at least the general—will be honor-bound to strike back," Markelson observed quietly.

That made up Jonmarc's mind. "It's very dark out here, don't you think? We were set upon by brigands in our sleep, without warning. They were after the king's tax money and our horses. We have a mandate from the king himself to rid the highways of robbers, and we defended ourselves." His men had gathered around, and he met each man's gaze as if daring them to disagree. "We've seen so many villagers on this trip, I couldn't keep one straight from another," he lied evenly.

He brought the heel of his boot down hard on Morton's dead face, smashing his features into an unrecognizable pulp. "As far as I'm concerned, we never saw these unhappy bastards before in our lives, and this is a tale we never need to tell again."

One by one, his soldiers nodded. They knew what he did, that the king's vengeance for an attack on his soldiers would be merciless, and that those who deserved the retribution were already dead. No good could come of punishing the rest of Ettenheld. *Technically, I'm asking them to commit perjury, if not worse,* Jonmarc thought. *Lying to our commanding officer, falsifying a report to the king, it could go badly for us if anyone found out. But it will surely go badly for the rest of the village if we tell the truth, and vengeance is already served.*

Yet he and the rest of his men came from villages much like Ettenheld. *Goddess knows, Ebbetshire had its own village idiots,* Jonmarc thought of his own home town. *I'd have hated to think that the fate of all our people depended on the actions of the dumbest men in town.*

"Let's clean up our camp and get the horses ready," Jonmarc said finally. "It's almost dawn. Let's see if there's a healer in Rendel's Pass."

THE SUN WAS BARELY above the horizon by the time Jonmarc and his men rode into Rendel's Pass, the next of the villages on their circuit. They had improvised a hammock for Kester between two of their horses, and it was sufficient to get him, alive, to the inn just outside of town.

Jonmarc spent his own wages to rent a room and buy the services of a healer. Imstaldt, the innkeeper, sent up a tray of food for Jonmarc's men and a pitcher of warmed wine and refused to take payment, insisting that they shelter and feed their horses as well.

"Will he live?" Jonmarc asked as the healer worked on Kester's wound.

Pillip, the healer, nodded. "He'll hurt for a while, but he'll live," he said, removing his hands to reveal a thin pink scar where there had been a jagged gash. "I'd suggest he avoid bandits for a while, and not go riding at full gallop, but he'll be all right."

"Thank you," Jonmarc said, adding an extra coin to the healer's wages in gratitude. The healer noticed and gave a nod of thanks.

"You're the kings' men, here to take the taxes?"

Jonmarc saw no point in evading the truth. "Yes," he replied. "In the name and power of King Radomar, with his regards for you and your people." It was the phrase he had been ordered to memorize, the official greeting and summons from the palace.

Pillip snorted. "I'm sure His Majesty's 'regards' are a mere formality," he said, sliding a skeptical look in Jonmarc's direction. "But those are pretty words." He paused to finish putting a poultice and bandage over Kester's nearly-healed wound.

"You won't have any problems in Rendel's Pass," he said, placing his vials and packets back into his healer's bag. "We're a pretty law-abiding sort in this town. The village fathers came around a week ago, gathering what everyone owed. They're not the kind to skim any off the top for themselves, so I suspect you'll ride out of here with what you came for."

"Much obliged," Jonmarc replied.

Pillip collected the last of his things and stood. "You're heading on down the road, to Treford and Chauvrenne?"

Jonmarc nodded. "And four more villages once we turn north again before we get back to the city."

Pillip adjusted his green healer's robe and slung his pack over his shoulder. "I don't think you'll have much trouble with bandits going that way, from what I hear of the travelers at the inn. Wouldn't imagine you'll get any grief from the villagers either, although you might have some trouble at Chauvrenne."

Jonmarc raised an eyebrow. "Why's that?"

Pillip shrugged. "Their harvest last year was pretty bleak. The river flooded, and it swamped their fields right after they planted. All that wetness meant the root crops got a blight, and there's a rumor going around that a rivalry between a farmer in Chauvrenne and the next village over led to someone putting a curse on their livestock. Lost every damn lamb and calf birthed over there, despite what the healers tried to do."

He met Jonmarc's gaze. "So don't be surprised if they try to pay you in turnips, or come up with less coin than the king wants. I've been called over there more than once, and the hardship is real." He shook his head. "Don't know if there's anything you can do about it, but you could rip up every mattress in town and hold a blade against their throats, and they aren't likely to have more than a few coins among the lot of them, not after the way last year went." He headed for the door. "Just letting you know in advance."

By the Dark Lady! This was supposed to be an easy run,

Jonmarc thought. He looked down at Kester, who was sleeping off the potions the healer had used. Much as he would have liked to have been on his way, the odds of arriving with all of his men alive meant letting Kester rest until morning. After the night before, he was in no hurry to camp along the road, and the room was already paid for. That meant that he and his men could sleep in shifts, eat a few good meals, and be on their way on the morrow.

Which might give me a chance to think of how to deal with Chauvrenne, Jonmarc thought. *Covering up for Ettenheld's madmen wasn't difficult, and we could argue that justice was served. There'll be no hiding the fact that we come up short with the tax money if Chauvrenne can't pay. Alcion's not going to like that. And if he decides to make an example of them, we're going to be the ones to enforce his punishment.*

Jonmarc had no idea how he would deal with that situation, and precious little time to come up with a solution. But there was nothing more he could do today, other than see to the needs of his men and meet with the village council so that they could leave with the tax money in the morning.

One step at a time, Jonmarc thought. *I'll deal with Chauvrenne when we get there.*

HARD CHOICES

HARD CHOICES

"We have no coin to give you," Sahila said.

"You don't have a choice," Jonmarc Vahanian argued. "General Alcion won't take 'no' for an answer on taxes. He'll have to make an example."

Sahila was a thin, wiry man in his early forties, one of Chauvrenne's village leaders, perhaps chosen to negotiate because he spoke excellent Common. Jonmarc had brought his squad of ten Eastmark mercenaries to collect taxes, and while the other towns had managed to make their payment, Chauvrenne was empty handed.

"Believe me, Captain, I know that," Sahila replied. The three other elders nodded, and Jonmarc could see in their expressions that they grasped the seriousness of the situation.

"Surely there's some way you can raise coin," Jonmarc argued. But he knew in his heart that Sahila was telling the truth. He and his men had been cautioned by the residents of the other towns where they had collected taxes that the year had gone particularly hard on Chauvrenne. Everything Jonmarc had seen since they arrived corroborated that story.

Chauvrenne, in the best of times, was not a wealthy town.

Like many of the other Eastmark villages, it was mostly self-sufficient, with farmers trading their produce for goods in town that they could not make. Since it wasn't on a main highway and did not benefit from travelers who needed to spend coin at an inn for food, lodging, and fresh horses, the residents got by mostly on barter, except for when they took their crops, crafts, and animals to market.

This year, a dam that burst after heavy snows melted flooded fields just after planting time and caused a blight on the crops. Many of the buildings had been damaged or destroyed, including the grist mill. Then the livestock took sick, whether because of tainted feed or, as some of the locals believed, a curse. Those hardships meant that there was little to take to market. The town's weaver, blacksmith, candle-maker, and beekeeper could hardly make up for the loss of more profitable animals and produce.

"What coin we were able to raise at market, we had to spend to buy food and seed," Sahila said. "Even so, you can see that none of us have been eating too much," he said with a self-deprecating, half-hearted smile as he held out his own bony wrist as proof. The other elders chuckled wryly, acknowledging the truth of the statement.

"A few years back, the same kind of bad luck hit one of the other cities," one of the other elders, an older man with a gray beard, said. "The General was merciful, and allowed them to make up the payment the next year."

Jonmarc sighed. "Then perhaps the general has grown more stern since then," he said. "Or maybe there are expenses to the kingdom that cannot be put off. I'm not privy to those things; I just know my orders. And my orders are to bring back full payment from every town on the circuit."

He hated the tone he had to take with Sahila and the others. They struck him as good people, much like the farmers and tradesmen of Ebbetshire. As a child, he remembered overhearing the whispered conversations of the adults when it was time for the king's soldiers to collect taxes. But that had been in Margolan, under the reign of King Bricen, by all accounts a more beneficent ruler than Eastmark's King Radomar. General Alcion was Radomar's brother, and in recent months, he had gained a reputation for ruthlessness that made Jonmarc suspect Alcion had ambitions for the throne. Such an endeavor would require money, lots of it, and so whatever grace Alcion had been willing to give in years past was no longer likely.

"We have nothing of value except the tools of our livelihoods," Sahila said, "and our land. Without those, we're beggars."

I did not sign on as a soldier to bully villagers out of their last mouthful of bread. Jonmarc tried to rein in his anger, hoping his feelings did not show on his face. Soldiers often found themselves administering policies they did not like, against people who had done them no harm. Yet his suspicion that Alcion's sudden hardline tactics were fueled by his own illicit ambition made his orders weigh heavy on his conscience.

"Talk about it. Come up with something. I'll be outside," Jonmarc snapped. He walked out of the small building the town used as its gathering place and out to the street, where his men were waiting.

"How bad?" Circan asked. As Jonmarc's second-in-command, Circan shared Jonmarc's opinion that Alcion would accept nothing less than payment-in-full. And while neither Jonmarc nor Circan had voiced their deeper concerns, Jonmarc had the distinct feeling that Circan—and the rest of his men—were uneasy with the direction things appeared to be headed with the general.

"Bad," Jonmarc replied and vented his frustration by kicking a rock so hard that it crossed the dirt road and ricocheted against the wall of the opposing building.

"Surely they've got some coins buried somewhere," Lieutenant Markelson said. He was the youngest of Jonmarc squad, and though he claimed to be seventeen, Jonmarc guessed the truth was even younger.

Jonmarc shrugged. "So far, they say not. Let's see what they can come up with."

Sahila came to the doorway for Jonmarc minutes later. The quickness of the elders' deliberation gave Jonmarc a good idea of what the answer would be.

"We have heard stories about General Alcion of late that make us all afraid," one of the elders said. He appeared to be the oldest of the group, perhaps in his seventh decade, his hands scarred and gnarled by hard work. "There are rumors that he seized the land from one town last season that could not pay, and forced its residents into the hills to make their way or starve. And it has been said, though I pray to the Dark Lady that it's not true, that in another town that disobeyed an edict, the townspeople were sold as slaves to the Southlanders."

Jonmarc had heard the same stories, from the soldiers forced to do Alcion's dirty work. And as bad as the rumors were, the truth was worse. *That was last year,* Jonmarc thought. *Something's pushed Alcion to get even more ruthless since then. I'm afraid that he won't be satisfied with half-measures now, no matter how brutal.*

"Then you know the stakes," Jonmarc replied. "For your own sakes, I beg of you, if any of your residents has coin, there's no benefit in withholding it. You are likely to lose everything if the taxes can't be paid."

Sahila nodded. "We know. And we have told our people

the bald truth. There has never been much coin in Chauvrenne, so I believe my people when they say they have nothing hidden away."

"Five of our young men have volunteered to go with you as payment," the middle-aged man said, and Jonmarc could see what the offer cost him in the man's eyes. "They're fit for soldiers. The price of a substitute for a wealthy man's son as a conscript would easily equal or better what we owe in taxes."

Sahila was right in figuring that young noblemen often paid commoners to take their place when the king called for conscripts. But it was Alcion, not Radomar, making the rules, and Eastmark had no mass conscription at the moment. *Besides,* Jonmarc thought, *Alcion probably figures that all the people in his territory belong to him anyhow. He'd see no reason to pay them as substitutes when he figures that he owns them, body and soul.*

"Surely your people earned some coin since market trading with the other villages," Jonmarc said.

Sahila shook his head, and his shoulders drooped. "It's been hard-scrabble for everyone around here lately. The people who live out in the forest or up in the hills used to come in every fortnight or so for supplies, but they've either moved on or made do because they haven't come to trade with us in months. We barely have enough livestock to pull our plows and give us wool and eggs, and after how bad the birthing season was this year—curse or blight—we've got none to spare, even to eat ourselves."

"Then you had best look to pack up what remains and leave, before Alcion sends us back to make an example of you," Jonmarc warned. His stomach churned. He had no desire to be the general's instrument of vengeance, nor did he want to see the village's bad luck taken out on his own men.

"We are discussing what to do," one of the elders said.

Jonmarc's eyes narrowed. "Discuss faster. It will only take us a few days to reach the city, and a few days to return. Make up your mind, pack your things, and be quick about it." With that, he and Circan left the building.

"Of all the stupid, dangerous, short-sighted—" Jonmarc fumed as he and Circan walked back to their horses.

"If they weren't going to be able to pay, it would have been nice if they had disappeared before this and saved us the grief," Circan said, agreeing with Jonmarc's unspoken thoughts.

Jonmarc sighed. "I don't know what's going to happen when we take this back to the general, but it isn't likely to be good—for them or for us. Damn! It's bad enough to be tax collectors, but terrorizing the peasants wasn't what I signed on for."

"We can go a little slower on our way back," Circan suggested. "Give them time to get going."

Jonmarc shrugged irritably. "Do you think they'll go?" He stared at the struggling village for a moment before he turned his horse back toward their camp. "I don't. They've stayed through a flood and blight, and Crone knows what other disasters. This is their land."

"What do you think the General will do?"

Jonmarc shook his head. "I don't know. But nothing good. Maybe a year or two ago, there might have been a way to work things out. But… people say he's changed. Now, he seems to want to make his authority very clear. And out here, we're his authority."

His team of men was equally glum when Jonmarc and Circan returned and shared their news. No one was foolhardy enough to openly criticize General Alcion, but there had been whispers in the ranks, enough for a newcomer and outlander like Jonmarc to hear. Just in the time Jonmarc had served the general, he could see the changes, and now it worried him more than ever.

"I'm not sure you've done your career a favor by leaving Chauvrenne as it is." Soster, the most experienced soldier of the squad, brought his horse up beside Jonmarc's as they rode back to the city. "If you'll excuse my bluntness, sir."

Jonmarc grimaced. "You're not saying anything I haven't thought."

"I've served for close to ten years," Soster replied. "Half of that time under General Alcion. He used to reward men who knew how to avoid a fight as well as how to win one. The king is set in his way about some things, like outlanders marrying Eastmark women, but on the whole, he's been good for Eastmark. No one doubted he was in control, but as kings go, he hasn't had a heavy hand."

"Then why the change?" The steady beat of their horses' hooves marked off the miles, bringing them closer to the city with every candlemark.

"Who knows?" Soster replied. "Certainly not hired soldiers at the bottom of the heap. King Radomar's probably in his sixth or seventh decade by now. Even if his health is good, people are bound to be thinking about succession. Alcion's younger, a military hero, and he's gone out of his way to keep his own troops from doing things that might upset the people."

"Like collecting taxes and enforcing unpopular laws," Jonmarc supplied.

Soster nodded. "Exactly. Even if we say what we're doing is on his orders, we're still outlanders, and not to be trusted. The changes started right about the time the general got himself a new group of advisors." He paused. "I guess it doesn't really matter why things changed. What are you going to do about it when we get to the city?"

153

Jonmarc had been asking himself the same question since they left Chauvrenne, and still did not like his choices. "The best thing I can think of is that the general sends us back to hand out whatever punishment he has in mind, and everyone's gone."

Soster shook his head. "Not likely to happen, especially since they sent five of their sons as tribute."

Jonmarc had argued with Sahila about bringing the boys, who were all just shy of conscription age, but the village insisted, hoping the gesture would move Alcion to be reasonable. The young men rode in a cart at the back of the group, and each time they stopped, Jonmarc woke hoping the boys had the good sense to run away. He was not surprised when they did not. Returning home without fulfilling their mission would have brought shame on them and their families. *In a way, my soldiers and I are stuck just like them. Deserters if we don't go back, worse—perhaps—if we do.*

THE CALDON ARMY compound was just outside the royal city of Talonia, third largest of Eastmark's cities. General Alcion's quarters were in the section of the camp for the Eastmark soldiers, separated from where the outland troops lived by the parade ground and common buildings. While his headquarters was unremarkable on the outside, the building was furnished to befit royalty. Rumor had it that when King Radomar was not in residence in the city's royal palace, Alcion availed himself of the accommodations.

Jonmarc stopped in front of the door to the general's quarters and collected his nerve. He had left the five prisoners with his men, still uncertain how to broach the subject with Alcion. Technically, Jonmarc reported to a major, and there were a couple more senior officers between him and the general. Yet perhaps because Jonmarc had been specifically requested by Alcion, he could not escape the general's attention. Some in the camp had been jealous, but Jonmarc did not view his visibility as a good thing.

I'd much rather explain this to a major than to the king's brother, Jonmarc thought. *And frankly, I wish I could hand off the responsibility to a senior officer, let their guts twist over what to do.*

"Captain Vahanian. You're expected." Alcion's valet met Jonmarc at the door and escorted him inside. Noorish carpets, finely woven and vividly colored, covered the floors. Inlaid wooden furniture and beautiful paintings made it clear that the general was more than just a senior officer.

The valet ushered Jonmarc into a well-appointed office. A massive desk dominated the room, inlaid with complex designs some said were magical. Magical or not, it was certainly expensive, a treasure only within reach of someone in the royal family. More fine carpets and two upholstered chairs made the office look more like a sitting room in a grand home. Paintings celebrating Alcion's victories hung on the walls, along with a tapestry that showed Eastmark's *Stawar* God conveying the crown to Alcion's ancestor.

The room was meant to convey royal and military power, along with great wealth, and it did not fail its purpose. Jonmarc did not think he could possibly be more ill at ease, but the reminder of Alcion's position managed to increase his nervousness.

A moment later, Alcion entered from a door on the other side of the room behind the desk. Tall and strongly built, the general looked every inch the hero the ballads celebrated. Complex black tattoos stood out even against his ebony skin, the mark of royalty. At one time, Alcion had been next in line for the throne, behind his older brother, King Radomar. The birth of Radomar's sons bumped Alcion down in the succession. Absent extreme circumstances, the crown would pass to Kalcen and his children. Alcion would remain a general—unless he took fate into his own hands.

Behind Alcion, a second man entered the room. He wore a dark cloak, and kept the cowl up, covering his face. The effect was unnerving, as was the fact that the man stood so still it hardly seemed like he was breathing. Jonmarc's stomach did another flip, but he tried to keep his face impassive.

Alcion took his time seating himself at the desk, shuffling a few papers around and making it clear that he would acknowledge Jonmarc when it suited him. Meanwhile, Jonmarc stood at attention, fighting the growing feeling that a bad situation was about to get worse.

"The tax money is short." Alcion's voice was clipped, and there was no question that the general was unhappy.

"Yes, sir."

"Why was this allowed to happen?"

The general peered at him coldly, but what made Jonmarc shiver was the sense that beneath his cowl, the faceless newcomer, perhaps one of Alcion's new advisors, was watching him very closely.

"We collected full taxes from every town except Chauvrenne, sir," Jonmarc replied. "Flood, blight, and a curse on its livestock have beggared the village. They had nothing of value to collect, even after we searched thoroughly. The village elders understand the severity of the failure, and sent five of their young men as conscripts in lieu of coin."

Alcion's fist slammed into his desk, and the sudden noise nearly made Jonmarc jump. "I don't need conscripts," he growled. "I have men aplenty for the ranks. Coin was due, and coin must be collected."

"And if there is no coin to be had, sir?"

"If I may, General, I suggest that an example be made of the villagers, something memorable so that others will know such behavior cannot be excused." The dark-robed man's voice sent a chill of recognition down Jonmarc's back, and it took all his willpower to keep from shaking.

He had heard that voice before, two years ago on a night of flame and monsters. A red-robed *vayash moru* mage had stopped him on the road and offered him the chance to earn enough gold to feed his family for a year, all for finding a worthless talisman in a burial cave. By the end of the next day, the monsters called by the grave jewelry had killed Shanna and their unborn child along with the rest of the villagers, and the village had burned to the ground, leaving Jonmarc the scarred sole survivor.

If he had any question about whether the general's advisor recognized him, he had his confirmation when the man let his cowl fall back, exposing deathly pale skin and a cruel smile of acknowledgment. The cloak's lining was red as fresh blood, and the mage let his fangs slip between his lips, just slightly, as if to make certain Jonmarc remembered him.

General Alcion nodded in agreement. "My thoughts exactly," he concurred. Seeing them together, Jonmarc no longer wondered why Alcion's behavior had changed.

Vayash moru *can glamour most people, bend them to their will*, Jonmarc thought. Although Alcion might not have needed much bending if the mage offered to give him the throne of Eastmark. Such an arrangement would, of course, bring benefits for Alcion's chief advisors as well, though not so much the people of Eastmark.

"You brought five young men back with you?" Alcion asked.

"Yes, sir."

"Give them a good dinner and see that they receive a measure of whiskey tonight. Tomorrow, bring them to the hanging tree."

"Sir?"

Alcion's smile was cold, his eyes hard. "They'll hang at dawn, and you can take them back to Chauvrenne when you go back to collect what is due the king. So that Chauvrenne understands that Radomar the Unforgiving does not accept their offering." He paused as if waiting for Jonmarc to reply. When Jonmarc did not, Alcion continued.

"You'll take the corpses with you, and tell anyone who asks how it was that the men died. To curb such behavior in the future." The cruel glint in Alcion's eyes told Jonmarc the general was enjoying this, though Jonmarc fought not to retch.

"When you reach Chauvrenne, give them back their sons," Alcion said with a cold half-smile. "Then gather the villagers in the largest barn, lock them inside, and burn it down."

"Burn—"

Alcion glowered. "I believe I was clear, was I not, Captain?"

Jonmarc swallowed bile and nodded. "Yes, sir."

"Captain Vahanian," Alcion added. "I expect you to follow my order to the letter. You failed me once. If you fail again, I will be forced to make an example of you as well. I don't wish to do that. You've served me well thus far, and I value my alliance with General Valjan. But I will do what I need to do to keep order. Am I clear?"

"Absolutely, sir."

"Dismissed," Alcion said. "You and your men will leave as soon as the bodies can be cut down from the tree."

Jonmarc gave a crisp bow because he did not trust his voice, then turned and forced himself to exit at a measured pace. Behind him, he heard the red-robed mage chuckle.

"The folly of outland troops is their lack of resolve, m'lord," the mage said. "Margolan is soft. Amazing it hasn't fallen to its enemies by now."

Can Alcion be mad enough to think he can wage war with Margolan and win, crown or not? Jonmarc wondered. King Bricen and his army were renowned among the Winter Kingdoms for their prowess in battle. *It's said King Bricen has the sorceress Bava K'aa to support him. Surely Alcion's mage is no match for a summoner like her.* Yet he knew that if Alcion had Eastmark's military might behind him, a war with Margolan would be long and costly, and could open both kingdoms to attack from across the Northern Sea.

Jonmarc's mind whirled as he replayed Alcion's commands. *He's going to hang five young men who would have pledged him their lives and swords, and murder an entire village, just to help turn the villagers' hearts against the king*, Jonmarc thought. The ploy was likely to work, especially if this was not the only time King Radomar appeared to order heavy-handed punishments.

The nobility are likely to be watching, too. They'll figure the king's gone mad, and be afraid he'll turn on them next. Some of them might even approach Alcion to see if he would consider saving the kingdom from Radomar. The plot was simple, and that made it even more dangerous. If the mage in the red robes used his magic or his *vayash moru* abilities to sway minds or nudge circumstances even farther in Alcion's favor, seizing the crown might be possible in a matter of months.

And my soldiers and I are the tools he'll use to turn the people against the king, Jonmarc thought sickly. *After he makes us murderers.*

First, Jonmarc stopped by the cooks' tents to make sure that the doomed young men at least received their meal and whiskey. If the cooks wondered about the order, they did not ask. Maybe they could piece the intent together from the look on Jonmarc's face. Despite his best efforts, he guessed that he looked as if he were going to the gallows himself.

Jonmarc walked the darkened streets of the army camp, trying to think of a way out for the villagers or his soldiers. Every possibility led to a dead end. He thought about seeking out the advice of a couple of the older outlander mercs with whom he had become friends, but discarded that idea as well. *No point dragging anyone else into this fiasco. And odds are good either the general or his mage is watching me. Well, let them watch.*

When he had encountered the red-robed mage before, Jonmarc had failed to live up to his half of their bargain. He had thrown the cursed necklace back into the caves where he found it, caves whose magic kept the *vayash moru* from entering. He had lost everything, and his deal had cost an entire village their lives. Fire had been the only thing that drove off the monsters that the necklace had called, and it had destroyed Jonmarc's life for a second time.

"A curse on you, boy!" the raider had shouted. *"May you lose all you love to the flame and sword, and the Dark Lady take your soul!"* Jonmarc had lost his parents, his brothers, and the village where he was born to the flames on a different night. Later, flames had taken Shanna and his new home as well. Now, another village would burn, and Jonmarc had no doubt that whether or not he followed his orders, the red-

robed mage would exact a thorough and merciless revenge that would cost him his life.

What to do? I can't see how to save the Chauvrenne boys unless I'm going to fight the entire base single-handed. And I can't follow my orders, by the Dark Lady! I'd be no better than the raiders that killed my folks. But what to do? Not just my life, but my men as well. What about them?

The bell in the camp tower rang ten times, and only then did Jonmarc realize he had been walking for nearly two candlemarks. He saw Circan heading toward him. "There you are! Everything all right, Captain?"

Jonmarc could only nod wordlessly. He dared not speak his fears or thoughts aloud, or he and his men would not leave Caldon camp alive. *I need time,* he thought desperately. *Time to come up with a plan, something to save my men even if I can't save the boys, maybe save the village—even if I can't save myself.*

"No, it's not all right," Jonmarc replied. He glanced around. Even at this time of night, there were too many eyes and ears to have the conversation in the open. "Come to my quarters. We've got trouble."

Circan and Soster joined Jonmarc a few minutes later in his quarters. Unlike Alcion's sumptuous accommodations, officers' quarters were only slightly less ascetic than those of their men, with a bit more elbow room and a tad more privacy. Jonmarc lowered the shades and lit just one candle, keeping it low to avoid setting them in silhouette.

"What's going on, sir?" Circan asked.

Jonmarc pulled out a flask, took a swig, and handed it to Circan. "He's going to hang the boys at dawn."

Circan exchanged an incredulous look with Soster. "Surely you heard wrong, sir."

Jonmarc shook his head and closed his eyes miserably.

"No. I didn't. They're to hang at dawn, and then we're to take the bodies back to the village, lock the villagers in their biggest barn and burn it down with them inside."

The two men sat in silent shock. "When the king hears—" Soster began.

Jonmarc met Soster's gaze. "We're to say that we act in the name of Radomar the Unforgiving," he replied, dearly wishing he could just drain the flask and make the whole bloody mess go away.

"That's not like the general, even at his sternest," Soster said. "I've seen him pardon enemy soldiers and commute the sentences for his own men who made mistakes."

Jonmarc nodded. "It's that advisor, the *vayash moru*."

"Foor Arontala," Circan said the name like a curse, but he kept his voice low as a whisper. "No one's sure where he came from. But that's what he's called—at least, that's the name he goes by here."

"Unless the general has other, secret, advisors—and he might—the ones he's been seen with besides Arontala are a few powerful nobles and the usual hangers-on that surround aristocrats," Soster added. "I don't think it's the nobles we need to worry about."

Circan nodded. "Agreed. It's not like in Trevath or Nargi, where the nobles are completely above the law. Radomar keeps them pretty well to heel."

And maybe wearing a collar and kept on a leash rankles, Jonmarc thought. *Perhaps Alcion has promised them more latitude under his reign.* Jonmarc ran a hand back through his dark, chestnut hair. "It doesn't really matter who's behind it, does it? Not now. We've got to carry out the order, or end up hanging with those boys."

Because if we don't do it, someone else will. There were always ambitious officers willing to climb the ranks and gain favors regardless of who got hurt in the process. Jonmarc had no illusions about that.

"When were you going to tell the rest of the men?" Circan asked quietly.

"I guess I can't put it off much longer," Jonmarc said with a sigh. "Come on. Let's get it over with."

The response was what he had expected. For a moment, his men stared at him dumbstruck, and then all at once, they reacted.

"Surely there's some other way, isn't there?" Markleson said. He was one of the most by-the-books soldiers Jonmarc had ever met, yet the revulsion in his expression matched Jonmarc's own.

"This can't be right. There's got to be a mistake," Ost argued. He looked up from the small piece of wood that he had been whittling and flicked a strand of red hair out of his eyes, searching Jonmarc's gaze for confirmation.

Penn said nothing. He rotated several clay balls in the palm of his right hand, constantly moving them around, over and under each other without even having to look at them. Jonmarc knew that juggling was Penn's way to deal with bad news.

Tor, their squad hedge witch, looked too devastated by the news to say anything. He just kept shaking his head, as if he were having a vivid internal argument with himself. Bann, Quan, and Henden were clearly angry. "—nowhere to appeal?"

"We can't do that!"

"What are you planning to do about it, sir?" The last voice was Henden's, and the flush of his face left no doubt about his feelings. Henden preferred to settle disputes with his fists, which were clenched, white-knuckled. This time, fighting could not solve the problem, and he looked angry and lost.

"I'm going to do what I can," Jonmarc replied. "There's no way to save the boys. I'm sorry. When we get to the village, we'll do what we can do."

His answer satisfied no one, least of all himself. Jonmarc went back to his quarters and had another swig of whiskey, knowing that nothing was going to make him sleep well.

JONMARC SLEPT little and was up before dawn. He had taken time to repack his bag with items he did not usually need for a regular assignment but could make good use of if things went as he feared they might. Then he left his bag packed by his door and headed out to make sure his horse was saddled and ready to go. After that, he walked out into the darkness to bear witness to what was about to happen.

I should have refused to bring them. This is my fault, Jonmarc told himself. The parade ground was empty except for Alcion, Arontala, the executioner and the five doomed young men. Jonmarc stood in the shadows across the way, where he could see but be less likely to be seen.

I had a hand in causing this. I need to watch what I've helped bring about.

One by one, Jonmarc's men slipped up beside him. No one said anything. None of them needed to.

The executioner might have drugged the boys, or perhaps given them enough whiskey to muddle their heads because none of the prisoners fought. Wrists bound behind their backs, heads down, the boys were herded onto the back of the same wagon that had brought them to the camp. This time, the wagon was parked beneath the hanging tree. Five nooses were visible by the torchlight.

Bastards. The height is wrong. Jonmarc had seen his share of hangings. There was an art to the executioner's work. A clean hanging meant that the distance the condemned man dropped was calculated to break his neck, and the noose was tied in a way to help that happen. Death was nearly instantaneous. If the hangman was sloppy or vengeful, the prisoner slowly strangled.

Jonmarc heard the crack of the leather whip and the hangman's shout to startle the horses, then the clatter of the wheels and the beat of hooves as the horse bolted with the wagon. He flinched but forced himself not to look away as the five bodies bucked and kicked. Tor groaned at the spectacle, while Rodd and Bann began quietly praying to the Dark Lady.

It seemed to take forever for them to die. Alcion and Arontala watched impassively. The executioner was hooded, so Jonmarc had no clue to his thoughts on the matter. After the bodies were still, Alcion made a motion, and the executioner led the horse and wagon around again, stopping beneath the dead men. His large knife cut easily through the heavy rope, and the corpses dropped into the back of the wagon limply, wrists still bound.

Arontala turned toward the darkness where Jonmarc and his men stood. "I hope you're prepared to head out. Your cargo is ready," Arontala said.

Minutes later, Jonmarc and his soldiers had grabbed their gear and swung up to their horses, with Suster volunteering to take first shift with the wagon, since his horse was the one in the traces.

Jonmarc did not know how much of the camp knew about the hanging, but word of such things spread quickly. Now, as he and his men made their way out of the camp in the dawn stillness, he felt as if all eyes in the camp were on them, accusing. He forced himself to keep his head up, back rigid, eyes straight ahead until they were out of the camp and beyond the Talonia city walls.

"Didn't even put a shroud over the poor blighters," Markelson said.

"That, we can fix," Jonmarc replied. He and the others pooled some of their coin to stop at the first town they came to that morning and purchase enough cloth to wrap the bodies and a large piece of canvas to cover the shrouded forms. The grave clothes did little to keep down the flies that buzzed around the corpses, but it gave the dead a measure of dignity and kept their forms out of the prying gaze of passers-by.

The journey back to Chauvrenne took most of the day. Much as Jonmarc wished to be rid of his gruesome cargo, the decisions that awaited them at the village were worse. A pall of silence fell over his men as they rode, leaving each man alone with his thoughts. Rodd played mournful tunes on his pennywhistle to distract himself, and Penn juggled, guiding his horse with his knees.

Jonmarc had made up his mind on what he would do. And as Chauvrenne grew closer, his resolve hardened. A mile outside the village, Jonmarc called a halt.

"This is as far as you go." He turned to his men who gave him questioning looks. "What happens after this is on my head," Jonmarc continued. "As your commanding officer, I order you to stop here and camp at the side of the road until morning. Then you return to Caldon and tell the general that I've deserted and taken the bodies with me."

"Beggin' your pardon sir, but not if we had to face the Formless One herself." Markelson was the least defiant of any of Jonmarc's soldiers, but now his chin was thrust out, and his eyes glinted.

"We talked about this last night after you were gone," Sosten said.

"Took a vote," Circan added. "Thought you might try something this, all noble and doomed. And we swore to a man we'd see this through with you."

"You don't understand what you're saying," Jonmarc argued. "Alcion won't just let us go. He'll hunt us. Unless we can get out of Eastmark, we don't stand a chance."

Circan nodded. "Aye. And we can't go back to Principality either, without making things complicated for the mercs there. The king might even hand us over, to keep the peace."

"We'd figured you weren't going to burn them, and we aren't, neither," Ost said. He had been whittling for much of the ride, and now Jonmarc got a glimpse of what he had carved. In Ost's hand was a small wooden medallion with the mark of the Lady, a passage token to bury with the corpses. Jonmarc did not doubt Ost had carved one for each of the dead boys. *He ought to just save time and make one for each of us. Our odds are slim.*

"I've already given you your orders," Jonmarc countered.

Circan chuckled. "And since we're already planning to commit treason and insubordination, sir, we politely intend to ignore them."

"Don't do this," Jonmarc urged. "We've had enough deaths already."

"The general's already shown his hand," Soster said. "He's shown what kind of man he is. If we went back, assuming he didn't hang us out of pique, what's to say that the next assignment wouldn't be to do the same thing? Or the one after that?" He shook his head. "We've agreed. This isn't what we signed on to do. War is one thing. This—this is murder."

Jonmarc looked each of his men in the eyes and saw the same resolve staring back at him.

"All right then," he said. "Let's go."

The village children spotted the soldiers long before they reached Chauvrenne so that when Jonmarc and the others rode into the small common ground at the center of town, most of the residents had already gathered. The elders were in the front, and Sahila stepped forward, acknowledging them with a slight bow.

"Honored soldiers. We did not expect you to return so quickly. Was our offering accepted?"

The smell of the corpses told the tale before Jonmarc could reply. Five women rushed toward the wagon, and collapsed, wailing and weeping inconsolably.

"There was nothing we could do to stop the general," Jonmarc said tonelessly. "He wanted to make an example of Chauvrenne so other towns would pay their taxes. But the worst is yet to come."

Angry shouts rose from the villagers as they realized what had happened, some of the men went to console the women, while others glared balefully at Jonmarc and his soldiers, on the edge of violence.

"What do you mean?" Sahila asked as the other elders crowded closer. "What can be worse than the murder of our sons?"

Jonmarc dismounted. It was a risk, facing the angry townspeople without the protection of his horse, but he wanted to look Sahila and the others in the eyes. "The general sent us with orders to kill all of you," Jonmarc said. "Orders we mean to ignore—but that makes us, and you, fugitives from the king."

"Kill us all?" one of the elders echoed.

Jonmarc nodded. "My orders were to lock you all in the

biggest barn and burn you alive inside it," he replied. "If you want to live, you're going to have to take what you can carry and run. Now."

Sahila spoke briefly with the other elders in low tones, then turned toward the assembly of townspeople, who were murmuring and glancing angrily at the soldiers. He shouted to the crowd in Markian, and from their reaction, Jonmarc guessed that Sahila was translating Alcion's judgment and Jonmarc's terse conclusion. Women shouted and began to weep. Men yelled curses and threats. Jonmarc's Markian was good enough to pick up the gist of most of what was said. From the way his soldiers moved closer together, still mounted and within easy reach of their weapons, he suspected that they also followed the conversation.

"Stop!" Sahila yelled as the crowd surged forward. He stood between Jonmarc and the angry townspeople. "These men have risked their lives to warn us. They don't intend to do the general's bidding. Harm them, and I will kill you."

Apparently, Sahila had a reputation for keeping his word because the villagers backed off. The glares and muttering did not end, but no one raised weapons, although Jonmarc could see that many of the people carried the tools of their daily work which could easily be used to fight.

"How can we leave? Where will we go?" one woman asked despairingly.

"How do we know the army won't find us?" a man demanded.

One of the other elders stepped up, an older man. As soon as he moved to speak, the villagers grew quiet out of respect. "There's not much left of Chauvrenne, after the flood and blight," he said. "Naught worth dying over. Some of our people have already left. It's time for the rest to move on —tonight."

"How can we go so soon?" a woman in the crowd wailed.

"Soldiers could be just a few candlemarks behind us, sent to make sure we do our job," Jonmarc warned. Since he suspected that the harsh punishment had been selected by Arontala to cause Jonmarc anguish, he would not be surprised to have additional troops—troops unlikely to abandon their duty for principle—on their way. "The general expects us back tomorrow with a full accounting. When we don't return, he'll know for certain. Other soldiers will come. They'll follow orders."

"Take only what you need to survive, what you can carry and still walk all night," Sahila yelled to the crowd. Leave your livestock, unless you can ride them or carry them. Take all the food you can carry, some seeds to plant, and your weapons. Leave the rest behind."

From what Jonmarc had seen, and what Sahila and the elders had told him before, the ravaged villagers barely had the clothes on their backs and a few ill-fed goats among them. Still, after all they had been through, abandoning the big of land they called home would be a deep loss. *Still better than being burned alive.*

"Hurry," Jonmarc urged, in Common and again in Markian. "You don't have much time."

"Go where?" someone shouted from the crowd.

Sahila turned toward the villagers. "Away from here. Off the main roads. Go into the forests. Don't travel in large groups. Don't tell anyone you're from Chauvrenne. Stay out of sight. You can be outlaws—or you can be corpses."

"Go!" the older elder shouted, waving his arms as if to shoo away a skittish animal. For now, they were more shocked than panicked, though fear would set in soon enough.

"What will become of you, since you've broken your orders?" Sahila asked, looking back to Jonmarc and his men.

"The same as your villagers," Jonmarc replied. "We'll be outlaws. Fugitives. The general will put a bounty on our heads."

Sahila nodded. "So I thought. Then you need to leave Eastmark."

Easier said than done since outside the army posts and the trading cities, few outlanders traveled the kingdom. Compared to the ebony skin of Eastmark natives, Jonmarc and his soldiers pale complexions would be impossible to hide."

"Do you have cloaks with hoods?" Sahila asked.

Jonmarc's men nodded. "Come with me," Sahila said. They followed him to a small wooden house that looked likely to collapse. Out back was a small garden. Sahila began gathering leaves, blossoms and stems into a bag, muttering to himself as he tried to move quickly.

"I've got a pot on the fire near to boiling," Sahila said. "I'm going to boil these up, and give some of the mixture to each of you to drink." He gave a rueful chuckle. "You won't like the results. It's going to make your skin look poxy and scaly, itch something awful, but it won't actually make you sick, but you'll look near enough like lepers that if you keep your hood up and don't get too close to people, they're likely to leave you alone." He added the plants to the pot and went out to pull some more from the garden.

"These will cook up quick," he said. "You'll drink the first mix, smear the second on your skin. It'll darken you up good." He grinned. "It'll let you pass from a distance, but it'll wear off after a couple of days, so put as much distance between you and here as you can, fast."

He tried to give them rations for their journey, but the

soldiers refused since each of them had packed all they could carry from camp. They unhitched the horse from the wagon and led the horses to a fenced enclosure where they would have pasture and water. "I don't have a doubt that Alcion will send someone to check up on us," Jonmarc said. "They'll find the horses when they come. We could ride them, but people will remember seeing soldiers on horseback more than beggars on foot, and if we stay off the roads, the horses are of little use anyway."

Jonmarc had worn other clothes beneath his uniform, intending to bury or burn it once he reached Chauvrenne. Now, he saw that his men had the same idea. In a few moments, their uniforms were heaped on the fire outside.

"There's a fire for the general," Henden said, dusting off his hands. Still, Jonmarc saw the same mix of anger, loss, and shock in his men's gaze that he was sure they saw in his.

"You'd best be going," Sahila said once he had dosed them with his brew and rubbed them dark as mahogany with the salve. "Get to the river—it's your surest guide."

"The Nu River's on the other side of Principality," Ost objected.

Sahila nodded. "Two smaller rivers pass near here, and both feed into the Nu. Thing is, there are only two good bridges—one north in Principality, and one south in Dhasson. Otherwise, you'll need a boat to get across, and the current's wicked this time of year. Only a few places you'll survive the crossing. Best places are along the Dhasson riverbanks. It's a ways south, but if you make good time on foot, you can be there in a couple of days."

South. Seers had warned Jonmarc more than once that if he went south, death would follow.

Death followed me anyhow, and I went north, he thought. *And I'm not going far south. Nowhere near Nargi or*

Trevath. Dhasson should be safe—safer than here, that's for certain.

"What about the others?" Jonmarc said with a jerk of his head toward the villagers. Some had already started down the paths into the forest, their belongings wrapped up in cloth and tied to their backs. Others scurried to prepare.

"I'll make sure they move on," Sahila promised. "It's a lot for them to take in, but we knew something bad would come of not paying the taxes. I argued for them to scatter months ago, but they wouldn't hear of it. Now, they'll listen," he said with a shrug. "Got a small shed out back that's barely standing after the last windstorm. Won't take much to bring it down in a heap. We'll put the bodies in there, then collapse it. Not much of a cairn, but it'll keep the animals off them."

"I'm sorry." The words were completely inadequate, but they were all Jonmarc had to offer.

Sahila met his gaze. "You've done all you can, and more than we had a right to expect. Now get out of here. The general may be angry at us, but you've defied him, and that's going to go hard if he finds you. So make sure he doesn't."

Jonmarc and his men walked to the edge of town, and looked toward the broad forest. "We can't travel together," he said. "Twelve men can't hide anywhere. Split up. No more than two in a group. Don't worry about the others. Just get yourselves to safety."

"I've been down toward Dhasson before," Circan said. "I'll go with you." Jonmarc nodded assent, and the others paired off. Jonmarc shook each man's hand, looking each in the eyes as he said goodbye, knowing that they were unlikely to all make it across the river alive.

"Been an honor to serve with you," Jonmarc said, his throat tight. "May the Dark Lady have her hand on you."

With that, they headed off in pairs, each choosing

different paths as the trail through the forest branched, and quickly leaving the footpaths altogether to avoid being seen. Before long, the others were out of sight and beyond hearing range.

He and Circan did not speak. They didn't need to. At most, they had a half day's lead on the soldiers who would hunt them, maybe less. Not nearly enough to get to the river, let alone to a crossing.

I'd still rather die with an arrow in my back than follow Alcion's orders. And with Arontala whispering in his ear, I'm pretty sure I was going to die sooner rather than later. I outran Arontala once. Let's see if I can do it again.

He focused his will on surviving, if just to spite Arontala and Alcion. Still, the curse the dying raider had placed on him years ago echoed in his ears, exacting its vengeance all over again. *May you lose all you love to the flame and sword, and the Dark Lady take your soul!*

DEAD RECKONING

DEAD RECKONING

Moss muffled the sound of running boot steps. Two young men dodged through the forest, fleeing for their lives. Branches snagged their skin, grasped their hair and tore at their clothing. Leaves slapped their faces. In the distance, hunting hounds brayed.

"They're getting closer." Circan ducked to avoid a low-hanging branch.

"Then we've got to get farther," Jonmarc replied.

A full run was impossible in the underbrush, but the two young men needed to put as much distance as possible between themselves and those who hunted them. That meant maintaining a steady jog despite brambles, uneven footing, and tree limbs that dipped low enough in places to smack the unwary traveler in the head.

"I thought we would have put the dogs off our scent when we waded down that stream," Circan said.

"We might have—if we'd had more time to put between us and them," Jonmarc's voice was strained, laboring for breath. "They probably figured out we weren't going north.

West would strand us at the river with no way to cross. East gets us nowhere. So we had to be going south." Their pursuers had likely forded the stream and set the dogs to sniff the riverbanks until they picked up the scent once again.

A few days ago, Jonmarc Vahanian and Circan had been mercenary soldiers under the command of Eastmark's General Alcion, brother to King Radomar. When the small town of Chauvrenne, ravaged by floods and blight, had been unable to pay its tax, Alcion had ordered Jonmarc's squadron to slaughter the villagers. Jonmarc and his men had sealed their fates when they warned the villagers to flee, and went on the run themselves, hoping to reach neighboring Dhasson and cross the Nu River to safety.

"How much farther?" Circan sounded as exhausted as Jonmarc felt. They had been moving almost constantly, snatching only a few candlemarks' sleep over the course of three days, and Jonmarc knew they were nearing their limit. Their pursuers could hand off the task to the garrison at the next town, and a fresh crop of hunters would join the chase, while the quarry grew harried and dangerously weary.

"No idea," Jonmarc admitted. "Not too much farther, if Sahila knew what he was talking about."

They had spent most of the last three days in the forest, resorting to roads only when there was no other choice. The food they brought with them would not last much longer, assuming they could elude capture. Despite the disguises Sahila had improvised for them, darkening their skin to fit in better among the Eastmark residents, hiding their features with a potion that raised welts and scabs, it would be foolish to risk exposure by traveling the highway for longer than necessary. The few times they ventured onto roads, Jonmarc hoped it would muddy their scent, make the dogs lose them amid the smells of horse dung and ox urine. Still, the forest had seemed the safer choice, at least before Alcion's pursuers had narrowed their lead.

Jonmarc's boot slipped on a wet patch of moss, and he went down hard, muttering a curse. He got back up, smudged the footprint in the mud as best he could and tried to find drier footing where he might leave fewer tracks.

By Jonmarc's dead reckoning, with the aid of his compass, they should be near the border between Eastmark and Dhasson. In theory, once they crossed into the neighboring kingdom, Alcion's soldiers had no authority to continue their search. In reality, out here far from guards or villages, no one would be the wiser if the Eastmark soldiers kept up their hunt. And if by chance Alcion's men encountered Dhassonian guards, Jonmarc suspected that those guards would turn a blind eye as the Eastmark soldiers apprehended their "criminals."

I wonder if the others have made it this far. Surely Alcion didn't send the whole army after us. Jonmarc's twelve men split into teams of two, each team heading out on different paths. There were thousands of soldiers back at the Caldon army camp, but Jonmarc could not imagine that the general would deploy them all to capture a dozen deserters.

Then again, we've struck a blow at his authority, and his pride, Jonmarc thought. *For Alcion, defiance is a capital offense.*

But it wasn't Alcion alone who was to blame, either for the harsh punishment for Chauvrenne or the increasingly heavy-handed rule the general administered. Jonmarc held Alcion's top advisor responsible, a *vayash moru* mage named Foor Arontala, a dangerous man whom Jonmarc had crossed long ago and for which he paid dearly.

Their plan had been to travel through the forest as long as possible until they were at the banks of the Nu River, and then to follow the river to the nearest crossing. The Nu was swift and wide in most places, meaning bridges were few and ferries were dangerous. Trying to swim across the mighty river was folly. Many had attempted such a feat; few had survived. Jonmarc was disinclined to tempt fate further since it seemed luck had already turned on him.

The hounds barked again, closer now, though in the forest sounds could be deceiving. The land here was rocky, with large outcroppings of boulders and sudden drop-offs they had missed so far largely by accident. Overhead, thunder rumbled, and Jonmarc prayed for a hard rain that would wash away their footprints and sluice the dirt clean of their scent, but he doubted that such a reprieve would come.

From Circan's frightened expression, Jonmarc knew his companion had figured the dogs had gotten closer, too. With more of a head start, they might have lost the hounds, but now, Jonmarc feared it was only a matter of time.

With luck, they'll shoot us in the back, a quick death. But he suspected that even in this, fortune was not on his side. Arontala would use Alcion to take his vengeance for Jonmarc's long-ago disobedience, and the price would be steep. As if the bargain had not already cost Jonmarc everyone he loved.

Up ahead, the forest cleared. If Jonmarc had figured correctly, based on the compass and what he recalled of a map, the river should be very close. Whether or not they stood a chance of crossing it remained to be seen, but a slim chance in the water was better than no chance at all where they were.

"I see them!" A man's voice rang out behind them, and both Jonmarc and Circan ducked and dodged, zig-zagging through the trees to present a more difficult target. Jonmarc heard the twang of bowstrings. Arrows thudded into the trees around them, embedding deep into the trunks and shredding leaves with their sharp tips.

"Faster!" Jonmarc hissed, though he knew Circan was running full out. The edge of the forest was not far now, and Jonmarc made a silent prayer to the Dark Lady to deliver them from their pursuers.

More arrows hit the dirt just behind their heels, slicing through the shoulder of Jonmarc's cloak. He and Circan were so close to where the trees opened up, and the Nu River presented a last chance for deliverance.

Circan's pained cry made Jonmarc's blood run cold. He turned to see Circan stagger, an arrow in his back, through the left shoulder. Jonmarc could hear their pursuers crashing through the underbrush, and he glimpsed the colors of their uniforms amid the branches and brambles. The dogs barked frantically, moments behind them.

"Leave me!" Circan said, sagging to his knees.

"Crone's tits! Get up!" Jonmarc ordered, backtracking a few steps to yank Circan to his feet. He got under his friend's shoulder and half-carried, half-dragged him toward where the forest canopy cleared and the riverbank ought to be.

The forest ended on a cliff.

Jonmarc saw a vast expanse of sky where the rocky land abruptly sheared away above the wide, deep Nu River below. The fall alone would likely kill them, if they didn't get filled full of arrows in the next few heartbeats, or mauled by dogs.

"Go." Circan gasped. Circan's blood ran hot across Jonmarc's arm.

Jonmarc never slowed his pace. He broke free from the shelter of the forest and ran at full speed off the lip of the cliff.

Gravity tore Circan out of Jonmarc's grasp. Their screams echoed from the rock, along with the curses of the soldiers who skidded to a stop on the cliff's edge up above. Jonmarc had barely enough time to angle himself feet-first into the water, trying to hit as cleanly as possible, praying the riverbed was deep enough that he did not smash to bits on submerged rocks. And then he was in the cold, fast-moving current, with a shock that addled him, plunging deep over his head. Instinct took over, and he pushed toward the surface; fear won out, and he stayed below as long as he dared, hoping that the river would carry them far enough to be out of bow range and beyond the grasp of their pursuers.

Jonmarc had grown up in a fishing village on the Margolan coast. His father might have been a blacksmith, but all the young men helped with the boats when the fish were in season. That meant he knew his way around water and currents, and something else important—how to swim.

He stayed beneath the water's surface for a long as his burning lungs would allow. When he finally burst through, he felt light-headed from the lack of oxygen, and he gasped for air, expecting an arrow in the neck at any second.

That's when he spotted Circan floating face-down a few feet away. Fearing that it was already too late, Jonmarc swam for Circan, managing to get an arm across his chest and pulling him over onto his back. Treading water, sure that any moment they were about to die, Jonmarc knew he had to get them to shore. More importantly, he had to get them to a place where they could get out of the water, somewhere a lot easier to access than the cliffs they left behind them. His strength was waning fast. Jonmarc struck out toward land, unsure whether to celebrate the fact that he was still alive, or mourn the fact that he might have lost his one opportunity for an easy death.

It took all of Jonmarc's strength to drag Circan onto the rocky shore and to heave himself up beyond the reach of the waves. He thought he had felt a pulse as he hauled Circan out of the water, but it might have been his own thudding heartbeat. Even if Circan was alive, he was in no condition to get up and run, and neither was Jonmarc. If Alcion's soldiers saw them surface, then it would only be a matter of time until they were caught.

Jonmarc crawled closer to Circan and checked for signs of life. Circan was alive—barely. That meant for Jonmarc, leaving on his own was not an option. He could have left a corpse behind without guilt. An injured comrade, never. Even if Alcion's soldiers didn't find Circan, the wolves and the crows would. *It would have been easier for both of us if we hadn't survived the fall.*

Jonmarc looked up and down the shore, eyeing the forest's edge. *A boat would be nice, or a cave,* he thought. Shelter or transportation. He saw neither. *I might be able to get us to the trees. Farther than that, doubtful. I'm not even sure I could get myself much beyond the tree line. Dragging Circan…*

He was halfway to the trees when the soldiers burst into sight. Their tracking dogs lunged from cover, teeth bared, snarling and barking. Four of the soldiers had crossbows nocked and ready, pointed at Jonmarc and Circan. At such short range, the bowmen could not miss.

"On your knees," the captain ordered. "You are under arrest, on the orders of General Alcion, for treason and desertion. You will be returned to stand trial and face the consequences of your actions."

Jonmarc was shivering uncontrollably from the dunking, bone tired and aching everywhere. He lunged at the nearest bowman, welcoming a quarrel to the heart, certain it would be far more merciful than anything Alcion and Arontala had in mind. On a good day, when he was in fighting shape, Jonmarc might have wrested the bow away and fought his way clear. Something heavy hit him in the back of the head, and he went down in a heap on the shore.

JONMARC AWOKE WITH A THROBBING HEADACHE. He tried to shift position and found that his wrists and ankles were shackled. With a groan, he managed to roll over onto his back. He was in the back of a wagon, and from the position of the sun, he figured that he had been out for several candlemarks.

Circan lay nearby where their captors had dumped him, which meant he had not regained consciousness. His shirt was blood-soaked, and while the plunge had broken off the shaft of the arrow that ripped open Circan's shoulder, the tip was likely still lodged inside. Jonmarc suspected they were unlikely to live long enough for that to be a problem.

Circan's breath was shallow, and his skin was ashen. *If he's lucky, he'll die before we get back to Caldon,* Jonmarc thought. Caldon was the army camp inside the royal city of Talonia, and Jonmarc was certain it was where they were heading. Alcion and Arontala would be waiting, with as many of Jonmarc's men as they could round up, and there would be a price to pay.

I wonder if Alcion would have been quite as bent on vengeance if it had been anyone else, Jonmarc wondered. *Arontala's never forgotten that I didn't deliver that talisman to him, though I never took his money either. The monsters that damned necklace called killed Shanna and everyone else —everyone but me. Hard to see how he's got a case for vengeance. I'd say I have the better claim. But powerful men don't like to be crossed...*

Especially if they were the immortal undead and a mage.

Jonmarc managed to roll back onto his side to keep the sun out of his eyes. The rough road banged him against the hard bed of the wagon, and from the pain he felt just about everywhere, he guessed the soldiers had gotten in a beating after he passed out. *There's worse to come,* he thought. *I wonder if the others got away. Maybe some of my men will get clear. Sahila and the villagers, that's going to be rough, but at least they're Markian. They can blend in once they reach another town or village. We never stood a chance.*

When the cart reached Talonia, passers-by stopped and jeered. Some threw stones or refuse. Humiliating prisoners was sport for onlookers, and public executions were well-attended spectacles. Jonmarc endured the ordeal stoically. Circan was spared awareness since he remained unconscious.

The Caldon army camp was another matter entirely. When the cart entered the gates, the entire force under General Alcion's command, Eastmark and Outlander, had turned out at attention. Soldiers lined both sides of the street, and it was clear that they had been told about the insubordination and desertion of Jonmarc and his men, even if Alcion had not fully shared the circumstances behind them.

Insults and curses were personal, from men Jonmarc knew by name, men he had fought beside and campaigned with. The shouts and threats were in both Markian and Common, but the intent was clear enough. Alcion might not have to execute him, Jonmarc thought. The crowd seemed angry enough to do it themselves.

He was too exhausted, frightened, and heartsick to make any response. Keller, Ronn, and Tamm, some of the few real friends he thought he had made beyond the men of his squad, were not on the front line. Jonmarc had no doubt that they were ordered to be present, but the fact that they were not among those pelting him with rocks and rotten produce was small comfort. He did not expect them to come to his defense, or be able to alter the outcome in any way. But at least they had not actively turned against him.

Well-aimed rocks left bruises and opened cuts on Jonmarc's face, sending fresh trickles of blood into his eyes. Soldiers grabbed him roughly and dragged him through the jeering crowd. They dropped him onto the floor inside the small building that functioned as the camp's prison and landed well-placed kicks and brutal punches that bruised ribs and caused him to retch up his last meal before throwing him into a cell. Circan's limp body was tossed in a moment later, to land with a dull thud.

"Got you, too," Markelson remarked. His words were slurred through swollen, bleeding lips, and one eye was purpled.

Jonmarc's heart fell as he saw Soster, Penn, Ost, and Quan in the cell. All looked as if they had been thoroughly beaten. Tor lay still in one corner.

"What about the others?" Jonmarc asked as he took in their battered appearance. Soster's arm hung at an odd angle, either broken or dislocated. Ost was missing his front teeth, and Quan's shirt was bloodied enough from a wound beneath it that Jonmarc feared the soldier might not live long enough to be executed.

"Henden is dead," Markelson replied tonelessly. "He went down fighting. You know his temper. The only way they were going to take him was by killing him. Don't know if it's true or not, but the soldiers said the General plans to gibbet us after he executes us, as a warning."

"Bann and Rodd haven't been brought in yet," Penn said.

The chains binding his hands made it impossible for him to juggle, but he rotated three small rocks in his palm, a nervous habit.

Maybe Bann and Rodd will make it, Jonmarc thought. Deep inside, he doubted it. Alcion's desire for vengeance burned too hot to allow anyone to get away with betraying him. He would hunt down the missing men, heedless of the costs.

"What happened to Tor?" he asked, looking worriedly over at the too-still body along the wall.

"They knew he was a hedge witch, so they dosed him with wormroot to dull his magic," Ost said. "He's out cold. Lucky bastard."

"The villagers?" Jonmarc asked. *Surely some of them will escape.*

Soster shook his head. "Alcion must have known you wouldn't follow orders. His men were less than two candlemarks behind us, from what I heard the soldiers say. The villagers had barely gotten to the road by then. Alcion sent troops to round them up and force them back to Chauvrenne."

He still means to burn them, Jonmarc thought with a sick feeling. *Everything we did was in vain. It's just more blood on my hands.*

Later that night, soldiers tossed in Rodd and Bann. They had been beaten so badly that their faces were unrecognizable. Rodd was coughing blood, and his breathing was labored, with a painful wheezing that made Jonmarc wonder if broken ribs had punctured a lung.

"Well, that's all of us," Markelson observed in a toneless voice that let Jonmarc know Markelson had figured out what lay in store for them. The heavy chains that bound their wrists and hobbled their ankles made it impossible to sit or lie with any comfort, and kept them from offering much assistance to the more seriously injured men.

"Here's your dinner," a guard said, pushing a bucket through the small door. Jonmarc knew from the smell it had been scooped from the latrine. "Deserters don't deserve food," the guard sneered. "Hanging's too good for you." He leaned close to the bars where they could see the hate in his expression.

"Too bad he isn't going to turn you over to us to take care of," he said. "We'd make sure you had plenty of time to beg for your lives. It can take days to kill a man, if you know how to do it right."

Jonmarc remained impassive, though the threat sent a chill down his spine. *Alcion's not going to waste food or a healer on us,* Jonmarc thought. *Not when he's got a gallows waiting for us in the morning. If we're lucky.*

"Oh, and congratulations on your promotion, Captain Vahanian," the guard jeered. "You know what that means, don't you? Ranking officers don't hang. They burn."

The guard slammed the door that separated their cell from the front of the building. Jonmarc turned to the others. "I'm sorry," he said. "I should never have let you go with me. I should have done what I meant to do: order you to stay behind long enough for us to get a head start, and then report me for desertion. At least then, it would only be me in the brig."

Markelson shook his head. "That's not true, Lieutenant. I mean, Captain. We had already resolved to see it through with you. Your orders wouldn't have changed a thing. And with Alcion's soldiers so close behind us, it wouldn't have made a difference."

Maybe not, Jonmarc thought. *But it wouldn't have made*

you traitors in Alcion's eyes. Maybe a few lashes, or some hard labor, even a demotion. But not this.

Soster rose and slowly shuffled his way to peer out the high, narrow window. "He's out there," Soster reported, and cursed. "Henden. The bloody bastards actually put his body in a gibbet for the crows, Crone take their souls."

Awful as the spectacle was for the living—and that was Alcion's goal, to inspire terror into the hearts of his men—Henden was beyond caring. Jonmarc rued not pushing the soldiers to kill him. As it stood, Circan and Tor might not regain consciousness enough to feel terror at their fate. They were the lucky ones.

Arontala wouldn't have let me take the easy way out, Jonmarc thought. *Sweet Chenne! How much of this was contrived from the beginning, so that Arontala could have his revenge over that damned talisman from the caves?*

The longer Jonmarc thought about it, the more he was certain that the task of collecting taxes had been given to him and his men intentionally to force him into a situation Arontala could exploit. *How long has Alcion been under Arontala's control? Dark Lady take my soul, might Arontala have arranged for the assassins in Principality, to maneuver me into position so Alcion would take note of me?*

It seemed unbelievable that one man could mastermind such a complex sequence of events. *But Arontala's a mage, and a* vayash moru, Jonmarc thought. *He can use both powers to control minds, tamper with memories, nudge circumstances to his liking.*

Why Arontala would care so much about the matter boggled Jonmarc's mind. *I'm nobody important. No one who poses him a threat. Why go to such lengths to destroy me, when I can't do him any harm?*

Yet Jonmarc had seen enough of high-ranking men to

know that any unpunished disobedience struck a blow against Arontala's power. *He doesn't dare let anyone get away with disobedience. It might set a bad example. And I've wounded his pride. That's what's unforgivable.*

It wouldn't be the first time a powerful man had done awful things to avenge his pride and maintain his reputation. Margolan's nobility was fairly well kept under King Bricen's thumb, yet there were stories of crimes gone unpunished and wrongs overlooked if the perpetrator was wealthy or well-connected enough.

It's probably all a game to Arontala, and we're just the markers on the board, nothing of consequence, Jonmarc thought bitterly. *We're only important if we get him what he wants—one way or another. After he's through with us, no one will dare defy him, or Alcion. And if I'm right, sooner or later Alcion will make his move to take the throne, and Arontala will have all the power he wants.*

Jonmarc had expected the executioners to come at dawn. But Arontala, as a *vayash moru*, could not go out in the daytime, and Jonmarc knew that Arontala would want to see every moment of the plot he had set in motion.

When sundown came, soldiers dragged Jonmarc and his men from the cell. "Watch your step," one of the guards mocked, stepping on the chain between Ost's ankles and sending Ost pitching onto his knees.

"We've got orders to deliver you for your trial," the second guard said. "You just have to be alive. They didn't specify what condition." With that, he gave Penn a shove against the doorframe, splitting open his cheek.

Jonmarc had nothing left to lose. He clasped his hands together and swung hard at the jailer, making sure the heavy chain's full momentum caught the tormentor squarely in the nose.

Rodd plowed his bulky frame into the second jailer, knocking the man off balance. Then he looped the chain between his wrists over the jailer's head and around his throat, jerking the jailer against his chest.

"We're going to die anyhow," Rodd grated through swollen lips. "You can come with us."

Three more guards appeared in the outer room. Rodd relinquished his hostage after tightening the chain enough that the jailer fell gasping to the floor. Their insolence earned them a round of blows from the new guards, but the satisfaction of not going out like sheep to slaughter lasted even through the beating. Two of the soldiers hauled Tor and Circan from the cell, though neither man had regained consciousness.

It was no accident that their route to the parade ground passed the iron gibbet with Henden's corpse suspended inside. The bars were worked in the rough shape of a man. That way whether it was a corpse or the battered body of a prisoner locked in the cage, the form remained upright. Crows had already pecked out the eyes and rats had gnawed at the fingers. The rest of the naked corpse would be food for scavengers for a few days, but it could take weeks for the remains to rot away, longer depending on the weather. The grisly spectacle and its smell would be a constant reminder of what happened to anyone who disobeyed General Alcion.

The hanging tree stood on the parade ground. Beneath its branches was a wagon. In the center of the grounds was a large bonfire, bright enough to make sure that all the soldiers standing at attention around the perimeter of the grounds would be able to see what was about to happen.

Jonmarc lifted his head defiantly to look at the man on horseback who sat at a safe distance, watching the preparations. Alcion's long black hair framed a face dark as night.

That alone told of his pure Eastmark blood. The intricate tattooed markings on his left cheek made it clear that he was also of royal blood.

Foor Arontala sat on a horse to Alcion's right. Arontala wore red robes that made his role as a mage unmistakable. His pallor left no doubt that he was *vayash moru*. The look of rapt attention and expectation on Arontala's face sickened Jonmarc and also sent a cold, hard knot to the pit of his stomach.

Soldiers with crossbows and swords forced Jonmarc and his men to kneel facing General Alcion. Circan and Tor were dumped unceremoniously beside them, face down in the dirt.

"Captain Jonmarc Vahanian," one of the officers read loudly. "You are charged with treason and insubordination. You failed to collect the king's taxes, willfully refused to carry out the village's punishment as commanded, and you led your men into treason. How do you plead?"

Jonmarc raised his head and looked straight into Alcion's eyes. "Guilty. And I'd do it again."

The guards nearest Jonmarc cuffed him hard enough across the mouth that blood started from his split lip.

"The penalty for insubordination and treason is death," the officer continued. "This is the sentence of General Alcion, in the name of King Radomar the Unforgiving. Let it be done."

Drummers started a slow, inexorable beat. Jonmarc looked at his men. He saw the same fear in their eyes that he felt, mingled with courage and defiance. More guards came forward to lead them to the wagon. Jonmarc waited, expecting to be led away with them. But two guards took him roughly by the arms and marched him toward a triangular wooden scaffold near where Alcion and Arontala sat on horseback, watching the spectacle.

"The General has arranged for you to watch the execution," said the officer who had read the charges.

At that, a rope was passed through the chain around Jonmarc's wrists, then yanked over a pulley at the top of the triangle to jerk him onto his tiptoes, suspended by his wrists. The chain tore into the skin, and the weight of his body quickly made his shoulders ache. Jonmarc now had no recourse except to watch his men hang.

The drums kept up their merciless beat. Eleven nooses had been prepared. Soldiers steadied the bodies of Circan and Tor so the executioner could fit the noose around their necks. The other soldiers were led, shackled hand and foot, to their places and the nooses dropped over their heads.

The executioner had a choice of whether to make the deaths clean and quick or not. The right position of the knot and the correct length of the rope could mean a snap of the neck when the wagon pulled away. Jonmarc's gut twisted as he realized that the ropes were the wrong length.

Circan and Tor might have already been dead. If not, they never regained consciousness. In the final moments, Markelson and Penn murmured quietly, praying for passage across the Gray Sea. Ost and Rodd looked stoic and stunned. Quan could barely stay on his feet, and the bloody stain on his shirt had grown larger.

"Crone take your soul!" Soster shouted, with a murderous look at Alcion.

"Go to the Formless One!" Bann yelled defiantly.

The driver's whip snapped, and the wagon lurched from beneath the doomed men's feet. For what seemed like an eternity, the prisoners' bodies bucked and jerked, convulsing and fouling themselves as they struggled for air. Jonmarc forced himself to watch, to honor their sacrifice, though bile rose in his throat.

"Charge!" The order rang out, and soldiers with pikes stormed forward in battle formation, running for the jerking bodies. As Jonmarc watched in stunned horror, the soldiers ran with their pikes lowered, and sank the blades deep into the dying prisoners, using their bodies as quintains.

"Again!" came the order. The soldiers made a second run, and then a third. Mercifully, by the third onslaught, the savaged bodies appeared to be lifeless, though they still dripped with blood. Finally, the bodies hung still, and the officer who had read their sentence turned toward Jonmarc.

"Your crime is greater than theirs since you were their commander," the man said, his hard expression regarding Jonmarc with disdain. "It is decreed that you be punished accordingly."

He gestured, and a soldier bent to retrieve something from the bonfire. It was a dark shaft, its tip glowing red as hot coals. As the soldier neared with the branding iron, two men stepped closer to Jonmarc and tore his shirt from his body.

"Traitors must be easily recognized," the officer said, and Jonmarc steeled himself for the pain as the soldier pressed the branding iron against the flesh of his left shoulder.

He gritted his teeth, swearing that he would not give Alcion the satisfaction of his screams. His breath came in shallow puffs, and his whole body tensed with the pain, which burned even after the hot iron was withdrawn.

"And now, as law decrees for defying the will of a Prince of Eastmark, forty lashes." The officer's voice was cold and emotionless, yet Jonmarc saw a flicker of satisfaction in Alcion's dark eyes, and the unmistakable glint of victory in Arontala's gaze.

The soldier who wielded the whip was built like an ox, with muscular shoulders and wide, calloused hands. He approached from the front, so that Jonmarc could see the whip, and as he neared he snapped the leather to make it crack in the air. If he hoped to see Jonmarc flinch, he was disappointed. Jonmarc stared him down, drawing on his rage and pain for strength.

"One." The officer counted, a drum gave a single, sharp beat, and the lash fell with a bloody snap across Jonmarc's bare back. The tripod held him upright, barely steady on his toes, and stretched the skin tight, increasing the pain of the blows.

"Two." Another drumbeat, another blow.

Jonmarc did not lose consciousness, nor did he beg for mercy. The lash rose and fell in a spray of warm blood, and Jonmarc clenched his jaw, choking back the screams Arontala coveted.

By the end, Jonmarc hung by his bonds, unable to force himself upright. His shoulders felt as if they were ripping from their sockets, the skin on his back was slashed open, and blood ran freely. A cold bucket of salted water doused his open wounds, and Jonmarc cursed at the pain.

"Put him in the wagon," Alcion ordered. "Take him to Chauvrenne. He chose the villagers over his duty to his uniform and to the king. Let him burn with them."

Jonmarc was tied to the back of a wagon, his wrists still chained, but the hobbles on his ankles replaced with rough rope. The soldiers hadn't bothered to give him a shirt or cloak. He was shivering with cold, which only made the pain worse. By rights, he should have been unconscious. That he was not made him suspect Arontala had used his magic to deny him the solace of shock until Alcion was through with him.

Every bump along the rough road to Chauvrenne was torment. His arms were numb for more than a candlemark from having supported his weight on the scaffold. The fresh burn of the brand vied with the deep cuts of the lash, making every movement agonizing.

Finally, they reached the village. Two of the soldiers dragged Jonmarc from the wagon. He stumbled and fell, hobbled by the ropes. He heard the whistle of a sword's blade and tensed, expecting to die. Instead, the blade sliced through the rope binding his ankles and cut painfully into his left calf. "On your feet," the soldier commanded, dragging Jonmarc to stand, and poked the tip of a crossbow bolt into his bloody back to direct him to move.

The villagers were herded into a barn, women, children, old and young. Now, soldiers pitched hay around the barn. More dragged branches from the woodpile. Behind them stood their captain, a man in the uniform Jonmarc had worn until just a few days before. Next to him were three barrels, and from the smell, Jonmarc knew their content: Oil.

"Nice night for a bonfire," the soldier who held the crossbow against Jonmarc's back murmured.

Soldiers opened the barn door far enough to push Jonmarc through. It took all Jonmarc's will to remain standing. He saw Sahila, one the village elders, and met his gaze. Sahila understood. They were going to burn.

The soldiers kept their crossbows trained on the barn doorway until the massive doors were shut and barred. One of the soldiers mockingly tossed Jonmarc's swords in behind him. Jonmarc looked to Sahila. "Any other ways out of here?"

"Nothing they haven't sealed."

Inside the barn, the soldiers' torches sent slivers of light between the old siding planks. Dust floated in the air, making it difficult to breathe. That dust would make the barn burn that much faster, once the flames came. Jonmarc looked around, desperate for inspiration. He spied a large iron ring in the floor.

"What's down there?"

"Grain bins and root cellars."

"How many?"

"Not enough."

"Get everyone you can below ground," Jonmarc said.

"Those bins could become an oven."

"Up here, we don't stand a chance."

Sahila nodded. Jonmarc watched him disappear into the throng. Jonmarc hobbled around the perimeter of the barn as quickly as his painfully bruised muscles would allow, but Sahila was correct: all the doors were sealed. Even if they found an opening, soldiers on the other side would shoot them down.

Smoke wafted through the small gaps between the boards of the barn walls. Flames licked at the old boards, casting eerie, dancing shadows. Jonmarc startled to see Sahila advancing toward him with an axe.

"Hold still."

"Screw that!"

"You want to die chained like an animal? Put your wrists on that beam, and close your eyes."

Jonmarc flinched as the heavy axe whistled through the air and clanged against his chains, severing them.

Sahila had gotten at most a third of the villagers into the bins, but the rest huddled in frightened groups. Outside, the flames burned higher. "Is there anything else below the barn? Even a dung pit is better than being in here when those rafters start falling."

Sahila thought for a moment. "Come with me." Slinging the axe over his shoulder, he led Jonmarc to a place in the center of the hard-packed dirt floor. He flung his axe, and it landed on its blade in the dirt, but the floor beneath their feet shook, just a bit. "Here. Dig here." Sahila motioned for several nearby men to join them. A hand's depth beneath the dirt, they hit wood.

It was growing warmer inside the barn. Jonmarc eyed the rising flames. They were running out of time.

Hacking with their tools and kicking with their combined strength, the men worked until the old wood splintered. Moist, cold air rose out of the darkness. "Caves. They run all through this area. Can't barely plant a field without someone falling into one. No idea what's down there or where it goes. Just remembered my father showing me where they'd closed over one when they built the barn."

"Anywhere's better than here. Let's get them inside."

The cave mouth was narrow, allowing only one person at a time to enter. One by one, the villagers descended, as the flames spread up the walls and to the barn roof. By the time the last of the villagers was down, bits of burning wood were falling around them. "Get in," Jonmarc said to Sahila.

"What about you?"

"I'll come. Just get in."

The roof creaked ominously as Sahila shimmied down into the cave. "Hurry."

Jonmarc needed no urging. He jumped into the hole, slamming painfully against one rocky side as overhead, the roof gave way. A shower of sparks and a hail of burning wood followed him down the shaft. He landed hard, and his leg folded painfully under him.

"There's no way out," Sahila said, helping him to his feet. "There are shafts—that's why we've got air. But not even the children could fit through them."

The cave was damp, helping to resist the blistering heat that seared down from above. In the distance, Jonmarc could hear screaming. Around him, babies wailed, and women sobbed. A few voices chanted in prayer, begging the favor of the goddess. Men cursed under their breath. They waited.

It took a long time for the fire to burn itself out. Hungry, thirsty, and cramped, they waited in the darkness until a night and a day passed, afraid that soldiers might be standing guard over the wreckage, waiting to shoot survivors. When Jonmarc finally climbed up the shaft, it took all his strength to shove aside a fallen beam that was still hot enough to burn his palms. Cautiously, he looked around, expecting to feel a crossbow bolt at any moment. He scrambled out and scanned the horizon. No soldiers awaited them. From the wreckage of the barn, the soldiers had felt assured there were no survivors.

Little of the barn remained standing. Charred timber covered the old barn floor. Sahila joined him, and together they ran to free the others who had taken refuge in the bins, throwing aside the wood that pinned the bin doors shut. They pulled back the doors, and the odor of burning hair and roasting meat rushed up to meet them. The huddled bodies of the villagers were covered by ash. No one moved. No sound came.

Sahila cursed. Jonmarc fell to his knees, unable to look away. From the cries of the men around them as they freed the other bins, Jonmarc knew there were no other survivors.

"Eastmark's not safe for you," Sahila said, turning to Jonmarc. "You've got to run again."

"What about them?" Jonmarc said, with a glance toward the villagers who had escaped with them into the cave.

"The soldiers have what they wanted. They think we're dead. They won't come looking for us this time. We have kin in the other villages. They'll shelter us. We'll survive," Sahila replied.

"I'm so sorry. I brought this on you."

"Would you have spared us by following your orders? We would all be dead. And you've paid dearly for your honor. We're grateful. But we can't protect you. You're Margolan-born. Go home where you'll be safe."

Safe. Nowhere is safe.

DESPERATE FLIGHT

DESPERATE FLIGHT

HE RAN.

Jonmarc Vahanian had been running—staggering—for two days. The village healer's hurried work barely knit the skin on his back where the whip had sliced, or the worst of the bruises from the beating, or the fresh brand on his flesh. The fragile, newly-healed flesh tore in places, bleeding through his ragged, soot-streaked shirt. He dared not stop, or sleep, or eat. Not yet.

If the general's guards caught up to him this time, he would suffer even more. Death would be a mercy withheld.

Once before, he had run through the Eastmark forest for his life. Then, the dogs and guards had caught him, dragged him back to watch the soldiers under his command hanged, the villagers he had tried to save burned alive.

This time, if they caught him, he would not go with the guards. This time, Jonmarc would fight to the death.

"There he is!" a voice shouted behind him.

He was two days out from Chauvrenne, the village General Alcion had burned for spite. Jonmarc was supposed to have died with the villagers. Some of the townspeople had survived. They could blend in, find refuge in other hamlets, and with the ebony skin and features of Eastmark natives, they would be difficult to easily spot. Jonmarc, an outlander mercenary, looked nothing like the Markians. He was lost, hungry, exhausted, and in pain, a long, long way from home.

A home he doubted he would ever see again.

"I see him!" another voice yelled.

The will to survive gave him a burst of speed. It was not enough. Jonmarc found himself ringed by three Eastmark soldiers.

"There's the traitor." The speaker weighted the word with contempt. "Take him."

Jonmarc wheeled into a high Eastmark kick, something the soldiers did not expect from an outlander. His boot caught the nearest soldier in the chest with enough force to send him back a few feet to fall on his ass. In one graceful movement, Jonmarc righted himself and came up with swords in each hand, surprising the second soldier.

Sword skills and fighting footwork came easily to Jonmarc. These soldiers must never have seen Jonmarc practicing in the salle or sparring in one of General Alcion's competitions. Outlander that he was, he rarely lost. Some men were good at ciphering. Others could play music or paint portraits. Jonmarc was good at fighting.

"Aiyee! He fights like a *dimonn*!" the third soldier cried as the tip of Jonmarc's blade caught his opponent in the gut, slitting him open like a fish. The fighting style was from Eastmark, but it was advanced training, rarely mastered. Jonmarc had a natural aptitude, backed up with obsessive practice. These soldiers were Markian, but it was clear their training had not extended as far.

"You'll pay for that kick!" the downed soldier growled, climbing to his feet. The second man had drawn his sword, but Jonmarc fought with a sword in each hand, a distinct advantage since his opponent lacked a shield to deflect the second blade.

Jonmarc swung with the blade in his right hand, and the second soldier parried. But the sword in Jonmarc's left hand laid the man open from shoulder to hip. He flinched with the pain, and Jonmarc's right-hand blade slashed back across the soldier's throat. Jonmarc pivoted as the soldier fell bleeding to the mossy ground, knowing that the third soldier was nearly on him.

"What kind of *dimonn* are you?" the soldier snarled. Being bested in traditional Eastmark fighting skills by an outlander, a *sathirinim*, was beyond the man's comprehension.

"Angry." Jonmarc used the man's confusion to his advantage. His opponent executed a clumsy version of the high kick Jonmarc had mastered. It took nothing for Jonmarc to dance out of the way of the man's boot, bringing one sword down in a crippling gash to his supporting leg. The soldier cried out in pain, blood gushing down his leg from a cut to the bone, and missed his footing, coming down hard onto the forest floor. Jonmarc drove his sword blade through the man's chest. Blood burbled from the soldier's mouth.

"That doesn't even begin to even the score," Jonmarc grated. He did not wait to see them die. He ran and kept on running.

I don't dare run into people looking like this, he thought. *I'm covered in blood and soot. I've got to clean the worst of it off and find some decent clothing if I'm ever to get through Dhasson and back to Margolan.*

The wide Nu River was too swift and wild to cross easily, and bridges that spanned the river were few. He dared not go north through Easkmark to the bridge that crossed to Margolan because General Alcion's troops—his former comrades—would be waiting for him. And they would carry out the death sentence he had so far, barely, evaded. Ferries cost money and ferrymen asked questions. Jonmarc could afford neither.

That meant his best chance was to get to neighboring Dhasson and cross over into his homeland from there. Even with a compass, that was a daunting task. He had no map, dared not stay on the main roads, and could hardly ask for directions. Reckoning by the stars was imprecise, but it was all that was left to him.

Perhaps on the main road there were signs to inform travelers when they crossed from Eastmark to Dhasson. Surely there might be guards, even tolls to pay to journey from one kingdom to the next. Here in the forest, boundaries were invisible. Jonmarc had to admit to himself that he had no idea where he was. All that mattered to him was where he wasn't —that he wasn't dangling from a noose in Eastmark.

He found a stream deep enough to reach above his knees and waded in fully clothed, hoping that he could wash himself and his badly stained garments at the same time. Without proper soap, it was hopeless to imagine that he would clean up entirely, but anything would be an improvement and might spare him being noticed, which would be dangerous.

"You there. Stay right where you are. We don't want no trouble—just your coin purse." The voice came from the stream bank, and Jonmarc saw two men emerge from the bushes near where he had left the bag of provisions Sahila had given him when he left Chauvrenne.

"Leave it alone, or you'll have plenty of trouble," Jonmarc warned.

The cutpurses looked to be in their early twenties, just a few years older than he was. Their clothing was mismatched and ill-fitting as if it had been stolen off wash lines. "All we want are your coppers, mate," the shorter of the two men said. "Ain't worth getting cut for, now is it? You look like a healthy sort. Won't hurt you none to skip a meal or two." The cutpurse patted his ribs in contrast.

"We just want your coins. Don't need the rest of it," the second man said. He fished through the cloth bag and cursed when he found nothing of value except the dried meat and cheese Sahila had scrounged to provision Jonmarc for his journey.

"I'm not in a generous mood." Jonmarc came out of the water at a run, both swords drawn. The cutpurses' eyes widened at the sight of the swords, far more resistance than they had bargained for. One of the men drew a wicked knife, while the other pulled a short sword from his belt.

"Aye now, if that's the way you want it, so be it," the skinny man said. "Don't say we didn't warn you."

Both cutpurses came at him at the same time. By the look of them, they had seen their share of fights. The taller man had a cut across his smashed nose that went from one brow to his chin on the opposite side of his face. The skinny man's left ear had a notch cut out of it, and he was missing several front teeth.

Then I fit right in. Jonmarc thought. A scar wound from his left ear down below his collarbone from his fight with a magicked monster the night Shanna died. Alcion's brutality gifted him with a number of new half-healed wounds that would scar, as would the places burning embers had fallen on him in the barn at Chauvrenne.

He drew on his pain and anger. Fear and frustration sent a jolt of adrenaline through his blood. With a war cry, he came up out of the water, not in the front assault the thieves expected, but with the complex footwork he had learned from his Eastmark sword masters.

Too late the cutpurses realized they had chosen the wrong victim. They were clearly used to fighting men with few battle skills or brute-force, straight-forward tactics. The thieves had not counted on cornering a desperate man, and Jonmarc hated what he had to do, just as he was certain he could give no quarter. *I don't dare leave them alive. They'd sell me out to the guards in a heartbeat. I am not going back to Eastmark.*

He ran the skinny man through with his first thrust. Getting past his guard was pathetically easy, and the man fell with a dumbfounded look on his face. The taller man stared wide-eyed at Jonmarc even as he slashed in panic to keep him back.

"Look, I'll be on my way," the man stammered. "No harm done. You keep your coin. I won't say nothing about Ted there," he said with a nod toward his dead companion. "Guards were lookin' for him anyhow. In fact, how 'bout I give you my coin, and you let me walk away."

"Where are we?" Jonmarc grated, easily parrying the man's strikes.

"Vassar's Woods," the cutpurse replied.

"What kingdom?" Jonmarc snapped, though since the man's coloring was similar to his own, he was nearly certain of the answer before it was given.

"Dhasson," the thief answered. He had not soiled himself, yet, which was to his credit, though Jonmarc could see in the man's eyes that he realized he was unlikely to emerge alive.

"How close to the Nu River?" Jonmarc thrust forward,

not intending to score but enough to scare the man into replying.

"Half a day's walk west," the thief responded. "But there ain't a crossing nor a bridge for another day, day and a half south, down near the Nargi border."

"Does the forest run the whole way?"

"I don't know," the tall man said. Jonmarc lunged toward him, and the man yelped as he beat back the attack with clumsy strikes.

"Thieves know the forest. How far does it run south?" Jonmarc demanded.

"Vassar's Woods is part of Rimkin Forest," the thief replied, his voice a few notes higher than normal with fear. "I heard tell it runs all the way down into Nargi, though don't no one ever go there," he said. "I seen a man once who said he traded with them. Hard folks they are, what with worshipping the Crone and all, and their Black Robe priests," the man babbled, trying to stave off the inevitable. "Said they fight men against each other down in Nargi like I seen men fight roosters or bears against each other for money. Bad place."

Jonmarc wholeheartedly agreed. "I've got no plans to go to Nargi," he said. His eyes narrowed. It was time to end the fight. He took no satisfaction in the decision to kill the cutpurse, though the man had probably knifed his share of marks. But he was equally certain that if he let the thief live, the man would betray him to the guards, no matter what promises were made.

The thief seemed to realize that, too. He did not wait for Jonmarc to strike but came at him like a coiled snake, his terror fueling his wild, brutal sword strikes. Jonmarc's fear was bone-deep and controlled, and he felt himself descend into the place of cold calculation his father had taught him to use when he butchered hogs. A soldier's detachment had seen the pattern in the thief's frenzied strikes, and when the opening appeared, he sprang into motion without conscious thought, driving his blade through the man's ribs.

"Pox on you," the thief sputtered. "Crone take your soul."

"Sorry," Jonmarc said. "I've been cursed already. She'll have to stand in line."

At least he had given them clean death; he told himself as he wiped his blades on the grass and washed up again in the stream. The altercation had taken a dangerous amount of time for a wanted man, but he searched the bodies for useful weapons and their coin purses, gaining two cheap daggers, a short sword, and enough coppers to buy him a few meals if he dared stop at an inn. He tracked the thieves' movements back through the underbrush to their squalid camp.

Obviously, the cutpurses had not been especially good at their craft, or they found few victims, because Jonmarc found only a cold campfire, two ramshackle lean-tos with tattered bedding, and a worn cloth bag of clothing and items probably filched from prior thefts.

Jonmarc had stolen the taller man's trousers since they had less blood and dirt on them than his own. He kept his own boots, as they were army issue and sturdy. Rummaging through the bag, he found a shirt and jacket that mostly fit and were far cleaner than what he had been wearing. Since the men wouldn't be coming back, he took the cleanest blanket, as well as the bread and dried sausage. He found a full wineskin, as he had no idea when he might get his next meal. Sure that he had lost enough time that the guards would be on him at any moment, he still hesitated for a moment to look back at the deserted camp.

Alcion's managed to make a murderer of me, despite Chauvrenne, he thought. *I could have let them live. I didn't.*

More blood on my hands. The Crone and the Dark Lady may have to fight over my soul when the final reckoning is done.

There wasn't time to linger, and he had already chosen his course, so there was no more reason to think about it. Forcing down his guilt, Jonmarc headed off at a jog toward the south.

The forest was thick and full of old growth, tall trees with scarce underbrush. Jonmarc jogged as long as he could, trying to put as much distance between himself and the dead thieves as he could, making up for lost time. By the time he slowed, the sun was setting, and shadows lengthened within the forest before the open lands grew dark.

Being alone in the deep forest at night was as dangerous as being on the open road, though the danger came from different types of predators. Jonmarc knew enough about hunting to recognize signs of the forest animals, and if there were deer and rabbits and other creatures about, there was sure to be wolves, especially this far from cities or a main road.

In the dying light, Jonmarc sized up his options. On the ground, he was easy prey—especially since he was bone weary and needed to sleep. He had seen no evidence of people in this part of the forest, so except for the guards looking for him, he did not expect to be happened upon by travelers or brigands. Wolves, on the other hand, were a very real threat, as were the foxes and *stawars* that lurked in the northern woods.

Many of the trees nearby were huge and old, their branches far too high to climb. But as Jonmarc ventured a little farther, he saw a tree with limbs sturdy enough to support his weight that were low enough to reach. He leaped and missed. Setting his jaw, Jonmarc leaped again, feeling the exertion in every aching muscle, and he caught the branch and pulled himself up. The effort strained the newly healed skin on his back, and he felt a trickle of blood on his skin.

From his new perch, Jonmarc surveyed the forest floor. The tree would not keep him safe from *stawars*, but it would stymie the wolves should they be drawn by the smell of his blood. The tree forked, and Jonmarc found that he could tie himself to the smaller trunk with the blanket and lodge securely enough in the cleft that he had a reasonable chance of staying aloft while he slept.

Below him, he heard footfalls on the leaves. Snuffling. Scratching. It was clear that the forest animals knew they hosted an intruder. Nearby, he heard the howl of a wolf and the answer of its pack. He was well-armed enough to fight one wolf, but a pack would strain the ability of the most expert swordsman. Jonmarc was glad he had decided to seek what shelter he could find before the wolves had come out to hunt.

Exhausted, Jonmarc rationed his food and wine, uncertain when he would have another chance to find provisions. He tightened the knot on the blanket that held him in the tree, then leaned back against the rough trunk and fell into a fitful sleep.

Jonmarc's dreams were dark. He saw his mother standing by the door to his boyhood home, calling to him to come in. Yet much as he tried to walk up the path, the doorway never grew closer. A new image came to the fore, Shanna's face wreathed in flames. He saw her standing in the fire but not consumed by the flames, cradling their murdered child. Shanna, too, was calling to him, and while he knew it was a warning, he could not hear her words. In the next heartbeat, he stood amid the burning ruins of his home town. It was the night the raiders came, the night everything died. One of the raiders lay dying at his feet, cursing him to lose everything he loved to the flames. That image remained, clear as it had been that awful night, until Jonmarc woke with a start and found the first rays of dawn glimmering through the leaves.

THE OLD COMPASS Sahila had given him validated the general direction Jonmarc had gleaned from the sun but gave him little indication of how close he was to the Nu River Bridge. He veered west, toward where the river ran its long course to the Northern sea, terrain rising all the way. The forest's edge opened onto fields and a roadway, too far from the river to see its banks. Jonmarc retreated to the shadows and kept on walking.

He wondered whether Sahila and the surviving villagers had found refuge. He thought about the cutpurses and wondered if their bodies had been discovered by the guards before the scavengers took care of them. He thought about his men, hanged and wronged. Jonmarc debated what he would do if he survived crossing the river. Return to Linton's caravan? Perhaps. See if he could sign on with King's Bricen's army now that he had real experience? Maybe. He had already decided that he could not return to Principality and the War Dogs. Captain Valjan would welcome him, but the reasons for his departure—desertion—from Eastmark would cause problems, and Alcion might well be able to recapture him and haul him back to finish what the general had started.

I could change my name. There's no one to know. Sign on with the guards far from the cities. Not the first time I've sold my sword. Bricen's a decent enough king. So's King Harrol here in Dhasson. Guess I might be able to hire on here. But it's too close to Eastmark. Too easy for Alcion to find me. I need more distance. Need to get as far away as possible.

Get as far away as possible. That phrase became a chant, the rhythm to his running feet. He stayed inside the forest's edge, running from dawn until dusk when he hauled himself up into another tree and tied himself to the limb for the night. Predators circled his tree, waking him. A dark shape clawed at the trunk but did not attempt to climb. The forest was alive with unsettling noises. Jonmarc heard the screech of an owl as it hurtled down to seize its prey and the death squeal of the small animal in its claws. In the distance, the almost-human scream of a *stawar* and the howl of wolves was a reminder, if he needed one, that the forest did not welcome strangers.

By Jonmarc's reckoning, he should be close to the bridge. He planned his escape carefully, considering his alternatives. If he reached the bridge at midday, he could try to blend in with the merchants and herders driving their wagons and flocks across the bridge to market in Margolan. In the bustling crowd, he might escape the guards' notice, since he had no papers and no way to forge them. At this point, he lacked even the letter of recommendation Linton had written to vouch for him to Valjan. All of that was back in Eastmark, far out of reach.

Or he could try his luck at dusk when the guards might be more interested in their ale and suppers than in watching the weary travelers making their way across the river at the end of a long day. In both cases, Jonmarc's plan was to keep his head down and attach himself to another group, close enough to appear part of the crowd, far enough back not to be questioned. He had bluffed his way out of tougher situations.

And if that failed, if he was turned back, Jonmarc resolved to find a boatman to take him across. He jangled the coins tied up in a rag at the belt of his stolen pants. The cutpurses had just enough money that Jonmarc might be able to hire a fisherman to take him across. That was risky. He would be remembered. The boat's owner might guess he was a fugitive and betray him. But the Nu was too swift to swim. He had to get across. Anything was better than being caught and taken back to Eastmark. Anything.

Jonmarc emerged from the forest late in the afternoon and made his way to the road that ran along the edge of the woods. He had looked over his clothing before nearing the highway to assure himself there were no bloodstains that might make fellow travelers or guards look askance at him. His clothing was ill-fitting and poor quality so no one would mistake him for prosperous. That was fine. With luck, they would not notice him at all.

He'd had to go out of his way for more than a candlemark to find a place where he could easily exit the forest near the road. At one point, farmer's fields and pastures forced the edge of the forest back in a wide arc. Jonmarc had no desire to cross such open ground if he could help it, nor to be chased by a penned bull or an angry farmer. So he skirted the fields and left the forest just below them, waiting until the roadway as clear for a moment so that, with luck, no one noticed him leaving the shelter of the woods.

Once he reached the road, he kept his head down and mingled with the other travelers. Traffic was lighter than he had hoped. A man drove an ox cart full of hay, and a shepherd prodded a flock of contrary sheep. Four men hunched along in a tight knot, bags on their shoulders and frowns on their faces. A peddler drove a ramshackle closed-sided wagon pulled by an old, swaybacked horse. Jonmarc fell in behind the sheep, thinking that he might be taken for a second shepherd if no one looked too hard.

From here, he could see the Nu River. It was a wide band of muddy water rippling with the current. On the other side was Margolan, and home. Just across, he spotted a large building lit gaily with lanterns though it was not yet dark. Streamers of red and orange fluttered in the wind, marking it as a brothel. If so, it was the largest one Jonmarc had ever seen, and bold to sit along the river by itself, instead of tucked into the shadows of the seedy part of town.

The Nu River Bridge was a massive structure. Heavy pillars of hewn stone rose from the tumultuous waters, tall, squat, and strong. Arches supported the weight of the bridge platform, stretching across to Margolan. Jonmarc had heard tell that the bridge, called the King's Penny Bridge for the toll charged to cross, had been built long enough ago that its builders adhered to an ancient code to assure the structure would last through the harshest storms. The first pillar raised was sunk atop the corpse of a child sacrificed for the occasion, an orphan no one would miss, but an acceptable offering to the Formless One nonetheless. The thought made Jonmarc shiver.

That was when Jonmarc realized his mistake. The Nu River Bridge was to his right, to the north. It looked at least a half a candlemark's walk distant. That could only mean one thing. He had misjudged either distance or speed and gone too far south.

He was in Nargi.

Jonmarc eyed the distance back to the dark shelter of the forest. It might arouse suspicion to suddenly turn around and come back the way he came. Hareing off across the open meadows and farm fields would definitely draw notice. But perhaps he could manage it, he thought, feeling an edge of panic. He remembered the fortune teller's warning to avoid the south. Now, the words took on new meaning.

He moved over to the edge of the traffic going north, toward the bridge, and bent as if to pick up something he had dropped. While he was squatting down, he turned in the opposite direction and rose facing south as if he had been going that way all along. None of his fellow travelers appeared to notice or care.

I didn't go far from where the forest is close to the road. I should be back there in a few minutes, and then I can go back into the woods and retrace my steps, come out on the Dhasson side of the border near the bridge.

It took all of his willpower not to break into a run. Jonmarc struggled to keep his gaze averted from the traders and farmers around him, avoiding eye contact and hoping he did not look foreign or suspicious. Nargi was known for being unwelcoming to foreigners, and he doubted that those outland smugglers who dared to enter the secretive, cloistered kingdom would be so bold as to use the main roads.

The spot where he had exited the forest was in sight. Jonmarc slowed his steps, hoping to allow the travelers around him to move out of sight without it appearing that he had come to a stop. When the road cleared for a minute, Jonmarc turned from the road and walked rapidly toward the forest edge.

"You there! Halt! The rough voice shouted in heavily-accented Common. Five soldiers dressed in what Jonmarc guessed were Nargi uniforms came into sight just as Jonmarc headed for the treeline. He could not imagine what infraction he had committed. In Margolan or Principality, it would have been assumed that he sought a bit of privacy to relieve himself. But Nargi was known for its harsh laws, merciless punishments, and complex web of proscriptions that covered every aspect of life. By all accounts Jonmarc had ever heard, Nargi was a place of horrors. He had no intention of being detained.

Once again, he ran.

The soldiers ran after him.

Exhausted as he was, sheer terror animated every muscle and sinew. Jonmarc found the strength to sprint across the small stretch of open land, hoping desperately that he might be able to lose the soldiers in the lengthening shadows of the deep forest.

Tall grasses slapped at his legs and cut his skin as he plowed across them. Vines threatened to trip him. His boot caught once, and he staggered, righted, and kept on running, eyes fixed on the sheltering darkness of the forest. He did not fear the wolves or the *stawar* as much as he feared the Nargi guards. Suddenly he realized that his greatest threat was not to be returned to Eastmark. It was to be kept in Nargi.

"Halt!" the voice called again, and repeated the order in a guttural language Jonmarc guessed was Nargi. He paid no heed, running at full speed beneath the tree canopy. Near the edge of the forest, where sunlight still reached the ground, saplings grew. Their thin branches whipped across his face and chest, threatening to put out an eye, cutting his skin, and ripping out his hair.

The soldiers crashed after him, angry at his insubordination. It was much darker beneath the canopy, but not full dark. The ground was largely clear of brush, but the land was hilly, littered with the fallen trunks of massive old trees, marked with boulders that had tumbled long ago, cleft with swales. Jonmarc assessed his options. The soldiers were almost on him. It was only luck that one of them had not put a crossbow bolt in his back yet. And still, no hiding place presented itself. Which left just one alternative.

Fight or die.

While he had been running, the five Nargi soldiers fanned out, and Jonmarc knew they were trying to circle him. Climbing a tree had gotten him away from the wolves and the *stawar*, but it would provide no escape from the guards.

Now, he wished it was the wolves he faced. He was too exhausted and injured to hope to fight off five men, and all the prayers to the Lady he might make was unlikely to provide him with rescue. He realized that he was going to die, and found that the knowledge pushed him into that cold place inside his mind. Jonmarc intended to make them work for their victory and to make his death as expensive as possible for them.

In one smooth arc, he dropped his cloak, pulled his swords and rounded on his pursuers. One of the guards had been closing from the left. Jonmarc wheeled into a high Eastmark kick and sent him flying, slamming into the trunk of a tree hard enough that he did not get back up.

A second guard shouted at him, and while the words meant nothing, the intent was clear. The guard swung his sword, his technique powerful but crude. He did not expect Jonmarc to block his swing, nor was he prepared to parry Jonmarc's second sword, which landed a bone-deep gash on the guard's left forearm above his vambrace.

A third guard came at Jonmarc, and Jonmarc reversed his sweep, striking low as the man went high. He slashed the guard's thigh and then landed a bone-crunching kick to the knee in the uninjured leg, downing the soldier and putting him out of the fight.

Guard Two came back for more, wary this time, as the fourth soldier closed the distance, trying to come up behind him. Jonmarc came up from his crouch with a roar. He blocked the second guard's swing with one sword while his second sword tore up through the guard's uniform, opening a bloody slash across the man's ribs. The second guard now had a knife in his left hand, and he managed to score a deep cut in Jonmarc's shoulder that made Jonmarc gasp in pain. Cold calculation saw an opening, and Jonmarc lurched forward in the instant the guard celebrated his hit, and sank his sword through the soldier's ribs.

Jonmarc felt the point of a sword in his back. The fourth guard was behind him, and the fifth man closed from the right. The soldier behind him shouted an order, but Jonmarc had no intention of dropping his weapon. Surrender was not an option. In the cold place in his mind, Jonmarc no longer feared death. If the legends were true, his family and Shanna along with many good friends would greet him on the other side of the Gray Sea. And if the stories were lies, then he would rest in the darkness. Either option was better than capture.

With a mad growl, Jonmarc dove to one side before the man behind him was prepared to run him through. He came up in a flurry of blades and vicious kicks. One kick should have taken the fourth guard in the belly, but the man turned at the last instant, absorbing the hit on his hip and rounding with his sword, slicing into Jonmarc's right arm deep enough that blood flowed down his forearm and over his hand.

Jonmarc wheeled to catch the fifth guard with a kick, but the man was no longer where Jonmarc had seen him a moment before. A sudden, sharp pain caught Jonmarc in his supporting leg, and he looked down to see the silver shaft of a throwing knife buried deep in his thigh. He went down, and rolled back up to his knees; swords gripped white-knuckled.

"I will not yield," he grated. "So if you want me, you've got to kill me."

He was bleeding freely from the wounds the Nargi soldiers had inflicted, and from a half dozen of the barely-healed injuries Alcion's guards had given him. Hungry, weary, and exhausted, he knew he was not far from death. If he could goad his tormentors into finishing him cleanly, it was the best end he could hope to make.

With a howl of rage, Jonmarc lurched forward, swinging for the fourth guard's ankles. But as he began to move, something heavy cracked against his skull from behind. His swords dropped from his hands, and he fell face-forward into the dirt, but he was conscious enough to feel a sword cut through his jacket and shirt and stab into the flesh of his back, right over his heart. Defeated, he lay still, awaiting the death blow.

The fourth guard's sudden shout surprised him. Now, the imperative was directed at the other guard, and in his hazy half-conscious blur, Jonmarc realized the two soldiers were arguing. He supposed it was over whether to hang him or run him through and while his preference was for the latter, he doubted they would weigh his opinion in their decision. Besides, speaking would require far too much effort and more energy than his battered body could muster.

Finally, the fourth guard kicked away Jonmarc's swords, then rolled him over with his boot. "Where are you from?" he asked in Common.

There was no point left in lying. "Margolan."

"Why are you here?"

"Lousy compass."

The guard regarded his answer with a smirk. He gave a kick to Jonmarc's boots. "Soldier?"

"Used to be. Not anymore." It was hard to think of the words to say, harder still to form sentences. Jonmarc's head pounded, and he was growing light-headed from his wounds. Blood soaked his shirt and pants.

"You fight like a *dimonn*," the senior guard said. "Our commander will have a use for you." He chuckled, a cold, bitter sound without humor. "You'll wish we had killed you, I wager, before long."

"I'm no good as a conscript," Jonmarc managed.

The two guards exchanged a glance. "Oh, you'll fight, that you will," the senior guard replied. "But in the ring. I daresay you'll win the commander plenty of gold. You'll make a champion fight slave—and the games will make him a wealthy man."

DEATH MATCH

1

DEATH MATCH

CAPTURED

JONMARC VAHANIAN DRIFTED IN AND OUT OF CONSCIOUSNESS. Awareness flitted just beyond his grasp. Slowly details filtered back to him. He remembered how he got here. Clearly, the goddess had not answered his prayer for death.

Jonmarc lay in the back of a wagon, wrists and ankles bound tight enough that his fingers and toes tingled. A filthy piece of cloth shoved into his mouth made him struggle to keep from retching, knowing that he would choke on his own vomit. Muscle and bone ached from his fight to win his freedom, a battle he lost. Even if it did take five soldiers to bring him down, even if he had three of them on the ground before he fell.

Mercy would have put a blade to his throat or driven a sword through his heart. But this was Nargi, and there was no mercy here.

Jonmarc willed himself to inventory his injuries. The deep bruises and gashes from his near-execution in Eastmark were still fresh. New slashes and bone-deep pain reminded him of every blow he failed to evade as he fought to escape.

"The General's going to find a use for you." His captor,

one of the Nargi guards, kicked Jonmarc in the knee to get his attention. The man spoke in heavily-accented Common. "You know what's in store for you, outlander? If you hadn't been as good a fighter, you'd be dead by now. But you fought like a wildcat, like you'd been possessed, and that's gold for a man like the General."

The gag kept Jonmarc from replying, but he knew the guard read the fury in his eyes.

The soldier leaned down close enough Jonmarc could smell old whiskey on the man's breath. "You'll go to the games. Heard about them? Blood sport. Fight to the death. The General'll see to your training. We'll see to breaking you, so you know your place," the guard added, clearly looking forward to his part. "Each game you win, the General keeps the bets. Each time in the ring, you face a tougher opponent. Win or die." He sat back with a laugh. "See how long you last."

Jonmarc turned away, and the guard kicked him in the ribs. He couldn't completely hide the groan as the soldier's heavy boot jarred already cracked bone.

"Don't know yet whether I'll bet on you or against you," the soldier mused. "Might bet on the other guy, on account of the cut you gave me with those swords. Huh. See how well you fight without them." He leaned forward again. "The matches are bare-handed, most of the time. Audience likes it better that way. More blood and the killing takes longer."

Jonmarc's stomach clenched. *Maybe if I rush the guards, they'll strike me down.* No one would search for him. The unit of men he commanded was dead, killed for following his orders, for refusing to burn out a village of civilians on the whim of an insane commander and his undead mage. The villagers he tried to save had burned anyhow, a handful of survivors scattered in the night, dispossessed, and hunted.

Fresh lashes from the commander's whip and seeping burns from the blazing barn still marked his flesh, a permanent reminder of his past, just like the scar that ran from ear to collarbone, an indelible memento of the night his world ended.

The Nargi army stockade sat back from the Nu River far enough to be defensible, just slightly out of sight of the riverbanks. His captors exchanged comments with the guard at the gate in the guttural, clipped tones of Nargi, discussing his fate in a language Jonmarc did not understand. One of the soldiers pointed and jeered at the bound captive lying bleeding in the back of the wagon. Jonmarc did not need a translator to get the gist of the other guards' suggestions, or much imagination to guess what they thought should be done with him.

A few moments later, the wagon rumbled inside the camp, and his keeper bent down with a knowing grin. "The boys at the gate said to bring you back if the General doesn't want you. Said they'd find a use for you," he added with a leer.

Jonmarc surged forward, managing a snarl despite the gag. Bound and hobbled, he could not make good on his threat, but the menace in his eyes made the guard sit back.

"Need to beat that attitude out of you," the guard snapped, but he kept his distance.

"Is he giving you a hard time, trussed up and gagged?" one of the wagon drivers mocked. "You know the General likes some spirit in his champions. The violent ones are more unpredictable. Bets go sky-high. Don't worry, he'll learn his place."

For the rest of the ride, the guard stayed back, as if he feared Jonmarc might manage to get teeth into him despite the gag. His expression promised vengeance, and it came as no surprise when a sharp punch to the kidneys brought Jonmarc to his knees as he stumbled from the wagon.

The guard grabbed a handful of Jonmarc's chestnut hair and yanked his head up and back, baring his throat. "Not so tough on your knees, are you?" the man hissed, giving Jonmarc a shove that sent him face down in the dirt when he could not catch himself with his bound hands.

"That's enough!" A Nargi captain strode forward, shoving the wagon guard out of the way. "Hands off the General's prize," he said, fixing the soldier with a glare. In the next breath, the Captain hauled Jonmarc to his feet by the shirt and sent him staggering as the too-short binding between his ankles made it nearly impossible to walk.

Jonmarc growled, shaking off the unwanted hand on his shoulder, only to merit being cuffed on the side of the head.

"You're no one's champion yet," the Captain said. "And you wouldn't be the first tough guy to die in his first match. Or have an accident in camp," he added with a jab to Jonmarc's cracked ribs. Jonmarc refused to look in his direction, but the threat could not have been any clearer.

The Captain manhandled Jonmarc into a wooden building, pressing the tip of a blade into the small of his back as a reminder. The quarters were austere, but the furnishings and few personal items suggested rank and money. A bed and a trunk sat against one wall, a desk and chair on the other, along with a small table and another chair. On the other side, a brazier took away the night chill. The Noorish carpet suggested wealth, as did the inlay on the trunk. A crystal decanter of brandy, in plain view on the desk, told Jonmarc the General was not a devout man.

A sweep of the captain's leg took Jonmarc's feet out from under him, dropping him to his knees.

"Don't move. Keep your head down." The cold steel of a knife blade slid between the filthy cloth gag and Jonmarc's cheek, and with a slight turn of his wrist, the captain managed to drag a thin, shallow cut down Jonmarc's face.

"Speak when spoken to, and not before," the Captain said, his Common so heavy with the harsh consonants of the Nargi language that Jonmarc barely understood his commands. The threats came through clearly, no translation necessary.

Footsteps sounded in the doorway behind them, and Jonmarc steeled himself, refusing to flinch, keeping his eyes on the ground. He squared his shoulders and straightened his back, determined to show that while he had no choice in the matter, they had not yet broken him.

"So this is the new prisoner." The voice belonged to an older man, and while the Nargi accent colored his words, Jonmarc bet that his was a more patrician upbringing.

"Yes, sir. Fought like a *dimonn* the men said. Not his first fight either."

"Strip off his shirt. Let me see."

The Captain's knife ripped up through the rags of Jonmarc's shirt, cold against his skin, and Jonmarc fought an instinctive shudder. The torn cloth parted easily, revealing everything.

"Interesting," the General said, and while Jonmarc had not yet raised his head to see the man, his polished black boots circled Jonmarc slowly.

"What do you make of it, Captain?" the General said.

"He's a criminal," the Captain replied, making no attempt to hide the disdain in his voice. "He's been whipped and branded, and there's bruising on his throat like he barely escaped the noose."

"Hmm," the General replied. "Yes. And yet these," he said, pointing to old scars with the tip of a knife, "look more like sword wounds." And this, "he added, touching the tip to the long scar that ran from Jonmarc's ear to his collar, "didn't come from a blade."

"Probably a brawler and a thief," the Captain said.

The General stood in silence for a moment. "What is your name?"

"Jonmarc Vahanian."

"Were you a soldier?"

"A mercenary. For the War Dogs, and for Alcion of Eastmark." Jonmarc couldn't stop the corner of his mouth from twitching up, just a bit. If the General knew anything of Principality and Eastmark, those names meant something, if only to suggest that Jonmarc was a better sort of ruffian.

"Curious. Why were you whipped and branded?"

"I disobeyed an order. One I believed to be wrong."

"An understandable punishment," the General replied. The knife blade touched the seeping burns along one shoulder. "And this?

"I failed to die in a burning barn."

"And this?" The tip touched the ragged tear that ran down the side of Jonmarc's neck.

"I fought a magicked beast and won."

"He lies," the Captain challenged.

Jonmarc shrugged. "Believe me or don't. You can both go screw the Crone."

A powerful backhanded blow nearly toppled Jonmarc to the ground. "Mind your mouth," the Captain warned.

"Tell your attack dog not to damage the merchandise," Jonmarc replied, ignoring his split lip.

"Nargi battle healers are remarkable," the General observed. "Bring a man back from the edge of death. Some say from beyond it. That gives him leeway, I think, to keep you in line."

The Captain yanked Jonmarc back to his knees. "We took

two fine swords from him. Proof that he's a thief. No merc carries weapons like those."

Jonmarc's jaw set at that, angry at losing the swords his father forged, the last two weapons made before brigands killed him. "Give them back," he demanded. "You want me to fight for you? I need my swords."

"Perhaps," the General said. "Quite a while before the matches allow weapons. You'll have to survive long enough to get that far."

"I want my swords," Jonmarc repeated. He had little enough to live for, but those blades were a legacy from his father, and he'd be damned if he intended to give them up easily.

"Then you'll have to earn them," the General snapped. Jonmarc raised his head then and fixed his captor with a deadly glare.

"I've earned them. Got the scars to prove it." *I killed the brigand who murdered my family, killed the monsters that slaughtered my wife and neighbors. Fought creatures and soldiers and criminals, won my place as merc. I've already damn well earned them and more.*

The Captain backhanded Jonmarc hard enough that his head swam. "Speak when spoken to. Keep your eyes on the ground."

Jonmarc swallowed back bile and lowered his gaze, locking his jaw hard enough that he thought he might crack a tooth.

The General gave a cold chuckle. "I like spirit in my fighters. You'll earn your place—in the ring or out under the dirt. Those scars on you—I might just believe you. Or maybe you were just slow enough to get caught."

"Cut the ropes and let me show you." No mistaking the intent in Jonmarc's voice, or the lethal look in his eyes when he slid his gaze sideways, enough to make eye contact.

The Captain raised his hand to strike again, and Jonmarc braced for the hit, but the General's arm blocked the blow. "No. I'm... intrigued. This one will be entertaining."

The General circled Jonmarc again, appraising. Jonmarc remembered buying horses for the caravan, sizing up the stallions and trying to decide which ones might be too dangerous to ride. Jonmarc's whole body tensed, gauging the moment to strike.

"I am your master," the General said, amusement gone from his voice. Jonmarc felt certain any infraction now would earn him a beating or worse. "You live at my sufferance, for so long as you profit me in the ring. Please me, win for me, and you'll find the rewards quite pleasant. Champions do well for themselves, though they will always be slaves."

He paused behind Jonmarc as if assessing the strength of his back, gauging his fitness to fight. "As a fight slave, you'll be fed, sheltered, and clothed. The healers will keep you in shape to fight, though they tend to leave the pain and scars as reminders to do better. Attempt to kill yourself, either to throw the game or escape, and you will be brought back. You will not enjoy the consequences."

Jonmarc kept his head down and said nothing, did not flinch away even as the General moved close enough that his coattail skimmed across the open wounds on Jonmarc's back. If the man wanted to put a shiv in his back or swing a blade through his neck, nothing would stop him. But Jonmarc knew the General intended no such kindness.

"Bring me the collar."

The Captain moved away and returned. Jonmarc heard the clink of iron on iron.

"Lift your head," the General ordered. The Captain

angled the tip of his sword against Jonmarc's chest, just above his heart, to make sure he obeyed.

The General gripped an iron collar, holding it out for Jonmarc to see. A solid band roughly two inches wide, hinged on one side, opening on the other with a hasp to lock it. Despite himself, Jonmarc could not completely repress a shiver.

"You will wear my collar," the General said. "My mark is on it, so there is no question when you fight contestants from other camps. You will wear it until you die. Do you understand?"

Jonmarc glared at him. The Captain back-handed him again, splitting his lip. "Answer the General!"

"I understand."

Jonmarc tried to hold himself motionless as the General placed the cold iron around his throat. He fought the urgent need to struggle, to escape, knowing that the guard would not hesitate to slide the sword between his ribs at the first sign of trouble. He stayed still, and hated himself for it, wishing he had the courage to force the soldier's hand, test the General's threat about bringing him back from the dead.

The iron collar closed around his throat, and he swallowed hard, his Adam's apple dragging across the metal that fit close against his skin. Not quite a noose, but just enough constriction to chafe, a constant reminder of servitude.

"Set it." At the General's order, the Captain went to the fire and returned with tongs holding a glowing bolt. Jonmarc's heartbeat raced, knowing what came next, bracing himself for the pain he remembered from Alcion' branding iron, willing himself not to cry out.

The Captain placed the bolt into the hasp, sending off a shower of sparks that burned into Jonmarc's shoulder. The hot iron warmed the rest of the collar until it felt like fire against his skin, heat radiating close enough to his ear that Jonmarc knew he would have blisters. His whole body shook, and he bit into his lip, tasting blood, to keep from crying out, tightening his bound hands into fists, his whole body drawn tight as a bowstring. But he refused to close his eyes, squeeze them shut against the pain.

Instead, Jonmarc raised his gaze to meet the General's. He knew his expression made clear what he dared not say. *I will kill you. Not today. But someday. Count on it.*

"Take him to the healers," the General ordered. "See that he arrives without further damage," he added, in a tone that told Jonmarc the Captain had other plans. "If you permit him to be injured, you will take his place in the ring until he recovers."

"Understood, sir."

"Wait for him until the healers are through. Take him to his cell. See that he has food, clothing, and bedding, and untie him. He must be able to rest before his first match."

The Captain steered Jonmarc out of the General's quarters, forcing him to walk in front of him, the tip of his sword between Jonmarc's shoulder blades. The ropes on Jonmarc's ankles permitted a halting gait, short enough that an attempt at speed would send him crashing to the ground. The Captain pricked his back with his blade, and Jonmarc knew the man would enjoy having provocation to rough him up.

As they moved through the camp, soldiers stopped to watch them pass.

"Is that the General's new toy?" one shouted. "Looks hard used."

"He'll be in the ring before long," the Captain replied. "Not sure I'd want to bet my money on him."

"He's pretty enough to have other uses if the fight don't

suit him," another soldier heckled, and others joined in laughing.

"Watch your mouth," the Captain snapped. "He's the General's prize."

"Not like he hasn't passed us a slave or two before," came the reply. "What do you think, outlander? Take your chances in the fight, or out here?"

Jonmarc kept his eyes straight ahead, his face impassive, trying to slow his breathing though his heart hammered in his chest.

"Leave him be," the Captain ordered. "Save it for the fight. Won't be long. General will want to test the merchandise."

"Oh yeah. Let's see him go up against Kelter. Go up and go down," one of the soldiers crowed. "You hear that, outlander? Kelter will take you apart."

"Outta my way," the Captain warned. "The sooner I get him to the healers, the sooner you can watch Kelter send him back to them again."

Holding himself rigid against the threats had Jonmarc shaking with harnessed adrenaline. He had no idea what fighting skills this Kelter person might have, but at least right now, he knew the Nargi also knew nothing about what he could do. *I've fought monsters and brigands, soldiers and assassins. I'll give them a show they won't forget.*

"We're here." The Captain gave a jab to emphasize his point. They stopped in front of one of the permanent buildings in the compound, a rectangular wooden building as nondescript as the rest of what Jonmarc had seen of the camp. A sign over the door in Nargi meant nothing to him, written in a language he had never even heard spoken until today.

Jonmarc entered with the Captain close behind him. Two older men in healers' robes looked up sharply, frowning at the intrusion. Questions asked, and answers given flew back and forth in the clipped, guttural language, and despite whatever the guard said, the healers looked no more pleased when he finished than when they entered.

"They don't like to heal outland scum," the Captain finally bothered to summarize. "Tried to send me away, told me to put you down if you couldn't heal on your own. I said you were the General's new fight slave. So they'll fix what might keep you from putting up a good fight, but don't expect careful handling," he added with a smirk.

The Captain left him to the healers, who if they could speak Common did not bother to do so. They poked and prodded Jonmarc's wounds, talking to each other in Nargi, conveying anything he needed to know with gestures or just pushing him into position. Jonmarc cursed them, winning himself a sudden, blinding headache from a healer who looked insufferably smug. Healers were not supposed to cause pain, but the rules obviously worked differently in Nargi.

Nothing about the healers' touch conveyed concern, just cold duty. They made no effort to hide their disdain, and Jonmarc suspected that their handling was rougher than required. He gritted his teeth, knowing that whether he intended to fight or flee he would have the best chance of surviving healed of his injuries.

The warmth of healing magic felt familiar from the caravan, from the War Dogs. He felt strength returning, and if these healers did not bother to temper the pain or erase new scars, Jonmarc could still tell that the severity of his injuries had lessened. They had barely finished when the elder healer grabbed Jonmarc by the shoulders and manhandled him up, making it clear from gestures and a shove between the shoulder blades that he should leave.

The Captain returned and exchanged more comments, and even without a translator, Jonmarc knew he was the butt of the joke. He cursed them under his breath, winning a cuff to the ear from the guard.

"Watch your mouth," the soldier warned. "I understand what you're saying. It won't go easy on you no matter what you do, but it can go harder, so keep your damn mouth shut and do what you're told."

Jonmarc bit back a reply because visiting the healers once had been unpleasant and he was certain a return trip so soon would be doubly so. They stopped in front of a small building with bars on the windows, the stockade jail.

"Your new quarters," the Captain said with a smirk. "Until you prove yourself. Make the General a lot of money, and you might get a nicer place. But you've got to live long enough to do that, and I'm not betting on your chances," he added.

"What happened to the last champion?"

"He died with his guts around his feet, and the General lost a lot of money."

He shoved Jonmarc into a bare cell and locked shackles on his wrists before cutting the rope that bound him, then did the same for his ankles. The iron weighed him down, but the few inches of movement they afforded were worth the burden. Jonmarc tried not to flinch as the iron door slammed shut. "At least you know you'll get food and water. The General will want you in fighting shape."

"When?" Jonmarc asked. "When is the fight?"

The Captain gave him a cold smile. "Tomorrow. You'll fight Kelter. He's a few cells down from you. Gonna be hanged for murder—unless he beats you. So he's got all the reason in the world to win. Smart money is betting you lose."

The Captain left the line of cells, though Jonmarc doubted

the jail was unmonitored. He sank down on the floor and rested his head in his hands.

Off the spit and into the fire. He ran a mental check of his body, verifying that the healers had truly reversed the damage, trying to sense whether they had done anything to him aside from healing him. *Would the General instruct them to alter him in some way, make him impervious to pain, or give him a short-term boost of energy or strength that might give him an advantage in the fight? Or might someone else with a bet on the line bribe a healer, have them set a weakness, in his heart, his joints, a blood vessel in his brain, that could be triggered by magic or just give way under stress, throwing the fight?*

Nargi forbids magic, he thought. *Or at least, some magic. Maybe they lump healing in with the priesthood.*

He had paid little attention to Nargi before this; there had been no reason to think about the kingdom, other than to remark about how it was best to stay out of it. *I completely bungled that.*

Is this better or worse than being caught by Alcion's men? Worse, he decided. Alcion would have brought him back to Eastmark in chains, had him whipped again, tortured. Possibly drawn and quartered, since hanging and burning hadn't worked. But then it would have been over. Alcion might have brought Jonmarc to the edge of death, revived him a time or two, just for vengeance, but eventually, the Eastmark commander would have tired of the game and let Jonmarc die.

He had no such assurances here. *Fight and die. Fight or die. Refuse to kill for their amusement, and they'll kill me. Kill men with whom I have no quarrel, who haven't wronged me, and I get to live to do it again. And again. Until a champion arises who can take me down, or the general tires of his toy or someone takes off my head, which even the healers can't fix.*

That was the crux of it, right there. Because while fighting and killing for the entertainment of some sick sons of bitches went against something deep inside Jonmarc, so did suicide.

He'd thought about killing himself more times than he wanted to admit. He had considered death when the monsters killed Shanna, creatures he had accidentally summoned, but his fault, nonetheless. Later, even though Linton and the caravan had welcomed him, there had been nights when Jonmarc felt too close to the past, too distant from the present, nights when the edge of his sharpened knife called to him. On those nights, he had tried the blade in hollow cuts along his forearm, just to see the blood bead up, proof that he was not as dead as he felt inside. It wouldn't have taken much on those nights to dig the razor-sharp blade just little deeper and warm himself in the hot rush of blood.

He hadn't done it then; could he do it now? Throw the game, let himself be killed, assure a violent enough death that the healers couldn't bring him back? Was he that certain that there could be no reprieve from his captivity, no escape?

Not yet. It'll be bad, going into the fight. But if Kelter had been condemned to die, maybe he's not any different from the bastards I've killed as a merc. He's not an innocent. Not helpless. And if he can win his freedom, he'll put me in the dirt without looking back. So I don't owe him anything. He's as dangerous as any brigand. By the Crone! How did it come to this?

Jonmarc looked up and took a deep breath, his course of action decided, at least for now. He would fight and do his best to win, to stay alive, and see what opportunities to escape presented themselves. He could always die another day.

His cell, though spare, offered more comfort than he expected. It held a cot rather than a pallet of straw on the stone floor and a blanket. One bucket of water looked clean enough to drink; the empty bucket on the other side clearly for taking care of his needs.

Dinner came on a flat board, shoved through a space beneath the bars of his cell. A hunk of roasted meat, a slab of buttered bread for a sop, and a wedge of cheese. Jonmarc sniffed at the dinner warily, alert for a trick.

"You think the General's going to poison you the night before your first fight?" the guard asked, his heavy accent difficult to understand.

"I don't know what to think." Jonmarc pulled the food closer. He could smell nothing either spoiled or poisoned, and while that didn't rule out a trick, his hunger overcame caution, and he ate quickly, not willing to risk having the food taken from him. When he finished, he pushed the board back through the bars and drank from the bucket.

"Why me?" he asked as the guard bent to retrieve the board.

The guard gave an incredulous snort. "You took down three guards by yourself, and fought the others hard, despite injuries. The General is… interested… to see how you'll do in the ring."

Jonmarc shook his head. "He would consider an outlander champion?"

The guard stared at Jonmarc as if he did not completely grasp the question. *Maybe it doesn't make any sense to a Nargi. Maybe if you're from here, that's just how things are, like the sky is blue and people can't fly.*

"Champions have to win. Doesn't matter where they come from. If they can't win, they're no use. The General has a proud record. Makes us a lot of money in bets too, which ain't so bad on a soldier's pay," he added with a smirk.

"So a champion fights other champions?" The scope of the ordeal he faced suddenly expanded beyond Jonmarc's expectations.

"Sure," the guard replied. "From all the garrisons around here."

Jonmarc considered that for a moment. "Suppose I beat Kelter tomorrow. What then?"

The guard gave him an appraising look. "Think you can?"

Jonmarc shrugged, though he suspected the odds were at least even for a win. "What if I do?"

"Well, you stay alive. And you'll move on to the next fight, whatever the General wants to throw at you. If he thinks you've got potential, he'll put you in training. Don't envy you none, no matter how it goes."

"Training?"

"Can't tell you much more than what I've heard. Wasn't assigned here the last time the General got a new champion. The matches will try to break you, see what you can take. Champion has to be tough, not just lucky."

Jonmarc leaned back against the cell wall. "How long as did the old champion last?"

"Almost a year, or so they say. Longer than most. New fighters usually die in the first match or two. We bet on how long they'll last, not whether or not they die."

"And what are the odds on me?"

The guard gave him a measured look. "You don't want to know."

The next day, Jonmarc found a new shirt and a clean pair of pants inside his cell. It seemed a shame to wear new clothing to a fight where they would end up covered in blood, but he could hardly go in his ragged shirt and tattered trousers. A different soldier replaced the guard who had talked to him the previous night, and this man showed no interest in conversation. *Guess he's betting against me.*

He had no idea when the fight would begin, and tension built in his gut. When two soldiers came to escort him to the fight, Jonmarc squared his shoulders and lifted his head. No matter what happened, he would not let them see his fear.

Midday two guards entered his cell, one of them holding a razor. "Sit," the one with the razor ordered. "Gonna get rid of that beard and cut your hair. For the fight."

Jonmarc complied, keeping a wary eye on the blade. Being clean shaven felt good, but he had always kept his hair shoulder length. He watched the long chestnut hair fall the floor in clumps as they worked. The remnants of his old life fell away with the clippings. Then he felt the blade against his scalp, removing the last bits of himself, reminding him that he was now a slave.

"So you're the challenger?" one of the other prisoners mocked. "Don't look so tough. Just a kid. Kelter's gonna murder you. Rip your guts out and pick his teeth with your bones."

"Shut up," one of the soldiers snapped, banging the grip of a knife against the bars so hard that the prisoner sprang backward.

"I saw Kelter's last fight," the prisoner shouted, undeterred once they were past his cell. "Couldn't make out no face on the loser. Pushed his nose up into his brain, clawed his eyes out. Just like he'll do to you."

Jonmarc did his best to ignore the taunt, but it still sent a shiver down his spine. He had fought *vyrkin* and *vayash moru*, seasoned soldiers, hardened mercs, and highwaymen who were stone cold killers. He had an advantage. He knew how true monsters fought. A madman could not do worse.

The guards led him to a small tent next to a much larger structure. Jonmarc watched them warily. "The shackles come off, but only if you do as you're told," the lead guard snapped, reaching out to unlock the manacles. Jonmarc rubbed the chafed skin as the second guard stepped forward, holding the tip of his sword against Jonmarc's chest as the other man bent to unlock the hobbles.

"Here," the first guard said, tossing a ball made from strips of cloth to Jonmarc. "Wrap your knuckles. It's allowed."

Jonmarc caught the object and unwound it. This, at least, was familiar, something he often did during sparring matches. "What now?" he asked, his hands moving by memory, wrapping the rags tight enough to offer some protection.

"Leave the shirt; keep the pants."

"Has Kelter fought in the ring before?"

The guard hesitated, then shrugged. "He's fought plenty; that's what got him where he is. Killed a man in a drunken brawl. Good soldier; bad temper. But he hasn't been in the games."

"What are the rules?"

"There aren't any," the second guard said. "Except surviving. No move too underhanded or violent, no places off limits, so I'd guard my nuts and eyes if I were you."

"Does it have to be a kill, or just putting him down and keeping him down?"

The guards laughed. "Oh, there'd better be blood. Your audience didn't come to see mercy. Whoever goes down goes out. Your choice on how to kill him, if you're the lucky bastard who survives. But you don't get a weapon."

Only when they reached the ring did the true reality hit him. He had pictured a crude enclosure from logs hastily pushed together and just as quickly kicked apart, something illicit on the edge of camp. He'd heard rumors of such things as a merc, not within the War Dogs—his captain would not have allowed it—but in other companies. Then, the fights were against the rules, continuing either through stealth or the complicity of officers, all evidence removed and memories conveniently blurry.

This was something completely different. The fight ring was a large tent with raised benches around an inner dirt area surrounded by a shoulder-high wooden wall. Above the benches were platforms rising close to the top of the tent, and he realized that was standing room for the audience, those who did not rank high enough to sit close to the action.

Dark stains marred the wooden walls, and the black smudges in the dirt made him look away. Jonmarc did not question the source. The crowd jeered as he entered, and the guards stayed behind at the entrance to the ring, ready to keep him from bolting, but not moving into the arena.

"Welcome the challenger!" a voice boomed. Gauging from the few cheers, most of the audience had wages riding on his failure.

"And the favorite." Cheers erupted from the stands. On the benches nearest the ring, the officers clapped their approval, leaving the vulgar shouts for the enlisted men. Their eyes gleamed bright with the expectation of blood, faces flushed, bodies taut with anticipation. The General sat in the center, face revealing nothing except curiosity, hands folded.

For the first time, Jonmarc got a good look at his opponent. Kelter might have been a few years older than he, a bit stockier. He had the muscles of a soldier, lean and hard. Jonmarc had the advantage with an inch or two of height; Kelter probably outweighed him by a stone. Kelter's grin made it clear that he expected to walk out a free man.

Jonmarc kept his face neutral, taking the moment to observe everything he could about his opponent, cataloging his stance for clues to old injuries, anything that might provide an edge.

The General called for silence with a clap of his hands. He looked down at the two combatants. "This ends when one man is dead. Begin."

Kelter moved as the words left the General's mouth, launching himself at Jonmarc and taking them both to the ground. They hit hard, Jonmarc on his back, air forced from his lungs by the fall and Kelter's weight on top of him. The crowd called for blood, jeering and shouting.

Kelter drew his fist back to land a punch and Jonmarc flipped them, pinning Kelter beneath him and striking hard.

Kelter bucked, trying to throw Jonmarc clear as he struggled for breath. Jonmarc hung on and moved to swing both fists together, when Kelter's knees came up with sudden force, barely missing a hit to his nuts, knocking him away.

Kelter sprang after him, but Jonmarc was ready, blocking the strike with his leg, rolling out of the way and gaining his feet, hauling off in a kick that caught Kelter in the belly.

The crowd howled, but Jonmarc dared not take his attention off his opponent long enough to determine who they favored, though he suspected they called for his death. Kelter staggered but did not fall, eying Jonmarc with a deadly look, keeping his distance until he dove forward with a feral roar.

Jonmarc almost dodged, but Kelter swung wide with one arm, clotheslining him across the chest. Jonmarc pivoted, grabbing Kelter's wrist as he turned, twisting his arm until the joint popped and Kelter screamed.

Kelter cursed under his breath, rage driving him on. He circled Jonmarc, feinting forward and dropping back, pleased with himself when Jonmarc mirrored him. He scythed one leg behind Jonmarc's knees, pitching him forward and throwing a handful of loose dirt in his eyes as he fell.

Instinct drove Jonmarc, and he rolled out of the way as he heard Kelter's boot crash down beside him, where his chest would have been. Jonmarc blinked furiously to clear his vision, relying on sound and the vibration of the ground, evading until he could strike back.

"Don't run from me, coward. Let me kill you like the outland dog you are."

Jonmarc's reply was obscene and creative. His vision slowly cleared, enough to make out the shadow form of his attacker, and he sidestepped at the last instant, driving his elbow down hard below Kelter's ribs, into his kidneys.

Kelter let out a grunt as the sharp bone connected with soft organs, and he stumbled away. Jonmarc's eyes burned and teared, but he had Kelter off balance, and he didn't know how many more falls he could take.

Jonmarc's boot snapped forward, pushing Kelter's right knee backward with a painful snap. Kelter went down with a scream.

This is it. Win or die. Goddess forgive me.

The crowd chanted for a kill, either of the contestants would do. Kelter scrabbled to find his way back to his feet, but Jonmarc wheeled into a high Eastmark kick, and the heel of his boot connected hard with Kelter's jaw, sending him sprawling several feet away.

"Kill. Kill. Kill. Kill." The crowd chanted in Common, feet stomping, their clapping pounding like a heartbeat.

Jonmarc shut out the noise. He was on Kelter in seconds, driving the breath from his lungs. Kelter's broken jaw made his face look melted, with blood dripping from his ruined lips and his eye already swelling shut. Jonmarc found the cold, lethal place inside himself where time slowed down, the refuge his father had taught him when they butchered hogs.

He knew how to fight, and he knew how to kill.

Jonmarc put his full strength into a hard punch to Kelter's throat. His knuckles hit flesh and cartilage, driving deep. Kelter's body arched, straining for breath that could not pass his crushed windpipe. His eyes widened, desperate and terrified. All around them, the crowd screamed for the spectacle, shouted for Jonmarc to move out of the way, the better for them to see Kelter's death throes. But to Jonmarc, nothing existed except the two of them, victor and vanquished, and in this moment, he could hang on to a shred of decency.

He pulled his arm back once more, this time landing a powerful blow to the side of the neck, where the artery ran. Kelter went limp beneath him, whether from the blow or the snap of his spine.

Jonmarc bowed his head, shoulders slumped, still kneeling on Kelter's corpse as the crowd screamed and chanted, clapped and stomped. Blood covered his ruined knuckles, spattered his bare chest, streaked down his pants. Some of it his own, most of it Kelter's. As the rush of the fight left him, pain returned. Kelter had landed several near-crippling strikes, which radiated pain in Jonmarc's bones and muscles.

Guards pulled him to his feet and kept him standing as his knees nearly buckled. They half-led, half-dragged him to the center of the ring, to stand before the General who looked down on him with a look of bemused surprise.

"Apparently the tale my guards told of your capture was accurate," he observed. "Well done. You will move on to the next level." The General's gaze moved to the guards who supported Jonmarc's weight. "Take him to the healers. See him to his quarters after."

Jonmarc remembered little of the trek across the compound. Neither of the guards spoke, and in a moment of lucidity, he wondered whether they had lost money on the fight. He doubted the dour healers were the gambling type, though they also said nothing to him as the guards manhandled him to the crude table.

When he regained consciousness sometime later, he lay on the cot in his room, no longer in pain. His bloody clothes had been stripped away and replaced, the blood that had covered his fists and arms washed clean, though the memory would never leave him.

Next to the bed lay a bottle of whiskey. Jonmarc had heard enough of Nargi to know its black-robed Crone priests frowned on alcohol, but apparently, those rules did not apply to a general and his favored fight slave.

"For your win," the note said in Common, tucked beneath the bottle.

Jonmarc sat up, stretched, testing his muscles to see what ached, but the healers had done their job well. *If the bruises are gone, you'd never know I killed a man with my bare hands.*

He reached for the bottle, freed the cork with a twist of his wrist, and let the raw liquor burn down his throat, hoping for oblivion.

2

DEATH MATCH

CLAY AND BLOOD

Two days after the first fight, a guard came to the cell door. No one else had come by except to push food beneath the door, dump water into his bucket, or clear away the foul contents in the chamber pot.

"Training time," the guard said, but despite Jonmarc's questions, told him nothing else. *Maybe he's still sore about losing his bet,* Jonmarc thought, trying not to think about the knot in his belly.

"Training" could mean a lot of things, none of them pleasant. Jonmarc's cell had a single window, high on the wall but not too far for him to gain a view of the parade ground. Drilling and turning out for inspection appeared to be a universal, no matter how different the customs or language. Earlier that day, he had watched the soldiers spar and drill with a quintain, practicing against a wooden arm and chest on a pivot.

Then he saw the captive dragged to the center of the parade ground, gagged, hands bound behind his back and shackled to his waist, ankles hobbled. Jonmarc went very still as he saw one soldier lift down the wooden effigy and slide an iron pole through the bound man's arms behind his back and then lift him up so that he hung from the hook in its place.

From here, Jonmarc could not see the eyes of the soldiers, only that they stood at rest while others fastened the captive into place. Their commander barked an order, and the soldiers formed a single line. Jonmarc swallowed down bile, disbelieving even as dread filled his belly with cold certainty.

Jonmarc did not need to understand the language to recognize the order to strike. One after the next, the soldiers surged forward—thrust, pull back, lunge—without hesitation or protest. He wondered what the poor dumb bastard had done to warrant becoming a human target. Treason? Insubordination? Cowardice? He would never know. When the last soldier finally moved away, a mangled corpse hung from the pole, run through dozens of times; clothing soaked crimson.

Jonmarc turned away, knowing that his hands shook, fighting the urge to throw up. The superficial similarities he had seen meant nothing. Nargi was not like Margolan or Principality; it was alien, unknowable. And for the first time, Jonmarc felt the cold certainty that he would die here.

When the guard came for him, Jonmarc wondered whether he would be the one doing the training or the quintain. He let out a breath that he had not realized he was holding when the guard led him past the training ground and tensed again as they approached the fighting ring.

"No one said anything about another fight," Jonmarc said, unsure whether or not this guard understood Common. He remained uncertain since the guard did not answer. The soldier grabbed Jonmarc's arm and pushed him into the tent.

Three healers were waiting for him, and Jonmarc stopped, confused. "What kind of training?" he asked, although they had never spoken to him in Common. By now, he suspected that at least one of them understood him, but not answering reinforced their position of power.

The guard unlocked Jonmarc's shackles and tossed them to one side. Jonmarc rubbed his wrists, glancing uncertainly from the soldier to the healers. "What in the name of the Crone is going on?"

That earned him a slap across the face. Seconds too late, he remembered that Nargi alone of the Seven Kingdoms venerated the Crone aspect of the Sacred Lady. "Watch your mouth, outlander. Show respect."

"How am I supposed to train if no one tells me what's going on?" Jonmarc forced his tone to be borderline civil, though he knew from the sour expressions on the healers' faces that he lacked proper deference.

One of the healers spoke to the guard, who turned to Jonmarc. "He says that with enough damage, you will learn your place. He says to warn you that despite the General's desire to win bets, disobedience and blasphemy will not be tolerated."

Jonmarc bit back the answers that came to mind. "No one's answered my question. Train how?"

The guard looked toward the robed men and nodded when a reply came. "Fight him," he replied, pointing into the shadows.

"Who?"

The tallest of the healers spoke a command, and Jonmarc heard a heavy rumble from the darkness on the other side of the ring. Ponderous footsteps echoed in the nearly empty tent, and Jonmarc steeled himself, unsure what to expect.

A clay figure emerged from the shadows, its movements heavy and sluggish. The dark smooth clay held the form of a man but without detail. The dark gray face had depressions for eyes and lips, an outcropping for a nose, but it lacked the finish of a true sculpture. The shoulders and chest spanned wide, but lacked definition for musculature. The mud man came to a stop a dozen feet from Jonmarc.

Jonmarc felt torn between curiosity and horror. He had heard tales of such things, "golems" some called them, but had never thought to see one, let alone be expected to fight such a thing.

He sized up his opponent. The golem stood a few inches taller than he, with broader shoulders and thicker arms and thighs. Had he been a living man, Jonmarc would have known the odds. He had fought opponents larger than himself many times, and he knew how to use their advantages against them; his agility against their too-tight bulging muscles, his speed versus their weight.

But for this adversary, he had no point of comparison. Magic animated it, but whether it worked like a puppet, its every move at the behest of its master, or had been imprinted with enough of a script to feign autonomy, he did not know. *Hollow or solid?* He wondered. The difference would dictate whether a blow from those giant fists hurt or killed.

"What do you want from me? What are the rules?"

He waited as the guard translated, then received an answer. "Fight your hardest. Begin."

The golem moved faster than Jonmarc expected, given its bulk. One massive arm swung at him, and he dodged out of the way easily, feeling the swish of air as the creature missed. He danced backward, having no intention of engaging this opponent until he had a better sense of its capabilities.

The next strike came with less warning and the margin by which Jonmarc evaded the blow narrowed. A third punch clipped the edge of Jonmarc's shoulder, sending pain flaring through the joint, giving him new respect for the golem's strength.

The mud man moved faster each time, and Jonmarc realized it anticipated his reaction after the first strike. This time, he dropped and rolled, coming up behind the monster, then dodging to the side. Momentarily confused, the monster hesitated, and Jonmarc hurled himself against its back, attempting to topple the clay creature.

Instead, he felt as if he had thrown himself against a wall. He bounced back, managing to keep his feet, but the golem did not stagger, solidly braced on its thick legs and wide feet.

It turned fast, scything its giant fist for Jonmarc's head. Jonmarc dropped to his belly and then rolled, barely getting out of the way of the golem's heavy foot as it stomped down inches from where his chest had been seconds before. Whether the golem "saw" through the eyes of the mage controlling it or by some other magic, Jonmarc did not know, but it was clear that its senses and reflexes were at least as sharp as a human opponent.

The lag between strikes grew shorter each time, and the blows more targeted. Jonmarc consciously varied his dodges, still playing a defensive game, looking for weaknesses he could exploit. He ran at the golem from behind and leaped onto its back, covering its "eyes" with his hands and locking his legs around its thick middle. The creature stilled, then brought one ham-sized fist down sharply on Jonmarc's knees, while the other slammed against the arms wrapped around its neck, and he felt the echo of the strike reverberate through the clay body.

Jonmarc dropped to the ground in pain, remembering to roll away from the golem's heavy feet only when a clay sole loomed over his head. It crashed to the dirt an inch from his ear with enough force to have shattered his skull. Jonmarc's right knee sent bright flashes of pain up his spine, and he thought his left arm might be broken from the creature's blow.

And yet… the shudder through the golem's body when it struck him told Jonmarc the creature was hollow. That his bones had not shattered beneath its punch supported that suspicion, since its limb would be even heavier if solid.

Hollow could be broken.

Jonmarc's arm throbbed, and pain from his leg lanced up his spine with every movement, but he had fought with worse. The golem turned, huge mitts already swinging, and Jonmarc dove to the ground, sliding across the blood-stained dirt. The creature followed, pounding closer, and Jonmarc rolled, gritting his teeth at the pain, coming up in a crouch with his discarded manacles clenched in his hands.

"That's it, a little closer," he muttered, biding his time. He dodged as the golem closed, still more agile than the bulky monster, and swung one set of iron chains and cuffs with all his might.

The heavy shackles hit hard against one thick clay arm with a satisfying crunch. Cracks spread from the point of impact, and the next hit broke all the way through, shattering the creature's right arm.

Breathing hard, trying to focus against the pain, Jonmarc mustered his strength and put his back into the next swing, hitting the golem in the left knee. He eluded the grasping left hand, moving back and out of range, then skittering forward to get in the second blow. The thick leg crumpled, and the golem listed to the left, falling on its arm with enough weight and force to crush the clay.

With his remaining strength, Jonmarc brought both sets of shackles down hard on the golem's head, smashing the dried mud form like an empty pot.

Sweating, bleeding, and heaving with pain and exertion,

Jonmarc forced himself to straighten and square his shoulders. "So much for your pet monster."

Jonmarc did not drop the chains he held, wary of another attack, wondering whether the mage-healers meant to send another conjured creature after him. He doubted he could survive a second fight, not with a broken arm and a battered knee, but he made his stand out of sheer defiance.

"You did well."

Jonmarc looked up in surprise at the tallest healer, startled that he deigned to speak Common to him. "Did that prove something?"

"Any brawler can fight a man. This required cleverness."

"Glad you liked the show." Jonmarc knew his flippancy might earn repercussions, but tamping down the pain made controlling his tongue less urgent.

The healer gave an order in Nargi, and the guard came forward to put Jonmarc in chains again. For a moment they faced off against each other, tension thick in the air. Jonmarc held the shackles in a white-knuckled grip, torn between a futile fight and inevitable surrender. The guard's expression showed clearly that he understood Jonmarc's hesitation, read it for what it was and stood ready to correct it brutally if Jonmarc were foolhardy enough to attempt making a break.

And go where? I'm locked inside a stockade, injured, and inside the borders of an enemy kingdom. I'd be dead before I got farther than the doorway, either from the guards or the healers.

Jonmarc hurled the chains to the ground in frustration. Before the guard could take a step toward him, white-hot fire burned through Jonmarc's belly, sending him to his knees, and then to the dirt when his injured leg gave way. Lightning laced through his gut as if molten lead coated his insides. He writhed, no longer able to distinguish between his broken arm, busted knee, and savaged innards, consumed by agony.

"A warning, in case such thoughts occur to you again," the tall mage-healer remarked.

Jonmarc panted, felt sweat streak down his face as he twisted, but nothing eased the pain. His jaw strained with the effort not to cry out, and his right hand tightened into a fist, digging his nails into his palm hard enough to feel warm blood trickle down his wrist.

"Consider this a foretaste, should you continue to defy us." As quickly as it began, the pain vanished, leaving Jonmarc spent and barely conscious, chest heaving and heart thudding.

The guard snapped the shackles onto his wrists, and Jonmarc bit back a cry as the weight jostled his broken arm. Cuffs closed around his ankles, and the guard hauled him to his feet, dragging him upright although Jonmarc's bad leg could not hold his weight.

"Healing is your reward for besting the creature," the tall robed man said. "Be warned that rewards can be withdrawn for intemperate behavior."

The three mage-healers turned toward him then, speaking Nargi's guttural language in low tones. Jonmarc gasped as fire flowed through his body, knitting broken bones and torn tendons, easing his blinding headache and his aching shoulder. Within minutes he could flex his damaged elbow and knee without pain, and his wounded leg did not buckle when he put his weight on it. The bruises he'd taken also vanished, leaving him as he had been when he entered the ring.

"Rest and eat. Tomorrow there will be another challenge," the tall mage said. "We shall see if you survive it, or deserve our services." With that, he and his fellow healers swept out of the ring without a backward glance.

"Back to your cell," the guard said, jerking hard on Jonmarc's chains and drawing his attention away from the departing figures.

THE NEXT "CHALLENGE" was a match, as Jonmarc discovered when the guard led him to the ring. The General sat in his usual place in the center of the best row of seats. Around him were men Jonmarc now recognized as his officers. Behind them on rows of risers, stood enlisted men. More viewers crowded into the standing spaces, and a second, unfamiliar group of officers sat cross from the General and his party. *I did well enough for him to bring in guests. Bigger bets. More at stake—he can lose money and lose face.*

"You've earned a new challenge," the General announced when Jonmarc stood in front of him. One of the guards unlocked his manacles and hobbles, with a poke to the ribs to remind him of his place. "Since Kelter proved no challenge, and you bested the golem, some of my best fighters want to try their luck against you. Let's see if you can hold your own."

"You don't want them anymore?" Jonmarc asked, quirking an eyebrow. "You want them dead?"

The officers snickered, and the enlisted men jeered. The General, however, merely gave him a look that mixed bemusement and condescension. "If they can't hold their own, they don't deserve to live."

Jonmarc shrugged. Prisoners, soldiers, or monsters, all were the same to him. He resented fighting for the crowd's amusement, but facing down opponents who chose to fight him, who entered the ring freely did not bother his conscience at all, especially since he knew they would willingly put him down like a rabid dog if they had the chance.

"Then let's stop wasting time," Jonmarc replied, challenge clear in his voice. For a moment, he met the General's gaze and saw grudging respect.

His first attacker came at him running. The man looked nearly as solid as the golem; thick arms and stout legs, and a wide, muscular neck. Neither of them had weapons, but the soldier's scarred and flattened knuckles testified that it was not his first bare-handed fight.

Jonmarc dodged at the last minute, earning jeers from the gallery but sending the stocky soldier stumbling as he did not meet the resistance on which he counted. While the soldier struggled to regain his balance, Jonmarc moved behind him, landing a hard punch to the kidneys.

The soldier staggered, bellowing in pain, but he did not fall. He turned, fixing Jonmarc with a murderous gaze, and feinted left while his left fist swung, catching Jonmarc with its full momentum.

Jonmarc took the blow on his arm and felt it through his whole frame. He ignored the pain, assured himself nothing had broken and ducked another swing that might have caught him in the head. He could absorb anything but a head strike; that would put him down for good.

He dodged another strike, moving out of range, ignoring the insults of cowardice from the crowd. He did not evade out of fear. Every step, every bob and weave, let him get the measure of his attacker, assess his tactics and habits, look for weaknesses. He could not let the shouts from the gallery rattle him, not with the stakes of the game.

"Come on, fight!" the soldier taunted. "Prickless bastard."

"Heard the same about Nargi men," Jonmarc replied, the conversation just between the two of them, with the onlookers too loud and distant to overhear. "That's why your women roll over and spread for outlanders. Like whores."

He calculated correctly, watching rage enflame his attacker. The man's face grew red, and his eyes narrowed. "That how you got here? Your mama fuck an outlander? A whole regiment of outlanders, whore-spawn?"

The soldier gave an incoherent shout and ran right for Jonmarc, meaty hands outstretched and grasping. Jonmarc grabbed one wrist, ducked under, and popped both elbow and shoulder from their sockets. In the same movement, he brought a kick behind the man's knees, sending him to the dirt, and stomped with all his might on the tendon behind the heel. He had no knife to hamstring the man, but if his full weight and the sharpness of the blow wasn't enough to sever the tendon, it would certainly keep him from getting back up.

He ignored the obscenities coming from the crowd, the empty threats shouted by the man he pinned. Jonmarc went to the cold place inside himself the way his father taught him when they butchered. He felt nothing and time slowed. He looked up at the General defiantly and brought his boot down on the back of the man's neck hard enough that the snap of spine echoed.

"Is that the best you've got?"

Two men rushed him, one from each side. Jonmarc longed for his swords, but sparring with the War Dogs and in the Eastmark army gave him the skills he needed, abilities hard-won with blood and pain. He swung into a high Eastmark kick, landing the sole of his boot hard on the ribs of one attacker, sending the man back on his ass. He ducked the blow the second soldier swung, going low with a kick to the man's knee that broke bone, following it up with a kick with his full might to the groin.

The crowd howled in shared agony with the downed man who cupped his crotch and screamed.

One down who won't be back up. Time to finish this.

The first fighter was on his feet again. He loomed tall and raw-boned, not as squat and muscle-bound as the other two men Jonmarc had faced, but more dangerous with a longer reach and more range of motion unhampered by girth.

"I'll make you pay for that."

Jonmarc did not bother answering. The man rushed toward his right shoulder. Jonmarc pivoted left, getting more height with this kick, and put his full strength into a hit at the soldier's sternum.

The soldier staggered backward, fear and surprise clear on his face as his hands went to his chest, grasping as if to restart the heart shocked into stillness by the violence of the kick. He sank to his knees, blanching, then pitched forward.

Jonmarc barely spared him a glance. Two steps brought him to the downed man, who still twisted in pain on the dirt. He flipped the man by the hips before the opponent could try to snatch at him with those big hands, then grabbed the man's head and gave a savage twist, breaking his neck.

Jonmarc glared up at the General, disregarding the howls of rage and cries of promised retribution from the audience. In the deathly cold of his mind, only he and the general existed. His expression held both Jonmarc's contempt for the Nargi, who forced him to kill, and for himself, for murdering on command. Their gaze locked, and Jonmarc saw the look understood and acknowledged.

Three men came after him next, ready for blood.

For an instant, Jonmarc wondered whether the General meant for him to die today. He had put three opponents down already, and while he had dodged the worst of their blows, he ached from the strikes that had landed, and his body felt the violence of his own moves. He could not fight like this forever, and he thought perhaps the sport was to see him break, like the proverbial straw on the beast of burden's back, and maybe that had been the wager of the day.

He realized an instant later that he no longer cared. Live, fight, and kill. Die, and find release—unless the black-robed bastards brought him back.

On the other hand, taking down Nargi's army a few sons of bitches at a time wasn't a bad way to go.

Jonmarc ducked one punch, but another hit hard, doubling him over. He drove his elbow into the throat of one attacker who to tried to throw him to the ground, and as he straightened, he slammed his head back into the face of a second who came up behind him. He heard bone break and figured he had smashed the man's nose.

He swore as a kick struck him on the left thigh, then put his weight on his right leg and kicked back. Jonmarc's foot caught one man on the chin, snapping his head back and sending him down in a pile. Another attacker tried to grab Jonmarc's ankle, but he moved too quickly to be caught. The other two fighters closed on him.

Jonmarc had no idea how much of the previous fights the two men had seen, but their eyes promised slow and painful death. With his swords, this fight would have already been over. His hands itched for the familiar weapons.

A punch caught Jonmarc on the jaw and he staggered as bursts of light exploded before his eyes. He returned the punch, and he felt bone and teeth yield beneath his knuckles. A backward kick sent the second opponent reeling, since the man had not learned his lesson about coming up on Jonmarc from behind. On the next strike, Jonmarc angled his knuckles flat and drove them into the throat of the man who had just boxed his ears.

A strangled cry squeaked past the man's lips before he toppled, gasping for breath. Before Jonmarc could assure the kill, the last attacker tackled him and drove them both to the ground.

Jonmarc landed hard on his belly, slamming face-first into the dirt. The weight of the man on his back made it difficult for Jonmarc to breathe, and he scrabbled to find purchase against the hard-packed ground.

"Outland scum. Whore-son. Pig fucker." The soldier snarled epithets, each worse than the last, but Jonmarc ignored him. He twined his ankle around the man's leg and shoved, moving him just enough off center for Jonmarc to push up hard, twisting to grapple face-to-face.

They went back down again, blows striking from all directions, both of them using every move they could to rip free from the other. Fists, palms, and clawed fingers slammed, slapped, and dug. Jonmarc narrowly evaded losing an eye, and the man beneath him struggled free from a hold that almost tore loose an ear.

Jonmarc turned his head to protect his eyes and closed his teeth on the soldier's bicep, clamping down with all his might until he felt blood start under his teeth and flesh rip loose against his tongue. The cry of pain and the instantaneous distraction it bought gave Jonmarc the chance to bring up a knee, hard, into his opponent's gut.

The soldier raked his nails down Jonmarc's face, then went for his throat. Jonmarc twisted free, reaching for a grip on his opponent's neck.

Blood covered both men, streaming from gashes and deep scratches, flowing freely from the bite Jonmarc inflicted. Jonmarc's vision swam, and broken ribs made it hard to breathe, even without the constant shifting of their combined weight.

His opponent's long fingers forced themselves beneath Jonmarc's chin, digging deep into the soft flesh, trying to crush his windpipe. Jonmarc brought a fist up hard into the other man's mouth, splitting his lip and showering them both with blood, then grabbed hold of the thumb of the hand wrapped around his throat and twisted until it snapped.

Instead of pulling back, the heavy man pushed forward, snarling in pain and rage. Jonmarc got one leg out from under himself, angling to bring his boot down hard on his attacker's tail bone. That sent the attacker reaching up and back, enough that Jonmarc could flip them both backward, still tangled together. He landed on the soldier's stomach, sitting hard with his full weight, and as the reflex forced his opponent to buck for air, Jonmarc slammed forward with the heel of his hand, breaking the man's nose and driving the bone shards up into his brain.

The body pinned by his weight and the strength of his knees spasmed, blood flooding from the attacker's nose and mouth. The dying man's eyes widened, his mouth struggling for a final curse, and then he dropped flat and limp.

Jonmarc staggered to his feet, facing down a bloodthirsty crowd. Even those who won their bets hated him for vanquishing so many of their own and surviving. One outlander, bloodied but breathing, and six dead Nargi soldiers. Jonmarc bit back a cry of pain as he squared his shoulders, limping to stand before the general.

"The match is ended," the General said, standing. This time, the gaze that swept over Jonmarc felt cold and utterly unreadable.

3

DEATH MATCH

DREAMS AND FAILURE

JONMARC COLLAPSED ON THE WAY TO THE INFIRMARY, FADING in and out of consciousness as the guards half-carried, half-dragged him across the compound. A portion—perhaps most—of the camp wished for his blood for losing their bet or killings comrades. The remainder won their bets, perhaps not unhappy that he rid them of someone they disliked. He knew the soldiers who escorted him now served as much to protect him from the wrath of the rest of the regiment as to prevent him from escaping.

Whether his injuries forced him into unconsciousness or the healers used their magic to make him less of a danger as they repaired his injuries, Jonmarc did not know. When he woke, he found himself in an unfamiliar room.

"Where am I?" he called out to the guard, the one he had nicknamed Nose for his prominent snout, the soldier who spoke Common.

"The General liked your performance," Nose replied. "Must have decided to keep you. Moved you out of the jail, into the old champion's quarters. Left you some whiskey, too."

Jonmarc looked around his new cell. Thirty paces by thirty paces gave him much more room than he had ever had, save for in the home he shared with Shanna. Two high windows, both barred, provided light and air. An iron grid for a door reminded him that he remained a prisoner, but unlike in the jail, the front wall was otherwise solid. Jonmarc had no memory of what the building looked like from the outside, but from what he could see, a hallway outside the door might mean that the guards could withdraw for short periods and leave him a bit of privacy.

These quarters were better furnished. A camp bed replaced his bare cot, along with a wooden table and chair. Better bedding, even a pillow. And near the door, a stand to hold a basin of water. Jonmarc read in their provision the implied contract, that they had been supplied with the knowledge that Jonmarc would not attempt to use them as weapons, recognizing that Jonmarc understood he had nowhere to run.

"When's the next fight?"

Nose shrugged. "Few days, I imagine. It'll take a while for him to send a rider out to the next garrison and announce a time, set things up. You won quite a bit of money for anyone who bet on you. The odds were against it."

"Did you bet?"

Nose shook his head. "I wouldn't be allowed because I'm your guard. Even if I could, I wouldn't. Don't care for it."

"The betting or the fighting?" Jonmarc found himself sincerely curious.

"Got no problem with a fair fight, two men who have a score to settle. But the games aren't fair. They're either rigged for or against the champion, to stack the odds. And nobody has a reason to fight that's not part of the game. So… it's what's done, but not what I do."

Jonmarc gave the guard an appraising glance. He had not

expected that answer, hadn't thought one of the Nargi soldiers might disapprove of something that seemed so thoroughly ingrained in their army culture. "Huh," he replied. "That why the General made you my guard?"

Nose shrugged. "I don't know. Perhaps."

"There's a word the crowd yells a lot when I'm in the ring," Jonmarc said after a long pause, more to pass the time than anything. "What does it mean?"

Nose looked away. "They are calling for your death."

Jonmarc guessed as much, but the memory of all those voices chanting sent a chill through him. "Your language is difficult. But it looks like I'll be here for a while." *Until I die.* "Can you teach me?"

Nose looked at him for a moment without replying, as if the request surprised him. "If it is not prohibited."

Jonmarc raised an eyebrow. "No one is going to mistake me for Nargi, no matter how many words I learn." His brown eyes were not dark enough to match the darker eyes of the Nargi, nor would anyone mistake his lighter skin for the swarthier tones of his captors, even when the sun tanned him copper.

Nose nodded. "All right. But you may not like what you hear once you know what they're saying."

That night, like so many others, Jonmarc dreamed of Shanna. *The three hard years since her death faded into nothing, and he saw her in the kitchen of the home they had shared in the village that gave him refuge.*

She hummed as she stirred a pot on the stove, and Jonmarc came up behind her, brushing aside her long blonde hair to kiss her neck, sliding one hand from her hip around to the swell of her belly where their child grew.

"Stop that," she chided in a tone that suggested the opposite.

"Why should I?"

"Because look where it's gotten us," she laughed, putting her hand atop his to press against her abdomen as the baby inside shifted.

"I like where we are," he murmured against her ear. She smelled of the herbs and plants she and her mother harvested, both of them hedge witches and medicine women. In her hair, he caught the fragrance of sun and marigolds, rainwater and rose petals.

"So do I," she said quietly, curling her fingers tighter around his hand. "But mama will have something to say about it if I burn the stew, and I've no mind to go hungry tonight."

Jonmarc drew her hair back to lay a trail of light kisses from her ear down her jaw. "I think I'll still be hungry later."

She giggled and shifted her hips against him, pressing into his groin, fully aware of the effect she had on him. Seventeen and not married a year yet. "Promise?"

He woke suddenly, cold and alone, the scent of marigolds a distant memory. Shanna and the baby she carried lay in cold graves far away in a distant kingdom, slaughtered by the monsters that gave Jonmarc the scar down his jaw.

He blinked back tears and swallowed hard. Even without the dreams, Shanna's death felt like a fresh wound. Losing her and their child to the monsters set him on the shadowed path that led him here.

Had they lived, he would have gladly spent his life in the Margolan Borderlands, a blacksmith by trade as his father had been. Shanna's death sent him running to Linton's caravan to flee from his past and from the red-robed mage whose promise of gold had sent him into the caves for a piece of grave jewelry. From the caravan, he kept on running, to Principality and the War Dog mercenaries, to Eastmark and a plum assignment gone terribly wrong, and then fleeing for his life, lost in the Nargi forest.

It won't be too much longer, Shanna. I'll be joining both of you. Soon, but not soon enough.

WEEKS PASSED IN a blur of fights and healing. In between, Jonmarc slept or lost himself as much as possible in the whiskey the General sent for a match well fought. He proved an apt pupil, learning the Nargi language faster than either he or Nose expected, though he doubted he would ever fully lose his Margolan accent. He even learned Nose's real name, though he never thought of him as anything except "Nose."

"Get up. We're leaving." Nose and a second guard came to the door of Jonmarc's cell. Nose held the wrist shackles, while the second guard held a sword and the ankle hobbles. The collar around his neck shifted, rubbing along the edge where the rough metal had already begun to scar the tender skin beneath. Not that anyone would see. The collar would remain so long as Jonmarc lived.

"Where?" Jonmarc asked, realizing belatedly he had processed both the question and his answer in Nargi without realizing it.

"The General wants to show you off. We're taking you to the next camp for a fight."

One guard held the sword while the other fastened the cuffs and chains. Jonmarc did not fight them, but he noted that the new guard did not lock the ankle chains quite right. He moved carefully as they led him to the wagon, cautious not to accidentally make the cuffs lock tight. *If I get the chance, maybe I can run. If they catch me, maybe they'll kill me, it would be a mercy. If they don't, we might be close enough for me to make it back to Dhasson. They won't dare follow me across the border.*

To Jonmarc's surprise, Nose did not get into the wagon with him. An unfamiliar guard, a young soldier Jonmarc had never seen before, climbed in to watch over him as they traveled. One guard rode up front to drive the horse team. *They must be sure of me to only send two guards. It's the best odds I've had since the bastards took me.*

"How far away is the camp?" Jonmarc asked, managing the question in Nargi.

"A candlemark," the guard replied in a bored voice. He watched the dark forest go by as the wagon rolled on, sparing little attention to his prisoner. Rain fell, turning the dirt road slippery and soaking Jonmarc to the skin. Clouds hid the moon and stars, and aside from the driver's shuttered lantern, the darkness was absolute.

The wagon jerked abruptly, throwing Jonmarc forward onto his bound hands. The driver cursed, growing louder as he climbed down to inspect a rear wheel gone into a hole in the road. While Jonmarc's grasp of the Nargi language remained elusive, curses and vulgarities had been among the first phrases he had learned.

"Get down here and help—the wheel's damaged." The driver stood up long enough to order the guard out to help. "And move his heavy ass out of the back. It'll be hard enough to fix the wheel without lifting his weight too."

The two guards argued for a moment, and then the second man yanked Jonmarc down from the wagon and sat him against a tree at the roadway's edge. He brandished his blade in warning. "Move and you'll be sorry," the guard threatened. "Don't get any ideas."

Jonmarc sat down without an argument, already determined to make a break or die trying. He maneuvered his ankles until he could reach the cuffs with his hands, and carefully worked the mechanism until the lock opened and he eased the chains to the ground.

The guards struggled with what appeared to be a cracked axle, and their argument pulled their attention completely away from Jonmarc. He waited until their backs were turned and then darted into the forest. Moments later he heard the guards' shouts, but he had already covered plenty of ground by then.

Jonmarc stumbled and staggered over the terrain, running blind in the dark forest. His bound hands were little use for him to keep his balance, barely able to deflect the branches and brambles that tore at his clothing and slapped into his face. He had no idea of direction without the stars to guide him, and for all he knew, he might step off a cliff or fall into a ravine at any moment.

Better than where I've been. Dead would be better.

He expected the guards to give chase, yet he could not hear footfalls behind him. *Are they afraid of the dark? Did I run off into a sacred forest?*

A shape moved on the path in front of him, and suddenly the darkness blazed with light. Jonmarc had only an instant to glimpse the tall black-robed healer from the Nargi camp before the light struck him, burning through his veins like fire, dropping him to the ground in agony.

Or maybe it's a trap.

The Nargi mage-healer said nothing, and that made the punishment even worse. Jonmarc had no chance to fight this kind of opponent, no magic of his own to counter the whipcords of light that struck again and again, driving out his breath and making his heart stutter in his chest. His head throbbed as if it would burst, and his skin felt charred as if the mage meant to burn it from his bones. Jonmarc writhed on the wet loam, his back arching, and screams tore from his throat until he tasted blood in his mouth. Convulsions seized him hard enough he thought bones might break or sinews snap from the stress. The white light held him, refused to release him to unconsciousness or death, pinning him in an endless loop of pain.

Finally, the light dimmed, and the fire receded. Jonmarc lay trembling in a puddle of his own vomit and piss, blood thundering in his ears, every muscle aching as if he had been ridden down.

Dimly, he realized the two guards stood a few feet away, watching silently. "Take him back to the wagon," the mage-healer commanded. "Return him to his quarters. The General will have a word with him."

Jonmarc lost consciousness as the guards hefted him between them and hauled him back through the forest, drifting in and out of awareness until they threw him into the wagon, blacking him out again. The ride back in the rain seemed to hit every rut and rock, banging him against the rough wood.

He fell when they pulled him to his feet by the chains on his wrists and retched into the mud. "Get walking," one of the guards ordered, hauling him up and shoving him forward. When he fell again and could not rise, the guards swore as they dragged him to his cell and shoved him in.

Echoes of the white fire pain shuddered through him as he lay on his back, gasping and twitching. Soaked to the skin, shivering with cold, Jonmarc heard footsteps heading toward him.

"Did you really think we were that stupid?" Anger and condescension mingled in the General's voice as the man stood at the cell door and regarded Jonmarc on the floor.

"There was no match. Just a chance for you to show how little you've learned."

"It was… worth a shot."

"Did you think you could run? Where you could hide?"

Jonmarc's voice was a painful rasp. "Didn't matter. I wouldn't be here."

"This is the only warning you will receive. You've gotten mercy only because you are an impressive fighter, but I will not countenance defiance. You've received no permanent damage. Your injuries will heal unassisted. Attempt to run again, refuse to fight, and I will give you to the troops as their quintain, with a mage standing by to keep you from dying. I will not be cheated of my champion."

Jonmarc closed his eyes and lay back in the cold puddle that dripped from his sodden clothing. *I've failed at everything. Failed to save my family. Drew the danger to the next village, and couldn't save them either. Brought the beasts down on us that killed Shanna and the baby. Made a mess of being a merc. Can't even escape right. Good for nothing except the ring, like a baited bear. I was a hired killer before—that's what a merc really is—but there was always a purpose. Now, killing for their entertainment, means I'm just a different kind of whore.*

He closed his eyes, praying for death, and knew that escape would be denied to him, too.

The next time in the ring, I'll fight just enough to make it look good, but I'll go down. I'll let him win. Make the crowd happy, and win my freedom.

No MATTER HOW much the General might have wanted to punish Jonmarc for his escape attempt, he needed his champion in fighting shape to win bets. After two days of agony, the pain finally subsided enough for Jonmarc to eat without throwing up and sleep undisturbed. Two more days found the last of the effects gone, and Jonmarc none the worse physically, though the memories of the mage-healer's torture would remain forever.

"Time for your match." Nose came to the cell door but did not look directly at him. Whatever slim accord they might have forged before Jonmarc's attempted escape had soured. *I'm a liability,* he thought. *If I try to escape again and he's been easy on me, they'll think he's complicit. He'll die with me. Can't blame him for watching his back.*

"So who's the sucker this time?" Jonmarc asked, making no attempt to hide his bitterness.

"A brigand. Caught him on the road waylaying travelers. It's a service to put him down."

"So the betting and cheering is just part of providing that 'service'?" Despite the language barrier, Jonmarc knew from the way Nose winced his comment landed as he intended.

"Things are what they are. Take what you can from it," Nose replied.

Jonmarc made no reply. Nose had been relatively kind to him; he could do worse for a guard. While he did not mistake that for any sort of friendship, he knew that a malicious guard would make things even worse. *And if this goes the way I'm planning, I won't be around to care.*

The night's audience shouted even more loudly than usual, and whether they knew about his ill-fated escape attempt or merely hungered for a blood fight, Jonmarc did not know. As he scanned the gallery, more soldiers seemed to be pressed in to the bleachers and standing space, their faces contorted as they yelled and cursed. The General sat in the center, watching Jonmarc closely, his face shuttered.

Jonmarc kept his expression carefully neutral and avoided making eye contact as if his plan might be guessed if the General looked too closely. He knew he would have to fight convincingly at the start, then make a few calculated mistakes, and if he did it right, neither his opponent nor the audience would be the wiser.

I'll make at least half of them happy by dying. Let them win their bets. Now that Nose had translated the shouted jeers, Jonmarc heard them calling for his blood. Usually, that raised his hackles and defiance fueled his anger. Tonight, he just felt cold and ready for it all to end.

The audience roared, and Jonmarc saw his opponent led in from the other side. The man stood a few inches shorter, but he looked strong, all wiry muscle. Old scars told a tale of life hard-lived, marring the man's hands, arms, and face. One eye did not open fully thanks to puckered skin at the corner, an injury that nearly cost the brigand his sight. No one could mistake the cold reckoning in the highwayman's eyes. Jonmarc felt his lips twitch in anticipation. He had picked the right killer to take him out.

"Begin."

Jonmarc and the brigand circled each other, looking for weakness. From the way the other man moved, Jonmarc mentally cataloged likely injuries, places to strike that would aggravate them. He bet the thief was good with a knife; maybe not as confident hand-to-hand.

The highwayman struck first, with a roundhouse punch Jonmarc saw coming and ducked easily, following up with a jab of his own that sent the man stumbling backward. The next strike came faster than Jonmarc expected, a blow from the left that caught him on the jaw. Blood started from his split lip and his vision blurred for an instant, but instinct served him, and his arm blocked a follow-up punch.

Jonmarc reminded himself of his intention, and let the next punch through his defense, taking it in the gut. The crowd screamed for blood, and the brigand gave a cold smile.

Jonmarc exaggerated his stumble, leaving himself open intentionally. A good fighter would seize the opportunity and go for the throat, landing the killing blow. Instead, the brigand circled behind and got in a blow to the kidneys. Jonmarc glimpsed the look on the man's face and realized he had misread his opponent.

The brigand didn't want to kill him. He enjoyed causing pain. Any resolution would be drawn-out and torturous.

To the Crone with that. I'll just have to die another day. Anger rushed through Jonmarc, and he straightened, coming back to the fight with a grim determination that seemed to register with the brigand, whose bravado slipped a bit after a look at Jonmarc's face. Jonmarc felt nothing but cold purpose as self-preservation won out over self-loathing, dismissing all thoughts of suicide.

Jonmarc's first punch got through the man's block easily, landing hard on his cheek and snapping the thief's head to one side. He swept his foot, catching the man behind the knees before he had regained his balance from the first punch, sending him to the ground in a heap. He did not begrudge his opponents their skill nor did he discount the strength of the need for self-defense. Yet the brigand's casual cruelty sent a deadly fury through Jonmarc. Much as he wanted to end his own life, he'd be damned if he'd go out suffering for the amusement of a sick son of a bitch.

His boot came down hard on the brigand's throat, and maybe it was his imagination, but the snap of the man's spine echoed in the huge tent, silencing the crowd for a heartbeat before the roar surged back louder than before. Cheers and taunts greeted him, as bets changed hands. The General gave him a measured look, and Jonmarc wondered if he had known all along what Jonmarc intended to do.

That's twice now, I can't even die right.

A bottle of whiskey waited for him in his cell. Not enough to kill him even when he drank it all. He knew that before he lifted the bottle to his lips, reminded himself as the rough liquor burned down his throat, but he never forgot why he sought oblivion, even when the room spun, and he sank to the floor. He finished the last swallow and felt rage return. So much anger, always just beneath the surface. At the raiders who killed his family, the beasts that killed his wife, the red-robed mage that sent the creatures, at the Eastmark general who betrayed his trust and the Nargi general who used him for profit. But always, mostly, anger at himself for failing.

The bottle shattered when it hit the wall, bringing an alarmed glance from Nose before the guard's disgust registered at Jonmarc's drunkenness.

"You know how hard that is to come by in Nargi? It's a waste when you guzzle like that."

Jonmarc made an obscene gesture and did not bother to answer, not that he was likely to get anything coherent past numb lips and a tongue that felt thick and leaden. *Not wasting it if I can't feel anymore. Can't think. Can't remember. Damn. Don't think there's enough alcohol in Nargi for that.*

The next thing Jonmarc knew, he heard voices quiet in the corridor outside his cell. He opened his eyes a crack and slammed them shut again against the light. Whether he had slept or passed out, he did not know and was not sure the difference mattered.

"So you're the General's great champion?" a voice mocked. Jonmarc fought vertigo to move just enough to glimpse the newcomer. Dorran, the General's second-in-command. He had seen the man before through the window of his cell, and even at a distance, Jonmarc pegged him for a ruthless martinet.

"Didn't think you were anything special," Dorran continued. "I've seen better brawls."

"General left orders for him to have space to recover, sir," Nose blurted, attempting to get Dorran to leave.

"Mind your task," Dorran snapped. "I go where I please. And it pleases me to get a look at the man who cost me my bet." He clucked his tongue. "I was counting on seeing you die. Rather thought I'd win, before you changed your mind." His tone turned as ugly as his words.

"Aren't you needed on the practice ground?" The General's voice cut off anything else Dorran might have said. For just an instant, before he schooled his features, Jonmarc saw anger and cunning in the man's face.

"On my way, General," Dorran said smoothly. "Just stopping by to congratulate the champion."

"Leave the champion to me. I'll be out to review the troops in a few minutes. Have them ready."

"Yes, sir." Dorran's footsteps receded, and Nose stepped closer.

"Keep an eye on him." The General's brusque voice had a hint of something that almost sounded like concern. Jonmarc couldn't be completely sure who Nose was to watch—Dorran or him. He had an odd feeling the answer might be both, for very different reasons.

"Beggin' your pardon sir, but he ain't goin' anywhere like that, 'cept to puke," Nose replied. "He'll be a sorry bastard when he comes around. Whiskey gets its revenge, if you know what I mean, sir."

A chuckle from the General suggested that he did indeed. "Don't let him choke on his vomit," he warned. "The healers said he took slight damage, but if something looks wrong, call for them. Haven't gone to this much trouble to lose him to a slow bleed."

"Spent the night calling for a woman," Nose volunteered. "Shanna. And a few other names I couldn't make out. He's a noisy drunk, and a miserable one, sir."

The General grunted in response. "I imagine he comes by that rage of his hard-earned. He did well tonight."

"The better he does out there, the worse it is back here, if you know what I mean, sir."

"Perhaps I've figured him wrong," the General mused. "I will reconsider."

4

DEATH MATCH

HOSTAGE

By the time six months passed since his capture, Jonmarc had bested the champions of the nearby regiments, and the General began to arrange fights for larger audiences. He never knew how much the winnings totaled when he beat his opponents, only that after big matches, the General sent more than one bottle, as if he understood how badly Jonmarc needed to lose himself and forget.

The morning after his biggest match thus far, Jonmarc roused slowly, aching everywhere. It took him a moment to remember why, and then a rush of memories filled in the gaps —except for when he had been unconscious or too concussed to remember. *Must have gotten worked over bad, if I still hurt. Healers don't usually leave the damage unless they're too spent to bother after they've fixed the big stuff.*

He lay still, focused on what hurt. His ribs felt bruised, though he assumed they had been broken before the healing. Stiffness in one shoulder made him suspect a newly healed break or at least a repaired dislocation. Muscles throughout his body ached, warning him that the healers had not bothered with bruising this time. The fact that he was breathing provided proof he had won, though his body told him otherwise.

"I didn't think you would ever wake up."

The stranger's voice, quiet and feminine, sounded from close by. Too close. Jonmarc startled, coming up in a fighting stance despite stiff muscles, fists clenched.

He found himself facing a thin, dark-haired woman dressed in a satin gown, one which accentuated her figure and displayed far more bosom and leg than propriety allowed. "Relax," she urged, but the smile she gave him did not soften the wariness in her eyes.

"Who are you?"

She gave a languid stretch, in case he had not fully noticed her attractiveness before. The movement seemed practiced, calculated. "I'm Thaine."

"What are you doing in my quarters?" Jonmarc looked around, trying to assure himself everything else remained as it should. Two unopened bottles of whiskey sat on a stand next to the bed, which told him he had been unconscious when the guards returned him to his cell. A tray of cold sausage, meat, and bread sat next to the whiskey, untouched.

"Your last fight must have impressed the General," Thaine replied. "I'm part of your pay."

"A whore?"

Thaine shrugged. "Says the man who kills people for his masters."

Jonmarc ignored the flash of anger her words provoked. "Is that any way to make a good impression?"

"Does it matter?" She met his gaze, an unspoken challenge between them. Beneath the defiance, Jonmarc read resignation, as if Thaine already expected how this would play out. That he would take his winnings as his due, whether that included the whiskey or her body, and "good impressions" had nothing to do with it.

"Seems a bit of a waste, with me passed out and all," he said, feeling a flush rise on his neck.

"Not all my skills are in bed," Thaine replied with an edge that made Jonmarc give her a second appraisal. He saw intelligence and bitterness in her eyes and wondered how she came to be a prisoner like himself. And despite the challenge in her tone, he saw fear in the way she held herself, braced for an inevitable violation. "I can nurse the sick. Cook, too."

"Not much need for cooking," Jonmarc said, suddenly aware that the guards had put him in his bed wearing only a thin pair of trews. "Guards shove food through the door a couple of times a day. As for needing a nurse, most of the time they patch me up pretty well. Guess I just needed more this time." He moved and winced as the bruises reminded him.

"You play *tarle*? I'm good at it," she said, naming a popular card game. "Dice, too."

"I can play. Not sure how well." That was a lie. He had routinely won a decent amount of money playing cards when he was a merc, even more betting on dice. Her eyes said she read the falsehood for what it was.

Jonmarc realized that he needed to relieve himself, and the cell provided only a chamber pot. The lack of privacy had not bothered him before, since the guards paid him no attention. Thaine's presence made him suddenly uncomfortable, though he suspected she had seen much worse.

"Turn your back."

"What?"

"Go to the door and turn your back." Jonmarc's gaze flickered to the chamber pot.

Thaine laughed. "You're kidding." His glare gradually

dissuaded her. "You're going to be shy about taking a piss in front of the whore you've been given to—"

"Just shut up and turn around."

Thaine stood and walked the few paces to the door, shaking her head in amazement, then turned her back. Jonmarc did his best to forget she was in the room and came back to sit on the side of the bed. "Finished."

Thaine chuckled as she walked toward him, hips swaying and gaze suggestive. "I can take your mind off those bruises," she offered, eyeing the dark blotches on his shoulders and chest where the last fight had left its mark.

"I'm sure you could. But no thanks."

Thaine stopped, raising an eyebrow. "You don't like what you see?"

Jonmarc felt his cheeks grow warm and turned away. "It's not like that."

"I'm not your type?"

Jonmarc gave a rueful chuckle. "No, that's not—"

"You don't like girls."

Jonmarc glared at her. "I like girls just fine. But I want my wife."

Thaine did not hide her surprise. "You're a prisoner, a long way from… wherever you're from. Pretty sure you're not going home again."

Jonmarc gave a bitter laugh. "Pretty sure you're right. And it wouldn't matter anyhow. She's dead."

Thaine paused, dropping the seductive swagger. "I'm… sorry. How long?"

"Three years."

That got her attention. "I'd guess the days of mourning are over, no matter how people do things where you come from. You telling me you haven't—"

"Don't want to talk about it."

Her eyes narrowed. "You aren't joking." Once again, she looked him up and down, evaluating, and he tried not to flinch under her gaze. "You look healthy to me. Unless one of those fights got you in the jewels—"

"Not the reason," he growled, looking away.

"So what's the problem? You take a vow to the Goddess or something? You're sure not a priest." Her smile turned predatory. "If it's just a matter of being out of practice—"

"This is a mistake," Jonmarc said, standing abruptly and pacing to the window. "You're not the first one to try to get me tumbled since she died." His friend Harrtuck had made repeated efforts until he finally realized Jonmarc was serious about not being ready to move on. He was certain the War Dogs placed bets on when he'd finally relent. He did not try to explain that the brief respite of a trollop's favor would do little to ease the ache inside, and he did not relish having to return to a cold bed alone after sharing the warmth of another, however briefly.

"I'll ask the General to send you back," he said, turning toward the door, intending to call for a guard. "You're very pretty. Not your fault." *I'm just broken.*

"Don't!" Her warning came out more sharply than she must have intended, given that the shock on her face mirrored his own. An instant later, her features schooled themselves into a mask that hid the fear he'd glimpsed. "Please," she said quietly. "Don't call the guard. We can work this out."

The bottom dropped out of Jonmarc's stomach. "Did he make a bet? Was there a wager on how long it would take for me to bed you? Maybe on how we'd do it?" His anger came through clearly in his voice.

Thaine took a step back, raising a hand in appeasement. "No. At least, not that I know about. I don't think so. It's…

customary… to gift a champion a companion for a fight well fought."

"And I'm lousy company, so why would you want to stay any longer than necessary?"

Thaine swallowed and looked away. "Because my survival requires that I please you. The man who brought me here made it very clear that if I failed, there was a barracks full of soldiers happy to have your leavings."

All whores were liars, to themselves and to their customers, but while Jonmarc did not doubt Thaine's capability for embellishment, he did not doubt the fear in her eyes. And while he had never cared for the idea of paying for a strumpet's attention, he knew Thaine was as much a prisoner in this matter as he.

"I'm not going to change my mind," Jonmarc warned.

Thaine managed a smirk that did not reach her eyes. "Less work for me if you don't. Though you're not hard on the eyes, battle scars or no."

Jonmarc fought a flinch at that. The last years had not been kind. Blades, claws, teeth, and talons from scores of fights left their marks on his arms, shoulders, back, and chest. Each one reminded him of how far he had come, how much he had lost. He had given no thought to what a woman might think of them.

"I'll probably need a nurse, on and off," he said, striving for indifference, as he were hiring a healer in the marketplace. "I come back in rough shape more often than not."

"I know how to make poultices and elixirs," Thaine replied. "And I'm very good at rubbing the knots out of sore muscles," she added. "That sort of thing might come in handy."

"I see you've met her." The General's voice made both Jonmarc and Thaine stiffen.

"We've met." Jonmarc's voice held no warmth, just shy of insolence. Every interaction with the General was a verbal sparring match.

"Pretty little thing," the General observed. Thaine's eyes narrowed, and while she did not flinch, Jonmarc saw the control it took to hide her reaction. "You've earned some companionship. The guards say you don't sleep well if you're not drunk on your ass. Perhaps she can help with that." He raised an eyebrow, his meaning clear.

"What's the catch?"

The General made a dismissive gesture. "Keep winning, keep your rewards. Behave badly, and you lose privileges." The threat could not have been clearer.

"Understood."

The General turned and walked away without another word. Nose followed him out and returned after a few moments. "There are extra pillows and blankets in the corner since it's two of you now," he said. "Got another dress or two for the lady," he added, blushing slightly. "Don't worry about me," he added. "I've got no mind to see things I don't have to."

Jonmarc cleared his throat. "Thank you."

Nose gave him a wry smile. "You know, I can almost understand you when you talk now. Good job."

Jonmarc no longer even thought about the fact that most of their conversations took place in Nargi. Apparently, his accent had improved.

Nose walked away to the outer room where the guards sat. Jonmarc turned back to Thaine. "Go ahead and put out the cards," he replied, grabbing one of the bottles of whiskey by the neck. He opened it and took a pull. "Got nothin' else to do."

Fights blurred, one much like the other except for the

scars. The healers liked to leave scars. Jonmarc suspected they could mend his skin unmarked if they wanted to do so. Perhaps they wanted to remind him of the power they held over him, to heal or kill, relieve pain or cause it. Or maybe they thought he valued the marks as trophies. Mostly they served as a rough calendar, a visual map to the passage of time. He'd had more than his share before being captured. The games had provided many more, despite his record of wins.

When he didn't have a fight, the time passed agreeably with Thaine, either playing cards or, after half a bottle of whiskey, telling stories. After fights, nights could unfold in two different ways. If Jonmarc nearly died, he stayed with the healers until his wounds were no longer life-threatening. He usually returned in a foul mood, eager to drink away memories until he passed out. Thaine had learned to give him space, keeping her distance except to pass him a bucket when he retched or pull a blanket over him when he succeeded in losing consciousness.

Fights that didn't almost kill him were worse. Those ended with him returning bruised and aching, and sitting sullenly while Thaine smoothed poultices over his injuries and rubbed the stiffness from seized muscles, Jonmarc drinking slowly and steadily to numb the pain and forget the faces of the men he had killed for sport.

Thaine seemed to know this fight had gone particularly badly when Nose and another guard half-dragged, half-carried Jonmarc to their quarters. "What happened?" she asked.

"Nothin'," Jonmarc slurred, finding that his vision wobbled when he tried to meet her gaze.

"Bad fight," Nose replied. Jonmarc tried to get his feet under him, but his boots scrabbled and shuffled on the stone floor, legs unsteady. Nose and the other guard hauled him into the room and dropped him on the bed.

"Healers didn't patch him?" she asked, and Jonmarc thought he heard censure in her voice, though he could not tell whether she directed it at him or at the mage-healers.

"Wouldn't, more like it," Nose muttered. "Colonel Dorran set up this match. Gave him a prisoner who wasn't a fighter."

Sprawled across the bed, Jonmarc muttered curses as he drifted in and out of awareness.

"He tried to refuse," Nose continued. "There wasn't any question about being a fair fight. And the General, he couldn't stop the fight after everyone had come. Don't think he knew what Dorran meant to do, but it was too late by then. So when he wouldn't fight, the General had the healers put a rage spell on him."

"Sweet Chenne," Thaine murmured. "And then?"

Nose sounded disgusted. "The mages are good at what they do. He fought like a man possessed. They both did." He swallowed hard. "Wasn't much left of the guy when the mages lifted the spell. He'd been dead for a while, and Vahanian kept swinging."

"Goddess." Thaine sounded sick. "What about Jonmarc's injuries? It looks like he took some hits."

"The rage spell worked on both men. It was.... bad."

Jonmarc lay on his back, eyes closed, partly to cope with the pain, mostly because he did not want to see their faces. Now that the spell no longer controlled him, shame filled him, twisting his stomach more than usual. He did not have to see to know that the prisoner's blood coated his hands and arms, splattered across his shirt and face, matted in his hair. He remembered flashes of the fight... enough to know it had been bare-knuckled murder. Even under the influence of the spell, the prisoner had no skill at fighting. He had been a trader who wandered into forbidden territory, and Jonmarc wondered whether Dorran had seized the man just to make sport at Jonmarc's expense.

"The General isn't worried about his favorite fighter being damaged?" Thaine challenged, anger cold in her voice.

"The mages made sure there was no serious damage," Nose replied. "Nothing broken. But he's still hurt pretty bad. Some of that blood is his. The prisoner fought like *ashtenerath*, like a madman."

Jonmarc flinched at the thought. He had seen *ashtenerath* a few times as a merc. They were men made into monsters, prisoners of war beaten and broken, dosed with drugs and dark magic until nothing of themselves remained, nothing except rage. They fought like *dimmons*, like rabid dogs, too badly damaged to fix. Killing them was mercy.

"Whiskey." Jonmarc's voice sounded like gravel; split lips slurred his speech.

"I'll need more fixings for poultices than usual," Thaine said to Nose. "Hot water and clean cloths." She rattled off a list of items for elixir and the poultice rub.

"I'll get them," Nose promised. "And the General said there'd be more whiskey than usual."

"Do you think Dorran arranged it the way he did for spite?" Thaine asked, dropping her voice.

"Maybe. He's a sly one," Nose replied. Since the new second-in-command had come to camp, enough tension had built that even Jonmarc and Thaine saw the changes. Nose said little, fearing reprisal if overheard, but what mild validation he could provide suggested that the friction they sensed between the General and Dorran was not imagined.

"Whiskey!" Jonmarc's body ached, and he knew he would be bruised from head to toe. Maddened by magic or just lucky, the prisoner's blows had come so fast and hard

Jonmarc could not deflect them all. He knew one eye would be swollen shut by morning, and he could taste blood in his mouth. His shirt stuck to him, wet with blood from gashes scored with the prisoner's fingernails and gouges torn with teeth. Desperate kicks bruised Jonmarc's ribs, and he was certain that his throat would show the bruises, just above his slave collar, where the panicked man had nearly throttled him.

"You drank all we had," Thaine reminded him. "You'll have to wait for more."

Jonmarc remembered the fight in flashes, as if he had been a mere spectator. He felt the memory of his punches in the aching bones of his hands and wrists, the strained muscles of his forearms and shoulders. He could hear the sound of bones breaking beneath his grip, of wheezing breath and a pained howl more like a wounded animal than a dying man. Yet none of those sounds had made him stop pounding away, each blow with his full strength, astride a body that soon fell still and silent. The crowd shouted louder than ever, hollering and cheering, reveling in blood.

When the rage bled out of him, Jonmarc had remained where he was, straddling the prisoner's corpse, fists blood-soaked and aching. It took minutes for him to regain the presence of mind to climb to his feet and stagger to review before the General. Dorran sat next to his commander, smug with victory, pleased at the carnage. The General's expression, dour as always, gave Jonmarc to think he did not share his second's pleasure.

Jonmarc heard the cell door clang shut and Nose's footsteps recede. Thaine sank down next to the bed and reached for him. He shrugged away. "Don't."

"You're hurt. You need tending to."

Jonmarc turned his head. "Deserve the pain."

Thaine shuffled close enough for her shoulder to nudge his. "You didn't have a choice. You tried to refuse."

"Could have let him kill me." The truth of it sat, naked and cold, between them.

"I've heard them talk about your fights, Jonmarc," Thaine said quietly. "You're a warrior. It's not in you to lay down and die."

"Wasn't a fight," he managed, his swollen throat forcing his voice to a whisper. "Was murder."

"It had to be you or him," Thaine replied. "And I'm glad you made it out." Her fingers brushed his arm. "Not your fault. I know something of what it is to be forced."

"Whiskey," Jonmarc said, quieter this time. His injuries throbbed, but the memories hurt worse, and he wanted to be numb.

"Soon," Thaine soothed. "Soon."

Before long, footsteps and the clank of the door signaled Nose's return. "Do you need help?" he asked Thaine.

"I can't get him out of his clothes myself, not when he's like this," Thaine replied. "You lift him; I'll strip off what's left."

Jonmarc groaned as Nose pulled him up to a sitting position and held him in place while Thaine dragged the rags of his shirt off over his shoulders. Dried blood stuck to scabbing wounds, and sore muscles protested movement. Nose eased Jonmarc's torso back onto the bed and helped Thaine manhandle him out of his trews.

"Not much left of his clothing," Thaine said when they were finished. "It's too far gone to mend or wash."

"There's new in his trunk. And I brought whiskey with the fixings you wanted. I'd best get back to my post."

"Some of these gashes are deep. They might go sour. Will the healers tend him if that happens?"

"The General is taking the regiment out to battle in the morning," Nose replied. "The mage-healers will go with him. Don't know when they'll be back."

"Well then. We'll have to do what we can."

Nose left them alone. Thaine poured whiskey and helped Jonmarc sit enough to sip, holding him in place until the cup was empty. "I'm going to need some of this to clean the wounds," she warned. "The healers must not have needed to earn their pay tonight."

"Don't bother."

Thaine gave a derisive snort. "Are you trying to die? Don't answer that. There's dirt in the wounds and bits of shirt. And those bites are already looking swollen. Now lie still and let me work."

Under other circumstances, Jonmarc might have given her a sidelong glance or a smirk at the innuendo, but not tonight. He clenched his fists in the rough sheets as she daubed at the wounds, first with clean water, then with whiskey. He sucked in harsh breaths as the alcohol burned at the raw flesh. Without needing to be asked, she gave him a second cupful, and he knocked it back, as much to dull the physical pain as the memories. Through it all, Thaine kept up a running patter, talking about everything and nothing, trying to distract both of them from the task at hand.

"Sorry," Thaine murmured as Jonmarc's body arched off the bed when she dribbled whiskey over the deepest gashes. His lips pressed together in a hard line, hands white-knuckled grasping at the covers, but he did not cry out. "It's deep. I'll need to stitch it up."

Jonmarc gritted his teeth as she drew the thread through his skin. "You're lucky my mam taught me to sew," she said, managing a wan smile. "I'll put a neat hem in you."

They worked through the first bottle of whiskey like that,

alternating cups and doctoring. After the burn of the whiskey on his torn skin, the poultices soothed, a sharp-smelling paste made from common plants. While the water stayed hot, Thaine made a healing tea, fortified with the fixings Nose brought.

"Whiskey."

"Tea first," Thaine replied, and after a glower, Jonmarc gave in, slowly sipping the brew. She let him lie down again when the cup was empty and began to bind up the worst of the injuries using strips of cloth from his ruined shirt.

"I don't like the look of that bite," she murmured, more to herself than to him. "Gotta keep it clean. Damn healers."

Pain and whiskey settled deep in Jonmarc's bones. The slightest shift of his body hurt, as did the rise and fall of his chest. "More."

Thaine opened the second bottle, and this time she poured a cup for each of them. "That's all for now," she warned. "Don't want to save you from blood loss and have you poison yourself on cheap liquor."

Jonmarc thought to make a reply, but exhaustion and drink finally let him sink into darkness.

Flames. Screams. The men of his village and his father, dead in the street from raiders' swords, the town engulfed in flames. Blood on the steel of his blade, and a curse to lose all he loved to the fire.

The scene shifted to another village, another fire. Shadow figures, monsters all, hunted in the alleys. Bodies all around. Shanna in a pool of blood clutching a misborn baby.

The thud of the gallows, the sway of hanged men's corpses, the hiss of a branding iron against his skin. Smoke and a burning barn, the stench of roasting meat, human corpses, children screaming and women wailing, then terrible silence.

He saw Shanna standing just beyond his reach, blonde and unmarred by tragedy, looking as she had when they first met. "Jonmarc." Her voice sounded clear and sweet, not choked by smoke or pain. "I miss you."

He blinked, and she held a baby bundled in her arms. Their child, the one who died before he could be born, cut from his dying mother's belly by a monster's sharp claws. "We're waiting for you. Come home."

He struggled to answer, but his voice refused to work, choked by smoke and tears, swollen from near-strangulation, rough with whiskey. "Shanna," he managed to croak, barely audible.

"Not far. Come home."

He reached out to her, almost close enough to touch, still just beyond his fingertips. "Shanna."

"Jonmarc." The voice sounded closer, clearer. He tried to reply and managed a groan.

"Jonmarc?" Uncertain this time, slightly afraid.

"Sorry," he slurred. "So sorry. Shouldn't have… gone to the caves. Damned amulet. Damned mage. All my fault. Called the monsters. My fault. Should have taken me. Sorry." The words came out in a raspy whisper, barely audible, distorted by whiskey.

A hand touched his shoulder. "It's all right, Jonmarc."

"Not right. You're dead. I should be… should be dead. With you."

"You're sick," a voice murmured quietly. "You've taken fever." Fingers brushed lightly over his cheek. "Got to cool you down."

"Don't. Let it take me. I'll come to you. Been too long."

"Not going to let you die." Something cool slipped across his skin, sending a shiver through him that warred with the fire. Surely the flames were close; he could feel them licking at his arms and legs, felt it burning in his core.

"Shh. Don't talk."

"Shanna—"

"It's all right, Jonmarc. You'll be all right." Another gentle touch to his face, the chill of water against his forehead.

"Shanna... don't go."

"I'm here," the voice promised. "I'm not going anywhere."

"Need you," he breathed. "Need you." Chills shuddered through him as the fever raged, soaking him in sweat and then letting him freeze.

He felt the bed dip and then she slid close to him, wrapping an arm carefully around him. "Shh. I'll keep you warm. Keep you safe. Sleep. I'll keep watch."

"Shanna," he murmured again.

"Let go," a soft voice said from beside his ear. "It's all right. I'll keep you warm."

When the fog of whiskey and fever finally cleared, Jonmarc struggled to wakefulness. He lay in his bed in his quarters and realized that Thaine slept pressed against his back. He shifted, surprised by her presence, and her breath hitched, then she settled once more.

Even asleep, tension had not left her features. Dark smudges marked beneath her eyes, and her face looked thinner. He could not remember how she came to his bed, but as his mind cleared and he cataloged the fresh stitches and bandages, and the sour smell of his own sweat, he could guess what had transpired.

Jonmarc lay still, unsure he had the strength to stand up by himself. He felt weak and hungry, and overdue to take a piss.

His entire body ached, though a vague memory suggested the pain was less than it had been before. His mouth was dry, and his throat felt like he had swallowed broken glass.

He untangled himself from Thaine carefully, aware of just how exhausted she must have been to sleep through his movement. Trying to sit up made him violently dizzy, so he slid off the bed onto his hands and knees and crawled to the chamber pot to relieve himself, humiliated by his weakness, and aware that the dim memories of the last fight gave him more cause for shame.

A bucket of clean water sat against the wall, just inside the door, along with a fresh wash rag. Jonmarc did not risk attempting to stand again; instead, he crawled to the doorway and soaked the rag, squeezing it over his head, mopping it down over his face and around the bandages on his bare chest.

"Two days."

Jonmarc looked up to find Thaine on her side, watching him from where she lay. "It's been two days since the fight. You've been out most of the time. Drunk for part, fever for most of it."

"You took care of me."

Thaine looked down and shrugged. "Healers didn't. Wouldn't. And they're gone with the General somewhere. Someone had to. Then the fever…"

"Did we—"

Thaine gave him a look questioning his sanity and shook her head. "You were mostly dead. I was worried about whether or not you'd keep breathing, let alone being able to—"

Jonmarc looked away. "Thanks." The cold water from the bucket dripped from his hair and ran down his cheeks and his neck, formed rivulets on his chest, washing away the sweat and nightmares.

"You need to eat." Thaine uncurled from her spot on the bed and stood up, walking to where Jonmarc sat. She offered him her hand, and he stared at her for a moment. "We're past the point of pride," she said, raising an eyebrow. "Unless you'd like to crawl."

Jonmarc frowned, but clasped her hand and let her help him up, allowed her to slip beneath his shoulder and help him hobble to a chair. "You'll feel better when you eat," she said in a matter-of-fact voice. "You haven't had anything except some broth that stayed down since the fight. If you're dizzy, that's probably as much the reason as anything."

She pushed a glass of water toward him. "Drink. You lost a lot when you sweated out the fever." His eyes flickered to the remaining bottle of whiskey, and she shook her head. "No. Not until you eat and drink more water and keep something down."

Thaine lifted a cloth that covered a slab of thick bread, slices of dried meat and hunks of cheese. "Have some of the bread first. It'll help your stomach."

Jonmarc made himself eat although the food tasted like ashes and he barely had enough spit to swallow. He felt the remnants of fever and hangover in every movement, and stiff muscles protested days of being bedridden.

Thaine moved to the door and called for Nose, then spoke to him and got a nod in return. She walked back across the room to get something out of his trunk and put a clean shirt and trews on top. As Jonmarc ate, she changed the poultice-smeared, sweat-soaked sheets and set the fouled bedclothes by the door.

"You'll feel better in a fresh shirt," she said, managing a tired half-smile. "And some hot water will loosen up those muscles." Only then did he realize that she had traded her dresses for an oversize shirt and trews as well, garments that looked like hand-me-downs from one of the guards. Her clothes were practical for nursing the sick, as was the way she wrapped her long dark hair back in a knot to keep it out of her face.

Food and water made a remarkable difference, and by the time Jonmarc finished what was on his plate and in the pitcher, he felt better than he expected, though still shaky, weak enough he doubted he could make it across the room without help. Bile rose in his throat. *Weak* was not something he could afford.

Nose came back with a steaming bucket of hot water and several clean wash rags. The water smelled of liniment, and Jonmarc took a deep breath, inhaling the vapors.

"Turn toward me." Thaine placed the bucket on the table, and Jonmarc shifted the chair so that he faced out, far enough away so that she could slip between.

Thaine dipped the rag into the water and hissed at the heat. After a moment, she wrung the cloth out and ran it down the back of his neck before spreading it across one shoulder. A moment later and she did the same to the other side, gently kneading over the warm rags.

"You don't have to—"

"Shut up. You can't, and there's no one else."

Jonmarc surrendered with a huffed breath. He had neither the strength nor the will to fight right now. He tried to relax, did his best not to flinch from Thaine's touch. There was nothing seductive in her manner, but smoothing the warm, herb-soaked rag down his body felt *intimate*, and Jonmarc shifted, unaccustomed to the vulnerability.

Until now, Thaine's efforts to nurse Jonmarc had been limited to patching up superficial wounds, rubbing the ache from stiff muscles and applying poultices to bruised limbs. Never quite such a full body effort, nor for as long a period of time. Jonmarc swallowed hard. He might be half-starved, beaten and dizzy from fever, but her touch sent a shiver through him and fueled an unwelcome heat low in his belly.

"Thaine, I—"

Thaine did not look up at him, continuing to draw the warm cloth down his sore arms, cleaning away sweat and flecks of dried blood from now-healing wounds. "Shh."

"I... can't."

Thaine rinsed the cloth again and returned, working on the other arm. "You called to her during the fever," she said quietly, still not meeting his gaze. "Shanna. You thought she came for you."

Jonmarc's cheeks reddened, and he swallowed again. "I dreamed about her. About what happened," he replied, his voice raw from reasons unrelated to the fight's damage.

"Years ago," Thaine said quietly. "Far away. You've been here a full year, longer than most champions survive. Every fight, you almost die. There's not much left for us. But this could be more than it is."

Thaine knelt next to him, slipping the cloth down over his bruised chest. She looked up, and this time, she met his gaze. "I know you don't love me. Didn't expect you would. But the nights are long and cold, and there's no reason not to take some comfort where we find it."

An understanding passed between them in that glance, and Jonmarc nodded. Thaine said nothing else, but she continued working the warm rags down his sore body, massaging tight muscles, releasing the pain. Jonmarc laid a hand on her shoulder, and she smiled.

5

DEATH MATCH

CHANGES

Six months passed filled with fights and pain, blood and the unspoken comfort of warmth in the dark. Jonmarc and Thaine found a rhythm that suited them, and if it wasn't love, it exceeded camaraderie and was far better than isolation.

"The camp is tense." Thaine spent her time observing the parade ground and what could be seen of the stockade from the windows of their quarters while Jonmarc trained in the salle. Reporting what she saw gave them something to talk about. "Do you know what's going on?"

Jonmarc shrugged. Even with his struggling grasp of the language, he picked up bits of conversations and hints of rumors. Few of the soldiers suspected that their outlander champion had a fair ability to understand the guttural, complex tongue even if his talent for speaking Nargi still fell far short of native. That meant the soldiers were willing to talk in front of him, say things they wouldn't otherwise. He'd learned a lot about the odds for upcoming fights that way, valuable information that helped him turn luck his way. But he found little to like in what he'd heard recently.

"Not really. Only what I can put together. There's tension between the General and Dorran. It's getting worse. Don't know why."

Thaine nodded. She said little about her past, but she spoke the language fluently, so Jonmarc did not doubt she made more of the conversations than he could.

"Your fame has spread far and wide," she replied in the same whisper, unwilling to have the guards overhear. "There's talk that one of the vampire lords came to bet on you."

Jonmarc looked up, remembering the red-robed *vayash moru* mage who had set him on the path to ruin. "Didn't think their kind was welcome in Nargi."

"With enough money to spend, you're welcome anywhere, or so I hear." Thaine did not try to hide the bitterness in her voice.

"So Dorran's jealous? Isn't he getting a big enough cut of the profits? Or is he still betting against me?"

"I think it's more than that," Thaine replied quietly, casting a quick glance toward the door to assure that the guards were not nearby. Jonmarc didn't think Nose would go out of his way to cause them trouble, a decent sort for a prison guard, but he knew better than to make the man choose between his prisoner and his own self-interest.

"Something about Dorran coming here in the first place. No one seems to know, but there are a lot of theories. That they knew each other before and had a falling out. That the General got a promotion or assignment Dorran wanted—"

"Dorran's younger by a decade," Jonmarc countered. "I doubt they were competing for the same promotions."

She shrugged. "It could happen. A slow-and-steady career soldier versus a young man with lots of promise."

"Maybe. But it doesn't feel right," Jonmarc said. Between

his time as a merc and what he had seen of the Eastmark army, he knew the military was home to as many petty rivalries as civilian life. Maybe more, since all that aggressiveness and testosterone, all that need to win and dominate had to go *somewhere* between battles.

"Maybe he's supposed to keep an eye on the General. Wait for him to make a mistake, do something that could cause a scandal." Assassins took all forms. Some were honest enough to use a knife. Others relied on insinuation and half-truths, knowing that gossip and envy could tighten a noose as expertly as a hangman.

"Could be. And maybe Dorran's been promised a move up in return."

They went through the motions of playing *tarle* as they spoke in low tones. The guards and soldiers around them were their only outside contact, the stockade their whole world. Dull as discussing their captors' lives might be, after a while, there was nothing much else to say.

Except that wasn't quite true. Jonmarc had told Thaine stories from his past to while away the candlemarks, tales judiciously edited, leaving out the most important parts. He did not doubt her own accounts were equally censored. They were comfortable with each other, and at the best of times, what passed between them might be fondness though not love. But neither were free to decide the terms of their relationship. Both remained prisoners, making the best of a situation that could be far worse, dependent on each other to survive.

Considering the possibilities, tenuous affection beat the alternatives.

"I don't know what's going on, but if it affects the General, it ends up affecting you," Thaine said, glancing up from her cards. Of course it affected both of them. If

Jonmarc's luck ran out, if he lost the General's favor, then Thaine's reason to receive preferred treatment—maybe her reason to live—vanished too. But she wouldn't presume to say "us," although Jonmarc knew the truth of it.

"Not like anyone's going to tell me," he replied.

"Still, stay sharp. If there's a plot of some kind, a conspiracy, Dorran might not be alone in it. Right now, as jealous as some people might be of your wins, they've made the General rich and money buys protection. Disgrace the champion, and the patron loses face." Thaine's voice sounded matter-of-fact, not at all like she had reasoned out a potentially deadly threat over a game of cards. Jonmarc wondered, not for the first time, how many state secrets were lost to pillow talk in brothels, how many ill-advised confidences sold to the highest bidder. Whores always made good spies.

"I'll keep my ears open. But I don't hear much gossip in the ring."

Training had begun in his first weeks as a prisoner-fighter. After the mage-healers put him through a match with the golem, they moved on to devising other ways for him to train. Always alone, so that no one—prisoner or soldier—might get experience fighting against him. Sometimes he sparred against quintains or scarecrows animated by magic to challenge his speed and dexterity. Now and then, a new golem tested his strength. The only certainty Jonmarc had about his time in the salle lay in learning to expect the unexpected, knowing the mages looked for ways to trip him up, hone his abilities by pushing him to the brink of self-preservation.

Jonmarc stood over his vanquished opponent, a particularly nasty animated effigy that had scored a few deep cuts with its blade. Blades were a new addition. Jonmarc's swords had been returned to him for the first time since his capture, the swords his father forged long ago. It had felt good to grip them, better to swing them, and while he had not fought with a blade in over a year, his muscles remembered. He might be sore tomorrow, it would take time to regain strength, but the satisfaction of fighting with his own swords made him happier than he had been in a long time.

"You did well." The General emerged from the shadows at the back of the salle as the mages relieved Jonmarc of his weapons. "This will add a new element to your matches."

Jonmarc straightened, trying not to heave for breath from the exertion of the fight. He dripped with sweat, and his heart hammered. "I get to use the blades in the ring?" He could not hide his wariness.

"There's a very big match coming up," the General replied. "A lot riding on it, and a more challenging opponent than you've had before."

Jonmarc glowered at him. "Not a *vayash moru*." His voice held a dangerous note.

The General hesitated, then shook his head. "No. Although I can't tell you exactly what you'll be up against—that was part of the bet. Hence your training becoming more rigorous."

"Do I stand a chance of winning?" He didn't doubt that a set-up rigged to have the great champion go down in a bloody spectacle would bring in a huge audience, if the General had tired of his services.

"I certainly hope so," the General replied. "I will be betting on you." He paused. "But the risks are… significant. And so I want to offer you something to fight for. Win this, come out alive and not hurt too badly for the healers to fix, and I will grant you anything you ask, short of harm to myself or my men, or your freedom."

That took Jonmarc aback. "Anything I ask?"

The General shrugged. "Within reason, and within my power to grant. That encompasses quite a bit."

"When do I have to tell you what I want?"

The General's lips quirked in not-quite amusement. "No hurry. After you survive would be fine."

"You'll remember?"

The General's eyes narrowed. "I keep my word."

"BE CAREFUL." NOSE'S quiet voice gave Jonmarc a chill of foreboding. Usually, when he came to take Jonmarc to the fight ring, Nose's forced cheerfulness showed his effort to say something encouraging when they both knew the night's outcome was uncertain. Tonight, Nose resolutely did not look up, and he sounded worried.

"Something about the match I should know?"

Nose shook his head, still not looking up. "No. If I knew anything, I'd tell you. Figure that's why no one's been talking to me. But whatever's going on is big. Everyone's excited, and the bets are crazy. So just... watch your back."

Jonmarc nodded. "Thanks."

He had not told Thaine about the General's promise of a reward. Jonmarc knew what he intended to ask, but that would wait until after—if there was an "after." Mentioning the General's veiled warning would accomplish nothing. Jonmarc's gut twisted with more apprehension than usual before a fight. He would have his swords again; that gave him hope. He had become a formidable bare-knuckle fighter over the last year, but even before that hard-won experience, he had been better than most in a fight with his swords. Whatever advantage his opponent held, Jonmarc knew that having the ability to fight with both his blades went a long way toward evening the odds.

Thaine had seen him off with prayer of blessing and a kiss. She had insisted on drawing protection sigils on his chest and back with herb-steeped water, swearing the effects would last even after sweat and blood washed away the invisible tincture. Thaine usually managed a façade of indifference when he left for the matches, but tonight she had not been able to hide her worry. That, coupled with Nose's concern, made Jonmarc edgier than usual.

The stockade was quiet for the time of night. Jonmarc had come to know its rhythms, to know more than he ever wanted to about the routine inside a Nargi army camp. Usually, he would hear the background noises he had come to associate with the outpost: distant voices, the creak of wagon wheels and sound of hoof beats. Now, it was too quiet, and only a few guards remained at their posts.

Jonmarc understood the reason for the silence when he neared the fight ring. Now he heard excited voices and the shuffle of footsteps. He had seen strangers from other camps arriving throughout the afternoon, reinforcing the suspicion that tonight's match held an unwelcome surprise.

Nose and the second guard stopped at the entrance to the tent, and a new team of soldiers escorted the General's champion into the ring. As usual, his wrists were shackled, though they had finally dispensed with the ankle chains a few months back, satisfied he had been broken to captivity enough not to repeat the mistake of running. His responsibility for Thaine's safety hobbled him more effectively than manacles, making him acutely aware that his actions had consequences. As much as Jonmarc had come to appreciate her companionship, part of him hated the General for knowing him so well, using his weakness against him.

A roar rose from the crowd as Jonmarc entered. He could usually guess the percentage of wagers for and against him by the cheers and jeers. Tonight, those betting on his death definitely outnumbered supporters, and he focused on keeping his expression neutral.

A glance at the stands told him that attendees filled the space to capacity. He recognized insignia from neighboring camps and thought he spotted a few well-dressed civilians among the crowd. The General sat in the center of the front row, his face unreadable as always. Dorran sat beside him, making no effort to hide his excitement.

A strange smell hung in the air, different from the press of so many bodies, of perspiration and adrenaline. The rank odor smelled of musk and decay, sweat, filth, and shit. Jonmarc already knew his opponent would not be human. Now he wondered what kind of animal, what sort of creature they intended for him to fight.

The guards removed Jonmarc's manacles and laid his swords on the ground a few paces away, backing well out of range before he could move for the weapons. At the General's nod, Jonmarc stepped forward and picked up the blades, taking comfort from their familiar heft in his grip.

The creaking of wheels made Jonmarc turn toward the far side of the ring. A large wooden crate on a wagon platform rolled slowly forward, pushed by soldiers who were each wearing chain mail shirts.

Haven't seen that before. Jonmarc felt a prickle at the back of his neck, a shiver of warning of something really bad about to happen.

The crowd screamed louder as the crate moved farther into the ring, into the light of the torches that surrounded the arena. A box of dark wood banded with iron rattled and banged ominously, the thing trapped inside eager to escape.

He guessed the box stood at least six feet tall, maybe more, and almost as broad across as his outstretched arms. The wood was stained almost black, and as the soldiers pushed it closer, Jonmarc could smell blood and unwashed skin, shit and piss, and stale, sour vomit. The thing inside roared and howled, and when a chill ran down Jonmarc's spine, he wasn't sure whether it was because the sound was too animal or too human.

"Begin." The General's voice carried above the din.

One of the mail-shirted guards had a long, sturdy staff tipped with an iron hook. He gave the heavy bolt securing the box's door a shove, and stood ready, staff held like a pike, to ensure the crate's occupant headed in the right direction.

Jonmarc moved into a defensive stance, swords at the ready. The door to the box slammed open.

Ashtenerath.

The creature launched itself at Jonmarc in a frenzy of limbs, teeth, and grasping, tearing fingers. It had been human once, before the torture and dark magic and the drugs ripped apart its sanity, taught it to hate and fear and fight. Beneath the filthy skin, tattered clothing, and matted hair, Jonmarc could make out a semblance of humanity, rabid and feral.

He had fought *vayash moru*, *vyrkin,* and magicked beasts, but *ashtenerath* were in a class all their own.

The creature dove for Jonmarc in a move no rational fighter would ever choose, all flailing arms and clawing, broken fingernails. Its unpredictability made it more dangerous than any beast. Animals hunted. Creatures whether the undead *vayash moru* or the shapeshifting *vyrkin* or the beasts born of blood magic—had patterns, ingrained ways of stalking and killing prey.

Ashtenerath no longer had human rationality and lacked the instincts of natural predators. All that remained was rage, pain, terror, and the strength born of panic. The wild swings were difficult to block, fueled by fury and coming from everywhere at once. Jonmarc's blades flashed in the torchlight, moving in a blur to fight off teeth, nails, and fists. His sword sank to the bone into his attacker's forearm, earning no more than a grunt though blood flowed freely. Another parry carved into the *ashtenerath's* opposite upper arm and Jonmarc knew the pain of that kind of wound, knew it should stagger a man. But the berserker kept coming, paying no mind to the blood that slicked its hands and soaked through its ragged shirt.

The crowd howled, sounding less human than the creature that grunted and snarled through stained, cracked teeth as it circled.

Claw-like nails raked down one arm as the attacker dodged in, ripping at Jonmarc's skin. He pivoted, stabbing one sword into his opponent's thigh, slicing into the right shoulder with the other. The *ashtenerath* did not slow its advance, flailing like a drowning man, wild-eyed. Despite Jonmarc's swords, the creature landed blow after blow, too many to fend off. Bare knuckles struck with enough force to break skin, and bony fingers tore cloth and skin, opening bloody tracks. Jonmarc swung again, thrusting with one sword as the other stopped the swing of a fist aiming for his head, missed a punch as his opponent dodged in suicidally close to pound a fist into his side that left him gasping in pain.

The *ashtenerath* threw itself at Jonmarc at waist height, taking him off balance, and they fell to the dirt. Jonmarc brought the sword in his left hand down like a flail across the mad man's back, opening up a deep gash from shoulder to hip, releasing the sword in his right so he could fend off snapping teeth and hands reaching for his throat.

The air in the arena tent was thick with torch smoke and the press of bodies. Sweat soaked Jonmarc's shirt and ran from his face. Though the night air outside had been cold, in here the stifling heat made it difficult to breathe.

The creature's teeth locked onto Jonmarc's forearm, and he brought his knee up hard into the attacker's gut, then rolled them so he could shift to bring his full weight down on the wild man's groin. That made the *ashtenerath* open its mouth to scream in pain, giving Jonmarc precious seconds to scramble free, panting hard, unwilling to think about the disease present in the berserker's saliva.

He dove forward to run the creature through, but the *ashtenerath* rolled away, scrabbling to get to its feet from a blow that would have kept a human opponent down. Before it could completely regain its balance, Jonmarc brought down his sword, aiming for the neck. His attacker shifted at the last minute, losing an ear instead.

Jonmarc dropped and rolled, coming up behind the *ashtenerath* and slicing through its hamstrings, a move he had learned from butchering hogs. Screaming like the damned, the *ashtenerath* fell to its hands and knees.

Jonmarc regained his feet and threw himself forward, bringing one sword down point first through the creature's back and into its heart, and in the next breath, severed the *ashtenerath's* head with the other blade. The body quivered as if its rage and madness might not need its addled brain to go on, and then collapsed in the blood-soaked dirt, twitching for a moment longer before it finally fell still.

Heaving for breath, bleeding from a dozen wounds and bruised from a score more, Jonmarc turned toward the screaming crowd, feeling nearly as full of fury as the dead monster at his feet.

He felt no triumph in the win, no exhilaration except for a

vague sense of surprise that he was still alive. The winners and the losers in the stands screamed epithets at him, and Jonmarc guessed most had lost their bets. He did not need to know the language to understand their bitter disappointment that he remained alive.

Dorran's expression mirrored the fury of the *ashtenerath*, and he looked for a moment as if he might come over the barrier to deal with Jonmarc himself before he squared his shoulders and schooled his features. In the General's face, Jonmarc saw cool regard, and only then did he remember the wager.

Belatedly, Jonmarc threw down his bloody swords. The soldiers came forward, two of them snapping the cuffs around his wrists and two more to drag the body of the *ashtenerath* away.

As the adrenaline of the fight left him, Jonmarc nearly fell to his knees, spent and hurting. He wondered if the *ashtenerath's* bite held poison and if it had already worked its way into his blood. If so, maybe the mage-healers could cure him, or maybe not. Either way, the pain would be over.

Guards came to lead him out of the arena, more of them than usual, and Jonmarc wondered if they were there to protect him from the angry crowd, from the men who had lost their wages betting on his death. For a moment he wondered whether the mob would descend on him and tear him to pieces. He heard the General shout for order, and the roar subsided, but by then the guards had surrounded him and hustled him outside, toward where the mage-healers waited.

The healers said nothing as they examined Jonmarc. Pain and exhaustion kept him silent as they cleaned his wounds with ruthless efficiency. They had nearly completed the bandaging when the General strode into the tent.

"An impressive show."

Jonmarc raised his head, daring to meet the General's gaze. "I didn't do it for a 'show.' I won to survive."

"Still, I've never seen another fighter on whom I'd bet against an *ashtenerath*. Your skills are… remarkable."

Aching and weary, Jonmarc had no time for pleasantries. "We had a wager."

The General nodded. "What boon do you seek?"

Jonmarc had known exactly what he would ask for from the moment the General made his offer. "Thaine's freedom, and safe passage for her across the Nu River to Margolan."

The General's eyebrows lifted in surprise. "You are not happy with her company?"

"She has been quite… suitable," Jonmarc replied, glancing away. He did not look forward to nights without Thaine's comfort, or to the aftermath of battles without her ministrations. But there had been too many close calls, too many nights lost to fever and blood loss when he nearly died, and he feared what would become of her when that day finally came.

"Then why?"

Jonmarc met his gaze again. "Because she is a slave. If I cannot free both of us, then I would see her freed and safe in Margolan."

"I can't guarantee you another whore."

"I'm not asking you to. But we had an agreement, and this is my request. Please—I did well for you tonight. This is what I want."

The General paused and then nodded. "Very well."

"I want to go along, when you free her," Jonmarc persisted. "You can chain me, hobble me. But I want to see it with my own eyes, see her across the river—in a boat with an oarsman, so she reaches the other side safely." The words tumbled out, Jonmarc adding details so the deal could not be twisted.

"All right. Tomorrow."

Jonmarc swallowed and nodded. "Good. That's good. I'll tell her tonight."

The General snapped orders at the healers and then left. Jonmarc remained where he stood, his stomach twisting in a sour mixture of relief and loss.

Thaine stopped pacing when Jonmarc entered their quarters and rushed toward him, already scanning him for injuries. "I heard… are you all right?"

Jonmarc could see the worry in her eyes and the playing cards on the table; evidence Thaine tried to distract herself during the match. Unsuccessfully, from the look of the scattered cards. "Sore. The healers patched the worst of it, and the rest will heal."

"Come. Sit down. Let me look."

Jonmarc let her guide him, swallowing hard, knowing it would be the last time. He smiled gratefully when she pressed a cup of whiskey into his hand and brought clean cloths and poultice for his bruises. He shut his eyes, focusing on the feel of her hands and the sound of her voice, committing them to memory. He did not regret his decision, but that did not make the letting go easier. Much as he had resisted Thaine's presence, he had grown used to the company, come to appreciate her wit and humor, her conversation and the comfort of her body in the night.

He remembered how he had been before Thaine, the coldness that settled deep inside him, numbing pain and loss, fear and grief, leaving only resolute survival. Despite his intention to remain detached, she had brought back a warmth he thought he might never feel again. He would be all the colder when she was gone.

Nose brought a better than usual dinner for them, another reward for Jonmarc's win, along with more whiskey. Jonmarc kept the conversation light during dinner, refraining from more than a glass of the whiskey, knowing he would need it more after she was gone. Despite Thaine's concerns for his sore muscles and newly-healed injuries, they made slow, careful love and fell asleep tangled together beneath the blankets.

Jonmarc woke when the sun lit the window. He remained motionless, listening to Thaine breathe, taking in the scent of her hair, the feel of her skin. He had been a coward the night before, putting off telling her of his wager, but he savored the memory of one last good evening. Now the time had come to pay the price.

"Thaine."

She murmured something and turned toward him, eyes still closed.

"Thaine, we need to get dressed. They'll be here soon."

She looked up at him, blinking away sleep. "Who? Why?"

Jonmarc pushed her hair behind her ear and skimmed his fingertips gently down her cheek. "I made a wager with the General. He promised me anything except my freedom if I won. So I asked for yours."

He saw confusion and then fear in her gaze. "What?"

"Safe passage across the river in a boat. To Margolan. You'll be free."

Thaine shook her head. "And you'll be alone."

Jonmarc sat up and gripped her shoulders. "Listen to me, Thaine. Dorran's scheming against the General. We've seen it. There's been talk about problems at headquarters. I don't think the General's going to be in charge too much longer, and if he's gone, if Dorran's in charge, I don't know what will happen."

"Dorran could lose."

"Or he could set me up in a match rigged to kill me. You know he'd make a fortune on a game like that if people knew they'd see the General's champion go down. And then what would happen to you?"

Thaine looked down. They both knew the answer to that question.

"Can't you talk the General into letting you go?"

Jonmarc chuckled. "No. He was very clear that my choices did not include my freedom. We always knew how this was going to end for me. I'll go down in a match, and the healers won't fix the damage. There are worse ways to die." *Like burning alive in a barn.*

"Thank you," Thaine said quietly, and although he read sadness in her eyes, she did not let herself cry. She cupped his cheek and pressed a kiss to his lips. "I know the risk, but I don't want to leave you."

Jonmarc met her gaze. "And you know that if Dorran wins, he'll take you away. I won't be able to protect you. So this is the only way."

Nose cleared his throat at the door. "The General sent word I'm supposed to make sure you're both ready to travel. He'll be here very soon."

"We'll be ready," Jonmarc promised.

THAINE WORE HER least revealing dress and a warm cloak. A small bundle held the rest of her clothes and a deck of *tarle* cards, her only possessions. They rode in the back of an army wagon. The General sat up front with his driver, while another soldier, one of the General's private guard, kept watch over the captives in the back. Jonmarc submitted to wrist and ankle shackles without protest. Rope bound Thaine's wrists for the ride, a formality, the General assured them, until she was in the boat.

Thaine sat next to him, pressed up against his side, her head on his shoulder. The closer they got to the river, the more Jonmarc worried. *What if it's a trick? What if the General goes back on his word? She can't swim with bound wrists. Will the guard throw her overboard in the middle of the river? Will he really take her all the way across and see her safely on shore?*

Jonmarc could envision any number of nightmare outcomes, but he could do nothing to avert any of them. In the end, it came down to trusting the General, and Jonmarc reminded himself that although the man had been stern, he had never been deceptive. Jonmarc hung on to that, trying to still his fear.

"We're here." The driver brought the wagon to a halt. Jonmarc rose to his knees and saw the Nu River a few dozen paces away, wide and swift. A small boat waited on the near shore.

Thaine stretched up to kiss him on the cheek, and then the guard took her arm and guided her out of the wagon. Jonmarc managed a sad smile and met her gaze, and then the guard walked her to the boat. The driver came to stand beside Jonmarc, reminding him not to bolt. As if there was anywhere to go.

The General remained in the wagon, watching everything, saying nothing. Jonmarc walked far enough toward the banks to see his homeland on the other side of the river. The Nu ran narrower here, and on across it lay a stretch of rocky ground and beyond that, Jolie's Place.

Thaine held herself stiffly, shoulders back, head up, giving away nothing to the guard who accompanied her. He helped her into the boat, and only then did she look back to Jonmarc one last time, before the guard shoved off and they headed out across the muddy river.

Jonmarc watched the small craft make its way despite the current, coming ashore closer to the downriver brothel than to the launch point. When the boat pulled up on land, the guard cut the ropes that bound Thaine's wrists, and she took up her bundle, lifted her skirts, and began the trek toward shelter.

Jonmarc turned back toward the wagon. "Take me back," he said quietly, suddenly tired. No one spoke on the return trip.

"Come on. Time to sober up." Nose's voice cut through the fog in Jonmarc's head.

"Leave me alone."

Six months had passed since Thaine left, though Jonmarc remembered little clearly except the fights.

Nose grabbed Jonmarc by the arm and pulled him out of bed, stumbling and swearing. He pushed Jonmarc toward the door, where one of the mage-healers looked on with clear disdain. Jonmarc staggered and almost fell, grabbing the bars to steady himself. The healer mumbled words of power and the alcohol-induced haze vanished, leaving him stone cold sober.

"Get dressed. Your match is in a candlemark."

Nose left food on the table and withdrew. Jonmarc stripped off his nightshirt and pulled on clothing for the fight, then sat down to a meal for which he had no appetite.

Six months of fights and practices he barely remembered, and nights he forgot entirely.

"What is it tonight?" he called to Nose, who came to the door, frowning with concern.

"A champion from one of the other garrisons. He's good, but I think you'll win."

The fights had increased in frequency, once or twice a week now. Jonmarc felt sure the fights were meant to keep the soldiers occupied, divert attention from the real struggle for power between the General and Dorran. Even Jonmarc sensed the tension in the camp, and he saw his suspicions borne out in the hurried manner and furtive glances as soldiers tried their hardest to ignore what was in front of them in order to do their jobs.

Afterward, once the healers had done all they intended to do for him, Nose guided Jonmarc back to the table and sat him down with a firm hand on his shoulder.

"I'll fetch the whiskey," Nose said, bringing a bottle and a cup. "Let me patch up what the mages couldn't be bothered to finish."

Jonmarc knocked back the first few fingers of whiskey and poured more. "Thaine teach you that?" he asked with a nod toward the poultice mixture.

Nose chuckled. "Some. But my mother and my grandmam showed me some, too, growing up. Handy thing to know."

"Tell the General to pay you more," Jonmarc said, voice still raspy from his opponent's thumbs digging into his throat.

"His orders are to keep you functional for the fights," Nose informed him. "And to not let you choke on your vomit in between."

Jonmarc gave a snort. "Nice." He sat silently for a few

minutes, breathing in the sharp smell of the healing mixture. "So what's going on out there?" he asked, dropping his voice.

"Nothing good," Nose replied.

"Even with the healers, I don't think I can keep fighting like this," Jonmarc said, wincing as Nose spread the poultice over sore flesh.

"I don't think you'll have to." Nose kept his head down, his voice almost a whisper. "There's a rumor that the General might be recalled. No one's sure why, but I've heard 'board of inquiry.'"

Jonmarc remembered the "trials" in the Eastmark army, more often than not just a show confirming a foregone conclusion. "If he goes, he won't come back, will he?"

Nose shrugged, which said everything he did not put into words.

"And Dorran?"

"Likely to be put in charge for the interim." Nose's voice remained carefully neutral.

"Funny thing, how permanent the 'interim' can be."

"Be careful," Nose said quietly. "You're known as the General's champion."

Jonmarc nodded. That meant Dorran would either consider him to be one of the spoils of victory, or another piece of the General's legacy to destroy. "Thank you," he said as Nose gathered up the bowl with the poultice and the clean rags. He might have meant for this night's help, or for everything, just in case he did not get another chance to say it.

"Best assignment I've had," Nose replied, not looking at him as he left.

Two nights later, the door rattled in the darkness. Jonmarc woke warily, wishing he had a weapon. He could see little from the moonlight that filtered through his barred windows, enough to make out a figure in the hallway.

"Get dressed. We need to hurry."

Jonmarc stared at the darkness, trying to make sense of what he heard. The General's voice, here, a candlemark or two before dawn.

"No time to waste." A second voice, Nose. Keys jostled, and the door swung open. "Come on."

Jonmarc had fallen asleep in his clothing. He reached for his cloak and wondered if this move had been planned far enough in advance to account for giving him less whiskey than usual. The buzz he had gained from finishing off a bottle candlemarks ago had long faded, leaving him clear-headed.

"Where are we going?" he murmured as Nose took his arm, noting that for the first time, no one moved to shackle his wrists.

"Away from here," Nose replied. "Hurry."

They left the camp on foot, slipping through the gate as a small grass fire took the guards' attention from their duty. Once they had gotten far enough away from the gates to evade notice, Jonmarc made out a small wagon and a horse tethered to a tree. "Get in," Nose urged, pulling him by the arm.

The General himself took the reins, urging the horse to move with as much speed as they dared in the moonlight. Jonmarc recognized the road. "We're going to the river?"

"I leave for the capital city tomorrow," the General replied from the driver's seat. "An inquiry. I don't expect to return."

"Then why— "

"You've made me a small fortune, for all the good it's done me," the General replied. "Dorran not only wants my command; he covets my champion. I can't stop him from taking my place. But I can cheat him out of his profit."

A number of possibilities occurred to Jonmarc, none of

them good. *They could slit my throat out here, and no one would be the wiser. Or leave me, as if I escaped, to give them an excuse to kill me.*

Then again, he was the General's property to do with as he willed. Which meant if the General wanted to slit his throat, he could have done it back in his quarters. Or engineered a match Jonmarc could not win or instructed the healers to stop his heart.

None of which explained why they came to the riverbank in the middle of the night.

"Your wager put the idea in my mind," the General remarked, climbing down from the wagon. "I didn't want to do it until I knew for sure. There was a chance that the inquiry might not happen. Didn't want to lose my champion if I didn't have to," he added with a forced chuckle. "But here we are."

"Not sure I understand."

The General turned to face him. "I'm giving you your freedom. Unfortunately, I don't have a boat tonight. But if you can swim the river, get to the other side, I won't send anyone after you. And if you can't—"

One way or the other, I'm still free.

"That's it? I just walk down to the river and get in?"

Nose hung back, watching but remaining silent. The General gave a curt nod. "Yes. That's it. We don't have time to remove your collar, but a blacksmith can see to that." He withdrew a bundle wrapped in cloth, and Jonmarc recognized the hilts of his swords. "But I did get these. Get moving. Someone's likely to notice we're gone."

"All right then." Jonmarc began walking, unable to quite get "thank you" past his lips for the man who had owned him. He steeled himself not to look back, expecting to feel a knife between his shoulders at every step, finally releasing his breath as he reached the rocky land at the water's edge.

A new terror seized him as he looked out across the swift, cold water. He could make out the eddies and current in the moonlight. Across the way, shadows shrouded the riverbank. Downriver, the lights of Jolie's Place stood out against the darkness. He wondered, not for the first time, whether Thaine had found sanctuary in the brothel, if she had stayed there or moved on. He might finally find out if he lived through the crossing.

Jonmarc drew a deep breath, tied the bundle with his swords onto his back, and waded in.

The current caught him almost immediately, pulling him with it. Cool air and cold water gave him a shock, and he knew he would grow sluggish soon with the chill if he did not move quickly. He struck out for the other side, glad that growing up in a fishing village meant that he knew how to swim and how to fight against the ocean tide, not too different from the coursing river's pull.

Something hard hit him in the shoulder, a piece of a tree, floating with the current. Jonmarc got a face full of water and came up sputtering, then angled toward the lights and pushed forward with strong, sure strokes.

His clothes pulled him down, held him back, but he did not fancy emerging naked on the other side, even if he might have been able to strip with the way the river dragged him. Twice he went under, getting water in his mouth and nose, gagging. He fought down panic as he struggled to clear his airway, unwilling to come so far only to drown mere yards from safety.

In a final burst of stubborn will, Jonmarc drew on his last reserves of strength and swam for the shore. As soon as he dragged himself up onto the rocks and the night air hit his wet body, he began to shiver violently. He collapsed onto all fours, coughing up river water, shaking it from his hair like a dog, sputtering for breath.

The river had carried him downstream from where he had gone into the water, to a stretch of riverbank just below the brothel, close enough that he could hear music and the sound of laughter. Lanterns lit the inside of the large building, and torches flamed around the outside. The wind shifted, and Jonmarc smelled roasted meat and baked bread. He staggered to his feet, eyes fixed on the lights, willing himself to put one foot in front of the other.

He almost made it to the wooden stairs. His head spun, and his body shuddered so hard with the cold that he could not walk. Jonmarc fell to his knees, wrapping his arms around himself for warmth. Then he pitched forward into the sand, and the lights faded into darkness.

GUARDIAN

1

GUARDIAN

JOLIE'S PLACE

"Kill him." The woman's voice sounded of smoke and whiskey, used to being obeyed. "He'll be nothing but trouble."

Cold, sharp metal settled against Jonmarc's throat. He struggled to open his eyes, to move, to fight, but his body betrayed him, leaving him only sound.

"Please no!" Another woman's voice, closer than the first, and then the feeling of warmth blanketing him, as arms wrapped around him. "I can explain. It's not his fault. He's in danger."

"He certainly is," the whiskey voice replied, but the blade lifted, and Jonmarc tensed for a blow that did not fall.

"Please," the second woman begged. "I can vouch for him."

"He's wearing a slave collar. We're only across the river from Nargi. They'll either come looking for him, or there will be reprisals. Sheltering him is more risk than it's worth."

"He was a prisoner. He protected me. Please—let me care for him."

"Perhaps you can let him wake up and tell his story," a

man interjected in a low, measured voice. "And then kill him if you want."

They might have said more, but darkness swallowed up Jonmarc, pulling him under, and the voices went away for a while.

Dreams replaced voices. *He felt the punches to his face and body, hissed as pain shot through him. Faces blurred, details muddied, but it always came back to the fight. The crowd screamed for his death, cursed his victory. He tasted blood.*

An iron collar around his neck marked him as a fight slave. He saw no mercy in the eyes of the man across the arena from him. Only one of them would leave. The crowd screamed in a guttural, clipped language, wagers placed on who would live and who would die.

Faces and fights blurred, too many to keep straight. Too many injuries, and far too much blood, his own and that of the men he killed to stay alive.

Older memories surfaced. Fire, raiders, and burning corpses. A cave, a talisman, and monsters that destroyed a village. A blonde woman's body, and a red-robed mage. Tents and horses, the smell of smoke and a blacksmith's anvil.

Uniforms. Battles. Then a burning barn. Running through a dark forest. Capture. The hiss of a branding iron against his skin and the smell of charred flesh. It always came back to fire.

Jonmarc's body burned, and he thrashed, soaked with sweat. Old wounds throbbed and bones ached. Voices came and went.

Sometimes, Jonmarc dreamed of water held to his cracked lips, or a hand smoothing a cool towel over his flushed skin. A voice he knew and almost trusted murmured soothing words, only to recede into darkness.

When he finally opened his eyes, Jonmarc Vahanian found himself staring at a wooden ceiling in an unfamiliar room. He smelled of sweat and sick. Breathing hurt, and his skin felt like it might peel away from his sore bones. He blinked, registering that his eyes hurt when he tried to focus.

"You're safe."

He turned his head just enough to see a woman sitting next to him. Her dark hair was caught back in a thick braid, and stains marked her plain linen dress.

"Did I drown?" he thought he remembered making it across the river, though his memory also served him up images of being pulled beneath the surface by the current, hit hard by floating debris and struggling for breath. Making it to the other side of the river had mattered a great deal, though at the moment, he could not remember why.

She smiled. "No, but it was a near thing."

He struggled to recognize her, and then the name came to him. *Thaine.* She belonged with the dreams, in the place with smoke and pain and blood.

"Do you remember?" she asked quietly, reaching out to touch his face with her fingertips, the touch of a lover, not a nurse.

"It's all mixed up," Jonmarc replied, wincing at the croak that was all the voice he could muster.

"You swallowed a lot of water and hit your head," she replied, carefully repositioning his pillow. "Then you caught fever and nearly died." Thaine bit her lip as if trying to decide whether to say more.

"Someone wanted to kill me."

Thaine looked away. "That was Jolie. She owns this house. Doesn't much care for Nargi. Didn't want them to come looking for you. Astir and I got her to change her mind."

Jonmarc raised a hand to his throat. He found nothing but skin and the smooth lines of two even scars. "I had—"

"Astir got the collar off of you. And I told Jolie some of what happened from before," Thaine murmured. "She's reserving judgment for now."

Jonmarc closed his eyes and sank back into the mattress. "Why heal me if she's just going to kill me?"

Thaine chuckled. "Pretty sure she's not going to kill you. How long you stay, that's another matter."

The things he wanted to say danced just beyond his ability to put sentences together. He sighed, then tensed at how the movement of his chest made all the muscles hurt and sent an ache through his ribs.

"Rest. You've had a bad time of it. When you're up to it, I'll tell you everything." She wrung out the towel and put it back on his forehead. "You're safe."

Jonmarc doubted that but he lacked the strength to argue, and this time when sleep took him, the nightmares did not follow.

The next time Jonmarc struggled toward consciousness, a sturdy hand fell on his shoulder, gripping him tightly and adding a light shake. "It's about time you opened your eyes," a man's voice announced, the words not quite hiding an undertone of relief.

Jonmarc frowned, sure he must still be asleep. That voice belonged to an old friend who should be far away from here. His companion began to laugh as if guessing Jonmarc's thoughts.

"Lucky for you, I frequent whorehouses," the man chuckled. "Luckier still that I've curried a bit of favor with Jolie, enough to get her to overlook you showing up here in Nargi clothing."

Jonmarc opened his eyes. Tov Harrtuck sat in a chair next

to his bed, still as broad-faced and barrel-chested as ever. "You're supposed to be in Principality," Jonmarc managed in a voice still far too raspy to be his own.

Harrtuck held a cup for him. "And you're supposed to be in Eastmark," he replied with a raised eyebrow.

Jonmarc looked away. "There were some problems with that." Most of his memories had returned; at least he thought they had. *Guess there's no way to know if I don't remember something until it bites me in the ass.*

"What happened?" Jonmarc asked, mustering the courage to look at his old friend. It had been over three years since they had fought side by side with the War Dog mercenaries, and so much happened since then. Jonmarc counted the years in the scars that crisscrossed his body. Harrtuck had gained scars, too. A deep cut marred his right eyebrow, a testimony to luck that he did not lose the eye. More recent scars showed on his thick, muscled arms. *Not out of the game, or if he is, he's left it recently,* Jonmarc thought.

"I came along in time to hear Jolie and Astir arguing over whether or not to kill the Nargi slave that crawled out of the river. Thaine was begging for them to hold off, and I heard your name. Thought I'd had too damn much to drink," he said, shaking his head. "Not that I didn't expect to find you in a whorehouse, but I'd heard you were dead."

"Nearly was, several times."

"Yeah. I can see that."

For the first time, Jonmarc realized that the clothing he wore was not his own. Someone had stripped him of his shirt and pants and given him fresh trews. He wore no shirt, and he knew Harrtuck could see the many marks the Nargi betting fights and his time in Eastmark had made in his flesh over the last few years.

"Thaine told me some of what happened," Harrtuck said,

and his gruff voice softened a little. "Damn, boy! You sure know how to get yourself in the thick of it."

Jonmarc shrugged. "What did you hear—before?"

Harrtuck leaned back, keeping his arms crossed. "About what happened in Eastmark? Word traveled fast. Captain Valjan was most unhappy."

Jonmarc did not doubt that the War Dogs leader took exception to the unjust court martial and botched executions, but it surprised him word made it back to Principality. "You were right," he replied. "I shouldn't have gone."

"What's done is done," Harrtuck dismissed. "Last I saw Valjan, he and the Dogs were still holding their own. Lost a few along the way." He mentioned names, and Jonmarc closed his eyes, remembering faces. "After what Alcion did to you, Valjan pulled the War Dogs back from Eastmark as soon as he could. It's a touchy thing to say no to a general who's the brother of the Eastmark king," he added. "But I suspect that Valjan got in a word to King Staden in Principality, who suddenly needed the War Dogs for his own purposes for the foreseeable future," he said with a smirk.

"Nice." Jonmarc fell silent for a few moments. "So why aren't you in Principality?"

Harrtuck looked away. "I'm getting too old for this shit," he said with a sigh.

"You're not that much older than I am."

Harrtuck shrugged. "Tell that to my bones."

Jonmarc snorted in agreement. "So why are you here? Aside from the whores?"

"I need a different reason?"

"There are a lot of brothels between here and Principality."

"True." Harrtuck stretched and circled his head until his neck gave a satisfying crack. "I left the War Dogs not long after you disappeared from Eastmark. Decided I wanted to come home to Margolan. Wandered around at loose ends for a bit, but I'm not much good at being anything except a soldier. So I joined up with King Bricen's army."

Jonmarc raised an eyebrow. "Next you'll want me to believe you've given up gambling."

"Don't talk nonsense," Harrtuck chided.

"What's Margolan like these days?" He realized with a pang that he had been gone from his homeland for nearly four years.

Harrtuck raised a glass of whiskey and took a sip. "Not too different, I guess. Bricen's been a good king, all things considered. As good as kings ever are. His army is disciplined and well-ordered. Valjan would approve," he added with a wan smile.

"Must be boring, after the War Dogs."

Harrtuck shrugged again. "Nearly dying gets old after a while. Stops being exciting, starts being insane. I figured I'd pushed my luck far enough. Not that the army here has nothing to do," he added. "The farther we get from the palace city, the more brigands there are on the roads. That takes up a lot of time. The captain gets asked to arbitrate sometimes when a village can't solve its own problems. Sometimes people bring us a murderer or a thief to deal with. Useful stuff."

"Is protecting the whorehouse part of your duty?"

Harrtuck chuckled. "Lucky for you, I'm on leave." He fiddled with his glass for a moment. "You know, when you're healed up, you could do worse than the army."

Jonmarc turned to look at him. "Are you crazy? I've got a royal death warrant from Eastmark on my head and probably a bounty from Nargi as well." *And a* vayash moru *mage who thinks I double-crossed him here in Margolan. This can't end well, no matter what I choose.*

"You think the Margolan army cares?" Harrtuck shook his head. "They won't, not once they see you fight. Since you're still alive, I'm going to assume you're even better than you were before, and you put everyone in the War Dogs to shame except for Valjan."

"I spent two years fighting in betting games for the Nargi. Now that I'm free, I don't want anyone picking my fights for me again, whether it's a king or a captain." Jonmarc's voice lacked its usual volume, but the bitterness came through just fine.

Harrtuck regarded him in silence for a few minutes. "Understandable. Just presenting an option. If you ever change your mind, I'll vouch for you."

"I won't—but thanks."

Harrtuck gave a curt nod and finished his drink. "I was supposed to fetch Jolie as soon as you were conscious enough to argue for your life. I'd better go do that, or she'll tan my hide."

"Too late to slip out the back?" Jonmarc was only mostly joking.

"Astir, her house manager, is *vayash moru*. Pretty sure he'd track you, even if you weren't half dead."

"Then I guess you'd better send her in and get it over with," Jonmarc said. He willed himself to sit up and paused as the room spun.

"Are you insane?" Harrtuck reached out to steady him.

"If this Jolie person is as tough as you and Thaine seem to think, I'm not facing her flat on my back." He glanced around the room. "I'd rather not do it half naked, either. Is there a shirt in here?"

Harrtuck found one draped over another chair and tossed

it to him. Jonmarc waved away help and managed to get it on over his head. He ran a hand over his short-cropped hair and decided that growing it back to its usual length would be a priority now that he was free.

"Should have left the shirt off. Ladies love scars," Harrtuck said with a smirk. He clapped a hand on his shoulder and left the room. Jonmarc doubted he could stand without falling, and moving made his head swim. He squared his shoulders and resolved to face the woman who held his fate in her hands with as much dignity as he could muster.

Jonmarc looked around his room for the first time since he had awakened. The room held a bed, washstand, basin, and two chairs, with a small chest in the corner and hooks on the wall to hold the occupant's belongings. It looked clean, better than most of the roadside inns he had visited in his travels. The rope supports of his bed were tight and the mattress newly stuffed, with sheets that looked freshly bleached. As he sat quietly, he could make out the sounds of activity around him. To one side, the rhythmic thumping of a headboard against the wall left little doubt as to what was going on. Muffled voices carried through the walls and from the hallway. He heard music and guessed that minstrels were keeping the crowd at the bar entertained. The air smelled of perfume, pipe smoke, and whiskey.

From what Thaine and Harrtuck told him, he gathered he was upstairs in Jolie's Place, one of Margolan's most famous brothels. The memory of losing his wife, Shanna, had been too fresh and sharp the last time he was in Margolan for him to entertain the idea of visiting a whorehouse. Even now, the thought held little appeal.

He had finally decided Jolie was not coming when the door opened.

"So you're Jonmarc Vahanian." Jolie gave him an

appraising glance that seemed to see down to his bones. She moved into the room with utter confidence and regarded him through narrowed eyes. Tall, regal, and curvaceous, Jolie's red hair framed angular features that were striking if not conventionally pretty. Jonmarc guessed that she might be in her fourth decade, though make-up and a good dressmaker could shave off years. She must have been stunning in her youth. Now, Jolie exuded a heady mixture of sexuality and power. Rings glinted on her fingers, while silver and gold bracelets adorned her arms. Her perfume, dusky and sweet, hung in the air like incense to the Dark Lady.

"Thank you for taking me in." Jonmarc had learned long ago that the easiest fights to win were the ones that did not happen. Since he was dependent on her goodwill for the moment, he decided to be conciliatory.

"That remains to be determined."

Movement in the doorway made Jonmarc look up, and he saw Astir step in behind Jolie. He was Jonmarc's height, with a slender but muscular build and dark hair caught back in a queue. Everything about Astir's manner gave a clear warning. Jonmarc felt the *vayash moru*'s gaze on him and fought back a shudder.

"What do you want from me?" Jonmarc asked. Best to get to the point. If she was going to throw him out, maybe Harrtuck could help him find another place to stay.

"The truth. What I've heard seems… difficult to believe."

Jonmarc resisted the urge to roll his eyes. "Sometimes it's hard for me too, and I lived it."

"I'd like to hear your version," Jolie replied. "Starting with how a Margolense like you came to be in Nargi."

Jonmarc regarded her for a moment, trying to decide how to frame his answer. Parts of the truth were not hard to tell. Others he felt less like sharing. Some were no one's damn business. "I was running away," he said finally. "Meant to cross the river in Dhasson, and ended up across the Nargi border by accident. Got caught by a patrol."

"Thaine says you fought in their betting games, that you survived two years as their fight slave," Jolie prompted. "From what I've heard of Nargi, I find that highly unlikely."

Jonmarc's eyes sparked with anger. "Believe what you like. You saw my scars. It's true."

"How did you survive so long? That's… remarkable."

"Remarkable" was not the word Jonmarc would have chosen. "Cursed," "fated," or "punished" might have come closer. "When I haven't nearly drowned, I'm a damn good fighter. Better than the opponents they set me up against, anyhow."

Jolie raised an eyebrow, and Jonmarc wondered just what Thaine had told her. "How did you get away?"

"The general who owned me was going to be recalled, and he wanted to spite his second-in-command, who was a nasty little piece of shit. Setting me free meant the guy who stabbed him in the back wouldn't make a profit from it."

"Thaine said you bargained for her freedom. Did you?"

Jonmarc looked away. "The General offered me anything except my own freedom if I won a big match. I asked for Thaine's."

"Why?"

Jonmarc looked back at Jolie as if he could not believe the question. "We were slaves. She was kind to me. Making the bargain meant I could repay her."

"A debt to a whore?" Jolie's expression and tone were hard to read.

"That's so hard to believe?" Staying upright took all of Jonmarc's barely regained strength, and the verbal sparring stoked his anger. "She didn't have a choice about being stuck with me, but she did choose to make the best of it. We protected each other. She patched me up."

"Why choose to give that up?"

"Did you miss the 'slave' part?" Jonmarc made no attempt to hide the impatience in his tone. He looked away. "The General let me know that if I got out of line, she'd be punished. Setting her free meant she couldn't be hurt—or used against me."

"What were you running from, when you ended up in Nargi?"

Odds were good that either Thaine or Harrtuck had already told the key points of his story. "I made some enemies in Eastmark when I served there as a merc. Got accused of things I didn't do; tried to outrun a death warrant." He glared at Jolie. "Look, if you don't want me here, I'll get Harrtuck to find me somewhere else to stay. Just say the word, and I'll go."

Jolie studied him for a moment. "I doubt you'd make it to the door."

"I'd make it. One way or another."

"I could use an extra pair of hands around here," Jolie said finally. "Clean up, make supply runs, fix things up, help keep order. Not very exciting for a hero."

Jonmarc did not miss the sarcastic emphasis she placed on that last word. "What's it pay?"

"Room and board, and some coin to spend once I see how you work," Jolie replied. "The girls are off-limits. Thaine's the exception—she told me you two were something over there," she added with a vague gesture toward the river, and Nargi. "That's between you and her." Jolie's gaze met Jonmarc's. "But understand that Thaine works here. She takes clients. If you have a problem with that, you'd better leave now. I won't put up with trouble."

"I won't make trouble," Jonmarc replied, pushing down the ramifications of Jolie's words to deal with later. "I can do blacksmithing, and I'm pretty good with tools. I can be useful."

"We'll see." Jolie turned and walked toward the door. After a few steps, she turned back to look at him. "Don't make me regret this." Astir leveled a warning look at Jonmarc and seemed surprised when Jonmarc did not shy away from his gaze. Mortals usually avoided a *vayash moru*'s gaze to keep from being brought under their compulsion. By some quirk of fate, Jonmarc had always been immune. Jonmarc took perverse enjoyment out of Astir's momentary confusion.

Once the door closed, Jonmarc fought the impulse to drop back onto the bed only because he knew it would hurt. He eased himself down and panted shallow breaths until the vertigo lessened.

I can do this. A roof over my head, food in my belly, and a way to earn some coin, without anyone trying to kill me. Not forever. Just until I figure things out, decide what to do next.

His thoughts moved sluggishly, but thinking about next steps kept him from wanting to throw up as his body fought the dizziness, and his abused lungs struggled for air.

He wondered whether Maynard Linton's caravan still traveled back and forth across Margolan, and where they might be right now. The caravan had been his salvation as the lone survivor of the monster attack that killed his wife and child and the others in their village. He had spent two years as a blacksmith's apprentice and sometimes guard.

I was welcome to stay. My choice to leave, to go to Principality and be a mercenary. Would I have done anything differently, if I knew how it would turn out?

He let out a long breath. *It's not like I planned for the way things happened. Eastmark seemed like a good opportunity—*

until that damned mage showed up and Alcion turned out to be a bloodthirsty madman. Nargi wasn't supposed to happen. I just had a lousy sense of direction.

Then again, his friends in the caravan had tried to talk him out of joining up with the mercs. Linton had made it clear that he had a place with them for as long as he wanted. The caravan had its share of dangers, but becoming a hired sword meant going looking for trouble. And a tour in Eastmark paid a premium because the hazards merited the bonus. *Can't say I wasn't warned.*

Jonmarc stared at the ceiling, thoughts still churning although the vertigo was gone. *I haven't forgotten how to work a forge. There are probably some blacksmiths that could use an experienced helper.* He could find a village, get someone to take him on in the forge, settle in.

Until things go wrong, and it's my fault they die, too. The first man he had ever killed, the raider who took his father's life, had cursed him with his dying breath to lose everyone he loved to the flames. Three times now, that curse held true. His parents, brothers, and neighbors. Shanna, their unborn child, and the village that had been kind enough to take him in. And then in Eastmark, the pyre that burned the bodies of his soldiers, executed for following his orders not to slaughter civilians, and later the townspeople who ended up locked in a burning barn anyhow for sheer spite.

Never again. He was not going to put another village in harm's way for giving him sanctuary. He would stay here until he had earned enough to get on the road, and then... he would figure something out.

He almost did not hear the door open. Thaine stood in the doorway. "Jolie says you can stay." The door clicked shut behind her.

Jonmarc nodded, feeling his throat tighten. He had grown

used to seeing Thaine in a simple shift back in Eastmark, like the plain clothing she had been wearing to care for him when he awoke. But the silk and satin of her gown and the ringlets of her long hair reminded him that things had changed. Jolie's warning rang in his ears. He and Thaine would have to sort things out between them. For a moment, he almost wished he was still unconscious.

"She said I could work here," Jonmarc replied, managing to leverage himself to a sitting position better than he had done on his first try. "Get my feet under me, earn some coin."

Thaine smiled, and he saw apprehension in her eyes. "That's good," she said, and Jonmarc did not doubt she had something to do with his good fortune. "Jolie runs a tight ship. It's not like… other places."

"Thank you."

Thaine looked down. "All I did was put in a good word."

"You didn't have to."

She met his gaze. "You bought my freedom."

He could not completely hide the wince her words caused. "People shouldn't be bought and sold."

A flush crept up her cheeks. "We all sell ourselves for something. It's how we get by. Your sword. My companionship. We do what we have to do."

Jonmarc had no intention of contending that point. Being a mercenary, a hired killer, was arguably far worse than sharing a stranger's bed. "I wasn't judging you."

"You knew what I was when they brought me to your quarters, back then." Thaine's eyes glinted with defiance.

Jonmarc nodded. "And you knew why I kept my distance." She had heard his fevered confessions, soothed his cries for Shanna when pain and whiskey dragged him under. When they had finally come together to take the comfort that they could, neither had pretended it was love. Fondness, affection, and a friendship borne of extreme circumstances, yes. Expediency, certainly. But not love.

"It's up to you," Thaine said, lifting her chin. "Some of the girls have lovers away from here. It just can't interfere."

Jonmarc felt his gut tighten. "I don't think I could do that," he said quietly. "I just couldn't."

"Most men can't." Her tone sharpened, whether with hurt or bitterness, he could not tell.

"I'll protect you," Jonmarc said, hoping she could see the sincerity in his gaze. "Do anything I can for you. Help you get the money to leave here if you want."

Thaine's chuckle was mirthless. "And go where? Do what? Go be a kitchen wench and give it up for free in the stable?" She shook her head. "Better money for easier work here. I know where I belong."

"You could change your mind."

Her gaze narrowed. "You've saved me once, Jonmarc. Don't think you need to make a habit of it. Jolie treats her girls well. Healer keeps us from catching the clap, and the guards she hires keep the customers from getting rough. None of us are here against our will. She pays decent and doesn't take most of it for herself like some. Got a roof and food. I've done worse."

He had never gotten the full story of how Thaine came to be in the Nargi army camp, or how she had come to be a whore. Then again, he had not told her his full truth, either. "Fair enough," he replied, surprised he still felt a pang of loss. "But we could be friends. I don't have many friends."

Thaine relented a little at that, and her eyes lost their defensive glint. "We can be friends," she said and gave him a sad smile. "With a little more history than most."

He nodded. "And I'm still going to watch your back."

"I wouldn't have it any other way." The silence grew awkward. "I need to go."

"Thanks… for everything."

"That's what friends do," she replied, ducking her head to keep him from seeing her eyes as she let herself out.

Jonmarc let out a long breath after the door latched behind Thaine. *That went as well as it could.* Most men would have jumped at the chance to have a woman like Thaine, regardless of the terms. He knew what he was giving up. And there would doubtlessly be long nights when he questioned his decision. But not really. Even after all this time, Shanna's death felt like fresh grief. Maybe it always would. Or maybe he was too much of a coward to risk another loss like that, to put someone else at risk from the curse.

The flames will take everyone you love.

2

GUARDIAN

THE SHADOWS FOLLOW

For as much time as Jonmarc had spent in pubs and inns, he had never thought about the dishes. Now, two weeks after being fished out of the river and granted a stay of execution, he knew more about dishes, pots, pans, and kettles than he ever thought possible.

"Hey! Need those tankards at the bar!"

Jonmarc muttered under his breath as he lugged a load of clean mugs to the bar. He set the tray down with a clank.

"Watch it!" Senn, the barkeeper, snapped at him.

Jonmarc turned back toward the kitchen with a tray of dirty tankards, surprised at how much his body ached. He thought he had recovered from the fever, but he knew his body had not regained full strength. Lugging trays of dishes and cords of firewood should not tire him, yet he felt unusually spent. He dumped the tankards into a tub of water and then went out back for more cordwood to stoke the kitchen fire.

"Have you eaten anything?" Amme looked up from where she stirred the gravy, meat, and vegetables that would become the filling for venison pie later that night. "There's bread on the table, butter in the crock."

"Senn'll have a fit if I don't get more tankards to him."

Amme put her hands on her hips. "Jolie'll have a fit if you take sick again because I haven't fed you. Sit. Eat. Leave Senn to me."

She looked so fierce that Jonmarc smiled and did as she bade. The warm bread melted the fresh butter quickly, and he shoved the piece in his mouth, hungrier than he was willing to let on.

"I'll save back some of the meat pie for you, once it's made," Amme said with a nod toward the rich stew in the cauldron. "Jolie told me your food was part of your pay. Said I was to see to it you ate."

Jonmarc murmured his gratitude through a mouth full of bread. Amme watched him eat and shook her head. She grabbed a bowl ladled out some of the venison stew, and handed it to Jonmarc with another chunk of bread. "Eat this. The pies won't be done for a while yet, and you look dead on your feet."

After everything he had survived in Nargi and before that, it chafed to be knocked off his game by a fever. And while he felt strength returning, he knew it might be another week or more before the last of the illness's effects were gone. "This is good," he said, and Amme grinned.

"It is, isn't it? Been cooking for inns and taverns my whole life, since I was a slip of a girl," she said. A glance at her face suggested she might have grandchildren of her own now. Gray hair framed a face lined by a life of hard work. "Been cooking here for ten years now, give or take. Miss Jolie, she's good to work for. You could do worse."

Jonmarc ducked his head, unwilling to meet her eyes. He knew he owed Jolie. And although she remained skeptical about his worth, he felt certain he could convince her otherwise, at least for as long as he needed sanctuary. "Better get back to work," he said, with a grateful smile. He put his dirty bowl in with the rest of the dishes to be washed and went to haul a new bucket from the well.

"Seems a waste putting a man like you on kitchen duty," Amme said when he returned and began to wash the dishes. "Not that I mind the help. You carry more in one load that the girls they usually give me can haul in three trips. And it's nice to have a supply of firewood stacked and ready, instead of me having to go look for it when dinner's already late. Still," she said. "Seems like there's more you could be doing."

Jonmarc shrugged. "I guess Jolie will put me where she wants to put me," he replied, unwilling to get drawn into a discussion. When he finished his task, he nodded to Amme in parting and then headed back to the bustling common room.

He paused for a moment in the entrance, trained by experience to size up his surroundings. After two years of nearly solitary confinement in Nargi, the common room seemed too busy, too loud, and too crowded. A minstrel warbled a song, trying and failing to be heard over the conversations. Pipe smoke hung in the air, casting a haze over the room. Bodies pressed too close in their attempt to get to the bar. The room smelled of sweat, perfume, and tobacco, with the bitter undercurrent of ale.

It took all of Jonmarc's will not to flinch at the raucous crowd. His time in Nargi had required constant vigilance, and the edginess that came with that hyperawareness had kept him alive. Now that he had returned to civilian life, he doubted he would ever adjust. His swords remained safe under his bed, unsuitable for this work, and he felt naked without them, though he had a knife sheathed at his belt.

Out of old habit, he scanned for threat. Several of Jolie's

girls circulated among the crowd, urging on the gamblers and flirting with the men spending money at the bar. He could not see Thaine among them, and he ignored the momentary flash of possessiveness he had no right to feel.

Neither Astir nor Jolie were in sight. Senn at the bar kept up a constant patter as he sloshed ale into tankards. Jonmarc's senses honed in on potential problems. One of the men on the right side of the bar stood several inches taller than Jonmarc and probably outweighed him by two stone. He would be hard to handle if he got out of hand. On the other side of the bar, a short, wiry man eyed the whores with an expression that set off Jonmarc's alarms. There was nothing he could do, not yet, but the predatory glint in the skinny man's eyes looked feral and dangerous.

Across the room, a game of dice prompted loud voices and drunken curses. Jonmarc glanced at Senn, but the barkeep shook his head. After a few shouts, the dice players settled down once more, with the loser intent on regaining his winnings. Only after the crowd shifted did Jonmarc see the three men near the fireplace. The tallest, a dark-haired man with a crooked nose, had a laugh like a braying donkey. A shorter man with blond hair tied back in a queue tried unsuccessfully to stifle his friend's loud outburst but did not seem too put out about the disruption. The third fellow had a wide face and short-cropped brown hair, with a belly that spoke of a liking for too much ale and leisure.

He guessed them to be early in their third decade, strongly built and dressed like traders or merchants. The three were obviously friends and clearly well into their cups, good-looking enough to attract the favor of two of Jolie's girls who smiled and flirted. Intuition told Jonmarc that out of the threats he had already identified, these three smug bastards were most likely to cause trouble. He grabbed a tray and busied himself picking up empty tankards and bowls, working his way through the crowd until he was close enough to where the trio stood.

"What say you keep us company, darlin'?" the tall man said to a pretty blonde woman who slipped through the crowd, dressed in a gown of blue satin and white lace. Erina was one of Thaine's friends, someone Jonmarc had spoken with once or twice. Despite the provocative cut of her gown, Erina somehow seemed demure, maybe even shy. He wondered whether that was a mask she created for herself since it seemed at odds with the demands of her profession.

"You fancy me?" Erina asked, tilting her head to look at the tall man.

"Oh yes," the speaker replied. "We all do. How about we go somewhere and play a game or two?" He reached for her wrist, grabbing and holding tight even as Erina tried to step away.

"You have to see Miss Jolie," Erina answered, and Jonmarc could see she was trying not to panic. "And decide which of you wants my company."

Tall man pulled her into the midst of their little group. "We all want your company, darlin'. Don't want to play favorites now, do you?"

Erina struggled to free her wrist without making a scene. "Sorry, that's against house rules."

The blond man laughed. "We can pay for it. Silver makes people forget about rules."

Tall man dug his fingers into her wrist. "We're used to getting what we want," he said, low enough that if he hadn't been standing close, Jonmarc would not have heard the threat above the noise of the crowd.

A glance around told him Senn was too far away and Astir still had not come into the room. Jonmarc set down his tray and turned to the foursome, catching Erina's eye. "Senn told me Jolie's looking for a word with you," he said, meeting her gaze and willing her to play along. "You'd better go find out what she wants."

"The lady is busy." The blond man moved between Jonmarc and Erina. "Go back to the kitchen."

Erina's gaze begged him to stay. "Let the lady go."

Fat boy snickered. "I don't see any 'lady' here, just a whore about to have a busy evening."

"Last warning," Jonmarc said quietly. So far, no one around them had picked up on the tension, crowding them together. The blond man took a step closer to Jonmarc, who slipped to the side, intentionally putting himself closer to Erina and her captor.

"Mind your own business," fat boy said.

Jonmarc twisted suddenly, landing a punch to the tall man's side that had the stranger doubling over in pain, followed by a kick to the knee that sent him to the floor. Erina tore loose and dove into the crowd. Blond man and fat boy turned on Jonmarc, and he saw the glint of a knife in the portly man's hand.

Shouts and gasps rose from the crowd, which had finally recognized trouble. Jonmarc ducked a swing of the knife, coming up behind the man and driving his elbow into his lower back, easily grabbing the knife away when the attacker stumbled. Tall man grabbed a bottle from one of the tables and held it by the neck like a cudgel. Before he could take a swing, Jonmarc wheeled into a high Eastmark kick, planting his boot hard in the tall man's chest, sending him careening back into the fireplace, where he hit hard enough against the stone to leave a bloody trail.

"Leave the girls alone," Jonmarc said, standing over the three ruffians. The blond man started to struggle to his feet, but Astir joined Jonmarc in a blur of motion, and grabbed the troublemaker by the throat, lifting him off the ground.

"I think it's time for you to leave," Astir said quietly, moving his gaze to each of the men in turn. Jonmarc did not know whether compulsion made them agree, or they were sober enough to recognize that the addition of a *vayash moru* to a fighter who had just handed them their asses could not end well for them. "Do not return. You are not welcome in this place."

The crowd parted to let them pass, and Jonmarc rubbed his left hand over his raw knuckles. He had broken a sweat, and his heart thudded more than the fight warranted, but despite his recent illness, he had held his own easily against the three men. That felt good.

Astir's unreadable gaze did not reassure him. "I'll see you in the kitchen," Astir said quietly as the crowd began to lose interest. Jonmarc nodded, pausing to right several chairs that had fallen in the scuffle and then grab his tray of dirty dishes. This time, the patrons parted when they saw him coming, not requiring him to push his way through their midst. Jonmarc heard murmurs behind him as he passed, and squared his shoulders. He had done a lot of things in his life that he regretted, but roughing up three troublemakers was not among them.

Astir awaited him in the kitchen when he arrived. "Do we need to have a discussion about not damaging the patrons?"

Jonmarc set the tray down and met Astir's gaze. Once again, the *vayash moru* seemed unnerved that a mortal could do so without repercussion. "Do we need to have a discussion about not letting the patrons damage the ladies?" He then proceeded to tell Astir what led up to the fight, gratified that the man listened in silence.

"You can ask Erina," Jonmarc finished. "She's probably

got bruises on her wrist."

"You're not fully healed," Astir replied. "You endangered yourself."

Jonmarc snorted. "Yeah, well. I didn't like what they said to Erina or how they grabbed her, and you weren't around. Besides, the three of them weren't really a challenge."

Astir gave him an appraising stare. "You did not think about your safety."

Jonmarc felt his temper rise. "No. I knew I could take them, even though I'm not at my best. And they were *hurting* her. They wanted to hurt her more. Thaine told me Jolie protects her girls. Well, right then, I protected Erina." He looked away and sighed. "Does this mean I'm dismissed?"

Astir was silent for a moment and then chuckled. "I understand why so many want to kill you, Jonmarc Vahanian. You are a challenge." He shook his head. "No. You are not dismissed. In fact, despite how much Amme has appreciated your help, I believe it's time to promote you to guardian. That's what Jolie calls security here at the house."

"Fine with me, but why do you need mortals when you could handle any threat yourself?"

"*Vayash moru* are tolerated in Margolan but not entirely welcome," Astir replied. "My presence serves as a deterrent, for those who recognize what I am. If I were to frighten the guests rather than instill a bit of caution, things could go badly. For myself, for Jolie, and for this house." He shrugged. "I will do nothing to compromise Jolie's position."

Vayash moru were not easy to read, both by their nature and by the advantage of having a long lifespan over which to practice hiding their emotions. Yet something in Astir's voice and manner gave Jonmarc to suspect he was fond of Jolie, perhaps more than as merely an employer. *Interesting*.

"You have an unusual resistance." Astir looked directly at

Jonmarc as if daring him to meet his gaze. Jonmarc returned the look; eyes narrowed in challenge.

"So I've been told. Just lucky, I guess."

"An advantage, working here," Astir replied. "Not that I would compel any of our people, although from time to time, it has been useful to… deflect… troublesome situations."

"I bet."

"Tomorrow, you'll work with Senn at the bar. Give you a chance to get to know the regulars, and Senn can fill you in about what's normal. Troublemakers don't tend to come back once they've been told to move on," Astir added, and Jonmarc could see just the tips of his elongated eye teeth beneath his upper lip. "But sooner or later, new fools find their way in."

"We get any other *vayash moru*?"

Astir nodded. "From time to time. Some of the girls will take them. I make our rules clear, and the penalty for breaking them. There have never been any problems."

"Soldiers?"

Astir's expression tightened. "A necessary, but less welcome group. We're within a day's ride of three garrisons. They are welcome to spend their money here, so long as they don't cause trouble. Sometimes, they forget. Some, like your friend Harrtuck, help them remember their manners."

"Oh, he'd be good at that," Jonmarc replied, smiling at the thought. "Probably be the highlight of his evening."

"Indeed." Astir frowned as he looked at Jonmarc again and tilted his head as if studying him. "You are injured, and the evening has strained your energy. Go and rest. I'll send someone up to tend to your wounds."

Jonmarc had forgotten about his bruised and bloodied knuckles, and the aches he could feel from where the three men had landed a few solid hits. Compared to the kind of damage he took in even his best fights in Nargi, the injuries were so minor as to escape his concern. Now that he thought about them, they throbbed, and he felt weary to the bone. "That's not a bad idea."

"I'll send supper and some whiskey up as well. You've earned your keep. And I'll make a report to Jolie. I believe she will be pleased." He chuckled, though Jonmarc did not get the joke. "You may indeed work out here, Jonmarc Vahanian."

To Jonmarc's surprise, working with Senn proved entertaining. Though his job revolved mostly around giving patrons a choice between ale, grog, and whiskey, Senn seemed to enjoy his work, bantering with the customers and earning extra coppers for himself in the process. Sometimes they chatted in the quiet before customers began to drift in. That time of day was Jonmarc's favorite, before the noise and smoke and crowds.

"So is it true?" Senn asked on Jonmarc's second night as his assistant. "That you escaped from Nargi? Fought in their games?"

Jonmarc shrugged and turned away. "Yeah. It's true."

Senn let out a low whistle. "Huh. Well, that will win some people their bets."

Jonmarc looked back at him. "Bets?"

Senn went back to putting tankards away and mopping up the bar. "Been rumors going around since the night they hauled you out of the river. Thaine and that Margolan guard wouldn't say much, and neither would Jolie or Astir. But I saw what you did with those three assholes who bothered Erina. That's when I figured the rumors were right."

Jonmarc shifted, uncomfortable to have been the topic of conversation. "I'm not from there. Just took a wrong turn and got caught. I'm Margolense. From the Borderlands." For some reason, it seemed important for Senn to understand that, and for him to pass it along to anyone inclined to care.

"Didn't take you for a Nargi. Can't imagine one of those Crone-worshippers would look kindly at working in a brothel."

"From what I saw, the Nargi did as they damned well pleased, Crone be damned," Jonmarc replied, grabbing a rag and scrubbing at a stain on the far side of the bar.

"Hey, didn't mean to cause trouble. Just asking," Senn replied. "After all, I'm the barkeep. Hearing people's stories is part of the job."

Something about Senn made total strangers tell him more than they intended. Only part of it could be blamed on the alcohol. Senn looked to be in his thirties, with thinning dark hair and a wide smile. His hazel eyes had an openness that set people at ease, and he was quick with a joke and a story.

"So, you know something about me. Why are you here?" Jonmarc's question was flippant, meant more to pass the time than out of real curiosity. He knew he would be moving on after he got himself settled, and had not expected to make friends.

Senn stiffened and turned away. "How do you think? Didn't grow up wanting to be a barkeep in a whorehouse. Lost some people, took a few wrong turns myself. Could have done worse."

The look on his face made it clear that questions were not welcome. Jonmarc wondered what losses had brought Senn here, though he could guess.

"Heard you used to be with Thaine," Senn said, turning the conversation back on Jonmarc.

"That was before," Jonmarc replied, focusing his interest on straightening the bottles behind the bar. "Just friends now." He wiped up some spilled liquor and flicked his cloth to dust the shelf. "You got a girl here?"

Senn ducked down to put away supplies below the counter. "I had a lover. He died."

Jonmarc silently cursed himself. "I'm sorry."

"He had a little brother, eight years old. Josef. Lives with me now. We get by."

That explained the young boy Jonmarc had seen around the place, fetching firewood and trapping rats. He had wondered whether the boy was the son of one of the working girls, or a village boy sent to earn some coin. "I've seen him," Jonmarc replied. "Cute kid."

"Yeah," Senn replied. "Deserves better, but I keep him fed and out of the rain, so it could be worse."

Jonmarc tried to forget that his own child would have been five years old. The child he had buried but never got to meet. He swallowed hard and kept his head down, glad Senn could not see his face. *Don't ask. Please, don't ask.*

"Astir said you're going to be a guardian," Senn said, and Jonmarc let out a quiet sigh of relief at the shift in conversation.

"Seems to be what I do best," Jonmarc replied, straightening. He still did not look at Senn, unwilling to trust his expression just yet.

"You could go into the army. Bet your friend could fix it for you."

"Had all I want of following orders," Jonmarc answered. "But keeping the peace, knocking a few heads together—I can handle that."

"Yeah, you've got it," Senn agreed. "So here's who you need to watch out for…"

THAT EVENING, Jonmarc felt a restlessness he could not ignore. His skin prickled, and he sensed pressure like a coming storm, though the night stayed clear. The crowd in the common room was in high spirits, spending freely on ale and food, betting on dice and cards. The girls circulated among the patrons, disappearing two by two upstairs earlier in the evening than usual. Even the musician sounded better than usual, though the ballad he was singing at the moment was one of Jonmarc's least favorites. Everything seemed to be going well, but he could not shake the feeling of something amiss.

Jonmarc's gut clenched at the smell of roasting meat. He knew Amme had venison on the spit, but in the shadowed places of his memories, he remembered a burning barn filled with trapped, desperate people and the stench of charred flesh. He felt himself pale and dodged outside, falling to his knees and heaving in the bushes. Jonmarc gasped for breath and shame flushed his cheeks. He reached out an arm to steady himself against the wall, and climbed to his feet, wiping his mouth with the back of his hand.

Goddess! I'm no good to anyone like this.

He took another deep breath, set his shoulders, and walked back into the common room. Senn gave him a look, and Jonmarc ignored the silent question. Two men in the far corner of the room had started to argue, and Jonmarc decided that breaking up their fight might be the perfect way to take his mind off his troubles.

"Take your argument outside," Jonmarc snapped as he pulled the men apart. They were two of the regulars Senn warned him about. Jedd stood as tall as Jonmarc but thicker-set, with mean, close-set dark eyes in a fleshy face. Netan was a hand's breadth shorter, with the look of a scrawny dog. This altercation wasn't their first, though so far at least they had done nothing bad enough to get themselves banned.

"He's cheating!" Netan spat.

"Like you've ever played an honest hand of cards in your life!" Jedd retorted.

Jonmarc hauled Netan free of Jedd's grip and easily tossed the man against the wall as other patrons shifted to give them room. "Everyone knows both of you cheat," Jonmarc said in a low voice. He kept one hand locked on Jedd's upper arm with a bruising grip that promised worse if the man did not hold still. "If you play a cheater, you get what you deserve."

"I want my coppers back," Jedd sulked.

"He stole my money," Netan accused, falling silent at the glare Jonmarc leveled in his direction.

"I'd say the odds are good you both stole from each other," Jonmarc growled. "So here's what you're going to do. You're going to take those coppers and pay them to Senn for your bar bill, and then you're going to leave for the night, you out that door," he said to Jedd with a tilt of his head to the right, "and you out that one," he added to Netan, flicking his gaze to the left.

"Now if you want to have a brawl outside, it's not my business unless you block the door," Jonmarc continued. "If that happens, I guarantee you that you won't be walking anywhere for a long time." He shoved Jedd hard enough that the man stumbled, careening into a table and sloshing the tankards of ale, which earned him a cuff on the ear and a torrent of curses from the angry patrons.

"Get going," Jonmarc barked at Netan, who scrabbled away from the wall and tripped over two people on his way out the door.

Some of the patrons stared at Jonmarc, who glowered in return. His expression and manner warned them to mind their business, and within a few minutes, conversation resumed. Jonmarc eyed the crowd for a moment longer, checking for additional threats, then made his way back to where he kept watch from the far corner of the bar.

"That went well," Senn remarked as he filled tankards.

Jonmarc shrugged. "Nobody bled. I count that as a win."

Senn gave him a look. "You've got a skewed way of looking at things."

"Comes with the territory." Jonmarc's promotion to guardian meant he spent four nights a week keeping the peace in the common room, or on rare occasions, intervening upstairs if a patron posed a threat.

Jolie's girls made the rounds, flirting and teasing. Thaine stopped at the bar to refresh a patron's drink, and looked over at Jonmarc. "Nice work," she said, her voice rough with the pipe smoke that filled the room. "Those two are trouble. Don't know why Astir doesn't ban them."

Senn looked up. "If we banned every idiot, there'd be no one left to buy ale." He gave a curt nod to the crowd at the bar. "Present company excepted." The men chuckled, acknowledging the truth in the comment.

Thaine headed back to her client, and Jonmarc made himself look away. He might not have loved Thaine the same way he cared for Shanna, but the thought of her with strangers bothered him more it should. He knew he had no right to object, that it felt more like protectiveness than jealousy, but he still kept his eyes averted when she headed upstairs to keep himself from fixing her client with a threatening glare.

"That's why we don't get involved," Senn murmured as he passed by on the way to grab a new barrel of ale.

"I'm not involved."

"Uh huh."

To Jonmarc's relief, Erina detoured from her rounds. "I didn't get the chance to thank you before," she said quietly. Jonmarc looked down to where long sleeves hid bruises on her forearm and wrist.

"It's my job."

Erina rolled her eyes. "Not then. Kitchen help doesn't usually come to the rescue."

Jonmarc could not resist a smirk. "Guess they had me in the wrong job."

Erina smiled as if they shared a secret. "Guess so." She turned serious. "Can you keep an eye out for someone for me? I don't want any more trouble."

Jonmarc frowned. "Sure. Who?"

Erina sidled closer, looking out over the crowd, and Jonmarc could read the worry in her eyes. "There's a guy who comes in here who makes me... unsettled. He fancies me, and he's never done anything actually wrong, but I'm running out of ways to avoid him."

"Does he bother the other girls?" Jonmarc asked.

Erina shrugged. "Some, but they'll take them. Well, except for Thaine and Jace—they don't like him, either."

"I'm not sure what I can do if he doesn't actually cause trouble," Jonmarc said. "Jolie won't be pleased if I start throwing out paying patrons."

She grimaced. "Yeah, that's the problem. It's just; something's off about the man, you know? Sends a chill down my spine. I'm used to being looked over and felt up, but he stares at me like I'm... food."

Jonmarc raised an eyebrow. "Is he *vayash moru*?"

Erina shook her head. "I don't think so. Astir keeps an eye on those pretty closely. He's just strange."

Erina described the man, and Jonmarc took note. "Are there any of the girls who won't mind if I steer him their way?" he asked.

"Pelli says it's all the same to her, long as they pay," Erina replied. "Renata doesn't seem to care, either. So whenever he shows up, I ask them to help me out." She looked away. "There are a couple of guys I take for them. It works out."

Jonmarc nodded, although he didn't understand, not really. Shanna had been his first, and then the grief over her death, the guilt and self-loathing and blame, meant he had not taken another lover until circumstances forced Thaine and him together in Nargi. He had plenty of opportunities, both with the caravan and as a merc. But he remembered how it had been with Shanna, everything tangled up together, and anything less held scant appeal. Maybe that would change, now that he was free again, but perhaps not. Being alone meant less to lose.

"I'll keep an eye out," Jonmarc promised. "And in the meantime, try to stay out of trouble."

Erina threw him a wink and her most flirtatious pout. "Now what fun would that be? Girl's gotta make a living." With that, she sauntered off, and Jonmarc knew the exaggerated sashay was for his benefit.

Candlemarks passed without incident. Jonmarc moved from one end of the bar to another, watching for problems, but tonight the customers were well-behaved. Senn cut off a few drunkards at the bar and Jonmarc escorted them out, but they went peacefully as if they had been waiting for the signal to call it a night.

When Jonmarc came back inside after taking the last drunk out to the road, he frowned as he realized a newcomer had entered through the back. He matched Erina's description of her stalker exactly. Tall, slender, with blond curly hair, cropped just at his collar. Too thin, but his corded arms suggested strength even without much bulk. He might have been in his late twenties or a decade older; it was difficult to tell. His features, while regular, were not remarkable. Then Jonmarc met his gaze across the room. He felt a cold tendril down his spine. The utter chill of the man's eyes seemed completely at odds with his casual manner and his smile.

Jonmarc scanned the room, and his gut tightened as he realized that Erina and Jace were the only trollops in the room. Jace took one look at the thin man and sat down in the lap of the man she had been seducing, initiating a kiss that caused the man's companions to prod him to go upstairs. The newcomer paid Jace no heed, making straight for Erina.

Jonmarc started forward, but Senn laid a hand on his arm. "Nothing you can do right now," he said, as Erina looked across the room, hoping for a reprieve. "The man might be a little strange, but if he pays and he plays by the rules, you can't turn him away."

"She should have a choice," Jonmarc said, feeling an angry burst of protectiveness as the man took Erina's elbow and guided her toward the stairs.

"And she does—to a point," Senn said quietly. "Jolie won't stand for anyone getting hurt. But it's part of the business, and Erina knows that. If the fellow steps out of line, feel free to break his nose. He might take the hint."

The look on Erina's face stayed in Jonmarc's mind as he moved through the room. He itched for a fight and caught himself hoping he would have an altercation to settle just to work off his anger. As if they recognized the danger, the crowd kept to their best behavior.

A scream from upstairs cut through the music and conversation and sent Jonmarc running.

He had his knife in his hand when he cleared the top of

the steps. Thaine and Pelli stood partially hidden by their half-open doors, covering themselves with their robes. "Down there," Thaine pointed. "Erina's room."

Jonmarc barged into the room, only to see the thin man leaping from the window and Erina lying amid bloody sheets on the floor. Thaine crowded in behind him and fell to her knees beside Erina, who gave a weak moan.

"Go," Thaine urged, "I'll see to her."

Jonmarc scrambled out of the window. Jolie's Place had been expanded over many years, a mismatched collection of boxy additions with a staggered roofline. Climbing in might have posed some difficulty, but dropping from one level to the next to get to the ground was easy. Jonmarc took off running, chasing after the thin man's dark form in the distance. He pressed for more speed, closing the distance, until the man dodged into the shadows of the trees that lined the road and emerged a minute later on horseback, galloping out of reach.

Jonmarc cursed, listening to the hoof beats recede into the distance. He doubled over, resting his hands on his knees as he caught his breath, and then straightened and headed back to the brothel. Much as he wanted to find an excuse for a fight in the common room, his worry for Erina overrode his anger. A glance at Senn told him that things were under control downstairs, and Jonmarc headed to the second floor, anxious to find out how seriously Erina had been injured.

Jolie sat on one side of Erina's bed, and Thaine on the other. A bowl of water, tinged pink with blood, rested on the mattress beside Erina, who lay still and pale. Thaine gently washed the blood from the slashes on Erina's arms, while Jolie bound the cuts with strips of cloth.

"I lost him," Jonmarc said, and at that, the others turned to note his entrance. "He had a horse hidden down the road a bit. Guess he thought he might need to make a quick exit." He paused. "How is she?"

"Hurt. Frightened. She's lost a lot of blood," Jolie replied, turning back to wrapping the woman's arms. "I've sent for the healer."

"Do you know why?" Jonmarc forced down a choking sense of guilt. Erina had asked for his protection, and he had failed her.

"He's been fixed on her," Thaine replied, anger clear in her eyes. "He says crazy things about her being his wife, his only one, about how she's his because of fate. I heard them arguing before she screamed. Wouldn't be surprised if he wanted her to run off with him."

"Do you know who he is?" Jonmarc asked quietly, meeting Thaine's eyes. He saw that she understood his intent.

"His name is Lem. Or at least, that's what he calls himself here," she murmured. "Don't know where he's from, but it's close enough he comes by often."

"He will not be permitted to return."

Jonmarc had not heard Astir approach. He wheeled on the *vayash moru*, feeling his fury rise.

"If you had been around, you could have caught him," Jonmarc snapped. "He outran me, but he couldn't have outrun you."

Astir regarded him with a cool expression that only made Jonmarc even angrier. "I was handling another incident. Two thieves were discovered in the stable, going through saddlebags. I went to deal with them. I returned when I heard her scream, but by then you—and the attacker—were already gone."

Jonmarc had to bite back his response. He knew he was looking for a fight, and knew equally well that Astir did not deserve his rage. A busy place like Jolie's had too much going on for any one person to handle everything. Still, he could not help feeling that had Astir responded more quickly, the attacker might have been caught. He turned away before his anger got him into trouble. Making an enemy of a *vayash moru* was never wise.

"I need to get back downstairs. I'll keep an eye out, and if he comes back, I'll take care of him."

Senn looked up when he returned, and when a lull provided the opportunity, Jonmarc filled the barkeep in on what happened.

"I should have gotten rid of him when he first showed up," Jonmarc said, as Senn slid a glass of whiskey his way. Jonmarc knocked it back, knowing it would do little to take the edge off his mood.

"This business draws its share of strange types," Senn said, keeping his voice too low for the customers at the bar to hear if they were inclined to focus on anything besides the drinks in front of them. "Jolie does better than most at keeping the girls safe, but given the work, there aren't any guarantees."

"Next time we get someone like that who bothers the girls, I'm not going to wait for him to cut one of them up," Jonmarc muttered. "Not if I'm on duty."

"Watch yourself," Senn cautioned. "Drive off the customers, and Jolie will hand you your hat."

"If that's what it takes to do my job, then let it come," Jonmarc replied. "She hired me to protect them, and that's damn well what I'm going to do."

THE NEXT MORNING, Jonmarc woke in a foul mood. His dreams had been dark. Nightmares filled with fire and blood awakened him choking back screams, drenched with sweat and shaking. He heard the thud of the gallows, the crackle of flames, and the snap of a whip. Magicked beasts pursued him down moonless roads, tearing at his back with their talons, snapping at him with sharp teeth. It had almost been a relief when the dreams shifted to the worst of the fights from Nargi, reminding him how it felt to beat a man to death with his bare hands, skin slick with hot blood.

He lay still until his heartbeat evened out and his breathing slowed, rubbing the heels of his hands against his eyes, wiping away the tears. Whiskey helped him fall asleep, and physical exertion deepened his rest for a while, but nothing ever made the dreams disappear. It had been better, for a while, when Thaine shared his bed. She had soothed him and stroked his chest, murmured reassurances and kissed him. He owed her for her kindness, and he missed her company, though he realized it was for all the wrong reasons.

By Chenne! I'm too broken to be of much use to anyone. He could taste last night's whiskey when he licked his dry lips. The bottle next to his bed lay on its side, empty. That his head did not ache only served to tell him that he had grown far too accustomed to drinking his pain away. He fully expected strong drink to do what his enemies could not: put him in an early grave. Jonmarc could not bring himself to care.

Mornings were quiet at Jolie's Place, one of the reasons Jonmarc liked that time of day best. He felt uncomfortable in the crowded common room during the evening amid so many strangers. For two years in Nargi, he had been quartered alone or with Thaine, seeing no one else except guards until a match. Before that, in Eastmark with his garrison and in Principality with the War Dogs, his world revolved around at most two dozen men whom he trusted with his life. He counted on their company, whether going into battle or heading to a pub.

Now, he had no one to watch his back, and it bothered him.

Senn was companionable, and Amme and her kitchen crew enjoyed teasing him and mock-flirting. Jolie and Astir were cordial but distant. Thanks to Thaine's vouching for him, Jolie's girls had adopted him as a big brother-protector. He rarely saw the other guardians, though they knew each other to nod in passing. All of which meant he felt deeply responsible and completely alone.

"I could use some help with these barrels." Senn's voice jarred Jonmarc out of his thoughts, and he hurried to give the barkeeper a hand.

"How's Erina?" Senn asked as he and Jonmarc grabbed a barrel from the brewery's wagon and began to haul it into the building.

"Thaine stopped down to tell me she was resting, and the healer closed up the cuts. It was bad, Senn. Real bad."

"Doesn't make sense, if this Lem fellow fancies Erina why he'd do that," Senn said, setting his end of the barrel down with a grunt.

"Maybe he got the message that he couldn't have her, and figured no one else could, either," Jonmarc replied, dusting off his palms on his pants as they headed back for another barrel.

"Shit," Senn muttered. "I've seen men swoon over the girls a time or two, mistake what they're paying for as the real thing. But they went away when someone explained it to them."

"So did Lem. But with a lot more blood."

"She'll be all right?"

Jonmarc blinked to erase the memory of Erina slumped

against the wall, covered in blood. He bent down to grab the next barrel. "The cuts will heal. The memories—they're the hard part." Perhaps a mind healer could blur the horror, blunt the remembered helplessness, but that kind of magic came dear, not easy to find.

"At least he won't be back," Senn replied.

A chill went down Jonmarc's back for no good reason at Senn's words. "Yeah," he said, ignoring the sensation. "There's that."

They unloaded the wagon, paid the driver, and Senn headed back inside. Jonmarc paused to take in the building from the stable side. Extra rooms and added wings made for an irregular profile. It sprawled higgledy-piggledy, and the mismatched sections gave it a certain charm. The frequent additions also suggested Jolie's business acumen. A storage building sat against one side, and across an expanse of dirt and patchy grass was the stable. The whole thing could use a good whitewashing, and Jonmarc noted where boards and shingles looked loose. If he stuck around, he could make himself useful and keep busy enough to drown out his thoughts by doing repairs to earn his keep.

He grabbed an armful of firewood and headed back inside. For the next candlemark, he straightened and wiped down the tables in the common room, helped Senn restock the bar, and brought up provisions from the root cellar for Amme, who fussed over him and fed him a freshly baked tart in gratitude.

Jonmarc could not help feeling edgy. Needing to keep busy, he had already finished the indoor tasks and started toward the stable. As a blacksmith, he had spent plenty of time with horses and farriers, and he thought he might be able to lend a hand. Just as he reached the door, he heard a dog barking frantically. He glanced over toward the stable, where Rufus, the barn dog was tethered with a sturdy rope to keep him from chasing the chickens. Rufus strained at his leash, barking desperately, and when Jonmarc turned, he understood the reason for the dog's agitation.

Flames engulfed the storage building, and in minutes, they would reach the rest of the house. Astir had gone to ground and Jolie had private quarters on the other side of the building, but Thaine and the rest of the women were asleep upstairs.

Jonmarc ran back into the common room. "Senn! Get Amme and everyone you can, grab buckets and form a line to the river. The shed's on fire!"

Before Senn could reply, Jonmarc headed up the stairs, shouting at the top of his lungs and beating on the doors as he ran past.

"Fire! Shed's on fire! Get up, get out now!"

Smoke already curled along the side of the building, seeping in through the gaps in the window frames. Jonmarc came back down the hallway, throwing doors open. "Come on! Move it! There's no time—wrap up and get moving!"

Thaine came out of Erina's room, and Jonmarc guessed she had sat up for the night with her friend. Dressed in their nightshirts, they made their way toward the stairs, Thaine guiding Erina with an arm around her waist as if she had had too much to drink.

"I'll get her out and come back to help," Thaine promised, but Jonmarc shook his head. The smoke made him cough, rapidly clouding the air.

"Stay out. Help with the buckets. If they don't put out the fire the whole thing is going to go."

Thaine gave a curt nod and maneuvered Erina down the steps. Jonmarc shouted and cursed. Twice, he went in and hauled sleeping women from their beds, herding the bleary-eyed strumpets toward the stairs.

Jonmarc coughed, gasping for breath. His eyes teared, and his throat burned, but he checked every room before he staggered down the steps. Smoke filled the common room, and he hoped it had merely been drawn inside through the open doors. He collapsed to his knees once he got outside, drawing in lungfuls of fresh air. In the distance, he heard shouts and excited voices.

When he finally got to his feet, he realized Senn had obeyed his frantic order. All of the kitchen help and the stable boys, as well as Thaine and the rest of the trollops except for Erina, had joined the line, passing every bucket, pot, and cauldron up from the river to douse the flames. At some point in the confusion, Jolie had joined them and taken charge of the bucket brigade, taking her place among those at the front of the line who threw the water onto the burning shed.

Jonmarc found a place in line, and lost track of time with the repetition: turn, grab, turn, hand off, repeat. Sweat and ash covered him as cinders rained down on the bucket line, burning where they touched skin. The faces around him are soot-stained and resolute, eyes red from smoke, tireless as they keep up a steady flow of water.

A cheer went up when the last of the flames died back. They kept on passing up buckets until the smoldering remains lay completely soaked, sending black rivulets of water beneath their feet.

Senn and Jonmarc moved up to poke at the remains of the shed and prod the blackened side of the main building. When they gave the all-clear, a weary shout rose from the others, who stumbled out of line and dropped to the ground, exhausted.

"I'm not looking forward to when Astir finds out about this," Senn said, kicking at a blackened piece of lumber.

"It could have been a lot worse."

Looking over the smoking ruins, Jonmarc could not shake a sense of foreboding. The timing of the fire seemed too coincidental after the events of the previous night. Lem's obsession over Erina had been too long-standing for him to suddenly give up. Lem could not have her and had not succeeded in his attempt to keep anyone else from claiming her. Jonmarc had no proof, nothing except his intuition, but he would have been willing to place a bet that Lem set the fire. Senn met his eyes, and Jonmarc saw his suspicions confirmed in the other man's gaze.

"So what now?" Senn asked quietly.

Jonmarc looked around at their exhausted companions. "Let's get everyone inside and fed, for starters. Then once the wreckage cools down, we'll cart away the remains."

"That's not exactly what I meant."

Jonmarc looked at Senn. "Don't ask questions you don't want to know the answer to. What you don't know, you can't tell."

"One of the stable boys lives in the next town over. Kettlesmith. He said once that he'd seen Lem in the village, thought he lived there. It's about a half a candlemark's ride from here," Senn said, staring off toward the river. "Just in case you ever decided to see the sights."

"Good to know."

Astir would not rise until sundown. Julie made a point of checking in with every person, summoning the healer to help with injuries and the effects of the smoke. Jonmarc spent the majority of the day helping Senn and Thaine get the house ready to be able to do business that night, wiping soot from tables and checking to assure the fire had done no real damage to the main building. When he had done everything he could to help, Jonmarc slipped away. He had the night off, and a plan for what to do with the time.

He stopped by his room to get his knife. Jonmarc hesitated, thinking about the swords beneath his bed. They were the last blades his father forged before the raiders killed him, balanced well with straight, true blades. Jonmarc owned nothing else of value, but he prized the blades as much out of sentiment as practicality. He remained grateful to the Nargi General who set him free for returning the swords to him before his escape. Since he had been at Jolie's Place, the swords had stayed beneath his bed, wrapped in a blanket.

He weighed his options and decided to leave the swords behind, taking only his knife. The swords would be too memorable, and he had no idea of the setting for the confrontation he sought. Best to keep it simple.

He made sure to slip out before the crowd gathered, even if it meant getting to Kettlesmith before the sun set. Jonmarc borrowed a horse from the stable. No one at Jolie's had cause to look for him, but if anyone noticed his absence, he knew Senn could come up with a plausible story.

The time on the road cleared his head, and despite his dark purpose, lightened his heart. He had not been free to ride a horse in nearly three years. Not since before the court martial in Eastmark, which felt like a lifetime ago. It all came back to him from long practice, and he let himself fall into moving as one with the stallion, enjoying having the road unfold beneath him. The rhythm of the hoof beats calmed him and steadied his nerves for what was to come.

He had no real proof to blame Lem for the fire, nothing but a deep, gut-level suspicion. An instinct he trusted enough to justify murder. *Not murder. Self-defense. Because that bastard cut up Erina and would have left them all to burn in their beds. And if he gets away with it, he'll be back, and maybe we won't be so lucky next time. This ends now.*

He slowed his horse as Kettlesmith came into view. Nothing marked the small village as out of the ordinary. Farms lined the road on the way from Jolie's Place, then more modest houses set closer together, and finally an inn at the outskirts of town. In the center of the village, vendors hawked vegetables and fresh meats in the marketplace, rows of open stalls selling everything from fabric to spices. Kettlesmith obviously relied on travelers and trade, since the cobbler, cooper, blacksmith, and chandler could not make a living solely on the occupants of the hamlet.

Jonmarc made a slow circle through Kettlesmith, thinking he might get lucky and spot Lem. He searched the faces of the merchants and the customers in the marketplace but did not see the man. He cursed under his breath. Even in a town that depended on outsiders for its living, people were likely to remember a stranger asking questions. And if those questions centered on finding a man who shortly afterward turned up dead, someone was likely to draw conclusions. If Lem found his way to Jolie's Place, it stood to reason other Kettlesmith residents took their pleasure at the brothel as well. Jonmarc did not want to be remembered.

He tethered his horse in the shade and made another circuit on foot. Lem did not have the look of a farmer, so Jonmarc felt reasonably confident ruling out the barns and fields he passed. Most people were working at this time of day, so odds were in his favor to find Lem out and about, instead of in his home. He might have fled, and Jonmarc had considered that possibility on the way to Kettlesmith, but he counted on Lem's obsession to keep him close.

Trying to avoid suspicion, Jonmarc lingered in the marketplace, buying some fruit and dried beef he did not really need. If he could not spot Lem in the village, he would have no choice except to go to the inn and ask around. Jonmarc had nearly resigned himself to that when he spotted a figure that looked familiar from the back.

"Excuse me," Jonmarc murmured, pushing through the crowd to follow. He nearly lost the tall man in the jumble of stands and shoppers, but he caught sight of his quarry again and closed the distance enough to confirm Lem's identity.

Jonmarc continued to follow Lem, hanging back enough to not be noticed. Lem did not seem to be aware that Jonmarc shadowed him, winding through the streets and leaving the busy market to turn down an alley to a shabby rooming house. Jonmarc lingered in the doorway of a nearby building, in case Lem had merely gone to visit someone, but when the man did not come out after almost a candlemark, Jonmarc felt certain he had tracked the arsonist to his home.

The smells of roasting meat and steaming vegetables filled the air, and Jonmarc took a chance that Lem would not go back out before eating his dinner. He returned to the alley and stared up at the rooming house, evaluating his options. Going in the front was too risky. He circled the building and noted a low roof and a drainpipe that could easily give him access to the second floor. He lingered at the windows, listening for voices, trying to get a glimpse inside.

Jonmarc quickly ruled out Lem being on the first floor. He climbed the pipe and slipped across the roof, glad for the lengthening evening shadows. The first window was dark, and he heard no movement inside. The second stood ajar, and Jonmarc easily pushed it wider. Lem sat with his back to the window at a table.

Spread in front of Lem was a coil of rope, a pair of manacles, a knife dark with dried blood, and pouches of ingredients Jonmarc bet were for some kind of curse. *He's planning to go after her... again.*

Jonmarc retraced his steps to the darkened window in the room next to Lem. He slipped in through the window, and when he assured himself that the room was empty, he readied his knife. He moved down the deserted hallway to Lem's door, which gave way easily when he shouldered inside.

Lem rose to his feet, a knife of his own in hand, and his posture gave Jonmarc to suspect the man knew something about handling himself in a fight.

"You set the fire at Jolie's."

Lem glared at him, keeping his distance, adjusting his stance. "She turned me down. I needed her to see that she made a mistake."

"And that," Jonmarc said, gesturing toward the rope and chains on the table, "was how you were going to show her? Convince her she was wrong by kidnapping her?"

"I love her!" Lem shouted. "She's all I think about, all I dream about. She belongs with me."

"She belongs where she is. Where she wants to be. Which isn't with you," Jonmarc replied. "Goddess—you could have killed her and everyone else if that fire took hold!"

"Better that than lose her," Lem shot back. "I'm not going to stop until I win her."

"She isn't a prize you take home from the fair."

"I'd rather die than be without her." Lem dove forward, slashing at Jonmarc with his blade. His swing went wild, driven by fury. Lem tried again, bringing the knife down in an arc that would have been lethal had Jonmarc not evaded the blow. Lem lacked training, but his madness-fueled unpredictability made him dangerous nonetheless.

Lem's next strike put him off balance. Jonmarc pivoted, using an Eastmark kick to disarm his opponent. The knife flew in one direction and Lem fell back on his ass. Jonmarc pinned him in one move, slamming a fist into Lem's jaw. "You almost killed a house full of people."

"I won't give her up. I won't, I can't stop."

Jonmarc's knife plunged down into the man's heart. "Yeah, you will," he muttered, stepping back from the growing pool of blood. He wiped the blade on the dead man's trousers and glanced around the room to assure nothing might lead authorities back to Jolie's Place—assuming that Lem's death would prompt notice by anyone other than the landlord. He grabbed a towel from the back of a chair and did his best to wipe the blood from his hands and face, counting on darkness to hide any spatter on his clothing until he could get back to the brothel. Satisfied, Jonmarc sheathed his knife and slipped back through the window.

Jonmarc breathed a sigh of relief to find his horse still tethered where he had left him. He swung up into the saddle and headed out of town, spurring the horse to a faster pace once they were on the main road. The trip back to Jolie's seemed to go much quicker than the journey into town, and Jonmarc felt surprised when the lights came into view before he expected to see them. He slowed his horse and came to the back of the stable, relieved that none of the stable hands were in sight.

Working quickly, he removed the saddle and tack, curried and wiped down his mount and returned with food and water, patting the horse's neck. "Just our little secret," he murmured, scratching the stallion behind one ear.

Jonmarc had just stepped out into the shadows beyond the stable when a strong arm swept him up against the wall as if he weighed nothing.

"You reek of blood." Astir loomed over Jonmarc, somehow seeming much larger than he had ever appeared in the light. Jonmarc willed himself to remain still, though his breath quickened and his heart thumped.

"I did what you couldn't—or wouldn't. I took care of the problem."

Jonmarc could meet the *vayash moru*'s gaze without surrendering to compulsion, but in the moonlight, he saw a much more deadly force glinting in Astir's eyes.

"Did anyone see you?"

Even with Astir's arm pressed so hard against his chest that he could barely breathe, Jonmarc managed to give the man a look. "No. Give me credit; I'm a soldier. I know how to do my job."

"Your job didn't include murder."

Jonmarc's eyes narrowed. "He was going to come back, and this time, he intended to take Erina with him. Had the rope and chains, and some conjure herbs to knock her out. Told me himself he wouldn't stop until he had her. You made me a guardian. I protect."

For a moment, Astir remained motionless as only a *vayash moru* could be, the utter stillness of the dead. When he loosened his grip, pulling his arm away, Jonmarc nearly fell as the pressure released him.

"Put this on," Astir said, removing his cloak and handing it to Jonmarc. "Go change, and then burn these clothes. Someone could smell the blood."

"You expecting more *vayash moru*?"

Astir's expression gave nothing away. "The night is full of many creatures, whose allegiances are unclear. Best to be safe."

With that, Astir strode off toward the brothel, leaving Jonmarc to make his way in the dark.

3

GUARDIAN

UNHEEDED WARNINGS

"Third time in as many weeks those *vayash moru* have been in," Senn said under his breath to Jonmarc, eyeing the two newcomers across the common room. They both knew their undead guests had hyper-sensitive hearing, but with the noise of conversation and the din of the musicians, Senn's comment was unlikely to carry far.

"What's Astir say about it?" Jonmarc replied, taking up his usual spot at the end of the bar, watching the room.

"As long as they pay their money and don't cause trouble, they're as welcome as anyone else," Senn replied with a shrug.

One of the *vayash moru* struck up a conversation with Pelli, who greeted him like she knew him. If she recognized what he was, it did not bother her. Both of the men were dressed as well as minor nobles, their clothing made from expensive fabrics and fine lace. Their boots alone probably cost more than what Jonmarc might earn in a year.

The men appeared to be in their thirties, though they could have been centuries older. The taller, sable-haired man had striking, angular features. His companion, a red-head, was equally handsome but in a softer, slightly debauched way. They carried themselves with a sense of utter confidence as if they owned the brothel and everyone in it. A sharp, sudden dislike stabbed through Jonmarc.

"Jolie all right with it?"

"If she wasn't, it would stop. Since it hasn't, I reckon she is."

Jonmarc's grip tightened on the edge of the bar as Thaine sat down with the second *vayash moru*.

"Easy." Senn followed his gaze and glanced down at Jonmarc's fist. "Just business, remember?"

Jonmarc growled a curse under his breath and forced his gaze away. Since the fire, the crowd had been less rowdy than usual. The debris from the ruined shed had been cleared away, the wall whitewashed, and lumber brought in to build a replacement. But Jonmarc still tensed if the smell of smoke came from the kitchen, and it had taken a few weeks for him to stop searching the crowd for Lem, although he knew the man was dead.

Thankfully, no one seemed to care. Lem's death passed unnoticed and unremarked, and if Erina and Thaine suspected that Jonmarc had put a permanent end to the problem, they said nothing. Neither did Jolie, though Jonmarc caught her gaze sliding sidelong to him on more than one occasion as if retaking his measure. *Or perhaps, deciding whether or not I'm too dangerous to keep around.*

Astir said nothing after that night, though it seemed to Jonmarc that something in their relationship had changed, an unspoken understanding. *One predator to another.*

Movement caught Jonmarc's eye. The red-haired man stood up, and Thaine followed a moment later. He slipped an arm around her, his hand at the small of her back, and they headed upstairs together. Not long after, Pelli and the other man followed.

The pang of jealousy caught Jonmarc unprepared, like a punch to the gut. He knew he had no claim on Thaine and no cause for the tangle of emotions that swirled through him. In the months he had been at Jolie's Place, he had seen Thaine go off with many other clients and had tamped down his misplaced possessiveness and the odd flutter of betrayal. Somehow, irrationally, the fact that the man was *vayash moru* bothered him even more than usual.

The thump of a glass with two fingers of whiskey in it jolted him out of his thoughts.

"On the house," Senn said with a look that gave Jonmarc to know the man guessed the direction of his thoughts. "Let it go."

When the house closed for the night, Jonmarc paid Senn for a half bottle of whiskey and headed to his room. A knock at the door made him startle. Finding Jolie in the doorway surprised him. She stepped in without preamble and closed the door behind her.

"You killed Lem."

Jonmarc nodded, wondering why she decided to bring up the incident now. "He was going to come back and try to take Erina away with him by force. I figured I could kill him then or kill him later."

Jolie's gaze slipped over him, appraising, and Jonmarc fought the instinct to flinch away. "Is it so easy for you to kill?"

He looked up, eyes narrowing. "I know how to fight. Killing is never… easy. But sometimes it has to be done. If Lem came back, there's no telling who else would have gotten hurt."

"I wasn't faulting you. I believe in practicality." Jolie

paused. "Thank you for protecting Erina—and the others. You ran into the fire to save my girls, and you got the bucket line going to save the building. I'm grateful."

Jonmarc shrugged, uncomfortable, and looked away. "You fished me out of the river and didn't kill me. Gave me a job and a roof and food. You didn't have to. So... we're good?"

A smile quirked at the corners of Jolie's lips. "Yes. We're good." Her eyes grew serious. "But I would prefer if you not make a habit of killing customers, even the problem ones. We exist here at the sufferance of the locals, and I have no desire to be forced to relocate."

"Understood."

"You're a good worker, Jonmarc," Jolie said. "You have a place here as long as you want."

"Thank you," Jonmarc said. He appreciated Jolie's welcome, just as deeply as he did not feel worthy of it. *Just a hired killer with a different target. At least I'm useful. Not much good at anything else.*

The bar closed, the patrons left, and the kitchen workers banked the fires for the night. Jonmarc finished the whiskey and headed out into the common room, looking for more. He looked up at the sound of footsteps. Thaine pulled a dressing gown around herself and headed toward him.

"You're up late."

He shrugged irritably. "Couldn't sleep."

"Me neither."

Jonmarc found the bottle he wanted behind the bar and left payment where Senn would find it. He stood up, surprised and annoyed to find that Thaine seemed to be waiting for him. "What?"

"Just thought you should know that you're quite the hero with the girls, after the fire and what you did for Erina."

Jonmarc turned away. "I'm a lot of things, but 'hero' isn't one of them. Just doing my job."

Thaine tilted her head, looking at him quizzically. "Pretty sure running into a burning building and killing a man goes beyond 'doing your job.'"

Jonmarc began to walk toward his quarters. "Don't know what you want me to say. I took care of things. It's done."

"How long are you going to stay here, Jonmarc?"

He stopped, surprised at her words. Of all the things he had expected Thaine to say, that question was not among them. "Until it's time to go," he said.

"Harrtuck could get you into the army. You could earn a commission."

"I've had enough of armies and orders. No thanks."

"You're better than this," Thaine argued. "You could leave here, be anything—"

Jonmarc wheeled to face her, his balance unimpaired by the whiskey. "You know what I am," he growled. "You know what I did... over there."

"You had no choice."

"There's always a choice." He remembered the nights he decided to throw the next fight, let his opponent kill him rather than continue the games. Every time, when it came down to it, self-preservation kicked in and he woke up, miserable and alive. "I just didn't have the stones to make the right one."

Thaine moved closer, and Jonmarc stepped back. "Jonmarc," she said, reaching out. He shied away as if burned.

"Don't."

"Haven't you thought about it? Where you could go? What else you could do? I have," she said, lifting her head. "I'm not going to be a whore forever, and I've got no mind to run a house like Jolie."

"I hope you make it," Jonmarc replied, meaning the words. "I don't have anywhere else to go."

"Someone once told me that there's always a choice," Thaine retorted.

"Choices have consequences," Jonmarc replied, his voice thick with liquor and self-reproach. "And mine have caught up with me. Leave me alone, Thaine. I'm more trouble than I'm worth."

He did not wait for an answer. Jonmarc gripped the bottle by the neck and headed back to his quarters. Thaine watched him go, and if she considered answering him, she thought better of it.

Despite the whiskey, nightmares came. *Flames and monsters. Gallows and the fight ring. Jonmarc flinched from the pain of Alcion's whip and gagged at the smell of his own flesh burning from the hot iron pressed into his back. The scene shifted, and he ran through the forest, pursuers close behind, narrowing his lead. Panic choked him, and his heart beat like it would burst.*

The dead accused him. He saw his brothers, gutted by the raiders' blades, staring at him with wide, angry eyes. His mother stood in the kitchen, holding the bloody ruin of her slashed belly together with stained hands, eyes fixed on him. "You failed us."

More faces, those of his friends and neighbors, and his father, risen from the pile of bodies where the raiders had dumped his corpse. He stood in the road in the middle of a burning village, blood running in a steady stream past his muddy boots. "Expected more from you, Jonmarc."

So many faces, so many bodies. Shanna held the bloody child the monster's talons clawed from her womb and stared at him balefully. "You brought this on us. You called the monsters. It should have been you."

The soldiers from his garrison stepped up through the shifting fog that obscured Shanna and revealed a different time and place. "We followed you, and you let us die. We died for your mistakes. You don't deserve to walk away."

So many faces. So many dead. This time, the revenants did not speak; instead, they emerged from the fog to stand in silent judgment, forming a circle. The villagers who burned in the barn in Eastmark. The friends he had been unable to save with the caravan. Every one of the men he had killed for the Nargi in the betting ring. They stepped forward to take their place, passing judgment with their gaze, fixing his fate with the look in their eyes. Slowly, they began to move forward, gradually tightening the circle, reaching for him—

Jonmarc woke with a gasp, sitting upright in his bed. The sheet fell away, and his sweat-soaked body felt the chill. His heart thudded hard enough that he felt the pounding in his ears, and as he pushed the hair out of his eyes, he saw that his hand shook.

He sucked in deep breaths, trying to calm himself. *Just a dream. Just a dream.*

Closing his eyes only showed him those accusing stares once more. *So much blood on my hands.*

A knock at the door sent a jolt of panic through him until he forced his breathing to slow. Amme stuck her head in.

"I was fixing the fire in the common room, and I thought I heard you call out. You all right?" Worry creased her forehead.

"Just a bad dream," Jonmarc said, hating that his voice lacked its usual timbre. "Goes with the territory."

"Get yourself decent and come get some breakfast," Amme said with a half-smile that told him she knew he had not told the entire truth. "Fresh pot of *kerif* is boiling, and

I've got eggs, potatoes, and bacon almost ready. Do you good."

Jonmarc murmured his thanks and watched the door close. He slumped back against his pillow, fighting a headache that threatened to blur his vision. His mouth tasted of old whiskey, and his stomach threatened to bring last night's binge back up. Jonmarc groaned and forced himself to get out of bed, trying and failing to revive himself with the cold water in the washbasin. He could already tell the day was going straight to the Formless One.

Breakfast sat like a stone in his stomach, which only served to darken his already foul mood. He moved through his chores by rote, but everything seemed off. Boxes fell, plates broke, and when he went to the stables, he only narrowly managed to escape being kicked by one of the horses. Jonmarc picked the jobs that kept him away from as many people as possible, but while his headache eased, nothing helped the anger that burned in his gut.

Anger at the raiders who killed his family and the monsters who slaughtered his wife. Rage at the Eastmark general who killed his soldiers, and the Nargi general who enslaved him. But most of all, anger at himself for the string of failed choices that brought him to this point.

Seemed like a good night for a fight.

Jonmarc had the night off, and some chores done for one of the stable hands got him a horse for the evening. He headed the opposite direction from Kettlesmith, toward the tavern he had heard about a few miles down the road. He took in its sorry appearance as he slowed his horse. The gray siding had warped in places, long overdue for a whitewash. The pub's thatched roof had not been properly tended, and he wondered how badly it leaked when rain fell. The stench of the latrine out back carried on the wind, along with the tang of the stable.

The One-Eyed Wolf Tavern looked as seedy as its patrons. Jonmarc pushed past a drunk passed out on the steps and shouldered his way to the bar. His nose twitched at the smell of unwashed bodies, stale pipe tobacco, and the unmistakable smell of dreamweed mingled with cheap whiskey.

"Bring me two for starters," he barked at the bartender, who regarded him with a flat gaze, unimpressed. Jonmarc knocked the first drink back, savoring the burn.

"Hair of the dog that bit you?" the bartender asked.

"Something like that." Jonmarc listened to the buzz of conversation around him and felt a tingle of adrenaline. What he needed, craved, was a good roaring fight. Something to get his blood going, to remind him he was alive. Something to deaden the memories and drown out the dreams, to lose himself in the moment.

Something that hurt, because only the living felt pain.

The second drink warmed him, sending a welcome tingle through his chest, cutting through the cold emptiness. He set the empty glass down with a thud. "Another."

The barkeep raised an eyebrow. "It's your funeral."

"I should be so lucky."

The One-Eyed Wolf lacked charm. It also lacked basic sanitation and fresh air. In the main room, men played darts and dice, arguing loudly about the outcome of their games. The whores looked tired and drunk, not even bothering to move from table to table. Jonmarc downed two more drinks before a voice he recognized caught his attention.

"Well look who's here. The whores' champion."

Jonmarc knew the voice but could not place it until he saw one of the soldiers he had beaten bloody and evicted from Jolie's Place.

"You come looking for trouble?" The second soldier also looked familiar. "Because you've found it."

Jonmarc rose from his seat, uncoiling with a lethal grace that should have been a warning. "I don't look for trouble, mate. I dish it out."

The man's companion snorted in derision as a third soldier joined them. "Big talk. I see three of us and one of you."

"One's enough."

The first man swung, a blow Jonmarc dodged easily. Jonmarc shouldered into the second soldier, knocking him off balance and into a table. Patrons scattered to get out of the way as the third soldier grabbed a chair, making a wicked swipe at Jonmarc's head. Jonmarc ducked, and the chair crashed against the bar, breaking the wooden legs.

Jonmarc drew his knife and grabbed a splintered chair leg from the floor in his left. He kicked at the remains of the stool, putting it at least temporarily out of reach of his opponents. The soldiers had also drawn blades, and Jonmarc knew from the way they held themselves that they had enough training to prove themselves a challenge.

Blood thundered in his ears, and adrenaline coursed through him. He wheeled into an Eastmark kick, planting his foot high on the chest of the second soldier and sending him flying backward, into two more men coming their way who looked intent on joining in the fray. Jonmarc saw a bottle swinging for his head, and turned, managing to take the blow on the shoulder. He lashed out with his knife, scoring a deep gash down the arm of the man with the bottle, who cursed loudly and dove forward, propelled by pain and anger.

Jonmarc thrust his blade into the bottle-man's belly, sinking in to the hilt. He turned, ripping the blade through flesh, in time to block an attack from behind. The soldier he kicked lay still amid the wreckage of a table, and his blade had taken down another man, but more of the guards' friends joined the fight as the pub's customers ran for the doors and the barkeep wisely cowered behind the counter.

Energy thrummed through Jonmarc's body. He had never enjoyed the fights in Nargi, though the spectators had clearly appreciated his skills. Now, fueled by fury and whiskey and the desperate need to make someone pay, Jonmarc felt more alive than he had since Eastmark. Cold clarity descended, letting him move smoothly through a sequence of attack and defense. This was the proficiency he loved as a fighter, the harmony of mind and muscle, sinew and strength. He was good at this, and the knowledge satisfied him at his core.

A blade dug into his shoulder. Jonmarc cursed, knocking the attacker's arm aside, clubbing him on the side of the head with the sharp chair leg and spattering them both with blood. The odds of the fight had deteriorated, despite his take-down of two opponents. Three men he knew he could handle relatively easily; he had fought as many at once in the ring. But five more soldiers wove through the scattered tables to back up their friends.

Jonmarc had no need for a rage spell to harness the anger within. Each swing of his blade or bludgeon, each slice of the knife or crunch of wood on bone satisfied old scores. *That's what Alcion deserved and his blood mage. This is for my men. For Shanna. My parents. My brothers. My village. For all the unfortunate sots I killed in the ring when neither of us had a choice.*

Reason gave way to primal fury. Jonmarc bled from a dozen wounds, some shallow, others much deeper. A fist caught him on the jaw, sending him reeling, and another strike from behind nearly sent him to his knees. Five of his attackers were either out cold or too badly injured to rejoin the fight. Some would recover; two lay dead, including the man who started the fight and his friend.

The three soldiers remaining came late to the fray, and were undamaged. Their eyes sparked with vengeance for their fallen and battered colleagues, and it occurred to Jonmarc that the brawl might have been unwise. Any chance the altercation might have had of ending well vanished with the first dead guard.

He caught one of the men in the throat with the wooden stake, watched as blood bubbled from his lips and he fell, hands scrabbling at his airway to clear it.

Too late, Jonmarc heard someone behind him. He felt the knife slip between his ribs and gasped, failing to block the second guard whose fist broke his nose. Another knife plunged into his thigh, and he went down amid a flurry of kicks and blows. Consciousness lingered, then slowly escaped his grasp, and one thought made it through the pain.

I'll see you soon, Shanna.

DARKNESS AND PAIN ENVELOPED HIM. Jonmarc rode a warm tide that threatened to drag him under. His body throbbed, aching but less acutely than he remembered in his last moments of lucidity.

Am I dead? He had imagined death differently, a destination across the Gray Sea rather than endless, empty night. Awareness faded in and out, and in the distance voices he could not distinguish rose and fell. He let the tide carry him, no longer caring whether he floated or sank.

He opened his eyes and saw a raven-haired woman walking along the shore. Her expression spoke of heartbreak and beauty, and her amber eyes met his, sending a shiver through his bones.

"Are you the Dark Lady?" Jonmarc asked, past the point of fear.

"So you call me. I am Istra."

Jonmarc found himself standing on the desolate shoreline, in the presence of the goddess. "You've come to take me?"

Istra fixed him with her depthless, amber gaze. "You are not finished."

"You've got that wrong. I'm completely finished. Wrecked. Done."

Istra's smile held secrets. "You've only begun your journey. Much has yet to be revealed. Without you, fates will change."

Jonmarc stared at the goddess, unafraid. "Fate won't notice one less burned out failure. Everyone I love, dies. Everything I do turns to ashes. I'm cursed. Take me: there's nothing for me here."

"It is not time. All men die, but today is not your day to cross the Sea."

"How must I atone before you will just let me go?"

"Live. Your atonement is worked out in every beat of your heart, every breath," Istra replied. "When the time comes, my hand will be upon you." Her image wavered and grew indistinct.

"Wait! I don't understand—"

Istra vanished, and the darkness rushed in, drawing him under and rolling him beneath its waves.

Jonmarc opened his eyes and found himself amid shadows. He recognized his room at Jolie's Place and recalled enough to wonder how he had returned. The last he knew, he fell to the assault at the One-eyed Goat, expecting to die in a pool of his own blood.

"Blood is too precious to waste." Astir's voice startled him. He had not noticed the *vayash moru* standing motionless in the darkened corner.

"How did I get here?"

"The barkeep at the Goat sent a runner to fetch us. We very nearly failed to arrive in time."

"Maybe I didn't want to be saved."

Astir regarded him for a moment. "In my existence, I have shed rivers of blood, some deserved, some not. I have failed those who trusted me and lost faith. I have felt the same loathing that consumes you. You stand in judgment of yourself, yet you have made the best of your lot."

"And you're going to tell me it gets better, if I just soldier on?"

Astir shook his head. "No. The pain never really goes away. It defines you, demands that your memory remain honest. But it is possible to move forward."

Jonmarc turned his face to the wall. "Not sure why I'd want to."

"The healer said you were beyond his grasp. And then he felt the breath of the Sacred Lady upon him, and his power pulled you from the void. Such things do not happen lightly."

"So I'm not allowed to die?"

"What the Lady wishes and what she permits are not the same. It would seem that she would like you to remain, but that does not mean she will prevent your death, if you are intent on dying."

Jonmarc wanted to argue. His body had been healed, but the scars on his soul remained raw. Yet he remembered the vision and the possibility that what he had seen might have been more than fevered imaginings made him doubt his purpose. He had long ago stopped begging the Goddess for favor. But the fact that she had taken note of him gave him pause.

"I'll think about it."

THE NEXT DAY, Jonmarc went about his chores, moving slowly and cautiously from his injuries. He looked up to see Thaine heading his way. Her hair hung loose around her shoulders, not in the fancy way it would be styled for the evening, and a dressing gown covered her night clothes.

"I heard you got hurt bad," she said, looking him up and down as if to check for any injuries that might have been missed.

Jonmarc grunted, not wanting to discuss it. "Just a bar fight. Not my first." The dreams and pain darkened his mood, and the tension between them had not lessened.

"I was worried."

"You've got more important things to worry about," Jonmarc said, intentionally keeping his distance. "Don't you have some undead aristocrat coming calling?"

"Don't—"

Jonmarc settled the armload of firewood by the hearth and looked up, hoping his eyes and expression hid his thoughts. He might not love Thaine like he had Shanna, but he still cared for her, and he knew in his gut the *vayash moru* noble would be trouble. He was almost completely certain his anger had nothing to do with misplaced jealousy.

"You can't trust him, you know that, don't you? They live

forever. We're like pets to them. What happens when you get older, and he doesn't? He'll either turn you or leave you, and then what?"

Thaine paled, and her body stiffened with anger. "It's not your business, is it? You said you didn't care—"

"I never said I didn't *care*. Just that—"

"Spare me." Thaine's eyes glinted. "You might not mind wasting your life, but Ellis could open up a whole new world for me, take care of me so I wouldn't have to do *this* anymore."

"Selling everything to one buyer instead of a dozen is still selling." It hurt to hear her talk so comfortably about the *vayash moru*, and he felt a little satisfaction seeing that his words stung.

"You want to be a hired hand in a whorehouse for the rest of your life? Fine. I'm going to make something of myself, and Ellis can help me. I can take care of myself."

Fear for her safety tangled with his pride and came out as anger. "You won't be safe with him."

"Astir and Jolie have been together for years."

Jonmarc rolled his eyes. "I don't like the look of Ellis. Sotted rich wastrel."

"That's not fair. You don't know him."

"I've seen his type. Arrogant undead bastard, thinks he owns everyone and everything. They're not like us. But you probably know that, since you've been sleeping with a corpse."

"We're done," Thaine replied, her voice shaking with rage. "Just leave me alone." She stalked toward the steps.

"Thaine—" Part of him wanted to apologize, but the rest of him rebelled, certain that if Thaine continued with Ellis something bad would happen. But Thaine never looked back;

she gathered her skirts and climbed the stairs before he could say more.

"Shit," he muttered as he turned back to his work. Everything had come out wrong, and he had botched his chance for his warning to be heard. He knew Thaine's stubborn streak and her independence. *I might as well have pushed her into his arms.*

He wondered whether he could get Astir to give Thaine a warning of his own, then recalled that Astir had known about Ellis and his friend frequenting the brothel and made no move to make them unwelcome. Maybe Astir trusted other *vayash moru* more than Jonmarc did, or perhaps he trusted Thaine to make her own decisions. Jonmarc told himself that if Ellis were an undesirable mortal lover, he would have backed off and let Thaine learn from her mistakes. But making a mistake with a *vayash moru* could lead to a far worse outcome than a broken heart.

Jonmarc glanced over his shoulder at the empty stairs as he picked up a broom and began to sweep, stabbing the bristles at the floor as he worked out his frustration. Trouble seemed certain, and once again he felt powerless to stop it.

JOLIE FOUND HIM just before dusk. Though the healer had fixed the most dangerous of his injuries, Jonmarc felt sore and stiff. He wondered whether the pain was left as an intentional rebuke, or whether he had taxed the healer's reserves to the point where non-essential injuries were left to heal on their own.

"I heard what happened. I expected better."

Jonmarc bit back the reply that came to mind. "I put down six of them. Eight was more than I bargained for."

"You nearly died."

"Not the first time."

Jolie's eyes glinted with anger. "Astir and I talked. We value your help—perhaps more than you value yourself. It might be good for you to get a change of scenery for a while —intending for you to return, of course, after a little break."

"What did you have in mind?"

Jolie leaned against the bar. Senn busied himself elsewhere, leaving just the two of them in the common room. "You have a logical mind. Good for business. I'd like you to learn more about how we get the supplies we need. I think you'd do well with that, and it would get you out of here for a while, give you a break. Clear the air."

Jonmarc opened his mouth to argue and shut it again without saying anything. He thought about Thaine and the vampire aristocrat, about Lem and the angry soldiers. Maybe Jolie was right. A change might do him good. He believed her when she said he would be welcome to return. Jonmarc respected Jolie for her plain speaking. If she said something, it was so.

After all, if she wanted me gone, she'd have no hesitation in making that clear.

"So, how does this work, sending me on a supply run?"

Jolie's expression softened, just a little, giving Jonmarc to know that his acquiescence pleased her. "I've been working with a smuggler I trust to get us what we need at a good price. He's sharp and wily, knows his way around, and he's good in a fight. He can teach you the business. That would stand you in good stead, whether you stay here or move on eventually." This time, a hint of a smile ghosted across her lips. "You are more than a quick fist and a sharp blade, you know."

Jonmarc did not plan to argue, though he secretly doubted she was right. "So I've been told."

"I sent word for my smuggler to meet us here. He should be arriving any moment."

"I'm here," a voice said from the doorway.

Jonmarc froze, then turned to face the speaker, stunned. "Maynard?"

4

GUARDIAN

OLD FRIENDS

"That's quite a tale, m'boy." Maynard Linton leaned back in his chair and stretched. The house was not open for business yet, and so the common room sat empty and quiet, except for Senn moving behind the bar.

Jonmarc and Maynard had a table in the back, with a pitcher of ale between them. Maynard had not been as shocked to see Jonmarc as Jonmarc had been to see him, giving Jonmarc to believe that Jolie remembered their past association from his confession.

"You and Trent were right, trying to talk me out of going to Principality and becoming a merc."

Maynard shrugged and took a swig of his ale. "It's what you had to do. Sometimes paths have to be taken. Shortcuts won't do."

Jonmarc grimaced and sipped his drink. "Maybe. Could have done without those lessons. Tell me about the caravan. Why are you here?"

Maynard looked away, and his expression grew pensive before he covered it with his customary joviality. "Ah well. The caravan ran its course, as all things do, I guess. It happens. We crossed back toward the Borderlands after you went off to Principality. But everything seemed to go wrong. People got sick. Animals went lame. We got into some trouble with the law," he added, rubbing the back of his neck. "The crowds didn't come like they used to."

"Competition?"

Maynard shook his head. "That was some of it. Some upstarts wooed away a few of our acts and most of our audiences. People had seen us—hadn't seen them. Just everything together—it got to be too much. Trent and Corbin and their families found a village and settled down," he said, mentioning the blacksmith that had been Jonmarc's mentor and the farrier who was his good friend.

"Seemed like we had people staying behind every village or two. Wanted to stop traveling, got tired of the life—once it started, it didn't take long until we didn't have enough people to put on the show or go on the road. So one night we broke down the tents, and everyone just seemed to wander away," Maynard said wistfully.

Throughout his time in Principality and Eastmark and during his captivity in Nargi, Jonmarc had pictured his friends with the caravan going about their familiar business, and taken comfort from the thought. Knowing that the troupe had scattered pained him like the news of a death.

"I'm sorry."

Maynard sighed. "Don't be. All things end. I sold off the equipment and kept my tent and a horse and wagon, and realized that I knew people all across Margolan to trade with, some legal, some not so much," he added with a grin. "Started out as something of a peddler, going village to village with wares to sell. That just kind of grew, once I realized that the different nobles had differing rules for their territories, and some perfectly reasonable goods weren't easy to come by—or legal for sale—in some places."

"So trading turned into smuggling," Jonmarc supplied with a fond smile.

Maynard grinned. "Exactly. I figured that I was already putting up with the risks of highwaymen and thieves by being out on the road and carrying money. Might as well turn a handsome profit for my pain. So I came back across the kingdom and realized that the river made it so much easier to acquire and sell goods with clients eager to remain anonymous."

"You mean, make a quick get-away."

"Exactly."

"And you got to know Jolie how?"

Maynard gave a knowing chuckle. "The road is a lonely place, m'boy. A man needs company from time to time."

Jonmarc rolled his eyes. "Too much information, Maynard. More than I wanted to know."

Maynard Linton stood a head shorter than Jonmarc, with a stout, solid build and skin tanned coppery from a life lived outdoors. A decade separated their ages, but Maynard had taken a shine to Jonmarc when he was just a young boy selling iron tools his father forged. When raiders killed Jonmarc's parents and slaughtered his village, Jonmarc had sought refuge in the only place he could think of—Maynard's caravan of wonders. After the hardships of the last four years, Jonmarc looked back fondly on his time with the traveling show and the friendships he formed there.

"Says the man who lives in a whorehouse," Maynard replied, raising an eyebrow.

"It's not like that," Jonmarc defended, then shook his head. "Jolie and Astir fished me out of the river when I escaped. Gave me a job. Which I've promptly screwed up."

For a few candlemarks, the dark mood that had overwhelmed him the night before had lifted, only to filter back slowly, like a malaise.

"I've known Jolie for quite a few years," Linton replied, refilling his tankard. "Even before the caravan broke up. She isn't a soft touch. But she likes you. Made it clear to me that she wasn't trying to get rid of you, just thought you needed time for things around here to cool off, maybe clear your head a little."

"She's probably right," Jonmarc agreed reluctantly. He shifted in his chair, wincing at the bruises from the fight. "Those men probably have friends who will be looking for my blood. Best for everyone if I disappear for a while."

Maynard looked at him for a long moment, and Jonmarc squirmed under the scrutiny. "What?" he asked, irritated and embarrassed.

"You were barely seventeen the night you showed up and asked me to take you on," Linton replied.

"Begged, as I recall," Jonmarc supplied.

"I was saving your pride," Linton rejoined. "You've grown up some since then." Six long years had made their mark, both in maturity and in the scars—visible and invisible—that the years left behind.

"I'm not a good man, Maynard," Jonmarc said, draining the rest of his tankard and wishing for stronger liquor. "You should know that before you take up with me again. I'm bad luck. People around me get hurt, even when I'm trying to protect them. If you're smart, you'll walk out that door without me."

"Good thing I'm not that smart." Linton poured them both a refill. "As for what makes a 'good' man, well, I've seen you fight for your friends and take crazy chances to save people, including my own sorry ass on more than one occasion. That's 'good' enough for me."

Jonmarc felt his throat tighten and looked away, not wanting Maynard to see the tears he blinked away. "All right," he said finally when he could trust his voice. "Tell me what we're going to be smuggling."

"We brought you here when you were dying." Jonmarc looked around the Floating City, struggling to remember.

"I can't say that I recall," Linton said. He drew up close to a stable on the banks of the Nu River a day's ride from Jolic's Place and hopped down from the driver's bench. Jonmarc climbed down from the other side and came around to join him as Linton spoke to the stable master. From their banter, Jonmarc could see that the two men knew each other.

"Not sure when we'll be leaving, so keep things close," Maynard instructed. The comment struck Jonmarc as odd, but the stable master nodded and palmed the silver coin Maynard gave him, more than adequate pay for stabling the horses for a few nights.

Jonmarc looked toward the river. The Floating City did, indeed, float, but it stretched the truth to call it a "city." Barges and ships of all types and sizes tied up to each other, forming an ever-changing configuration that bobbed with the current. A few regulars formed the core: pubs and brothels and hardy merchants. Seasonal traders came when their produce and products were available and left when they sold out of their wares.

The less reputable merchants tended toward the outer fringe where they could quickly cut their mooring ties and leave at the first sign of trouble. Those included traders of banned goods and stolen merchandise, gambling ships that took advantage of their customers, smugglers, and outlaws. Small houseboats tied up and cut loose throughout the day and night as the denizens of the river area came to trade.

The whole ramshackle temporary construction bobbed up and down with the flow of the river. Lanterns glowed in the windows as the late afternoon shadows lengthened, and Jonmarc remembered that come nightfall, those lights would be reflected on the swift black water like fallen stars. As they walked nearer, Jonmarc caught the mix of smells he recalled from his last, desperate visit: cooking fires and pipe smoke, raw whiskey, unwashed bodies, dead fish, and piss. Music carried on the night air, along with the distant jumble of voices, the barking of dogs and the squawking and squealing of the livestock brought to market.

They headed for the rickety gangplank that led to one of the larger, more permanent ships. A man greeted Maynard with a shout and a rapid conversation in the river patois, a language Jonmarc did not understand. He hung back, unsure whether the newcomer meant welcome or warning, until Maynard and the stranger thumped each other on the back and broke into loud guffaws. Reassured, Jonmarc moved up to stand beside Maynard. He caught his own name among the foreign syllables and gathered he was being introduced when the stranger clapped him on the shoulder, then laughed when Jonmarc froze as if unsure whether to fight or run.

"Torsen says you look like you'll make a proper smuggler, with work," Maynard translated. Torsen added an aside that made Maynard smirk and which he did not bother translating. "If you're going to do much of this kind of thing, you'll have to learn the language."

"I learned Nargi; I can learn this," Jonmarc muttered.

Torsen looked up, and his expression darkened. He

snapped something at Maynard that sounded distinctly less jovial than before and eyed Jonmarc warily. Maynard gave the man a stern look and answered in a reproving tone. Whatever he said satisfied Torsen, who relented, but still looked askance at Jonmarc as they walked onto the gangplank.

"I wouldn't mention your 'friends' across the river around here," Maynard warned under his breath. "They've been known to cause trouble for the river folk, even had some people go missing who were out in open water nowhere near their shores. You don't want to be lumped in with them."

Jonmarc frowned. "Does that happen often? Having… them… show up on this side of the river to cause problems?"

Maynard paused before they entered the crowd. "River folk are a wary bunch. King's guards, local constable, the soldiers across the river, all come sniffing around sooner or later, making trouble for someone. Add in thieves, people with old grudges and unpaid debts and most people learn to mind their business and watch their backs. It's a good lesson to heed," he added, arching an eyebrow.

Jonmarc followed Maynard up a gangplank to a hard-used houseboat with a wide open deck around the central cabin section. As soon as they reached the ship, they were greeted by a tall, broad woman whose wide smile revealed missing teeth. He remembered the woman everyone called "Mama" from his last visit, and from her reaction, she had not forgotten them. She let out a shriek of glee and wrapped her arms around Maynard tightly enough that he gasped for breath.

A moment later, Mama released Maynard and grabbed Jonmarc as she babbled in the river patois. Maynard seemed to enjoy the look on Jonmarc's face as he tried to squirm free of the awkward hug. "Mama says she's glad to see us both looking well," Maynard translated. "And she's happy I brought you with me. She knew you were going to Principality to be a merc, and she says she worried about you."

Mama finally released Jonmarc and motioned for them to follower her into the main cabin, where she immediately began bustling around to set out food and some of the raw, home-brewed liquor for which the Floating City was well known.

"Does my heart good to see the both of you," Mama said, switching to heavily-accented Common for Jonmarc's sake. She brought a plate of meat, bread, cheese, sliced fruits, and vegetables over to the table and returned for a jug of moonshine and cups for all three of them. "Eat," she urged. "Then I want to hear your news."

"Tell us what we've missed," Maynard said as he reached for some meat and bread. Jonmarc sniffed the clear liquid in his cup and raised his eyebrows at its strong odor. Maynard knocked back half of what was in his glass and thumped his chest with one fist as he gasped for air. "That's good 'shine.'"

Mama beamed. "Of course it is. Made it right here." She leaned back, crossing her arms over her ample bosom and watched them eat as if they had been starving. "Been a while since we've seen you, Maynard, and you were half dead then. Lots of things happened in that time."

"Give me the highlights."

Jonmarc ate as Mama rambled on, filling Maynard in on gossip about the merchants and their regular customers. Maynard grunted from time to time as he ate and drank, looking unfazed by the harsh liquor beyond a flush to his face. Jonmarc sipped cautiously at the drink and fought for breath from the burn of the raw moonshine.

"Good, ain't it?" Mama encouraged, and Jonmarc managed another sip under her gaze before she returned her attention to Maynard.

From time to time, Mama lapsed into the patois, and from Maynard's reaction, he guessed her comments were unflattering comments about some of the denizens of the Floating City. "The king's soldiers leave us alone, mostly," Mama continued, switching back to Common. She pushed more food toward Jonmarc, who held up a hand to stop her, but she pretended not to notice. "Came 'round a few months ago looking for a pair that murdered some guardsmen over a horse. They weren't none of our regulars, so we gave them up, tied up pretty as a package, and the soldiers went away."

Maynard shoved a piece of fruit in his mouth and nodded in reply. Jonmarc took another sip of the moonshine and felt his blood warm

"Been more thieves and pirates on the river than usual," Mama observed. "Best you be careful if you're of a mind to go out there. Trouble from the other side of the river, too."

"Oh?" Maynard asked, making an effort to appear nonchalant.

Mama nodded enthusiastically, glad to have an audience for her tales. "Oh, those Nargi bastards been causing trouble, that's for sure. Not sure what's got them riled up, but seems you can't go out on the river without keeping an eye out for them."

"What are they doing?" Maynard wiped his mouth with his sleeve.

"They might be having their own problems with the pirates and smugglers, but they aren't too particular who they chase," she replied. "It's gotten so most of the boats trying to go all the way past Nargi skirt in real close to this side of the shore, even if they scrape bottom, rather than take chances. Don't forget that, or you'll be in for some hurtin'."

"Anything else?"

Mama's expression darkened. "Been some men gone

missing in the last few weeks—and not for the usual reasons. There's talk the Nargi snatched them, but you know how folks are. More likely their past caught up with them, or some-such. But it's worth saying, just because."

Jonmarc averted his eyes. If Dorran had been successful at ousting the General, he might be flexing his newfound muscle, seeing if he could cause problems for a trading hub he would consider villainous. The Floating City had its share of shady characters and no few outright criminals, but after what Jonmarc had seen in his time in Nargi, he could not consider the larcenous merchants of the river market nearly as bad as the blood sport his captors had loved.

Maynard thanked Mama and paid her for the food and drink, hustling Jonmarc out onto the rickety bobbing decks that connected the ships before Mama thought to ask Jonmarc to account for what he had been doing since she had last seen him. Jonmarc breathed a sigh of relief as they made their way through the rough crowd.

"What did you make of all that?" Jonmarc asked quietly as they shoved past those who stopped to haggle with the peddlers who spread out their goods on tattered cloth at the side of the walkway.

"Never a good thing when those bastards across the river get involved," Maynard growled. "But I can't see how it has anything to do with you. We'll just steer clear of them; plenty of jobs to do without taking a risk of getting boarded by them. Don't want to be handing you back."

Jonmarc repressed a shiver. "Glad to hear it."

"As for the rest—Mama knows everybody and hears all the gossip. Once you've been around for a while, you'll start recognizing names. Most of what she said was just trading tales, but now and again, you get a bit of news you can use to your advantage."

Jonmarc kept his expression neutral as they wove their way through the press of unwashed bodies. He did his best to ignore the rats that skittered past and turned away from the cheap whores who called out as he walked by. Maynard's smile became a feral grin, and Jonmarc thought his friend looked alive with the hunt as if the deals to be made and the bargains to be had represented a keen challenge.

Maynard finally stopped in front of a shabby boat lashed to the other skiffs and barges around it. A wizened man rocked in a chair on the weathered deck with his wares spread at his feet. Jonmarc immediately recognized the brass and silver jewelry as protective amulets. Some looked old, and he recalled the pilfered grave jewelry that had led to so much bloodshed years before.

"Watch and learn," Maynard murmured as he stepped forward, waiting for the merchant to wave him on board.

Jonmarc hung back as the two men greeted each other in the river language and then began to argue about prices, slipping between patois and Common until Jonmarc's head hurt from trying to follow the dispute.

"You're going to push me into an early grave, Linton," the amulet seller groused. "I've got a bad heart, and having you pick my pocket does me no favors."

Maynard made a dismissive gesture. "You should be acting in the theater over in Palace City, Gav—got a real flair for drama. It's my pocket being picked; I wager I'm giving you the best price you've seen in a fortnight for that trash."

"Trash!" Gav clutched his chest as if wounded. "These are Goddess-blessed by the Oracle herself! You know the real thing when you see it. I should call the law on you—trying to take advantage of an old man!"

Maynard snorted. "You call the law on me? You do that, and they'll haul your sorry ass away without giving me a second look. Stole them from the Oracle's more likely. But I'll grant you—they're real, though you're overcharging like the shameless whore you are. Go ahead, pack them up. Just this once, I'll let you think you've put one over on me."

Gav gathered up the amulets and put them into a lidded basket. "You gonna carry them with you?"

Linton looked over to the shadowed doorway to the boat's cabin, where a pair of dark eyes glittered, watching them. "Nah. I'll give two coppers to your boy there if he'll run this back to my wagon for me." A boy of about ten summers edged from the darkness. "Mind you—if you try to cheat me or the wares are missing, I'll be back, and it won't be pretty," he warned. Gav said something to the boy in patois, and the child nodded solemnly.

Maynard gave the messenger directions to the stable and the wagon, then concluded his business with Gav and steered Jonmarc back into the crowd. "Best we be gone before he thinks too hard on that 'deal,'" Maynard said.

Jonmarc hung back and watched Maynard bargain and cajole his way across the Floating City. He had witnessed some of Maynard's negotiating skills back with the caravan. In those days, he had gone along as extra muscle, for protection and cargo handling. Now, Maynard seemed to view the outing as the first step in Jonmarc's education into the nuances of river smuggling.

While some passers-by eyed them as if sizing up a challenge, more saw Maynard coming and gave way, with a nervous glance at Jonmarc striding behind him. They stopped every few feet as Maynard greeted someone he knew, or merchants hailed him. From what Jonmarc could tell without speaking the patois, Maynard got on well with most of the regulars and commanded respect from those who looked askance at his passing.

Jonmarc tried to eavesdrop as much as he could when they passed through the crowd, which split between speaking the river dialect and using Common. Hushed tones and the buzz of the crowd made it impossible to follow any conversation for long, but more than once Jonmarc picked up comments about Nargi soldiers causing problems for river pilots, and dark speculation that those guards might have had something to do with men gone missing.

I never heard anything about the General bothering river traffic in the two years I spent in Nargi. What's Dorran's angle? A possibility occurred to him. *The General made sure Dorran couldn't profit from putting me out to fight. So maybe Dorran needed a new way to make money—like river piracy and slaving.* The likelihood of his guess being the truth made him shiver.

At each merchant where Maynard bargained a purchase, he sent the goods back to the wagon with a runner. They wound back and forth across the constantly-shifting landscape of a "city" perpetually re-made with boats coming and going, with rickety walkways, gangplanks—and in some cases, bridges—connecting everything so as to be both navigable and easily reconfigured. The boats rose and fell beneath them, forcing Jonmarc into a sailor's rolling gait.

He kept watch while Maynard did his dealing, and as he stayed alert for pickpockets and robbers, he wondered how the toughened men and women came to be here. *Probably like me. They just fell and kept on falling. River pirate is one step less honorable than merc, maybe one up from whore. But one thing's certain—we're all at the bottom of the barrel.*

Raised voices brought Jonmarc's attention back to where Maynard and the last merchant on their list were engaged in a shouting match. The merchant, a short, grizzled man with a lantern jaw, leaped to his feet, stabbing a finger at Maynard as he shouted and cursed. Maynard leaned in, shouting back, his face flushed with anger.

Jonmarc's hand fell to the grip of the knife in his belt, and he eyed the narrow gangplanks, trying to figure out their options for escape. At first, the altercation garnered no notice from those around them, but gradually a crowd began to form. Jonmarc glanced down the walkway to the left and saw three brawny men shouldering their way through the spectators.

"Maynard! Time to go!"

Maynard looked over his shoulder, threw a handful of silver coins at the merchant and grabbed the contested bundle from the man's table, taking off at a run with Jonmarc hard on his heels.

Between the pitch of the boats on the ever-moving river and the staggering gait of pedestrians, Jonmarc stumbled along behind Maynard, trying hard to keep his feet under him. He heard shouts behind them, both the aggrieved merchant and the guards calling out in vain for them to halt. Linton moved faster than his stout body suggested, easily keeping up with Jonmarc's pace.

"It's a long way back to the wagon," Jonmarc panted as they careened around a corner, knocking bystanders out of their way.

Maynard did not respond to him, but instead tossed a few coins to the right and left as they passed between two rows of produce merchants. A shouted order in the patois had the vendors scrabbling for the coins and then hastily pushing their carts to block the walkway. One of the sellers tipped over his high stack of baskets and vegetables, making the path impassable even if the carts were dragged out of the way. Through it all, Maynard never broke stride, leaving Jonmarc to suspect the former caravan master had used the ruse before. A few shouted well-wishes validated his suspicion. Finding out just what the argument entailed would have to wait until they reached the safety of the stable.

The Floating City presented a maze of possible routes, and Maynard dodged and wove, frequently changing direction and leading them on a path Jonmarc could never have retraced. Where the opportunity arose for some minor vandalism to block the way behind them, Maynard never failed to take advantage. Given that the gangplanks and walkways crossed over individual boats, any path rendered unusable required pursuers to backtrack to find a similar path across other ships. Each time blockages forced the guards to revise their route, they not only lost time but the cabin section of the boats blocked the line of sight, making it more difficult to pick up the fugitives' trail as their lead lengthened.

Night had fallen, and the Floating City glowed from lanterns hung on poles and strung from ropes over the walkways. Their light glimmered off the dark river water. Jonmarc's breath came in rapid gasps as he followed Linton onto what appeared to be a derelict barge. Rats skittered out of their way. No one had lit lanterns here, and heavy shadows hid the rotting deck. Jonmarc tested the boards beneath his feet and felt them give disconcertingly.

Maynard charged on, either knowing the way or too foolhardy to slow down. Cursing under his breath, Jonmarc followed, unsure whether he would fall through to the hold or be ambushed by a cutpurse before the night was finished.

"C'mon boy! Not much farther now."

Jonmarc had little choice but to follow since he certainly could not go back the way he came, even if he could remember how to retrace his route. Maynard led him around the outside of the ship's central cabin and off a ramshackle dock that swayed dangerously with every step as if its moorings would snap from their weight and motion at any minute.

Jonmarc felt the dock give way as he ran toward the end, the warped, rotting boards splintering under his boots. He leaped for shore, clearing the last few feet to land on the bank and stumbled to keep from falling to his knees. Maynard grabbed him by the arm and yanked him forward.

"Can't stop. Almost there."

Together they fled into the scrub on the riverbank, running in the shadows in a path that paralleled the water. From here, Jonmarc could see that the Floating City spanned a much larger area than he first suspected. When they first crossed over from Mama's houseboat, he thought the moored boats might have only ranged for a city block or two, a few dozen large craft at the most. Following Maynard on his errands, Jonmarc kept revising his estimate higher, losing count of how many boats tied up to each other or to the docks that wound between them in some places. But from this perspective, he could see that the bobbing "fleet" of mismatched ships numbered closer to one hundred, stretching all along the banks. He would have to ask Maynard to tell him more about the flotilla, assuming they survived long enough to have that conversation.

"Up ahead."

Jonmarc squinted, making out the shape of a building in the moonlight that shone through the trees at the edge of the wooded area. From the way Maynard sped up, he guessed it was the stable. He glanced behind them, even though he had not heard any footfalls to suggest their pursuers had followed them off the tethered boats.

When they finally broke from the cover of the trees, a movement in the shadows next to the stable had Jonmarc drawing both his long knives.

"You made it back," the man who stepped from the stable doorway greeted them, and Jonmarc remembered him as the one who welcomed them warily on their way in.

"Always an adventure," Maynard said with a broad grin, clapping the man on the shoulder. He handed over a jangling purse of coins. "You're a good man. Everything set?"

"Loaded and harnessed. Get out of here before someone comes looking."

Maynard gestured for Jonmarc to follow him into the stable. A single lantern hung from one of the support posts, enough to see that their wagon was indeed filled with the crates and boxes they had purchased and the horses stood impatiently in their traces.

"Up you go," Maynard ordered, sending Jonmarc around one side and up onto the driver's bench as he went in the opposite direction, untethering the horses, swinging up to the seat next to him. With a cry and a snap of the reins, Maynard sent the horses galloping out of the stable and out into the darkness.

"Some night, eh m'boy?" Maynard grinned at Jonmarc as the wagon careened down the road.

"Are you insane? We're going to break an axle!" Jonmarc hung on with all his strength, trying not to let his teeth clatter every time the wagon hit a rut.

Maynard cast a look over his shoulder and reined in the horses, slowing their pace to a fast trot, which to Jonmarc's mind still tempted fate in the darkness. "Got everything on our list, and none the worse for the wear," he exulted.

Jonmarc stared at him as if Maynard had lost his mind. "You're counting this as a success?"

"Still alive, aren't we? No one's bleeding, and we've got the goods." Maynard's smile widened.

"What about the next time? You don't think that vendor's

going to remember what you did?" Jonmarc paused, recalling that given the language barrier, he hadn't completely followed the altercation that led to their hasty exit. "Speaking of which—what exactly made him so angry?"

Linton's laughter carried on the night air. "I insisted on paying him in silver. He wanted coppers—the better to cheat the tax man—and I didn't have that many on me. I didn't shortchange him. He got the full value. Josah is a particular son of a bitch who gets his trews in a twist if everything isn't just so. Odds are, he'll have shipped off downriver by the next time we visit, if he can even remember his own name— let alone that argument—with as much *potcheen* as he drinks."

Jonmarc shook his head. "Amazing you're still alive."

Maynard guffawed. "Coming from you? That's rich. I think we're going to make a fine team."

5

GUARDIAN

A NEW PATH

JONMARC AND MAYNARD TRUDGED INTO JOLIE'S PLACE JUST before dawn, after the bar and the common room were closed.

"That was a great first run, m'boy," Maynard said, clapping a hand on Jonmarc's shoulder. He pulled the benches away from a table and hauled himself up onto it, wadding up his jacket for a pillow and shaking out his cloak to use as a blanket. "Tomorrow, we'll talk about the next one. So get some sleep. You'll need it."

Jonmarc retreated to his room and set the lantern on the desk. Something about the brothel felt wrong, though nothing looked out of place, in the main room or in his own quarters. He tried to write off his uneasiness as the stress of the day catching up to him, but he did not believe himself. Jonmarc pulled off his boots and fell across his bed, fully dressed. Whatever was amiss would have to wait until later in the day to be reconciled, when he could ask Senn or Jolie whether anything had happened. His instincts served him well in battle. Now, he only hoped that he still had time to fix the source of what left him disquieted.

By the time he woke, the sun hung low in the sky. He ran

a hand back through his hair and grimaced when he realized he had slept in his clothing. His muscles protested, stiff from the rough wagon ride the night before. Jonmarc stumbled toward the basin of water near the door and sluiced the cold liquid over his face, sharpening his focus. Belatedly, he realized he needed a shave.

He paused long enough to change into a clean shirt before heading into the common room. Senn gave him a nod from behind the bar and then tilted his head toward where Maynard lay snoring atop one of the tables.

"It's still early," Jonmarc observed, ambling toward the bar. Senn turned away as he approached, busying himself restocking the jugs and bottles, and the same cold intuition Jonmarc had felt the night before solidified in his gut.

"Did something happen while Maynard and I were out?"

Senn kept his back to him. "You know this place. Never a dull moment."

"Senn—" Jonmarc's voice dropped lower, a warning.

Senn froze, then squared his shoulders and went back to unloading a crate of bottles, one that had been among the supplies Jonmarc and Maynard had retrieved from the Floating City.

"Thaine's gone."

"What do you mean, she's gone?" Jonmarc's voice, low and dangerous, assured the question would not be ignored.

Senn let out a long breath. "She left. With Ellis. Took her stuff. Not coming back. Jolie gave her the payout she was due —Jolie always gives the girls who leave a bag of silver so they can start over. If they come back—and some of them do —they have to repay her." He shook his head. "But I don't think Thaine will be back."

Jonmarc leaned against the bar, feeling as if his knees might go out on him. He told himself that he had no claim on

Thaine, that it had been his choice to break off their relationship. He didn't regret that; deep inside, Jonmarc knew he was far too broken to be worth anything to someone else. Seeing Thaine go off with someone who might be good for her, it would have hurt, but he still would have wished her well. But Ellis… he did not trust a *vayash moru* to keep Thaine safe, even if Astir and Jolie proved that such a thing might be possible.

"Do you know where they went?" As soon as the words left his mouth, Jonmarc regretted the question. Thaine was free to do as she pleased, and he had no right to stop her. Going up against Ellis and his buddies would be as suicidal as it was unwelcome.

"No. And I wouldn't tell you if I did. Let her go, Jonmarc."

Fair enough. "Gimme a whiskey."

"You're working tonight."

"Not gonna get drunk. Just taking the edge off. You think I can't kick someone's ass with a little brew in my veins?"

Senn glared at him, but he poured the amber liquid into a glass and set it down with a *thunk*. Jonmarc slid a coin toward him. "That's for now," he said. Several more coins joined the first. "And that's for the rest of the bottle, after closing."

The nagging feeling of uneasiness did not let up after Senn told him about Thaine. As the liquor burned down his throat, Jonmarc had to admit that he knew Thaine would leave. She had made it clear that she wanted more than this life, and he could not blame her. *But not with a fucking vampire.*

He tossed off the rest of the whiskey and pushed the empty glass back toward Senn. "Thanks," he muttered, leaving it open whether the information or the whiskey earned his gratitude. By that point, Maynard had stopped snoring and blearily got to his feet, nearly sending the table crashing to the floor as it tilted under his weight.

"Think I'll go take a piss," Maynard mumbled, walking for the door with a saddle-sore gait.

"There been any trouble other than Thaine leaving?" Jonmarc asked, looking around the room and wondering when the crowd would begin filtering in.

"Like what?"

Jonmarc shrugged, not entirely sure what he meant himself. "You know. Trouble. Fights. Thieves. That sort of thing."

Senn frowned. "No more than usual. Couple of drunks who thought they could take on the whole bar—and couldn't. A pickpocket who wasn't good at his job. One fellow tried to leave with a better horse than he came in on—Astir took care of him. Don't think he'll be back."

Darkness had fallen, and a few early patrons were finding their way into the common room. Before too long, Erina and the other women would come downstairs in their finery, a musician would begin to play, and the night would begin in earnest.

"I'm going to walk the property," Jonmarc said, pushing himself away from the bar. The idea came to him suddenly, but with such urgency that he knew he had to follow his hunch.

"You feeling all right?" Senn asked, raising an eyebrow.

"Yeah, yeah. Just got a funny feeling that something isn't the way it should be. Probably nothin'."

Jonmarc stopped in his room and withdrew the pair of swords from where they lay wrapped beneath his bed. He had not needed them since those last few fights in Nargi, and his long knives were equally lethal and less visible, fine for the situations he faced at the brothel. Buckling on his belt and scabbard grounded him, and he let his palm linger on the fine steel of the blades, remembering his father forging them so long ago. He sheathed the swords and headed out.

Jonmarc rolled his shoulders, trying to work off the tension thrumming inside him like a persistent itch. Something felt wrong. Something bad was coming. He walked the perimeter of the grounds slowly, moving silently. In the months since he had been at Jolie's, Jonmarc had been outside at night many times, and always before the cacophony of sounds mocked the thought that the darkness could be still. Crickets in the grass, foxes in the brush, frogs down by the river, the wind in the trees and the distant slap of water against the banks—all of it formed a constant night song in counterpoint to the music and voices that carried from inside the brothel.

Tonight was too quiet.

He had a sword in his right hand as he made his way along the thin scrub of brush at the edge of the grounds. Enough light flowed through the windows of the brothel for him to see, despite the dark of the moon. He sniffed the air, unsure what he tried to scent, finding nothing except the smell of wet grass and leaves, and the fishy odor of the river as the wind changed.

He froze, and raised his face to the wind once more. He caught a whiff of something else blowing up from the river, a scent he had not smelled since he left Nargi. Before his captivity, he had never eaten a dish containing *asafetida*, a pungent spice, but Nargi food was redolent with the seasoning, so much so that the distinctive smell clung to the skin and clothing of those who ate it regularly.

He had never smelled it before—not in Margolan, or Principality, or Eastmark. It didn't belong here. Yet the scent hung on the night air, heavy as perfume, and Jonmarc's lips drew back in a feral smile.

Mama and merchants warned about Nargi raiders. It only figured that Dorran would eventually come after the prize asset that the General cheated him out of—his best fight slave. Nargi soldiers were here, now. And it would never even occur to them that Jonmarc would smell them coming.

Jonmarc edged closer to where the land sloped down to the river. The light from the brothel faded before it got to the water's edge. A single wooden staircase led up from the bank to the house on the cliffside above. He remembered collapsing at the foot of the steps the night he swam for his freedom.

Four dark figures made their way up the stairs. Below them, Jonmarc could just make out the shape of a boat pulled up on the riverbank.

He unsheathed his second sword and moved closer. Four against one. He had fought—and won—against those odds as a fight slave barehanded. This time, his opponents would be armed—but so was he. They might be Nargi soldiers, but he was Eastmark trained, and every time he had faced down a Nargi in the ring, he had bested his opponent.

Then, he had been forced into fighting for survival.

Now, he fought willingly to protect his friends. Those unlucky Nargi bastards had no idea what was coming for them.

Jonmarc emerged from the shadows to block the top of the stairs. "Looking for me?" he asked in fluent Nargi.

"The Commander said you'd be here. You're coming back with us," the soldier near the top of the stairs replied as his companion took a step back.

"Screw that." Jonmarc swung his sword, not surprised when the soldier parried, but his second sword slashed into the man's left shoulder before a lunge and thrust had Jonmarc backing up a step to avoid the blade.

Two soldiers crowded up the steps, while at the base of the stairs, he saw three more men coming his way. *Four I can handle. More than that…*

Even with blades in both hands, keeping his opponents at bay required all of Jonmarc's skill, especially since he dared not allow them to move forward lest the reinforcements join the fight. He went to the cold, analytical place in his mind that let him see a fight in slow motion, allowed him to track and respond to his attackers' movements like a precise, complex dance. The clang of swords broke the stillness of the night air, though the sounds of music and laughter from inside the house assured none of the patrons were the wiser.

Jonmarc felt a rush of air, saw a blur of movement, and suddenly one of the men on the stairs went flying over the side of the steps to hit the cliffside with a sickening crunch and fall to the rocky beach below. A heartbeat later, the same thing happened on the other side as a second soldier plunged to his death, screaming. Astir stood on the stairs, blocking the ascent for the three remaining Nargi.

"You don't belong here," Astir told them. "I will make sure your commander knows not to waste more of his men."

Before Jonmarc had a chance to see what Astir intended to do, he sensed someone behind him. "Leave some for me," Maynard said, moving alongside him and throwing himself into the fight.

Jonmarc dove forward, taking advantage of the distraction as Astir grabbed one of the Nargi and disappeared into the darkness. Jonmarc's blade slipped beneath his opponent's guard, sinking deep into the man's belly. The soldier clasped one hand to his bleeding abdomen, and Jonmarc's kick sent his blade into the brush. The man's companion cried out in rage and used the opportunity to move behind Jonmarc and on to solid ground. He threw himself at Jonmarc in a flurry of sword strokes. Jonmarc mirrored his movements, parrying with both blades, watching for a moment of weakness.

Maynard shouted taunts at the two men he kept from attacking Jonmarc's back as they moved up the stairs. Maynard's accent mangled the language, which appeared to be limited to an impressive number of obscenities and curses.

Jonmarc narrowed his focus, moving to block his remaining opponent at every turn. He saw determination on the man's face and knew he intended to complete his mission at all costs. The attacker's sword skills served him well, as Jonmarc pushed him harder, attacking with both his swords and gradually scoring a dozen gashes on the guard's forearms, shoulders, and thighs.

"Give up, and I'll make it quick," Jonmarc grated.

"Come with me, and this can be over."

"Not happening."

Maynard shouted with victory as one of his two attackers fell in a bloody heap. Jonmarc went on the offensive, coming at his opponent with a series of fast, hard strikes, including a deep slash to the man's forearm that made him drop his weapon. Jonmarc spun into a high Eastmark kick that sent his attacker sprawling, then lunged forward, sinking one of his blades into the soldier's chest, taking him through the heart.

Behind him, Jonmarc heard the unmistakable sound of a sword slashing through flesh and bone. He turned in time to see Maynard's last opponent fall, headless, down the stairs.

Astir emerged from the darkness, unmarked and apparently undamaged. "There are no more Nargi on this side of the river," he announced. "I left one on the other shore, badly injured but alive enough to tell his commander the cost of making landfall where they do not belong. I doubt we will see another foray."

Jonmarc wiped his bloody swords on one of the dead men's uniforms, pausing while he caught his breath. "How did you know to come out here?"

Astir gave him a look as if he were simple. "I heard you—and I heard odd noises that did not belong. I came to investigate."

Maynard cleaned his sword, kicked one of the corpses to assure the man was indeed dead and ambled over to join them. "You're just damn lucky I had to piss," he said, grinning as if it had all been a fine adventure.

"We've got to get rid of the bodies," Jonmarc said, sheathing his swords.

"The river's as good a place as any," Astir said. "I've already taken care of the ones below."

Working together, Jonmarc and Maynard pitched the dead guards off the cliff, then descended the steps to haul the remains to the water's edge and heave them into the swift current. The wind promised rain, which would wash the bloodstains from the grass. None of the patrons ever came out to the cliff anyway. No one would notice.

"Thank you," Jonmarc said, once they had all regrouped behind Jolie's Place.

Astir inclined his head in acknowledgment. "You are most welcome."

Maynard clapped him on the shoulder. "Damn, boy, you're even better with those swords than I remembered. You did yourself proud."

Jonmarc looked out toward the dark river, and then back to Jolie's. "I'm a danger to all of you if I stay here," he said, realizing the truth. "I'm surprised Dorran didn't send someone sooner. But now that he has—he won't rest until he either kills me or recaptures me. And I'm not going back there."

"If they return, we will deal with them," Astir replied.

Jonmarc shook his head. "It's too much of a risk to the girls, the staff, the customers. I'm too tempting a prize sitting still on the other side of the river. He'll be back."

"Then accept my offer and move on," Maynard said, meeting Jonmarc's gaze. "I could use a smuggling partner, and you already have Jolie's blessing. I certainly trust you to have my back, that's for damn sure. You'll be a moving target—harder for this Dorran fellow to find. Make yourself a good bit of coin while you're at it."

"You are most welcome to stay here, and if not, Jolie has already told you that you're always welcome to return," Astir said. "She is pleased with your services. The choice is yours." He turned and strode back to the house, leaving them alone.

"Ask me again in the morning," Jonmarc said, feeling the adrenaline of the fight leave exhaustion in its wake. "I'll tell you then."

To Jonmarc's surprise, Jolie, Senn, and the rest of the women were waiting in the common room the next morning when he emerged from his room carrying a sack with all his belongings and his swords in a carefully wrapped bundle.

"Astir said he thought you'd be moving on," Jolie said. She nodded to where Maynard sat at one of the tables. "And Maynard says he's offered you a job."

Jonmarc nodded, feeling a flush come to his cheeks. He had made up his mind overnight and expected to go looking for Jolie to share his decision. Now that the moment was upon him, he felt awkward. "It's too dangerous for me to stay," he said. "Dorran will keep on trying, and someone will get hurt. It's better if I move on."

Jolie regarded him with a look that let him know she understood that his worry about another Nargi attack formed only part of his reasoning. "That's too bad. You're a good guardian. Best ever—except for Astir. I like you. Any time you want to come back, you've got a place here. Even if you're just passing through."

"Thank you… for everything," Jonmarc replied. He knew leaving was the right thing to do, but he had grown fond of Jolie and all the house regulars. Oddly enough, he knew he would miss them.

"Time to go, m'boy," Maynard said, rising and walking over to stand next to him. "Jolie's got a house to run—and we've got a full day's ride to where we're going. Big trading market. Deals to be made, fortunes to be earned," he said with a broad smile, eager to get going.

"Come back anytime," Jolie said. She raised a hand in blessing. "And may the Dark Lady's hand be upon you."

SMUGGLER

1

SMUGGLER

NEW VOCATION

Hooves pounded on the road behind them, closing the distance. Jonmarc Vahanian urged his horse to go faster, as his companion pulled ahead of him. He dared not turn around to see how narrow the gap had grown between them and their pursuers. Any moment Jonmarc expected to feel an arrow between his shoulders or the blade of a throwing knife in his back.

He gritted his teeth, hunched over his mount's neck, and dug in his heels, willing the sleek black horse forward. He understood now why Maynard Linton, his business partner, had insisted that they buy the swiftest stallions they could afford.

Smugglers needed to be able to leave town in a hurry.

"Come on," Jonmarc urged, snapping the reins as if the horse were not already running full out. Moonlight lit their way, but it also revealed them to their pursuers. In the twenty-three years of his life, many things and people had tried to kill Jonmarc. Every time, he had fought his way clear. He had no intention of dying on a dusty back road at the hands of the half-trained guards of a backwater duke.

Just for a moment, he feared fate might have other plans.

"Now!" Maynard's voice rang out over the still night air. He and Maynard passed beneath the low boughs of old trees overhanging the road. Their knives glinted, and then a whoosh of air and the fall of a gray curtain of rope separated them from their pursuers.

The old fishing nets fell to the ground with a thump, blocking the road. At the speed the guards behind them were riding, it would be all they could do to avoid running headlong into the nets, which would be enough to tangle their horses and perhaps throw the riders from their mounts. At best, they would be forced to slow down and find a way around the nets if they wanted to continue the chase. That would be difficult, given the lay of the ground on either side of the road, a feature Jonmarc and Maynard scouted by daylight when they set the trap.

Maynard whooped in triumph as he and Jonmarc thundered away, the curses and shouts of the frustrated guards carrying on the night air. Even so, they did not slow their pace until they had covered another league and only relented to a walking pace after a candlemark passed without a sign of their pursuers.

Jonmarc rode up beside Maynard, who reached out and clapped a hand on his shoulder. "And that, m'boy, is how it's done!" Maynard's wide smile and the light in his eyes told Jonmarc that the older man considered the evening's work to be a fine lark.

"You're insane."

Maynard laughed. "Maybe so, but you agreed to be my student, so what does that say about you?"

Jonmarc grinned in reply and reached down to pat his horse's neck. "You knew I was crazy when you asked me to come with you."

SMUGGLER

Maynard reached inside his jacket and withdrew a flask. He opened it and took a long swig of whiskey, then passed it to Jonmarc, who did the same. "It's not crazy to do what you're good at, and you are a natural-born smuggler."

Jonmarc gave a disbelieving snort and returned the flask. "Somehow, I don't think smuggling is the kind of thing you're born into."

Maynard shrugged. "Maybe not, but then you've only fate to thank for the set of skills you've got."

Jonmarc sobered at that, turning away. Luck and fate were rarely on his side. He knew what Maynard meant. Jonmarc's combat skills came naturally, honed by time as a soldier and a fight slave, earned one bloody conflict at a time. Years as a mercenary in Principality and Eastmark and then as a prisoner in Nargi taught him those languages. He learned a blacksmith's trade from his father and gained proficiency traveling with the caravan of wonders Maynard used to manage. Along the way, he had learned to ride and hunt, rig tents and tend bar, and a number of other less savory abilities, like how to pick a lock, slit a throat, or evade a bounty hunter. And far too early, he had learned how to dig a grave.

"Stop that," Maynard chided, as if he could guess the direction Jonmarc's thoughts had taken. "We're going to celebrate tonight. Find ourselves an inn and some supper, and have at that bottle of Tordassian brandy we snagged for ourselves."

With effort, Jonmarc pulled himself from his memories and managed a smile. "Think our client will notice that he's short a bottle or two?"

Maynard answered with a wicked grin. "He isn't—that's the beauty of this. The exchange rate worked in our favor. The duke sent us with orders to get him twenty bottles. My haggling got us two extra. Consider it a bonus for a job well done."

They had been hired through intermediaries to smuggle the brandy across the border of Duke Celeran's lands, an ascetic man whose severe and unpredictable bouts of devotion to the Sacred Lady led to conflicting and often incomprehensible edicts. A recent ban on liquor prompted a wealthy man within Celeran's borders to take matters into his own hands and arrange for private delivery. Either someone tipped off the Duke's guards, or luck just did not favor them tonight, because they had run right into an ambush.

Jonmarc and Linton remained alert, but they finished the trip home without further incident. "I'd say this calls for a little celebration," Maynard said. Jonmarc felt no surprise when they ended up at the stables by the banks of the Nu River, right next to the Floating City.

After six months of smuggling with Maynard, Jonmarc had just begun to get his bearings on the jumble of boats, ships, and barges that made up the Floating City. Stories varied as to how the Floating City got its start. A few of the ships closest to the shore remained constant, but the rest—dozens of watercraft of all sizes and descriptions—varied by week or even by the day.

Some of the smaller boats lashed up to the sides of the larger ships to offload their cargo, sell perishables like fish or fresh vegetables, or find buyers for stolen goods. In other places, wooden docks floated on empty barrels, providing mooring places for boats to come and go as they pleased. Some stayed for days, others less than a candlemark. The Floating City constantly changed, yet as Jonmarc grew more familiar with its people, he learned that in many ways, it always remained the same.

"Drink up!" Maynard ordered as a tankard of ale thumped

down on the bar in front of Jonmarc. For the moment, they were safe within a houseboat run by a large woman whom everyone called Mama, one of the few boats which never left its moorings.

"You're trouble on the hoof, that's for certain, Maynard Linton!" Mama shouldered her way through the crowd. "Shouldn't let you into a respectable place like this." That drew guffaws since nothing in the Floating City verged close to respectability. Humor blunted Mama's words, and Jonmarc noticed her gaze flick over them, looking for wounds.

"You two make it back all right?"

Maynard flashed a smile of pure bravado her way. "Don't we always?"

Mama snorted. "Must have hit your head while you were out. Patched you up more times than I can count, and your ungrateful ass can't even remember?"

Maynard held up a hand in appeasement. "You know I do, Mama. You're the best."

"Damn right," she agreed. "You heard much from Jolie lately?"

"Just what she needed us to pick up for supplies," Maynard replied, as Jonmarc looked away. Jolie ran one of Margolan's most infamous brothels, not far from the Floating City. After his escape from the Nargi, Jonmarc had found refuge at Jolie's Place, doing chores and protecting the "girls" and the regulars from unruly customers.

"And you? How are you faring?"

It took Jonmarc a moment to realize that Mama had spoken to him in the river patois and that he had understood her without needing to pause to translate. "Still alive," he replied.

The patois was the language of thieves and smugglers, whores and criminals. Jonmarc had never heard it before his association with Maynard. *Then again, I hadn't been a thief or a smuggler.* Though Eastmark made him a criminal with its wrongful court martial and the bounty on his head, and Nargi forced him to fight for the entertainment of his captors. *So I guess I've been a criminal and whore as well.*

"Anything interesting while we were gone?" Maynard asked Mama. The press of bodies in the houseboat made the small space too warm, pungent with the smell of sweat, whiskey, and smoke. Rough men with hooded eyes desperate to drink away their memories and misdeeds filled the bar. Jonmarc fit right in.

"The usual," Mama said with a shrug, glancing toward her bartender to assure all was well and nodding when he signaled assent. "Fights, a couple of knifings, that sort of thing. Business has been good."

"Are you Maynard Linton? With the caravan of wonders?" The speaker, a wide-eyed young man who appeared to be a few years younger than Jonmarc, pushed his way through the crowd.

"Who wants to know?"

"I'm Petyr, and I can juggle fire and do trick knife throwing. I want a job with your caravan."

Petyr looked so earnest, Jonmarc hated to see him disappointed. Maynard tried to stifle the smile that quirked at the corners of his mouth. "Are you any good?" Maynard asked.

"Oh yes," Petyr assured him. Before they could stop him, Petyr pulled three throwing knives from his belt and sent them flying in quick succession to thud into the narrow gaps between the bottles of liquor at the back of the bar, sticking point-first into the wall.

"Hey!" the bartender roared. "What in the name of the Crone do you think you're doing?"

"Sorry!" Petyr squeaked.

Mama hustled around the end of the bar and yanked the blades free. "You got good aim, sonny, but take it outside. Don't need no trouble, you hear me?"

"Yes ma'am," Petyr replied, pale and abashed.

Jonmarc clapped a hand on his shoulder. "Not a bad demonstration," he said, barely choking back a laugh, "but you're lucky you didn't start a riot."

"I don't have a caravan these days," Maynard said, eyeing the boy with amusement. "Don't know if I ever will again. But I'll keep you in mind if I start it back up."

"Thank you, sir! You won't regret it!" Petyr took one look at the bartender's dark expression and made himself scarce. The patrons at the bar went back to their drinks, and after a moment, the bartender turned to his work once more, casting a wary glance now and again toward the door.

Jonmarc reached for his drink, chuckling. "Well, that was different."

Maynard sighed. "Nice to know people remember the caravan. And maybe I will get one going again—but not for a while. I needed a break."

Mama slipped into the crowd, keeping an eye on her unruly brood. Maynard motioned for the barkeeper to refill their drinks, then stepped away from the bar with a motion for Jonmarc to follow him. Together, they made their way toward the back of the boat, to a small room lit by a single lantern. Business might begin at the bar, but terms and details were handled in private.

"Took you long enough."

"Nice to see you too, Rania."

Maynard moved out of the way, giving Jonmarc the first glimpse of their contact. He felt a jolt of surprise to see a woman in her mid-twenties, within a year or so of his own age. Her dark red hair was plaited into a thick braid that

437

wrapped around her head, providing no leverage for an attacker to grab. Her dress fell ankle-length, but as she rose in greeting, Jonmarc saw that it lacked the layers of underskirts favored by "proper" ladies and that high slits on either side revealed trews beneath. Practical apparel for someone concerned about being able to run and fight.

"So this is your new hired hand?" Rania ran an appraising glance over Jonmarc. "I've heard he's good with his sword." Her smirk and the tone of her voice made the innuendo impossible to miss.

"Play nice," Maynard reproved. "Rania, this is Jonmarc. Jonmarc, meet Rania—our contact for the next job."

Jonmarc responded with a nod. Rania's eyes narrowed, assessing, and then her expression cleared. Most people on the river went by a single name. No one asked for more, and fewer still believed any names given were more than aliases. "Jonmarc" might be common enough to avoid arousing suspicion, but too many people might find "Vahanian" interesting for all the wrong reasons.

"Sit down," Rania said. "I've got a job I think you'll like."

Maynard angled his chair so that his back was to the wall. Jonmarc turned his so that he had a clear view of the doorway. "Tell us about it," Maynard replied.

Rania leaned back in her chair, stretching. Her long, lean body arched, and Jonmarc could not avoid noticing. His last relationship ended months ago, and current circumstances did not lend themselves to long-term plans. It had been a while, longer than he wanted to recall. He shifted in his chair and looked away.

"It's in Principality," Rania said. "And it involves gems."

Maynard guffawed. "Smuggling gems out of Principality?

That's like smuggling water out of the ocean! Why would anyone want to do that?"

On face value, the prospect seemed ridiculous. Principality, on the other side of the Nu River near the sea, led the rest of the Winter Kingdoms in the mining of precious gems. After centuries of warfare among the other kingdoms over who would control the horde, a truce had finally been brokered wherein Principality became its own sovereign entity, trading its riches with the other nations yet beholden to none. To assure its independence, Principality offered sanctuary to the best mercenary armies in the Winter Kingdoms, in exchange for a vow that those same mercs would protect its borders and never hire their swords against it. A few years ago, before his time in Nargi, Jonmarc had been one of those mercs. Those memories felt like they belonged to a different lifetime, and another man.

"Not out of Principality," Rania chided. "Into Principality."

"Who's got anything Principality doesn't already have?" Jonmarc asked, curious.

"Ever heard of *zanite*?" Rania countered. Her expression suggested she enjoyed the game as much as the win. And right now, she reveled in doling out her secrets.

"It's rare, if it even exists," Maynard replied, frowning. "Rumor has it that just a few slivers of *zanite* can be used by witches with the right talent to do all kinds of spells. Cure wounds, heal the plague, re-attach a severed limb—just about anything except raise the dead."

Rania's smile broadened. "Very good. Most people haven't heard of it at all—but you're only half right. *Zanite* can cure—but it can also focus energy for other spells, the kind that require a mage to store some magic to draw on later

If, for example, someone wanted to sink a ship, or maybe blow a big hole in something."

"And of all the kinds of gems they mine in Principality, I'm guessing *zanite* isn't one of them?" Jonmarc said.

"Exactly. Not only that, but *zanite*'s dangerous in the wrong hands, so its import is tightly controlled. Principality is touchy about who can make use of the *zanite* that does come into the kingdom. There's never much of the stuff available to start with, and that just cuts the supply and makes the price go up, up, up," she said with a predatory grin.

"And you've got a buyer?" Maynard's tone suggested his impatience with Rania's storytelling.

"More than that—I've got a seller." Rania's blue eyes fairly glowed with triumph. "Just a few ounces, but it's worth more than gold. The buyer will pay his price—plus our premium. No questions asked."

"Any idea what the buyer wants to do with the *zanite*?" Jonmarc asked. "In case it has something to do with one of those big explosions?"

Rania shrugged. "None of my business—and none of yours, either. Although I'll tell you what he told me—he's got a sick daughter, and the healers can't do any more for her. Needs the gem to try a desperate cure."

Maynard chuckled. "And you believed him?"

Rania's sly grin turned feral. "Of course not. But that is what he told me."

"So why do you need us?" Jonmarc asked. "You've got it all set up."

"Muscle," Rania replied. "I need bodyguards I can trust, and I'll pay you well for the effort. I'd be a fool to walk into the hand-off alone."

"In other words, you need bodyguards who won't slit

your throat and take the *zanite* and sell it themselves," Maynard corrected.

"That too."

"Who do you expect to come against us?" Jonmarc leaned forward. "The client?"

Rania shook her head. "Doubtful. What I've got is the real thing, so he'll want to keep me—us—alive in case we can supply more. But if anyone else's gotten wind of the deal, things could go badly."

Jonmarc knew that "anyone else" included the king's guards and whatever mercenary groups might be helpfully watching the coastline. "What's the plan to hand off the rocks?"

"This is so much more than 'rocks,'" Rania replied, rolling her eyes. "We pick them up from my supplier, take a boat across the river, and meet with the buyer's representative. Get the money, and get out of there."

"Why do I doubt it's going to be that easy?" Maynard muttered.

"If I thought it would be easy, I wouldn't need your help," Rania snapped. "That's why I'll be paying you—well." She named a figure. "Each."

Back in his merc days, that much money would have been four months of pay. If Rania was prepared to hand over twice that amount—for him and Maynard—her own take had to be substantial. From the way Maynard's eyes narrowed, Jonmarc suspected his friend's thoughts had taken the same turn.

"That's a good start," Maynard drawled. "But there are two hand-offs involved, and two chances for big problems. Plus the river crossing. Add thirty percent—each—and we're in."

"Twenty percent."

"Twenty-five."

When Rania hesitated, Maynard started to stand.

"All right," she huffed. "Twenty-five percent more—each. But that's final."

She gave in quickly enough that Jonmarc wondered whether Maynard should have asked for more.

"Where and when?" Maynard asked. "And don't forget little details that are nice to know sooner rather than later. Like whether either the buyer or seller is a mage."

A slow smile played over Rania's lips. "No mages—at least, none that I've been told about."

"Not exactly a solid 'no,'" Maynard said.

Rania shrugged. "It's the best I can give you. I'd expect the seller and the buyer's rep to bring guards. Be fools not to—and I don't think they're stupid. As for when—meet me here tomorrow at sundown. I'll give you the details then. What you don't know, you can't tell."

"Thanks for the vote of confidence," Jonmarc muttered.

"Just taking care of business," Rania replied. She rose, indicating that the meeting was at an end. "See you in a few days, boys." With that, she sauntered out.

Jonmarc exchanged a look with Maynard. "Do you think she'll double-cross us?"

Maynard stared after her. "Odds are fifty-fifty. But I don't think she'll get us killed on purpose—at least, not unless it's the only way to save her own skin."

"You're not making me feel good about this."

Maynard met his gaze. "You've heard about 'honor among thieves?' Rania's as close to that as it comes. I don't entirely trust her, but she doesn't have a reputation for betraying her business partners." Jonmarc noticed that Maynard stressed the word "business" just a bit and drew his own conclusions.

"If this *zanite* is as hard to find and powerful as she says—"

"It is."

"Then even if the seller and the buyer's rep are on the level, everybody and his brother will want to steal it before we hand it off, and Rania's going to have a king's ransom in gold on the way home."

Maynard nodded and clapped him on the shoulder. "And that, m'boy, is where we earn our keep."

They met the seller in an abandoned fishing village a few candlemark's ride upriver from the Floating City. The dilapidated buildings that remained told Jonmarc the villagers left long ago. Old docks canted in the water, barely standing on rotted supports. Shadowy hulks—all that remained of long-vacant homes and shops—stood like silent, ghostly sentries.

Jonmarc felt a chill down his back. He had not thought about his own village for a while, but he knew it would haunt his dreams tonight. Nothing about the forsaken town suggested that it perished in flames at the hands of raiders, but even so, his imagination wasted little time supplying unwanted details.

"You with me?" Maynard elbowed him in the ribs as they walked their horses toward the large building.

"Yeah. Just having a look around."

Both Jonmarc and Maynard were well-armed, living up to their role as bodyguards. Rania had at least as many blades concealed on her person as they did. What struck Jonmarc as unusual was Rania's insistence that they bring crossbows. He scanned the dark, empty ruins of the village, senses at high alert; certain something watched them from the darkness

"Did you bring the money?" The deep voice came from the shadows alongside the run-down market building. Jonmarc could make out the outline of a man's form, but nothing more.

"Did you bring the gems?" Rania countered.

"All is as we agreed. You know what to do."

Jonmarc and Maynard moved forward, each gripping one side of a mid-sized chest. They walked halfway across the open ground toward the stranger, then set the box down. Rania struck a spark and lit a metal lantern, holding it aloft over the chest so that the gold inside gleamed.

A second figure stepped up beside the seller, also nearly hidden in the darkness. He made a motion with his hand, and the light over the chest flickered then steadied.

"Full payment; real gold," a low voice said.

Jonmarc and Maynard exchanged a glance, surprised that their contact brought along his own mage to assure the deal. Rania's demand for crossbows suddenly made more sense. Blades against magic were nearly useless, but a crossbow could move almost as fast as thought.

"Now let me see yours," Rania said, refusing to step away from the gold.

The mage walked toward her, holding a much smaller box in front of him. Rania held the lantern up, but the light did not reveal the face beneath the mage's cowl. When he stood just a few paces away from her, the man opened the lid. The lantern's glow glinted off shards of lilac-colored crystal.

"Prove it," Rania ordered.

The mage gestured once more, and the shards in the box flared with an ethereal light far beyond the capability of Rania's lantern. The light vanished as quickly as it appeared, and the box lid flipped shut.

"All right," Rania said. "Put it down beside the gold. You

step to the left, I step to the right, we take our boxes and back away. No sudden moves. On three."

Jonmarc held his bow steady on the mage, while Maynard trained his weapon on the figure by the wall. If being in the sights bothered either the seller or his witch, neither showed it.

Rania picked up the box and took careful steps away from the meeting point, never taking her eyes off her counterpart. The mage lifted the much heavier chest as if it weighed as little as the gem box, and moved cautiously back to the wall. Jonmarc could not see his face, but he felt the witch's attention on him and the weapon he held.

"If the buyer wants more?" Rania asked when she stood safely between Jonmarc and Maynard. Neither man lowered his weapon.

"You know how to find me. Do not reveal your source. I also know how to find you."

Jonmarc bristled at the implied threat, but Rania put a hand on his arm. The two figures melted into the shadows, and a moment later, they heard hoof beats headed in the opposite direction.

They did not speak until they were back at the horses. "You're sure the *zanite's* real?" Jonmarc asked.

Rania's fingertips brushed over the Noorish inlay on the wooden box. "Yes. I've seen *zanite* glow in the presence of magic. I'm sure."

"That went pretty smoothly," Maynard ventured as they swung up to their mounts.

Rania gave a wry chuckle. "That wasn't the hard part. Getting in and out of the hand-off—that's going to be the challenge."

They rode through the night, making rough camp for a few candlemarks when they could ride no longer, taking turns sitting watch as the others slept. As soon as they and their horses had rested and fed, they took off again, pushing as hard as they dared for the two days it took until Principality lay across the Nu River. They rode along the river's course until they reached a point on a hand-drawn map Rania produced from the pouch on her belt.

"The Gray Cliffs," she said, pausing beside the river's edge to point across to the other side.

The boat for the river crossing sat ready on the shore where Rania's contact had secured it earlier. They all agreed that the less time the *zanite* remained in their possession, the safer for all of them. That meant they would finish the deal tonight.

Jonmarc looped his reins over a low branch and patted his horse's neck. "We'll be back soon," he said quietly and hoped luck made that true. The night seemed too quiet, and once again Jonmarc raised his head, alert for danger, but nothing moved along the riverbank. The nearly full moon cast sharp shadows, bright enough to see all the way back to the tree line. Nothing looked out of place, but Jonmarc could not shake the feeling of being watched.

"Come on," Maynard urged, and together they shoved the boat into the shallow water, holding it while Rania climbed aboard with her precious cargo. Maynard followed, and Jonmarc gave the boat its final push, climbing over the prow without managing to get too wet.

"I hope you know where we're going," Maynard muttered as he and Jonmarc picked up the oars. "I can't land a boat on a sheer cliff."

Rania chuckled. "The cliffs are full of caves along the water line. Some of those caves lead up to the bluff above.

Smugglers have used them for generations. Too many inlets and too many caves for the guards to track, assuming they cared."

"You'd better be right about that," Maynard replied.

Rowing helped to center Jonmarc and burn off the tension. Throughout their journey, he had never caught sight of pursuers, and at times, the feeling of being watched eased, only to return again. He felt it more strongly now, uncertain as to whether the attention felt hostile or protective. Intuition had saved his life more times than he could count, but when he had mentioned his concern to Maynard, the older smuggler had brushed it off, assuring him that all would be fine. As their boat neared the forbidding wall of rock on the other side of the river, Jonmarc's gut told him this meeting would not go as smoothly as the last.

"There! Do you see it? An opening in the rock—and a place to tie the boat," Rania directed.

Jonmarc eyed the cliffs. "What's to keep them from having a mage who draws on the *zanite* and blows us away?"

Rania's smile turned into a smirk. "Salt cliffs. Natural magical dampener. Pretty sure that's why the fortress was built on top, long ago. Creates a stalemate—you can't use magic, but neither can your enemies."

Maynard said little during the trip. Instead, he kept his gaze on the dark waters of the river as they flowed past. Jonmarc wondered if Maynard were privy to a secret he had not shared since it was unlike him to be so distracted during a job. Jonmarc kept his attention on the cliffside, alert for archers. He did not like how exposed they were, navigating their small boat into a narrow channel. Too many possibilities for things to go wrong; too many opportunities for betrayal.

"We're here," Rania announced, leaning forward to loop the rope around a pylon at an old dock within the cliff's fissure. Despite the dock's age, it looked well-maintained, suggesting to Jonmarc that the inlet remained in active use.

"Not much of a party," Maynard noted, finally breaking from his thoughts. "Where's everyone else?"

"They'll be along," Rania replied. She lit a tin lantern and held it aloft. "Follow the path."

Jonmarc took point, carrying his sword in one hand and a long knife in the other. Rania followed, gripping the box with the *zanite* and a wicked blade. Maynard followed, equally well-armed, guarding the rear.

The path led upwards, and Jonmarc could see an opening into the cliff wall at the end. Flickering light affirmed that they were, indeed, expected.

"How do you know where we're going?" Jonmarc asked.

"The messenger gave me directions," Rania replied. "Which I memorized. Can't go having a map laying around."

The path ended at the cliff face, where a doorway had been carved into the salt and rock. Jonmarc had to admit the location's natural protections made it a formidable redoubt, since salt not only dampened magic but also repelled vengeful spirits and other types of supernatural threats. "We going all the way up to the top?" he asked when the entrance led to a set of carved stone steps.

"No. There should be a room that opens off the stairway partway up. Don't know whether it used to be a storage room, or whether it's always been a meeting place, but that's where they're waiting."

Lanterns lit the way well enough for them to see, although they did not completely dispel the shadows. Being inside the cliff made Jonmarc uneasy as if he could feel the weight of the rock around him, compressing his chest, making it difficult to breathe. Maynard looked equally uneasy, and Jonmarc wondered if he, too, had the sense that something would go wrong.

Fifty steps or so up the long stairway, a passageway led off to the left, hewn into the rock. His shoulders brushed the sides of the passageway, and he could not stand to his full height. *Did the ones who built this purposely make it too narrow to draw a blade?* Jonmarc wondered.

At the end of the passageway, more lanterns provided a welcome glow. Jonmarc stepped out of the gloom and into a room big enough to hold a dozen men. To his relief, only three figures awaited them.

"Did you bring it?" The speaker sat behind a substantial desk with intricate Noorish inlay that provided a silent testimony to wealth and power. The man wore a black tunic and trews, stark except for the gold chain at his throat from which hung several protective charms and talismans. He appeared to be in his fourth decade, his features made more severe by his completely shaved head and the rough, purple scar above his left temple.

On either side of him stood bodyguards. Jonmarc sized them up immediately. The man to the right looked like a soldier from his stance and build. The taller man on the left struck Jonmarc more as a scholar or a mage than a fighter, though the swords that hung from his belt suggested that he would not be defenseless if attacked.

"Of course I did," Rania answered, shifting so that the box she carried could be more easily viewed. "Did you bring our payment?"

The bald man gave a cold smile. "Of course." His hand slipped beneath the desktop to retrieve a heavily weighted bag whose contents clanged metallically.

"Show me."

Their host dumped out the contents of the bag. Gold coins

shone in the lamplight. Jonmarc hoped no one could hear him catch his breath. He had never seen that much gold before. Without being asked, the bald man counted out the coins. The pile held enough for Jonmarc's and Maynard's share plus a generous amount for Rania.

"Satisfied?" the man asked.

Rania held out a small glass vial. "If you please," she said, her tone pleasant but her expression firm.

Irritation flickered in the bald man's eyes, but he took the vial and sprinkled drops of its contents across the pile of gold. Nothing happened. He handed back the vial. "Good enough?"

Rania nodded. "Very good."

The man went to put the gold back into the pouch, but Rania cleared her throat. "Leave it in plain sight," she ordered. "We'll bag it."

Again, a look of annoyance crossed their host's face, but he said nothing, merely nodding and pushing the gold off to one side, clearing half of the desk. "Your turn," he said, raising an eyebrow as if the statement were a dare.

Jonmarc stood to one side as Rania moved forward. He and Maynard mirrored the position of the bald man's two companions, keeping a cautious eye both on the bodyguards and on the gold.

"As promised," Rania said, setting the carved wooden box on the table and opening the lid. She did not spill out the precious *zanite*, since many of the fragments, though small, were quite valuable. The *zanite* formed just a single layer on the bottom of the box, a king's ransom for not-quite a handful of crystals.

"They're real," Rania assured without being asked. She did not look surprised when the bald man nodded to his tall companion, who moved closer to the box and stretched out his hand.

"No touching until it's paid for," Rania warned. The mage gave her a look but did not reach into the box. Instead, he held his hand palm down over the box, and closed his eyes, as if listening for a song only he could hear.

"It's genuine," he reported a moment later, opening his eyes. "And very high quality."

The bald man nodded and looked back to Rania. "You can obtain more if we need it?"

"There's more—if the price is right," she replied. Rania nodded toward the items on the desk. "So how about I collect our gold and your people come around to the other side where you can take your box. That way we each only handle our own goods and nobody gets fidgety."

Jonmarc and Maynard flanked Rania as she slowly moved toward her end of the table, while the bald man's companions did the same. Rania took out her pouch and carefully counted the coins as she dropped them into the bag. Jonmarc could see that Rania gave each coin a careful look as she handled it, alert for any tricks. She replaced the pouch in a leather satchel that hung from a strap across her body.

"Pleasure doing business with you," she said with a grin that reminded Jonmarc of a satisfied wolf.

"You've been most professional," the bald man said, closing the lid on the *zanite* box and slipping it into a satchel of his own.

"We are very professional," Rania agreed, "which is why we're going to leave first. You and yours stay here until we're down the stairs and out to our boat. I wouldn't want to damage our new friendship, but if I see anyone follow us or get between us and the boat, I'll think the worst and act accordingly." This time, her smile bared teeth.

"As you wish," the bald man replied. "My patron has no

desire to damage his access to such a rare and exceptional resource. We will do as you bid."

Jonmarc, Maynard, and Rania retreated warily, weapons ready. True to their host's word, no one followed them down the long stairs, and no guards were in view when they crossed the path to the boat.

"Doesn't look like anyone's touched it," Maynard said, eyeing their boat before permitting anyone to climb in.

"Let's get out of here before they change their minds," Jonmarc muttered. For once, Rania looked to be in wholehearted agreement.

The dark, swift river looked wider than on their first trip. The current rippled the surface, and Jonmarc repressed a shiver remembering the chill of the water on the night he swam for his freedom. He stared across the river, following the silver reflection of moonlight when a movement in the shadows brought his instincts to the fore.

"We're not alone out here," he murmured and reached for his knife.

Maynard turned to Rania. "Something you want to tell us?"

She shook her head, eyes wide in the gloom. "This isn't my doing. And if it's the buyer, he'd have had an easier time coming after us before we left land."

Two small boats glided toward them, one from each side. Jonmarc remembered how he had the feeling of being watched when they crossed the first time; now he wondered if he had somehow sensed the newcomers.

"Stop rowing." The voice came from the boat on the right. Despite the shadows, enough moonlight spilled over the water for Jonmarc to see three men in a craft not much larger than their own. Two of those men held crossbows trained on them. A glance to the left showed him three more men in a similar boat, also holding crossbows ready to fire.

"What do you want?" Maynard's voice held a note of command as if he did not understand that they were the prisoners.

"Our friend said he got called in to guard a buyer of some insanely valuable rocks. *Zanite*. Worth a fat king's weight in gold," the speaker replied. "He figured that if you could get some for the buyer, you knew where to get more. So you're going to row back across, nice and easy, and you're going to take us to your seller, and give us some of those fancy rocks."

"It doesn't work like that," Rania snapped. "We don't know where the *zanite* is mined. The seller brings it when we've got the money to pay for it—which you don't have."

"Ah, that's where you're wrong. The seller just has to believe you have the money. And I bet you're a pretty good liar," he added, giving her the once-over.

Jonmarc's mind raced, assessing their options, none of which were good. The bandits' crossbows could shoot them dead long before Maynard and he could maneuver their boat close enough to use a blade. Any fight out here on the water was suicidal. The Nu's cold, swift current could overwhelm even a strong swimmer. Jonmarc had barely survived his escape, crawling out half-drowned and freezing onto the rocky shore. He did not care to tempt fate a second time.

On the other hand, their odds looked bleak if they went along with their captors. He doubted Rania's supplier would be so easily fooled, or that he would come to a meeting without significantly armed back-up, given the merchandise. There were a million ways the situation could go wrong, and few gave them a good chance of survival.

No matter what happened, Jonmarc was sure of one thing: He was not going down without a fight.

"All right," Maynard said, hands raised in surrender. "Hold your arrows. We'll row to shore. You can follow."

Rania and Jonmarc turned toward Maynard, incredulous that he had given in so easily. His face revealed nothing of his thoughts, but as Maynard bent to pick up his oar, he brought his heel down hard three times on the bottom of their boat.

Jonmarc exchanged a glance with Rania, who shrugged, looking equally perplexed.

"Put your back into it, m'boy," Maynard growled. "Do it now."

Trusting that Maynard had more in mind that being in a hurry to be taken captive, Jonmarc pulled on the oar with all his strength, matching Maynard's rhythm. After several strokes, they had pulled ahead of their pursuers.

"We can't outrun them, if that's what you're thinking," Jonmarc hissed. "And they've still got crossbows. They could drop us before we could climb out of the boat."

"Patience," Maynard murmured. "And stay low."

A moment later, something beneath one of their attackers' boats sent a rush of water skyward, tossing the boat into the air as if it weighed nothing, and spilling out the men into the cold, fast-moving current. An instant later, the same thing happened on the right.

"Now!" Maynard urged, and Jonmarc did not need to be told twice. He and Maynard rowed with all their might, as Rania steered the rudder.

"What just happened?" Jonmarc asked, chancing a look behind them. He saw the brigands' boats overturned, and the silhouettes of men bobbing in the water. Then, a man's hoarse scream split the night, and one of the figures vanished, pulled down beneath the water by an unseen force. Another scream followed a few seconds later, again and again until no sign of the men remained, nothing but the upended boats silent on the dark surface.

"Maynard?" Jonmarc's voice did not completely hide his fear.

"Row for shore. We'll be all right." Maynard sounded convinced, but Jonmarc could not help throwing a glance behind them now and again, sure that whatever had caused the destruction would soon come after them. Rania said nothing, tight-lipped, holding the rudder so hard her knuckles were white.

Jonmarc let out a breath he had not realized he was holding when they finally pulled their boat up on shore. Fear turned to anger as he helped Maynard drag the boat onto the rocky beach. "You want to tell me what happened back there?"

"Ah, here they come now," Maynard said, as if he had not heard a word Jonmarc said. He gestured toward the river, from which four soaking wet figures emerged. It took Jonmarc a moment to realize what was wrong with their movement until he realized he had not seen them swim up and climb out on their hands and knees, as it had taken his full strength to do once before. Instead, they walked out, as if they had walked across the bottom of the river bed—

"By the Crone's tits!" he muttered under his breath, fist clenching. "Maynard, are those "

Maynard smile broadly. "*Vayash moru*. Friends of Astir's. Willing to be our bodyguards, for a reasonable fee." He looked insufferably proud of himself.

"You could have told me!" Rania's face flushed with rage. "This was my operation tonight!"

"No offense intended," Maynard replied, slipping into his caravan master charm that won over many an audience. "You hired us to be your bodyguards. I just hired someone to guard the guards."

"You're paying them out of your part of the money," Rania snapped. With that, she stalked away toward where their horses stood tethered, and they heard her ride away.

"Good work," Maynard told the *vayash moru* who stepped in front of the others. "Quick, efficient. Payment for a night's work and a good meal, all at the same time."

"I wouldn't touch something that polluted if I were starving," the *vayash moru* replied, disdain thick in his voice. "It would be like drinking a spittoon."

Maynard carefully counted out four gold pieces while assuring the others did not get a good look at how much was in his pouch. "As agreed," he said, placing the coins in the leader's hand. "Nice working with you. I might have reason to call on you again."

The *vayash moru* shrugged. "Maybe. You know how to contact us." The four men moved in a blur of speed that left a rush of air behind them.

Maynard turned to Jonmarc, grinning in triumph. "Not a bad evening, eh m'boy?"

Maynard's grin slipped as Jonmarc seized him by the lapels and backed him into a nearby tree. "We're supposed to be partners," Jonmarc said through gritted teeth. "You kept them a secret from me."

"Easy," Maynard said in a placating tone. "It was all for the best. Didn't want either of you two to tip our hand. Ace up the sleeve and all."

Jonmarc thumped him harder into the tree trunk. "If we're going to be partners, then we don't keep secrets, aces or not," he growled. "Get this through your head. I am not expendable."

2

SMUGGLER

THE BARGE

"Nice to see everyone looking well," Jonmarc said to Senn as the two of them unloaded casks from the back of Maynard's wagon.

"Yeah, well. You know how it is here. Mostly the same from day to day, except when it isn't." He grinned. "A lot duller since you left."

Jonmarc slapped him on the shoulder. "See, I knew you'd miss me."

Coming back to Jolie's Place, Margolan's most infamous brothel, always felt bittersweet to Jonmarc. He had lived at the house for a year and fiercely defended its regulars and guests as one of Jolie's "guardians." In the end, that same desire to keep them safe forced Jonmarc to leave, once he realized that if he stayed in one place, the Nargi captain who lost his best fight slave would keep sending people to hunt him down until he was dead or captured. People could get hurt. Reluctantly, Jonmarc knew it was time to move on.

"You look like you're doing pretty well for yourself," Senn observed. "Haven't missed too many meals," he added, with a joking poke at Jonmarc's ribs. Senn tended bar at the brothel, and he had always been a good friend to Jonmarc.

"Food's not as fancy in the kind of places Maynard and I go," Jonmarc replied with a grin. "Nothing to compare with what Amme here puts on the table."

"I'd say smuggling agrees with you," Senn said, helping Jonmarc with another barrel. "You didn't seem like you'd be happy staying in one place for long."

Jonmarc ducked his head, letting his long chestnut brown hair hide his face. Once, years ago, he never questioned the idea of staying in the fishing village where he had been born, or if not there, at least nearby. Too much death, fire, and blood lay behind him now to think that he could settle down like that again. "It's a big world," he said, hoping the cheer in his voice didn't sound as forced to Senn as it did to him. "Be a shame not to see as much of it as I can."

Senn gave a snort. "You can keep it. I'm happy hearing stories about other places, but I know when I've got a good deal where I am."

Jonmarc helped him set down the heavy cask, then rose and mopped the sweat from his eyes with his sleeve. "If you've got the whiskey, I've got the stories," he said with a grin.

"Now you're talking," Senn replied. "Once we're done unloading, I know Amme will insist you have a plate of whatever she's making for tonight. Wouldn't hurt to stick around long enough to give your best to Jolie and the girls before you go, either."

Jonmarc had expected as much, and Maynard sent him on his delivery run alone, knowing he would want to visit for a while. He and Maynard had found a temporary place to stay in one of the houseboats moored at the Floating City, and while bobbing on the river current made for a good night's rest, Jonmarc was happy to spend time on dry land when the opportunity presented itself.

He and Senn made quick work of the rest of the wagon load. Along with the casks of ale and brandy, Jonmarc brought the hard-to-find spices Amme requested and bolts of Noorish silk and brocade for the gowns worn by Jolie's "girls." Smuggled goods, all of them, secured for a fair price at the cost of Jonmarc and Maynard risking life and limb.

"There you are!" Amme, the brothel's cook, came out of the kitchen, dusting her hands on her stained apron. "It's good to see you, Jonmarc." She squinted as she gave him an assessing look, eyeing him with concern. "Not too thin—that's nice to see. Not bleeding either—always a plus."

Jonmarc rolled his eyes and chuckled. While Amme had made certain he had all he wanted to eat while he lived at the brothel, she had also seen more times than he cared to remember when he had come out of one fight or another worse for the wear. "I'm just faster with my fists, Amme. Better with practice."

"Humph. Best fight is the one you don't get into," she huffed. "Well don't just stand there. Come in and get fed. Still a growing boy."

At almost twenty-three, Jonmarc hardly qualified as a "boy," but Amme was old enough to be his grandmother, so he let the comment slide. True to her word, she had a plate of venison and potatoes for him at a table in the kitchen, along with half of a warm, crusty loaf of bread. Senn came in a few moments later with a glass of whiskey and set it down in front of Jonmarc.

"Now let's hear some of those stories," Senn said, pulling up a chair across from Jonmarc as Amme bustled around the kitchen. Mornings at the brothel were quiet, empty of customers. The staff had chores to do in preparation for the evening's patrons, but most days, the mornings and early afternoons provided a much-needed respite.

"Not much to tell," Jonmarc said between bites. "The less you know about where and how Maynard and I obtain your supplies, the safer you are. You can always claim ignorance if the guards ever come calling."

"Come on," Senn coaxed. "You can do better than that." Amme looked over from where she stirred a pot on the hearth and raised an eyebrow, seconding Senn's request.

"All right," Jonmarc relented. He regaled them with a few of the more spectacular escapes he and Maynard had made, carefully editing out places and names to assure they would not provide evidence, should they get repeated to someone who might care. His tales entertained them, and Senn fetched him a second whiskey to keep the stories flowing.

Jonmarc finished off the last of his food and sipped the whiskey. He missed the easy camaraderie he had found at Jolie's Place, and while he enjoyed his new venture with Maynard, Jonmarc knew he could not have safely remained here at the brothel. He felt a twinge of sadness that this sanctuary had been denied him.

"Jonmarc! It's so good to see you, *cheche*." Jolie swept into the kitchen, at full volume and larger than life. She wore a linen dress, plain compared to the gowns she favored in the evening, but even so, Jolie's presence demanded attention. "Maynard is treating you well, I see?"

Jonmarc stood and accepted Jolie's hug. "For the most part, yes. Except for the running for our lives part."

Jolie laughed, a raucous sound that promised good times. Her husky voice suggested whiskey and pipe smoke even when she was not playing the role of the seductress. Jonmarc knew for a fact Jolie no longer took customers herself, preferring to remain in the background, overseeing her very profitable enterprise with the help of her *vayash moru* manager, Astir.

"I think that's something you're very good at, am I right?" She looked around at the new items Jonmarc and Senn had unloaded from the wagon. "You got everything on the list?"

Jonmarc nodded. "Even brought a few extras I thought Amme and Senn might want," he said. "And they did."

Jolie patted his arm. "Already thinking like a businessman. I knew Maynard would be a good influence."

Jonmarc laughed. "You remember that I knew him from before, with the caravan? Whatever you do, don't tell him that he's a 'good influence.' He won't sober up for a week." Maynard Linton had an excellent nose for business and the skills of a natural-born showman. But his regard for the law had always been open to creative interpretation, and now that he no longer had the caravan to slow him down, Maynard had become even more daring than before.

"Well then, you'll have to be his good sense," Jolie replied with a smile. She grew serious. "I am pleased to see you healthy, if not completely safe. It's a good move for you."

They both knew he could not have stayed, and Jonmarc felt eager to change the subject. "How are the girls?"

Jolie leaned against the wall and crossed her arms. "A few new ones have come since you left, but most are still here. It's the way of things." Jolie had a reputation as a fair madam who protected her trollops and made sure they were well cared for. Astir and her guardians made certain nothing got out of hand.

Jonmarc wanted to ask after Thaine, but he knew better. He thought he saw the acknowledgment of what he did not say in Jolie's gaze.

"Haven't had any more problems with the Nargi," she

said, changing the subject. "I suspect they got the 'message' you and Astir sent them the last time." One dead body and all those missing soldiers should have gotten their point across loud and clear.

"That's good. Anyone else try to tear up the place?" Jonmarc had settled more than a few fights. Ruffians never expected to find someone with his fighting experience playing bodyguard to whores.

"Nothing worth telling, *cheche*," Jolie replied. "Your friend Harrtuck stopped in a few weeks ago, let me know we probably wouldn't see him for a while. His new assignment takes him to the Palace City, and maybe if he's fortunate, to a place in the King's Guard."

Jonmarc let out a low whistle. "Good for him. Though I can't imagine Harrtuck on good enough behavior to be anywhere close to King Bricen." Tov Harrtuck had been Jonmarc's friend and mentor when he joined the War Dogs mercenaries several years ago. Now that they had both left the mercs, Harrtuck had returned to what he knew best, being a soldier.

"Tell Astir 'thank you' again for me," Jonmarc said. "Some friends of his helped Maynard and me out of a tight spot a few weeks back."

"So I heard," Jolie replied. "And you can remind Maynard that I did not send you to him for him to get you killed on a damn fool errand."

"I'll be sure to do that." As glad as Jonmarc was to see everyone, he knew it was time to go before the silence between them stretched into awkwardness. Given the regular supply runs he and Maynard made for Jolie, it would not be more than a month or two before he would be back. "You have a new list for us? That last one took some time to piece together. That's the thing about contraband—it's not quite like going to market."

Jolie chuckled. "Ask Senn for the list on the way out. Some Tordassian brandy would be nice; we get some patrons with deep pockets now and again. I like the silk you brought me. The girls always need new dresses. I added some satin and lace to the list for next time."

"Always the best for you, Jolie," Jonmarc said, bending to give her a peck on the cheek in parting.

Jolie laid a hand on his shoulder. "You take care, Jonmarc," she said, all joking gone from her eyes. "Astir asked me to give you a message. His dreams have been dark, of late."

"I didn't know *vayash moru* dreamed."

"They don't, always. But sometimes, he sees portents and omens. Such a dream came to him twice now, about you."

"Me?" That got Jonmarc's attention.

"He doesn't know the meaning, only that he saw Istra, the Dark Lady, lay her hand on you."

Jonmarc gave her a sharp look. "Blessing or punishment?"

"He could not tell. It was just a glimpse and then gone. But he is sure of what he saw."

"Sometimes dreams are just pretty pictures," Jonmarc protested. "Imagination. Nothing more."

"And sometimes, they are not," Jolie countered. "I have learned to trust Astir's intuition. You should, too. And you know you can come here, whenever you need to."

"Thanks," he replied, fighting not to show just how much her offer meant. "You know I won't be a stranger."

Her grip tightened. "One thing I did hear. Dhasson has hired mercs from Principality to watch their borders. If your travels take you that direction, be careful."

"I'll pass that along to Maynard," Jonmarc assured her, and waved goodbye to Amme and Senn on his way out. Although the empty wagon should have meant that he made a faster return trip, Jonmarc did not urge the horse to full speed. Jolie's Place was as close to a home as he had known since raiders destroyed his village eight years before. As much as he looked forward to visiting when he brought a delivery, leaving put his mood off for the rest of the day.

"I'VE GOT A new job for us, m'boy!" Maynard greeted him when he returned to the houseboat.

Jonmarc grabbed onto the cabin doorway to steady himself as the boat rocked. It always took a moment or two to adjust his balance. The houseboat resembled a small barge with a box on top, seaworthy but unimpressive. Inside, the cabin looked like a room at a down-at-the-heels inn, hard-worn with few comforts. Two cots took up one side of the room. In the center, a small table sat bolted to the floor, and two chairs hooked in to rings on the deck to keep them from sliding when the wind or the current rocked the houseboat. Two large wooden boxes attached to the deck held their gear and belongings, while a third box filled with woven baskets stored food that would keep.

Water came from a spring on the shore, since no one in his right mind would drink from the Nu anywhere near the Floating City. A counter on the other side of the cabin had a slab of slate bolted to it, with a small brazier fastened securely on top. Their few pots and utensils hung on the wall. He had made do with much less.

"What kind of job?" Jonmarc asked, slinging his satchel down on the chair. "It better be good. My ass is numb from the bench on the wagon, I pulled a muscle helping Senn unload the casks, and I haven't eaten since lunch. I'm tired, hungry, and cranky so please—some good news would be nice."

Maynard chuckled and slid a jug of ale across the table. Jonmarc took a deep swig and wiped his mouth. "There's vegetable soup with some chicken warming on the brazier," he said with a nod toward the counter. "Got some bread left, too, if it hasn't gone moldy. Maybe some cheese." He waited while Jonmarc grabbed a bowl and helped himself, then sat down at the table.

"I've got a client who wants us to smuggle a shipment of Noorish inlaid boxes into Dhasson."

"Why does he need them to be smuggled? Surely Dhasson can get its own Noorish boxes."

Maynard leaned back. "Sure—but the legal way means fees to the king, bribes for the guards at the border, maybe some more fees to the merchant's guild in the city if they've got one. Eats into profits."

"We're not talking about smuggling anything in the boxes, are we, Maynard? Like dreamweed?" Jonmarc looked up from his food. "Because I don't have many scruples left, but I won't move dreamweed—or slaves."

Maynard nodded. "Understood. I told you up front when you signed on—neither do I. So the boxes are empty. I specified that—and we'll check. Otherwise, we meet up with a barge that will be floating off the Dhasson coast in a remote stretch at a certain time. Most of the risk is on them—the boxes are legal to buy here in Margolan, and legal to resell."

"Except for the part about taking them across kingdom borders," Jonmarc replied with a mouth full of bread.

"If it were legal, we wouldn't make the extra percentage," Maynard said.

"What about Raina?"

"What about her?"

"Is she in on it?" Jonmarc asked.

Maynard shook his head. "No. Don't need her. Why split the profits more than we have to?"

Jonmarc took a few spoonfuls of soup before he answered. "Jolie warned me that Dhasson has beefed up its border patrols—with Principality mercs."

Maynard cursed under his breath. "Lovely. That will make buyers nervous, and make them lay low until things go back to normal. Bad for business." He took another swig from the jug. "Shouldn't cause problems for this job, because we're coming in from the river. Whether the buyer can get the boxes where they've been sold is his problem, not ours."

"Just passing along information," Jonmarc replied, finishing his meal and sitting back. "Jolie said to tell you hello."

"Fill me in—I'm sure you heard all the news."

Jonmarc grabbed a tin cup and filled it with ale to leave Maynard the rest of the jug, then passed along the gossip he had gained at the brothel. "They wanted stories about the smuggling life, so I shared a few—stripped of any incriminating details," he added.

Maynard rose from his chair, wobbled a bit with the bob of the current and the ale in his stomach, and clapped Jonmarc on the shoulder. "You're shaping up into a fine smuggler, m'boy. Always knew you had it in you."

"What do you know about Rania?" Jonmarc asked, stretching his legs and enjoying the ale which, for once, was actually drinkable.

Maynard turned to look at him and raised an eyebrow. "Not much. Why do you care?"

Jonmarc glowered at the implication. "I don't care," he

snapped. "But she seems to be someone you've worked with quite a bit in the past, and if she's going to be around, I like to know what I'm dealing with."

Jonmarc watched Maynard's expression, and thought perhaps his sharp comment to Maynard about expendability had been taken to heart. For once, the former caravan master seemed contrite, as if playing his cards close to his vest was so much of a habit he had forgotten he was doing so.

"Out here on the river, people write their own stories about themselves," Maynard replied, finishing off the jug and grabbing another from the bin. He set it on the table between them with a thud. "Names and histories are what you want them to be. Goddess, we've certainly done some of that ourselves."

True enough. While Maynard knew nearly all of Jonmarc's history and Jonmarc knew a good bit of his, few others aside from Jolie and Mama knew their true past. In the Floating City, they both went by their real names, but outside the City, they went by a variety of aliases, and he assumed that was true for their counterparts too.

"I'm in the mood for a good story," Jonmarc replied, refilling his cup.

"I've been working with Rania for several years," Maynard replied. "She ran some jobs for me on occasion back when I had the caravan, and we'd come this far east. Kept us supplied with materials for the artisans and some of the more exotic items we had for sale."

"Tell me she didn't get you the *stawar*," Jonmarc said, remembering the black predator cat that was rarely ever seen outside its Eastmark home.

Maynard chuckled. "No. Although another smuggler did —and that was quite the tale. Those Markians don't much like having one of those cats taken out of the kingdom."

"Because it's the symbol of their god," Jonmarc supplied. While Eastmark gave lip service to the eight-faces of the Sacred Lady as did the other Winter Kingdoms, they still hung onto older deities, including the *Stawar* God, consort of the goddess.

Maynard made a dismissive gesture. "It's a symbol, not the real thing," he replied, rolling his eyes.

"What do you know about Rania? Even if she's made up a tale, there's usually a small truth in a lie."

Maynard refilled Jonmarc's cup and took a generous swig from the jug. "Orphaned young, and for a girl on the streets, that's got to be as rough as it gets, so if she's still alive, she came up the hard way. No living relatives, no long-term 'entanglements.' Good with a knife, fast on her feet, can punch like a sailor. Probably not above sleeping with someone who's got what she wants, but she's nobody's whore. Anyone who can survive in the smuggling business for as long as she has is nobody's fool, either."

"So you trust Rania?"

Maynard met his gaze. "I didn't say that. We've done business together. She's good at what she does, and she gets the job done. She's less of a pain in the ass to work with than some of the other smugglers out there, and so far, she hasn't stabbed me in the back. But there's always a first time."

"Lovely business," Jonmarc muttered.

"Not much difference from the caravan trade, or have you forgotten?" Maynard asked, raising an eyebrow.

Jonmarc had not forgotten, no matter how much he might like to wipe out some memories. The caravan had been betrayed several times by one of their own, someone seeking to gain by selling them out to brigands, slavers, angry guards, or vengeful bounty hunters. They had faced down true monsters and restless spirits, fought rogue *vayash moru*, and battled the worst nature could throw at them.

"No, I haven't. I couldn't." They buried too many friends along the way for those nightmares to ever leave him.

"You saw the dark side of the merc business," Maynard added.

"Can't argue that."

"And you know for a fact that being a tradesman doesn't guarantee safety."

Jonmarc had to look away. Raiders burned and looted the fishing village where he had grown up, killing his blacksmith father and weaver mother along with all their neighbors. Monsters destroyed the village that took him in as a lone survivor. Since then, Jonmarc had not stopped running.

"No. There's no such thing as a safe place."

It might have been his imagination, but he thought he saw a glimmer of sadness in Maynard's eyes at that. Maynard covered it quickly. "Unfortunate truth, m'boy. One you've learned the hard way yourself."

"So about this job." Jonmarc looked away, eager to steer the conversation to safer topics. "Are we going to have Astir's friends backing us up?"

Maynard reached back and rubbed his neck; a sure tell that the man was not entirely happy with circumstances. "No, not on this one. Something about Dhasson—they wouldn't explain, just turned me down flat. Even the undead have politics—imagine that."

"Then what's our ace? Because I don't want to swim home or end up floating downstream with an arrow in my back."

"Believe me when I tell you, I'm in total agreement. That's why we're meeting on the barge. Technically neutral territory—not Dhasson, not Margolan. Both sides row in and back. Put the barge in the middle of the river at midnight, lift anchor and no one's the wiser."

"And the buyer was all right with that?" Jonmarc gave Maynard a skeptical look.

"Better than all right, m'boy. I think that arrangement sealed our deal. Hard for either side to cheat."

"Whose barge?"

Maynard chuckled. "That's where it helps to have friends. Got a guy who owes me a favor who hauls heavy cargo down the river. He'll drag the barge out at midnight, and bring it back before dawn, no questions asked. In between, he'll row himself back to shore—he's may not be asking any questions, but he's not an idiot."

"That could work," Jonmarc said as he mulled it over. "The middle of the river is too far out for an archer on shore to hit—found out their range the hard way," he added, wincing at remembered pain from the Nargi arrow he had taken in the back. "We'd see anyone else who was out there in a boat, and so would they." He nodded. "I like it."

"Good. Because we're going to make some nice money from the deal." Maynard named a figure, and Jonmarc's eyebrows rose.

"No one pays that much money for an easy job," Jonmarc warned. "What didn't your contact tell us?"

Maynard considered his question in silence. "It's not that the boxes are Noorish—neither Margolan nor Dhasson have issues with the Noors. There's nothing in the boxes. Getting around taxes and tariffs keep smugglers employed. So I don't have an answer for you, but you raise a good point."

"Let me guess—you've already taken possession of the boxes," Jonmarc said with a weary sigh.

"This isn't a business that rewards delays."

Jonmarc brought his hand down hard on the table. The

loud *smack* resounded in the small cabin. Maynard jumped. "Dammit, Maynard! If I just wanted to die, there are easier ways to commit suicide."

Maynard held up a hand in an appeasing gesture. "I've got no death wish; you know that. But I examined those boxes myself. I checked them for magic and for curses. Nothing. Maybe we're better off knowing."

Jonmarc leveled an angry glare. "We're never better off not knowing. Ignorance gets people killed—people like us."

"We'll both go have a look at them tomorrow," Maynard promised. "Maybe you'll see something I didn't. We don't have to deliver until midnight."

"Midnight tomorrow?" Jonmarc echoed.

Maynard looked away and rubbed his neck again. "Yeah. You know it's dangerous to hold on to cargo for long. I would have done it tonight, but it's gonna take that long for my friend to get the barge—"

Jonmarc stood up, banging against the table hard enough that it would have overturned it without the fastenings to the floor. "Do you remember what I said about not being expendable?" he snapped, voice rising with his anger. "This is part of that. Dammit, Maynard, if we are a team, then I know about these things before they're a done deal. I get a say. Shared risk, shared reward—that should mean shared decisions. Because I've got a feeling this is going to bite us in the ass."

Anger colored Maynard's cheeks. "Then it's amazing I'm still alive since I've been doing this a long time without asking your permission."

"Don't let your pride get in the way," Jonmarc retorted. "What about two heads being better than one? This isn't about who's in charge. It's about us not getting killed. I've been through the Dark Vale since we were back in the caravan. I grew up. Learned a thing or two about fighting. I want to help, but you have to let me in on the plans."

For a moment, Maynard tensed up and started to stand. Jonmarc feared they might come to blows. Then the older man remained seated with effort and forced his hands to unclench. "You're right, dammit." The words were rough like Maynard had dragged them out unwillingly. His eyes still glinted with anger, and his face still flushed, but he took a deep breath, and let his shoulders drop. "You're right."

"Yeah?" Jonmarc remained standing, far enough from the table that he could scramble back should Maynard decided to follow through with that punch.

Maynard ran a hand over his face and back through his hair. "Yeah. This isn't the caravan. I've got no reason but habit not to treat you like a partner on this. So… we'll handle this job, and do it differently next time. That work for you?"

Jonmarc knew it was as much of an apology as he would get and took it for the peace offering it was. "I can live with that," he replied. "Now, how are we going to live through this deal you've cooked up for us?"

The next night came far too quickly. Jonmarc and Maynard stood on the riverbank, and Maynard raised a spyglass to his eye. "The barge is right where it's supposed to be," he said in a hushed voice. They were alone, but both knew voices carried across water.

"What you expected?"

Maynard shrugged. "Too dark to see much except an outline, but it should work. We just need a floating platform to make the hand-off." In the distance, they heard the bells of a distant town ring eleven times.

"Let's go," Jonmarc murmured.

They took care to row silently, keeping low against the boat. Jonmarc had argued for them to go early and be in possession on the barge before their counterparts showed up, and for once, Maynard agreed. Jonmarc listened for any hint that the buyers might also be heading over before the meeting time, but they heard nothing except the lapping of water against the sides of the barge.

Jonmarc tied off their boat to the side of the barge and drew himself carefully over the edge of the deck, then rolled to a crouch. He reached down to give Maynard a hand up, moving as quietly as they could.

The old barge looked barely seaworthy. Peeling paint above the waterline made Jonmarc cringe at the thought of what rot lay beneath the surface. A repair to the front corner suggested that the barge had run aground at least once. The deck showed traces of long-ago paint, visible in the mismatched colors of multiple coats; all scratched down to the wood in places. A small cabin for the barge's captain looked like it would barely hold a cot. Soot and cinders darkened a spot near the cabin, suggesting that cooking outdoors worked better than in the small wheelhouse.

Otherwise, they had a clear view of the deck. No crates, no cargo, and no people—unless they lurked on the other side, remaining in their boat. Wordless agreement sent Jonmarc and Maynard moving to flank the cabin, knives drawn, alert for a trap. Jonmarc flung the door open and blocked the doorway, but moonlight laid the small space bare.

"It's empty," Jonmarc reported. "So I guess now we wait."

They did not wait long. Maynard gave a jerk of his head to indicate a change in the night sounds. The rhythmic lapping of the water on the far side of the barge shifted to the soft bump of wood against wood. Jonmarc and Maynard moved carefully away from the cabin toward the middle of the barge, staying close enough to their boat to make a run for it. The precious cargo of boxes remained in the cabin.

Two men climbed over the side, then froze as they realized that, despite arriving before midnight, they were not alone.

"I expected to pick up my cargo," Maynard said, the code to alert the buyer that his contact had arrived.

"I'm amazed this old crate still floats," the taller of the two strangers replied, completing the code.

Jonmarc and Maynard relaxed their stance, enough to put the newcomers at ease. "You have the payment?" Maynard asked.

The tall man nodded. "You have the goods?"

"Show me the gold," Maynard answered. "Then I show you the boxes. We trade, everyone goes home happy."

The tall man's looked annoyed at Maynard's glib reply. His companion's face remained impassive, and Jonmarc realized that the second man's focus was on the river around them, as was his own.

The speaker withdrew a pouch from inside his coat and counted the gold coins into his palm. Maynard watched, judging the shine and size of the coins and the sound of their clink as they fell together to assure that they were genuine.

"Satisfied?" The man's voice held an impatient edge.

"Keep that pouch where I can see it," Maynard replied. "We'll bring the boxes." He glanced at Jonmarc, who drew his sword as he took the few steps to the cabin, never taking his eyes off the three men in the center of the barge. He brought out their cargo. The bag bulged, large and unwieldy, but lighter than it looked.

"Show me."

Jonmarc took out one box and displayed it as best he could in the moonlight. Meticulously-pieced ivory inlay made complicated patterns against the dark, polished wood of the box lid. Inside, deep blue satin lined the box. When the tall man nodded, Jonmarc placed the box on the deck and did the same with the other twenty. Their buyer relaxed a bit as the last box met with his approval.

"Very well," the man said. Leave the boxes where they are. I will place the pouch here. We'll move carefully to take what is ours and leave. Pleasure doing business with you."

Before Jonmarc had a chance to shout a warning, black-clad figures swarmed over the edge of the old barge's deck.

"In the name of King Harrol of Dhasson, you are under arrest. Give yourselves up!"

"Screw that," Jonmarc muttered, wheeling into an Eastmark kick that caught the closest soldier in the throat, dropping him to the deck. He twisted, swinging his sword for the chest of the fighter's comrade, blocked from a killing blow at the last second as the stunned soldier realized their quarry intended to fight. Jonmarc gripped his knife in the other hand. The familiar cold focus of battle settled over him, letting him think clearly above the rush of adrenaline and the pounding of his heart.

Maynard had thrown himself into a vicious knife battle with the two guards within reach. The former caravan master might not have been a soldier, but he had survived enough bar brawls and deals gone wrong to have plenty of experience fighting dirty.

Ten soldiers had come over the deck, Jonmarc counted, against the four of them. Both the buyer and his bodyguard also fought two men each. Jonmarc had dispatched one almost immediately, but the dead man's companion seemed eager to avenge his fallen partner and flung himself at Jonmarc in a flurry of hard thrusts and slashes that took all his skill to counter. Out of the corner of his eye, Jonmarc spotted a guard closing on them, while another soldier headed toward the bodyguard, who had also dropped one of his opponents.

Jonmarc landed a deep cut to his attacker's shoulder, while the man opened a gash on Jonmarc's forearm in response. From the way the men fought, Jonmarc felt certain these were mercs. The king's soldiers fought with trained precision. These men attacked with a no-rules ferocity Jonmarc had only ever seen from other mercenaries. He wondered if his attacker recognized the same from him.

Before the next merc could join the fight, Jonmarc threw himself to one side, rolling and coming up in a crouch behind his opponent. In one smooth movement, he drew his blade across the man's hamstrings, smiling coldly at the scream and spray of blood that followed as he dropped. He counted on an instant of surprise as the merc behind realized what happened, and Jonmarc lunged for the man with a wild cry, inflicting a punishing series of fast strikes. His blade bloodied his opponent in a half dozen places. Though the mercenary's instincts served him well, it wasn't enough to keep him alive.

Jonmarc spared a glance to see that Maynard and the bodyguard had teamed up after Maynard dispatched his first attacker, with two opponents still standing against them. The buyer held his own with a sword and had felled one of his attackers. Six of the mercs lay dead or injured on the deck, telling Jonmarc that the bodyguard had also scored a kill. The remaining hired soldiers made no move to run, though clearly, the night had not turned out as they expected.

A near miss from his attacker's blade brought Jonmarc's focus back to the fight, and he feinted to one side with his knife, then went for the kill with his sword. The merc evaded the knife, only to leave himself open for Jonmarc to sink his blade deep into the man's side. Blood washed down the man's dark pants, soaking the deck as he collapsed in a heap.

Jonmarc ran to join Maynard and the bodyguard. Another soldier lay on the deck, head missing from his shoulders. Jonmarc guessed the kill belonged to Linton, given his preference for a heavier sword. The merc turned to counter Jonmarc's sword strike, but Jonmarc changed the angle at the last moment and nearly took the merc's arm off at the elbow. The injured merc staggered from pain and shock, and the bodyguard turned, slipping a blade between the merc's ribs from the back.

The last mercenary fought like a *dimonn*, knowing the odds had turned against him. The buyer with the help of his bodyguard made short work him, taking down the last of their attackers.

"Think they'll send more?" Breathless and bloodied, the buyer looked completely rattled.

"Doubt it," Jonmarc replied. "They didn't expect a fight—certainly not the kind they got."

"No need to leave evidence." Maynard grabbed one of the dead men by the arm and hauled the corpse to the edge of the deck, heaving him overboard. Jonmarc and the bodyguard did the same, though the buyer stayed back. Whether his injuries prevented him from helping or he remembered he meant to remain aloof, Jonmarc neither knew nor cared.

"We'll be going now," Maynard said, scooping up the coin bag. Neither he nor Jonmarc turned their backs to the others. The bodyguard quickly repacked the boxes into the bag and hefted it to his shoulder before they made their way toward the other side of the barge. Within minutes, Jonmarc and Maynard were back in their boat, rowing for shore.

Now that the fight was over, Jonmarc felt every slash of his attackers' knives with each pull on the oars. From

477

Maynard's grunts and curses, his companion struggled similarly. "We'll get back and get patched up," Maynard said after a long silence. "A bit more work than we counted on, but still a good payout for the effort."

Jonmarc turned to stare at him. "A good payout for the effort? We were ambushed by ten mercs."

"We beat them. Got our coin. Delivered the goods," Maynard replied, taking the battle in stride. Jonmarc had forgotten how vexing the man could be. "Only thing is, I don't know how I'm going to explain all the blood on the deck."

"Guess that's one less friend you can call in a favor from," Jonmarc said, glad to see the shore so close. He jumped out when they beached, grabbed the rope and hauled the boat onto the rocky ground. Maynard got out, hauling the pouch with their payment, and together they made their way back to the houseboat.

"Think we could smuggle anywhere besides the river for a while?" Jonmarc asked after he sat down on his cot and stripped off his shirt so that Maynard could bind up his wounds. "I'm tired of being seasick."

Maynard brought him a cup of whiskey, and a handful of cloth strips ripped from old shirts. "You'll get a stomach for the water, sooner or later," he said, eying Jonmarc's injuries. Born of the experience from far too many fights in Nargi, Jonmarc already knew that only two required doctoring. The rest were shallow.

"You're just saying that to shut me up."

"Yep." Maynard poured some of the whiskey on the open cuts, smirking as Jonmarc cursed at the pain. He sewed up the worst two gashes and smeared a foul-smelling ointment over them when he was done. "That should hold you."

"My turn," Jonmarc replied. Maynard had taken a couple

of bad gashes, but considering the odds, both had escaped relatively unscathed. Jonmarc had him mended in no time, and they finished the rest of the bottle at the table.

"You ever figure out what was so special about the damn boxes?" Jonmarc asked, raising a glass in a cynical toast.

"Actually, I believe I did," Maynard replied, clinking glasses together. "They're specially made to increase a man's fertility and guarantee him a son."

Jonmarc choked on his whiskey. "Say again?"

"I put it together from some of the things the seller said. The wood is birch—which people connect with fertility. The patterns are supposed to be lucky in that way—and the inlay is made out of the right kind of bone."

Jonmarc raised an eyebrow. "The 'right' kind of bone? What do you—" He broke off as Maynard gave him a meaningful look. "Oh."

"So apparently, twenty wealthy men in Dhasson needed a little help in the bedroom—and we are the richer for it."

Jonmarc downed the rest of his whiskey in one shot. "I'm sorry I asked. But you were right about one thing—it's unlucky to hold on to cargo longer than you have to. Wouldn't want any of that 'luck' from the boxes to rub off."

3

SMUGGLER

CROSSROADS

"You said you wanted to be in on the plan from the start." Maynard clattered around the small galley of the houseboat, clearly annoyed.

"Do I get a choice about which plan? Because stealing a necklace sounds like theft more than smuggling."

"Hang you either way, if we get caught."

"Thank you for that—not making your case any better, if you hadn't noticed," Jonmarc shot back.

"Actually, it's stealing and smuggling. First, we steal the necklace, then we smuggle it back to Principality, where it will be returned to its rightful owner."

"Says the man who hired you to steal it, so forgive me if I don't trust his word."

"You're too young to be so cynical."

"You're too old to be so dumb." Jonmarc folded his arms across his chest and glared at Maynard's back as the man stirred the fish stew.

"Would it ease your conscience if I told you that we were stealing it back, from the person who stole it originally?"

"And I'm wondering when thieving became part of the deal."

Maynard ladled the stew into two bowls, which he carried to the table, then returned for a cutting board with bread and cheese. "Smuggling is already stealing—at least, according to the king's guards."

Keeping up his righteous anger took more effort with the smell of hot stew and warm bread in front of him. "That's different. We're doing them out of some tax money. Not breaking into someone's house to—"

"Reclaim it for the person from whom the current 'owner' stole it first."

"Some days, I sort of hate you, Maynard," Jonmarc replied through a mouthful of bread.

"You wanted to know."

"And when would you have told me? When we were picking the locks or after we were riffling through the man's jewelry case?"

"Probably in between those two points," Maynard said, with a look on his face that let Jonmarc know the other man meant to be aggravating.

Jonmarc dug his spoon into the stew with more force than necessary. "I did not escape from Nargi just to end up in the king's dungeon."

"And you won't, m'boy, if we plan this carefully."

"Start by telling me who hired you and what's in it for them." Jonmarc dipped a hunk of bread into the broth and did his best to eat slowly, not wanting to make Maynard any more irritating by admitting how good the stew tasted.

"The person who hired us represents a Principality duke who was indiscreet. He had an affair with a woman who stole the necklace from him. He wants it back. Family heirloom and all."

"Can't he just send the guards after her? He's a duke."

"The woman fled to Margolan, and sold the necklace. It's passed through several hands, and it now is in the possession of a wealthy landowner who bought it for his wife to apologize for an... indiscretion."

"Why doesn't the duke just send someone to buy the necklace outright? Why bother with all this sneaking around?" Jonmarc finished his stew and pushed the bowl aside, then took a long draught of ale.

"Inquiries were made, and the landowner and his wife don't wish to sell."

"Does he know it's stolen?"

Maynard shrugged. "I don't imagine he cares, especially if the gift is gaining him favors."

Hard to argue with that. "How did you manage to get noticed by this duke anyhow?"

"I've done a few runs for him on some hard-to-find items for his collections, through intermediaries, of course," Maynard replied, but he did not meet Jonmarc's gaze.

"So you've stolen things for him before."

Irritation began to outweigh Maynard's good humor. "Stop saying that like it's a bad thing. It's just business."

"Not when it could have us dangling from a noose," Jonmarc countered.

Maynard rolled his eyes. "It wasn't exactly stealing. The duke had contracted for a shipment, and the supplier delivered short. Cheated the duke. I merely offered to obtain the rest of his rightful order—for a fee."

Jonmarc rubbed his hand across his mouth. "So the duke has lousy taste in women—and bad luck in business. Are you sure he's got the money to pay us?"

Maynard nodded. "He's always paid well, with a bonus if... complications ... are avoided."

Jonmarc snorted. "Yeah, because this duke of yours has so much good luck like that. Seriously?"

"I didn't say whose complications we were avoiding," Maynard replied. "Look, I know there's risk, but if there weren't, we would be merchants, not smugglers. He's held up his end of the bargain before, and everything I've been able to find out about this landowner says we can nab the necklace when he leaves to go hunting. He's very much the sportsman, goes out on a hunt several times a month. While he's gone, there's a very small staff at his home, since the wife goes to visit her family. He sends all but a few servants away until he returns. We slip in, grab the necklace, slip out, and we're done."

Jonmarc's expression made his skepticism clear. "When I said I wanted in from the beginning, I reckoned that from the point we decide whether or not to agree to do the job, not after we're already committed. In case you weren't clear."

Maynard scowled. "I'm clear."

"So how do we know when he's going hunting again?"

"I've got someone watching the house. There's always a flurry of activity before a hunt—horses and hounds being brought in, people coming and going. My informant just has to tell me when that happens, and we're in."

"Are you planning to kill your informant afterward? Or will he be informing on us next—once the necklace happens to go missing?"

Maynard gave him a horrified look. "By the Lady, no! He's a cousin on my mother's side. And I've cut him in for a nice percentage."

Jonmarc covered his face with his hand. "I should have known. Thieving runs in your family?"

Maynard grinned. "Yes, actually. But that's beside the point. This is business."

"Same thing."

"Often, yes."

In the week before the hunt began, Jonmarc and Maynard made their own trip to carefully check out the estate and its lands. Squire Lorans's lands include fields and barns, plus ample acreage for hunting. Jonmarc could only guess that the current squire or his ancestors had done a service to the king to gain such a holding.

The house, while large, lacked the opulence of a noble's manor. It stood three stories tall, made of brick, situated on a hill so its owner could survey his lands. Careful to avoid being seen, Jonmarc and Maynard studied the approaches and alternate escape routes, checked the proximity to the nearest regiment of the king's guards, and looked for the best places to hide their horses.

"I still don't like this," Jonmarc paced the cabin of their houseboat. "I've got a feeling there's more to this that we don't know."

"Probably," Maynard agreed. "There always is. We're just the delivery men for cargo that is part of grander schemes. I accept that—because I'm just as happy not to know those big plans. Gives fewer people reasons to try to kill me."

"There's a long enough list for that already." Jonmarc combed a hand back through his hair. "How do we get into the house?"

"We don't. You cause a distraction, and I steal the necklace."

"What kind of distraction did you have in mind?" Jonmarc asked, unsure he wanted to hear the answer.

"Fire usually works well."

To Maynard's vexation, Jonmarc made them go over the plan multiple times looking for alternatives and weaknesses.

He could not shake a sense of foreboding, but he knew that it was too late to back out of the agreement now.

When the time came, Jonmarc found himself waiting in a copse of trees at the edge of the estate's lawn. The master of the house, his friends, and their hounds had departed early that morning, bound for Lorans's hunting lodge deep in the woods. Jonmarc and Maynard had watched the servants leave soon after. Light from within the house confirmed that a few of the staff remained behind, and as night fell, the grounds grew eerily quiet.

He already had his diversion in mind. A small stone building sat several yards away from the main house, and from the cords of wood stacked against its wall, Jonmarc bet it was a smokehouse. Setting the wood ablaze would bring the servants running to one side of the house, while Maynard entered—and hopefully, exited—from the other. Putting out the fire and cleaning up would take time, meaning fewer people in the house to notice intruders—if they were lucky.

Jonmarc circled back around to await his cue, remaining still and quiet in the shadows. He heard motion in the darkness, coming from along the edge of the stand of trees. Jonmarc weighed his options and swore under his breath. If he hesitated to go after whoever lurked along the tree line, he risked a knife in the back. Yet investigating the unwelcome newcomer jeopardized his timing to set the fire.

Expediency won out, and Jonmarc crouched low, sticking to the shadows to track the watcher in the forest. Moving silently, he closed the gap between them, coming from behind. The stranger did not glance his way until he dove to tackle his opponent, knife in hand.

"You!"

Before Jonmarc could register the voice, an arm lashed out, and strong, thin fingers gripped his wrist, forcing his knife clear of their bodies as they crashed together to the ground.

"Don't stab me!" Rania lay pinned beneath him, her face darkened with soot, eyes wide.

None too gently, Jonmarc hauled her to her feet, one hand clamped on her arm and his knife still in the other hand. "What are you doing here?" he hissed.

"Probably the same as you—stealing something."

"Who hired you?"

"The duchess. You?"

"Son of a bitch. The duke." Jonmarc and Rania glared at each other for a moment. "I don't have time for an argument," he snapped. "Either join in with us, and we give you a cut, or I knock you out and leave you here, and you can hope nobody finds you."

Rania's first reply was as anatomically impossible as it was creatively obscene. Jonmarc raised an eyebrow and lifted the solid pommel of his knife in a warning.

"All right," she muttered. "I'm in."

Jonmarc gave her a skeptical look.

"Trust me or don't trust me, but we've got a necklace to steal."

"Nice," he said, keeping hold of Rania's arm and moving them toward the smokehouse. "Get going." When they reached the smokehouse, Jonmarc let go of her arm. "Stay in front of me where I can see you," he hissed. "Stack the wood around the outside of the shed." He pulled flint and steel from a pouch on his belt, along with a skein of wool for kindling.

"Where's Maynard?" Rania asked as she moved to help with the wood. She remained within his line of sight, taking care not to get too close and present a threat.

"With luck, inside."

The seasoned wood crackled and easily burst into flame.

In minutes, fire ringed the shed, dancing high along the walls, easily visible from the main house.

"Come on," Jonmarc urged, with a jerk of his head toward the shadows. "Ladies first," he smirked, intent on keeping Rania in front of him.

She glowered but complied. "I didn't have to accept your offer," she muttered. "Could have kept the whole payout for myself."

"Only if you'd have gotten to it first," Jonmarc replied, just above a whisper. He guided Rania back toward where he kept watch for Maynard.

"Servants are coming to deal with the fire," Rania said, pointing to where several dark forms ran from the house carrying buckets.

The blaze would be easy to put out and had little danger of spreading, but in the precious minutes while three servants doused the fire, Maynard had easy access to the inside of the manor.

"Shit," Jonmarc growled. "Who are they?" Rania followed his line of sight to see two more dark figures moving toward the front of the manor from the other side.

"Common thieves?" she mused. "It's no secret that the owner is out on a hunt."

"Unless it's a set-up. Maybe someone is betting on us all getting tangled up with each other and embarrassing the duke, his wife, or the landowner—maybe all three."

"What are we going to do about it?" Rania's tapping toe made her bias for action clear.

"Take care of the complication," Jonmarc replied, lifting a crossbow. At the same time, Rania withdrew a length of leather from her belt and fitted a smooth stone into the sling.

"I'll take the one on the right," she said.

They fired their weapons nearly simultaneously. The

interlopers froze at the twang of the crossbow, which covered the nearly silent *hiss* and *snap* of the sling's release. One man fell with a quarrel in his chest, as the other swayed, head snapping back with the impact of the stone, and then crumpled.

Minutes later, a man dressed in black slipped from the entrance. Rania reached for her sling, but Jonmarc caught her arm. "Relax. It's Maynard." Even at a distance, Maynard's silhouette and gait assured Jonmarc his partner was on his way.

"What about the two dead men on the front lawn?" Rania asked as Maynard sprinted toward the rendezvous point.

"What about them? I don't imagine they'll be missed."

Rania rolled her eyes. "No one's going to think they just committed suicide."

Jonmarc shrugged. "Who cares? Sends a message to Lorans that he was careless. And the duke and his wife can hardly turn us in without admitting their part in this."

Maynard jogged up to them and did a double take at Rania. "What's she—?"

"Not now. Let's get out of here. The fire won't hold them much longer," Jonmarc cut him off.

"My horse is back there," Rania said, jerking her thumb toward where she had emerged from the forest.

"Did you steal it?" Jonmarc asked.

"Yes, but—"

"Then consider it a loaner. You can ride behind me." Jonmarc grabbed her wrist, and they headed at a dead run toward where they had left their mounts tied. Along the way, Rania jerked free of his hold, and she refused a hand up to the horse, swinging up behind him with practiced ease.

Jonmarc and Maynard urged their horses as fast as they dared go on the rutted forest road. Jonmarc expected pursuers to emerge at any moment and braced to dodge a hail of arrows. When they had ridden for half a candlemark without unwanted company, he finally relaxed. Maynard slowed his horse, and so did Jonmarc.

Only then did he become conscious of how closely Rania pressed up against his back, and how snug her arms felt around his waist. He heard her laughter at the wild ride and realized how much Rania relished the thrill of the chase. He shifted in his saddle, uncomfortably aware of his body's response, and tried to pass it off as the rush of adrenaline from a dangerous job. He did not fully believe himself.

When they reached the old barn that was their safe house that night, Jonmarc was doubly glad they had shied away from taking a room at an inn. It would not do for them to be remembered, and while showing up late at night flushed from a chase might or might not be noted, bringing a pretty redhead up to their room certainly would be memorable. And tonight, neither Jonmarc nor Maynard intended to allow Rania out of their sight.

"It's like you don't trust me," Rania teased, in a mock pout.

"We don't," Maynard replied, putting his feet up on a crate as he lounged in a mound of hay. He pulled out a flask and took a swig, then held it out to share, only to realize both Jonmarc and Rania held up their own flasks in salute.

"How are we going to explain this?" Rania asked, her voice rough with smoke and whiskey. "Your client didn't want his wife to know the necklace was missing. Obviously, she figured it out. Odds are she didn't want him to know she knew."

Jonmarc shrugged. "Maybe. Unless she's the one who brought the money into the marriage, in which case, she's sending him a message."

"And planning to make his life unbearable," Maynard added.

"Serves him right," Rania replied and took another mouthful.

"Don't have much choice," Maynard said. "Either we say nothing, deliver it up to the duke and let his wife believe you failed and ran off, or we push the issue, force them into caring and sharing, and present the bill together."

Rania made a face. "Don't like either option, and I doubt the duke and his wife will, either," she said. "Even though we're returning with the goods, they won't both pay up. I think the less we admit, the better. Wouldn't be the first time a smuggler bailed out when a job went sour. The wife isn't one of my usual clients, and I don't think she's connected to my buyers, so the damage to my reputation shouldn't be too bad," she added with a wicked grin.

"How did you hear about the job?" Jonmarc asked, taking up a spot facing the opposite direction from Maynard. He knew without needing to discuss it that the two of them would be sleeping in shifts, both to watch over the stolen necklace and to assure that Rania didn't take off in the middle of the night—with or without the jewelry.

"You know how it is," Rania said with a one-of-those-kind-of-things shrug. "Word gets around. I've made a bit of name for myself with some of the high-born ladies who occasionally need a little something taken care of for them that they can't ask the menfolk to help with."

"Something like blackmail, stealing back love tokens, that kind of thing?" Maynard asked.

Rania nodded. "Funny thing, but it's hard for a lady to get the kind of service she deserves from your run-of-the-mill rogue. They like me because I understand them."

"Or at least, their money," Jonmarc supplied.

"That, too."

"How were you supposed to deliver the necklace?" Maynard stretched, taking a final pull from his flask and settling back in the hay.

"Her lady's maid was supposed to meet me at the Fox and Hare tomorrow night," Rania replied. "Do the hand-off out by the summer kitchen, where no one would look twice at a couple of women." She paused, sipping from her flask. "You?"

"Similar," Maynard replied. "A hand-off to a go-between." His deliberately vague response prompted a sour look from Rania. "What?" he said, noticing her annoyance. "You don't think I'm going to just give it up to you."

"I told you mine."

Maynard snorted. "Which we aren't using anymore."

"Maybe, maybe not," Rania replied. "How much did the duke offer you?"

Maynard named a sum. Jonmarc knew it was less than the true amount, but still high enough to afford Rania a tidy profit for her collusion.

"Less than I would have gotten solo," Rania groused.

"What you would have gotten solo was a mild concussion," Jonmarc reminded her. "Or at least rope burn after I tied you up and gagged you. This is a much better deal for all of us."

"I still have the feeling you don't completely trust me," Rania said.

"We don't," Jonmarc and Maynard said in unison.

"After all, you didn't tell us about your deal with the duke's wife," Maynard pointed out. "So you can hardly fault us for the same."

"Maybe I'll let it slide this time," she said, grinning. She claimed a pile of horse blankets for her bed. The scratchy wool smelled like the animals but probably held less vermin than the straw.

"I'll take the first watch," Maynard said, standing up. "You can have my spot until I need it," he said, offering his place to Jonmarc.

Several candlemarks later, Jonmarc startled awake to Maynard's hand on his shoulder. "Your watch," Maynard said.

"Rania?" Jonmarc asked, with a glance toward where their unexpected companion lay on the blankets.

"Not a sound out of her," Maynard replied. "But if she happens to get chatty while you're on watch, just keep your wits about you."

"I'm a big boy, Maynard. I can take care of myself."

"Uh huh. But until that piece is safely delivered, and the money's in hand, keep distractions to a minimum."

"Got it." Jonmarc got to his feet, yawning and stretching, wishing for a strong pot of tea to chase the sleep from his mind. He settled for splashing cold water from the horse trough on his face. "Go rest," he told Maynard. "I'll take care of it."

Jonmarc paced the barn to stay awake and keep an eye on the perimeter, never letting Rania out of his sight. He half expected her to cozy up to him, taking advantage of a rare moment alone. When she did not, he fought back an odd sense of disappointment, even as his estimation of Rania as a professional rose. For tonight, at least, she appeared to be honoring their contract.

The pre-dawn silence gave Jonmarc too much time to think. It had been a few weeks since he roused to nightmares in the dark. Maynard had been patient, and not too surprised. Then again, they both had a lot of miles behind them, not all of it pleasant to remember. Maynard also tossed in his sleep, though his dreams seemed less horrific than Jonmarc's, or perhaps dulled more by time.

Smuggling kept him busy, and the bouts of action and danger took the edge off his restlessness. Maynard proved to be as good a business partner as he had been a caravan manager, and most of the time, Jonmarc enjoyed his company. In the months since he had left his job at Jolie's Place, Jonmarc had picked up a good bit of the river patois, and if he had not quite mastered it like a native, he could at least understand most of what people said and reply coherently.

To his relief, there had been no further incidents with the Nargi. *Maybe Dorran's discovered that being a general takes more time than he expected. Can't spend all day betting on the games and dealing out payback on old scores.*

He was equally happy to have put enough distance between himself and Eastmark to decrease the danger from the death warrant Alcion and his mage Arontala had put out for him. Though he occasionally missed his time with the War Dog mercenaries, Jonmarc knew he did not dare return to Principality, at least, not while the bounty remained on his head in neighboring Eastmark. With his old friend Harrtuck gone to Margolan's palace city with the army, Jonmarc heard nothing about his old merc company. He wished them well, though their business did not lend itself to happy endings.

In the stillness of the old barn, Jonmarc's thoughts returned to Rania. If she feigned sleep for the chance to catch him off guard, her act was convincing. So far, she had played straight with them on every deal, and while Jonmarc agreed with Maynard about being cautious, he hoped their collaboration continued.

Thaine had been the last lover he had taken. Maynard urged him to try the companionship of the barmaids and serving girls in the taverns, but that hurried trysting held little appeal. He still cherished Shanna's memory, still grieved the loss of his young wife, but after so many years, he could not blame that loss for his choice to remain unattached. Thaine's company had been thrust upon him by his Nargi captors as a reward, and her safety dependent upon his compliance. Theirs had been an alliance of captives, though the fondness and friendship had been real enough.

Jonmarc watched Rania sleep and felt a stir of desire. Pretty, independent, and able to hold her own in a fight—verbal or physical—Rania intrigued him. He did not need Maynard's cautions to limit his expectations. Anything that might happen between them would be temporary, a way to work off the stress of their dangerous job, a mutual diversion. Then again, Jonmarc had nothing more to offer someone.

Settling down just gets the people around me killed, he thought. *I'm cursed, like the raider I killed said. Everyone I love dies. I'm a wanted man, a criminal with a death sentence, a thief and a killer. I'd soil anyone decent who got close to me. At least Rania takes me for what I am.*

Maynard muttered something and rolled over in his sleep. Rania shifted but did not wake. Outside, the sky began to lighten with dawn, and in the distance, a rooster crowed. Jonmarc gently toed at Maynard's boot.

"Wake up. It'll be light soon."

Maynard swore and grumbled, but got to his feet and shook his head, clearing away the last traces of sleep. Rania woke on her own and gave a long, casual stretch that Jonmarc found difficult to ignore. She winked at him, letting him know she had caught him looking.

"Let's get on the road," Maynard said.

"A CROSSROADS AT MIDNIGHT? Are we summoning the Dark Lady or collecting our fee?" Jonmarc stormed. Maynard let him vent his misgivings, leaning back in his chair aboard their houseboat, while Rania looked on in amusement.

"Not too many people around, and plenty of freedom of movement," Maynard remarked. "I picked the spot because it's flat and clear—plenty of visibility in all directions, so no one's going to sneak in a regiment of soldiers."

"It's dark and in the middle of nowhere," Jonmarc argued. "Which means it's ideal for an ambush."

"Which we would see and hear coming a mile before they reached us," Maynard said.

"I could back you up with the crossbow," Rania offered.

"No." Once again, Jonmarc and Maynard answered in unison.

"You're going to stay with the horses," Maynard replied. "Make ready for a quick get-away. Besides, you don't need the duke's go-between getting a good look at you—since you defaulted on the deal with his wife."

"Plenty of red-headed Margolense smugglers," Rania muttered. "I could be any of them."

"Right," Jonmarc said in a tone that conveyed his disbelief.

"Fine. I'll watch the horses," Rania snapped. "But I've got money riding on this deal, too, now. So I'll be watching your backs, and if something does go wrong, just remember who it'll be saving your asses."

They passed the day in the houseboat with games of cards and dice, betting with dry beans since none of them wanted to wager real money. Given that they all cheated and all knew each other's tells, Jonmarc felt no surprise that by suppertime, the piles of beans in front of each of them were roughly equivalent.

"I usually win at least a few silvers or two when I play at the inn," Jonmarc said, reaching out to scoop the beans from the last round into his pile.

"That's because you're playing rubes and locals, not card sharps as crooked as you are," Maynard said with a snort. "And besides, I taught you how to cheat."

Jonmarc raised an eyebrow. "Only partly. Learned a thing or two from the mercs. Had to cheat carefully, or you could end up with a busted nose."

"Is that how it happened?" Maynard replied, eyeing the small bend in Jonmarc's nose.

"Just the first time," Jonmarc answered, dealing another round of cards.

"I usually let the marks play the game and collect my—I mean, their—winnings afterward." Rania's voice held a sultry note, and the smile that quirked at the corners of her lips suggested she had a record of success. Tonight Rania wore a functional outfit—boots, trews, and a man's shirt cinched with a belt, but beneath the homespun clothing she had a slim, lithe figure and for a moment, Jonmarc allowed himself to picture her in a form-fitting satin gown. He felt no surprise at the idea that aided with flattery and good whiskey, Rania could relieve a mark of his winnings and having him thanking her for the favor.

He vowed to keep that in mind as a cautionary tale, but his imagination had other ideas.

"You usually work your jobs solo, don't you?" Jonmarc asked Rania, not looking up from his cards.

"It depends. I try not to get too attached. Safer that way. Friends and family are just hostages to fate, waiting to be taken."

Jonmarc could not disagree. "But you make an exception to the solo work now and again?"

"When the job requires it," Rania replied. "Bigger jobs, bigger risks, and more pay-off means I can pay for the extra assistance."

Maynard cleared his throat, impatient to play the game. "Loser at the end of the night buys a round of drinks for the other two at Mama's tomorrow night," he said.

"Sounds good, since I know I won't be losing," Jonmarc replied.

Rania's finger circled the top of her glass idly as she studied her cards. "Just remember," she goaded, "I want the best whiskey in the house."

"Which will be the stuff Mama brewed up last week," Maynard said. "If the kitchen staff didn't use it for rat poison."

Despite the jibes and friendly competition, none of them focused fully on the game. They paused to listen each time the bell tower struck the hour, watching as the candle slowly sank from one notch to the next.

"You think the duke's man will try anything?" Jonmarc said when they finally called the game a draw.

Maynard considered for a moment. "Hope not. Then again, anything's possible. But I've done work for the duke before, and he's kept his word, so let's see if he's as good when the stakes are personal instead of business."

They reached the crossroads just before midnight and found it deserted. The light of the half-moon barely illuminated their way, requiring them to bring partly-shuttered lanterns to keep from breaking an ankle on the rutted road.

"Think he'll show?" Jonmarc asked, making a slow circle in the center of the intersection to assure no one lurked in the fallow farm fields that spread out on all sides of them.

"Yeah. Too much embarrassment at risk for the duke if he doesn't regain the necklace. Though his wife hiring her own thief gives you an idea of how much credit the duchess put in his abilities."

A few minutes later, they heard hoof beats and saw three riders approaching in the moonlight. Jonmarc and Maynard kept their swords sheathed, but drew back their cloaks so that the newcomers could clearly see that they were armed. Jonmarc had never met the duke or his emissary, but Maynard stepped forward as if he recognized the lead rider. The trio halted their approach a dozen feet from where Jonmarc and Maynard stood in the center of the road.

"Did you bring it?" The lead rider was a man in his fourth decade who looked too rough to be a bureaucrat and too refined to be hired muscle. Jonmarc suspected he was one of the duke's enforcers, someone who handled distasteful tasks discreetly.

"We've acquired what you wanted," Maynard replied. "Did you bring the money?"

"Show me what you have."

"Show me the money," Maynard countered.

The lead rider motioned to the man at his left, who swung down from his horse and took a bag of coins from his saddlebag. He hefted the bag and let the coins inside jangle. The man on the right also dismounted and stood waiting by his horse.

Jonmarc thought he saw something out of the corner of his eye in the open land off to the right. He stared out across the fallow field, eyes narrowed, watching carefully, but saw nothing except the breeze swaying the weeds.

"Count them," Maynard said, keeping his gaze locked with the man in charge. The newcomer's assistant signaled the third man and poured out the coins into his cupped hands. Then he counted aloud as he dropped the silver coins, one after another, back into the pouch.

"Keep the pouch where I can see it," Maynard ordered, unwilling to allow a switch to be made. The assistant placed the pouch on the road, and both men backed away, hands raised in front of them.

A glimpse of movement in the empty field on his left took Jonmarc's attention for a moment, but when he looked out over the moonlit land, he saw nothing but tall grass. *An animal*, he thought, *or maybe the wind.*

"Give us some proof that you brought what you promised," the lead man said, pulling Jonmarc's attention back to the hand-off.

Jonmarc withdrew a pouch from his belt and slowly removed the necklace, holding it up for inspection.

"Very nice," the leader said. "Put it down by the coin purse and step away."

Jonmarc moved to do as the man bid when a new voice interrupted.

"Stay where you are. Put your hands in the air."

Across the seemingly empty fields, figures rose from the tall weeds, their backs camouflaged with mats of woven grass slung over their backs. A dozen men ringed the crossroads, and all held swords.

Jonmarc exchanged a glance with Maynard. *They don't look like any highwaymen I've ever run into. It's a deserted place to lie in wait for random travelers, and too much of a coincidence that they are here for the exchange,* he thought.

"Exander. Why am I not surprised," the lead man said, scorn clear in his voice. "How long have you been lying on your belly in the dirt, waiting for your big moment?"

"Nothing is too difficult or tedious in the service of m'lady," Exander replied. "You're one to talk, Rofus, the master's good little errand boy."

Rofus, the lead man of the original three riders, made no

attempt to hide the disdain in his expression. "Does that include becoming a brigand?" he challenged. "Because here you are, holding us at sword's point, on a dark road. How far you've fallen, defending that sullied bitch."

Exander drew his sword. "You've got little room to talk, cleaning up your master's disgrace. The necklace didn't belong to him, and now you're sent out to deal with ruffians to steal it back."

By now, Rofus's two helpers had already taken their swords in hand. Jonmarc and Maynard took two steps backward, unwilling to be drawn into the fray, but the ring of armed men surrounding them made escape impossible.

"So you've come to steal it from me?" Rofus challenged. "How noble."

"M'lady wishes to regain what is rightfully hers," Exander replied, his voice cold and sure. "And to send a message to her husband that he will hear without mistake."

"Which would be?"

Exander's smile raised the hackles on the back of Jonmarc's neck. "Your deaths, and the deaths of the thieves you hired."

Five against a dozen, assuming that Rofus's men would ally with him and Maynard, at least for the duration of the fight. He did not trust Rofus, but Exander's intentions were clear.

The twang-thud of a crossbow broke the silence, and Exander staggered, hands clutched across the tip of a quarrel protruding from his chest. As he fell to his knees, the sharp crack of a whip split the stillness, and then a wild-eyed horse came galloping straight for them.

Everyone seemed to move at once. Rofus charged forward, reining in his horse to make it rear and kick its front hooves at the two nearest attackers. Jonmarc and Maynard wheeled, each closing the gap with the closest opponent and launching an all-out attack. Rofus's two men did the same, showing themselves to be far more accomplished with a blade than Jonmarc would have expected. Another quarrel felled one of the attackers near the rear of their party, and Exander's men looked around, panicked, to find the location of their hidden assailant.

Leaderless and besieged, Exander's men had no choice except to fight. Jonmarc downed his first opponent quickly, stalking a second man who eyed the bloodied corpse of his comrade with wide, panicked eyes. Maynard traded blows with another of the attackers, forcing the man on the defensive. Rofus rode down another man, who went down screaming under the hooves of Rofus's stallion.

Another twang sounded, and one more of Exander's men dropped to the ground with an arrow in his back. The odds were steadily improving, Jonmarc thought as he parried a clumsy thrust by his latest opponent, then delivered a series of pounding blows that set the man on the defensive and forced him backward.

Half a candlemark later, Exander's men lay dead in the dirt. Rofus cleaned his blade on the tunic of one of the corpses and turned back to where the coin purse and the bag with the necklace lay undisturbed in the middle of the crossroads.

"I assure you, we knew nothing of Exander or the duchess's plans," he said. He lifted the coin purse and tossed it to Maynard, who caught it on sheer reflex. Rofus picked up the bag with the necklace, looked inside to assure its contents, and tucked it beneath his coat.

"Obviously, since your men are bloodied, too," Maynard replied. Rofus and his assistants had acquitted themselves well in the fight, but they, like Maynard and Jonmarc, were bleeding from gashes on their forearms and shoulders.

"The duke is grateful for your service," Rofus said, looking on with amusement as Maynard also checked the contents of the coin purse.

"He bloody well should be, since we were pulling his ass out of the fire," Maynard muttered. "Maybe he'll have a care about where he takes his mistresses and keep them away from the family jewels."

Rofus's gave a wan smile. "Would you like me to convey that to the duke?"

Maynard glowered. "That won't be necessary."

Rofus and his men swung back up to their mounts. "A pleasure doing business with you," he said as he turned away.

Jonmarc and Maynard remained where they were until Rofus was well on his way. "You can come out now," Maynard called to Rania.

Rania emerged from the trees, leading two horses by their reins, with the crossbow slung over her shoulder. "Lucky you had me around," she said with a smug smile. "Saved your asses, just like I said I would."

"Hey, where's my horse?" Jonmarc glared as Rania's smile broadened.

"Skittish thing," she said, clucking her tongue in mock dismay. "Bolted when I cracked a whip. Nice diversion. Probably find its way home in a day or two."

"How in the name of the Dark Lady am I supposed to get back to the river without a horse?" Jonmarc demanded.

"You can ride behind me," Rania said, swinging up to her saddle. "Unless you'd rather walk."

"I'm heading over to Mama's for a drink." Maynard tossed his sword belt and scabbard onto his bed. "Don't wait up."

"Think maybe you should stop bleeding before you head for the bar?" Jonmarc asked.

Maynard shot him a tired grin. "Nah. Mama doesn't care. Long as my money's good."

Jonmarc sat down on his cot and grimaced as he shrugged out of his cloak and shirt. Blood stained his sleeves, but closer examination showed only one wound deep enough to bandage.

"You want some help with that?"

Jonmarc might have been exhausted, sweating, and bleeding, but even that could not erase the memory of Rania's body close against his on the ride from the crossroads and a hunger he had not felt in far too long that burned low in his belly.

"Yeah, I could use some help." Even to his own ears, his voice sounded low and rough. "Not going to be able to reach that shoulder cut myself."

"I'll take care of you." Rania's voice held the promise of much more than first aid.

She crossed the small room to grab a bottle of whiskey from the table and found the bandages in a drawer where Jonmarc directed her. She returned and let her fingers brush against his good shoulder, a light caress.

"You've got a lot of scars," she said, settling behind him on the bed, one knee on either side of his hips.

"I get around."

"So I've heard."

He had no desire to discuss the past. "How bad is the cut?" he asked.

"You'll live. Apparently, you've had worse." Rania

shifted behind him. "You know how this works. The whiskey's going to hurt like a son of a bitch."

"Just do it." Jonmarc tensed, locking his jaw and shutting his eyes, stifling a curse as the alcohol burned on the raw wound, cleansing it.

"There was a jar of ointment in with the bandages," Rania said. "You want me to use it?"

"Yeah," he said, letting out a long breath. "Better safe than sorry."

She smoothed the salve over the wound with gentle strokes, and then carefully wrapped the cloth strips as best she could to cover the gash. "It's not too deep," she said, knotting the fabric. "Couple of days, and you won't even feel it."

Rania's hands slipped over his bare back, then up to his neck, gently massaging sore muscles. "You're tense."

"It's been a rough night." They both knew where this was heading, like steps to a dance they had practiced. *It's probably a bad idea,* Jonmarc thought. *Maynard's right. I'd be stupid to trust her. And I don't. Not really. But… it's been a long time.*

Rania leaned closer and pressed her lips to his neck. "Relax," she murmured. "I'll take good care of you."

4

SMUGGLER

BETRAYAL

A MONTH PASSED, AND THEN TWO. JOBS FOUND THEM, sometimes on leads from Rania, more often through Maynard's contacts. The river patois no longer sounded strange to Jonmarc, and it surprised him to find himself thinking in the language that had become familiar. Rania came and went, working her own deals.

When she came back, Rania and Jonmarc took up again as if she had never been gone. While she was away, Jonmarc kept busy. They had made no commitments, and Jonmarc did not expect exclusivity, but he had no desire for other companionship. Easier for everyone to keep things simple and casual.

"The life suits you, *cheche*," Jolie said when Jonmarc brought the list of contraband provisions Astir had requested.

He shrugged. "More than some other options, I imagine." He looked around, taking in the familiar surroundings. For as long as he had spent living in the brothel, now he felt antsy, like he no longer belonged here.

"Life moves on, doesn't it?" Jolie did not expect an answer to her question. "Changes and stays the same. Most of the girls who were here when you first came have gone.

Senn's still here; probably always will be. Amme took sick a while back, and it got bad, but she pulled through."

"Glad to hear it." He had never considered the brothel to be home, but the pang of wistfulness he felt surprised him as Jolie cataloged the changes.

"You want to come in for a drink?"

Jonmarc shook his head. "No thanks. I'd better get back." Old memories would just wrap tighter around him the longer he stayed.

"You're welcome anytime, Jonmarc," Jolie said, giving him a kiss on the cheek. "Take care of yourself."

"You too, Jolie."

She laughed, throaty and whiskey rough. "Always, *cheche*. It's what I do best."

The visit left him out of sorts, and he guessed anger came easier than sadness when there had really been no choice about his options. Staying at Jolie's, no matter how comfortable, put them all in danger. That threat might never go away so long as he lived, but at least being a moving target improved his odds.

Maynard sat at the table in the cabin of their houseboat and looked up from his ledger as Jonmarc walked in. "Everything go all right?"

Jonmarc nodded. "Same as always. Jolie sends her love. Mostly the same, a little different."

"I can make the run next time if you want." Maynard's offer let Jonmarc know that the other man read Jonmarc's mood.

He shrugged. "Won't change anything. I'll do it. But thanks." He nodded toward the ledger. "Problems?"

Maynard took a sip of his cup of *kerif*, which Jonmarc suspected to be laced with whiskey. "Last month was slimmer than I like. We've got a bit set by, for emergencies, but a big job or two would fatten the coffers."

Before Jonmarc could say anything, someone knocked at the door to the houseboat's cabin. Maynard slipped a knife from his belt and held it behind his back as he moved to answer the door.

"I came to see about that job—with the caravan." Petyr stood in the doorway, tossing three ball-shaped lanterns with flames alight from the top of each sphere. The fire traced a circle in the air as Petyr juggled them with easy skill. "I can do five, but I thought you'd get the idea of it with just three."

"Put those things down before you set the boat on fire!" Maynard thundered. Petyr looked abashed, and caught the balls in sequence, blowing out the flames.

"I haven't caught anything on fire—by accident—in a long time," Petyr replied. He brightened. "So can I have a job?"

Maynard let out a weary sigh. "Boy, I told you before. If I had a caravan, I'd hire you. But I got out of the caravan business, and I don't know when—or if—I'll get back in. Maybe not until you're a grown man with children of your own."

"I can wait," Petyr said eagerly. "I saw your caravan of wonders when I was a small boy. Never seen anything like it. Knew right then I wanted to run away and join up when I got old enough."

Maynard passed a hand over his eyes. "I'm... flattered," he said. "But it doesn't change the fact that I don't own a caravan. So maybe you can get a job at one of the taverns, and if I ever lose my mind and start up again, you can run off and join us then."

Petyr looked crestfallen. "The tavern masters all are afraid I'll set the whiskey fumes on fire, and they say the patrons won't like my knife throwing."

Jonmarc privately agreed with the assessment but kept his thoughts to himself.

"Maybe you could be a street performer," Maynard suggested, sounding a bit desperate to get rid of their unexpected visitor.

"You think so? I hadn't thought of that!" Petyr's grin lit up his face. "Thank you! I won't disappoint you!" He ran off, and Maynard slumped against the door as he closed it behind the boy.

"You've just about guaranteed that boy is going to get himself arrested," Jonmarc said, biting back a laugh.

"Not my fault. He'll be an independent businessman."

"He'll be a busker and a beggar."

Maynard shrugged. "Pretty much the same thing, most days." He dumped a generous measure of whiskey into his *kerif*, making Jonmarc wonder whether the mug was straight alcohol by now. "As I was saying, about fattening up the coffers—"

"Got something in mind?" Jonmarc poured himself a cup of the dark, bitter drink and saved its warmth as he joined Maynard at the table.

"I heard that some extra cargo is coming in on a boat from Principality in a couple of days," Maynard said, leaning back in his chair. "Unregistered gems, Eastmark silver, that kind of thing. I know the captain, and if he was able to arrange the haul he intended, we could take the cargo off his hands and sell it, make a tidy sum for ourselves." He grinned. "Might even be some bottles of Trevath port in the haul we could keep for medicinal purposes," he added with a knowing wink.

"How reliable is your captain friend?"

"About as much as any of my other friends," Maynard

replied. "If he brings in what he thought he could get, we could go inland for a while, maybe up to Ghorbal."

Ghorbal was a trading city on one of the tributaries that fed the mighty Nu River. Jonmarc had never been there, but Maynard spoke of it as a mix of good business and fine sensory delights. "You ready to get away from the river?" Jonmarc asked, curious about Maynard's sudden wanderlust.

"Might not be a bad idea. We've been here for a while, maybe too long," Maynard replied. "Isn't wise to stay in one place. The past catches up to you."

"Something brewing that you haven't mentioned?" Jonmarc asked. "Heard some gossip I need to know about?"

Maynard shook his head. "Of course not. I'd tell you— we're partners. Just… a feeling like we should be moving on." He gave Jonmarc a sideways look. "Unless you've got an arrangement with Rania—"

Jonmarc looked away. "Nothing like that," he replied. This last job of Rania's had taken her away for more than a week, and he found himself growing restless in her absence. Much as their nights together sated his physical needs, he remembered why he had usually turned down the offers of casual companionship when he was a merc. *It's not enough. Like being hungry right after a meal.*

"You're the marrying kind, Jonmarc, in a business that doesn't suit that," Maynard observed as if he had read his mind.

"That was a long time ago," Jonmarc replied, without meeting his gaze. "Almost another life."

"Doesn't change facts," his friend said.

Jonmarc shrugged ill-humoredly, unwilling to admit how much Maynard's words echoed his brooding on the way back from Jolie's Place. "Not in the cards," Jonmarc said, taking a long drink of his *kerif* and wishing he had spiked his cup. "I'm bad luck. Surprised you've hung around this long."

Maynard grinned. "Well, no one accused me of being clever," he joked. "But I'm willing to take my chances." He pushed back his chair and stretched. "Just thought a change of scenery might do us both good. Mix it up some. It's been long enough since I've worked Ghorbal the folks I've been trying to avoid should have moved on or given up by now."

"That's comforting."

"Fact of life, m'boy. And it occurred to me that perhaps we've been tempting fate staying close to the river for so long, as far as your 'friends' go."

The same thought had crossed Jonmarc's mind as well, but when he had tried to raise his concerns before, Maynard had brushed him off, insisting the river and the easy access to Principality and Dhasson were the best way to teach Jonmarc the smuggling trade.

"What's to smuggle in Ghorbal? Pretty far inland from the river."

Maynard grinned. "Fresh customers. On the river, everyone's a smuggler. Easy in, easy out. Takes more skill, experience, and connections to get the goods from the river all the way to Ghorbal without getting caught or double-crossed. But once you do, it's a big trade crossroads for all of eastern Margolan. With a thriving black market in everything that's hard to find or illegal."

"And more of the king's guards to crack down on troublemakers?"

"That just keeps it interesting," Maynard said and slapped Jonmarc on his good shoulder.

"Sounds good to me." Jonmarc twisted, trying to ease a kink out of the muscles of his back. The idea of pulling up stakes and going elsewhere appealed to him far more than he expected, as if it answered the itch in the back of his mind that had kept him on edge these last few weeks.

"When?"

"Once we work the job I've got lined up."

Jonmarc looked away. "You planning on bringing Rania in on it?"

"I'd rather not. Besides, she's not even around. No reason we need her help, and it'd be nice not to have to split the take three ways. Why?"

"That's fine with me. Just wondering." Jonmarc felt a little guilty at the sense of relief that accompanied Maynard's comment. He suspected that Rania's long absences were leading up to her vanishing altogether, and while that would not break his heart, his pride preferred that he be the first to move on.

They sat in silence for a few minutes and Jonmarc finished his cup of *kerif*. He rose to pour another, and this time, added a splash of whiskey for good measure. "So, you ever think of starting the caravan back up?" he asked, sitting down again.

Maynard gave him an appraising look. "Sometimes. In moments of weakness—or temporary insanity. Why?"

"Just wondered." Jonmarc knew that his nostalgia for Maynard's traveling show glossed over the darker times. He had been raw when he had sought sanctuary, still reeling from Shanna's death and the murders of the villagers who had taken him in. Running from his past, from the curse of a dying raider, from a red-robed *vayash moru* mage with a grudge.

When he let himself think on those times, he remembered the camaraderie of the campfires, his friends Trent and Corbin, and the excitement only a village boy could feel suddenly thrust into a world far beyond his imagining. He did not dwell on the shallow graves in roadside fields or the brigands, bounty hunters, slavers, and witches that had cost the lives of some of those fellow travelers and earned him both experience and scars.

"I might, sometime," Maynard said, as if the conversation had not fallen awkwardly silent. "Didn't burn all my bridges. Be a whole new crew though, if I did. Some of the performers and merchants might find their way back once they heard we'd gotten it going again, but others... well, they've either settled down or scattered, the ones that aren't dead or in jail."

Jonmarc smiled at Maynard's casual inclusion in his plans, the confident 'we' that presumed Jonmarc would come along for the adventure. And maybe he would, depending on what options presented themselves. Restarting the caravan was an attractive daydream, but for now, Jonmarc knew neither of them were ready to make that commitment.

"How soon will your captain be ready for us?" Jonmarc asked, tossing back the rest of his coffee and then rising to stretch.

"Two nights from now. I suggest that we be packed and ready so we can ride for Ghorbal that night."

Jonmarc raised an eyebrow. "That hot, huh? You sure this is a good idea?"

"Of course it's not, m'boy! If it weren't risky, everyone would be doing it, and it wouldn't pay nearly as well."

"Pretty sure there's a flaw in your logic somewhere," Jonmarc observed, laughing. He hated to admit that he loved the risk and adventure almost as much as Maynard. "Who put you on to it? Raina?"

Maynard shook his head. "No. Heard from Sirian, an old contact of mine, out of the blue. Didn't know what had become of him, and he'd apparently been here and there along the way, but he found his way back to the river—as people do—and had been talking to the captain, who needed a go-between. Ran into me at Mama's, and mentioned the job."

"He didn't want it himself?" Jonmarc distrusted unexpected generosity.

"Sirian?" Maynard guffawed. "It's not his kind of job. Too big, too hard to fence the goods afterward. He's more of a card sharp and a pickpocket, and a damn fine snitch. Tends to know everything about what's going on, and happy to share the information for a price."

"You trust him?"

Maynard shook his head. "Boy, why do you keep asking that question? Of course not! I can count the people these days I trust on one hand—me, you, Jolic, Astir, and Mama. But Sirian's information checked out. I got in touch with the captain directly, and he confirmed everything. It's real."

Maynard's assurances should have eased the tightness in Jonmarc's gut, but he still felt on edge. "Just… be careful," Jonmarc said. "Call it a hunch. I have a feeling something's going to go wrong."

"I've never known you to look on the bright side," Maynard replied. "I'd be worried if that changed now."

Jonmarc mustered a weak smile. "Yeah, well it's kept me alive so far. Humor me."

Maynard sobered. "I take your hunches very seriously, m'boy. I'll sniff around some more, but so far, everything about this has been legitimate—well, you know what I mean."

FEAR AND ELATION thrummed through him as Jonmarc packed up his belongings. The houseboat didn't afford them much room, and years of living on the road—first with the caravan and then as a mercenary—taught him to travel light. The time he had spent as a guardian at Jolie's Place and then sharing the houseboat with Maynard was the longest he had stayed in one place since the raiders killed his family over eight years before. Maybe that explained why the thought of moving on appealed to him. Part of him clung to the belief that if he could just move fast enough, the curse that dogged him could not catch up. The rest of him knew better, knew fate could not be beaten in a foot race.

Jonmarc packed up and haggled for a wagon while Maynard ran a few last-minute errands. One of those, Jonmarc knew, was to let Jolie know they would be leaving for a while so that she could make other arrangements for provisions. Fond as Jonmarc was of Jolie and his friends at the brothel, he knew it was time to move on, and suspected that Jolie could guess the reasons why.

Maynard had lined up buyers for the haul, managing to scrape enough money together to front the amount the captain had demanded for his contraband. A wagon and their horses waited in an abandoned barn for them to make their getaway.

"Why here?" Jonmarc hissed as they made their way to the quay along the river in a trading village that sat several miles upriver from Jolie's Place. The night air smelled of wood smoke and dead fish.

"The river's deep enough for him to anchor his bigger boat and row in to shore here," Maynard replied under his breath. "And the village is apparently used to people coming and going at all hours, so no one's going to pay much attention."

"I'll be happy when this is over," Jonmarc muttered. The knot in his gut had not loosened all day, although Maynard reminded him several times that nothing seemed amiss. Their rendezvous point lay ahead, a hard-used warehouse along the docks. Light rimmed the edges of the closed door, suggesting that their seller awaited them inside.

It's just last-job jitters, Jonmarc told himself, glad for the weight of his two swords on his belt. *We'll get the goods and take off for Ghorbal, and good riddance.*

Maynard led the way into the warehouse. An unfamiliar man stood next to a tin lantern, face illuminated in the shuttered glow. "Hello, Sirian. Where's the captain?"

Sirian took a step backward, away from the light, as men rushed forward from the shadows to grab Jonmarc and Maynard, holding them tightly, knives pressed against their throats.

"I'm sorry," Sirian murmured, then he turned toward the shadows that ringed the warehouse. "I told you they'd come."

"Of course they'd come."

Jonmarc startled at the voice. Rania strode out from the dark edge of the building, with two men beside her. One of the men had the ebony skin of a native of Eastmark, while the other had the dark hair and dusky skin of a Nargi.

"What's going on, Rania?" Jonmarc managed to keep his voice cold and steady, doing his best to ignore the knife edge against his skin. Maynard cursed loudly, struggling until his captor drew blood in warning.

"You're worth a lot of money, Jonmarc," Rania said, an expression of pity and sadness on her face. "Dead or alive, depending on who's paying. Too much money to pass up. Maynard was right: I really can't be trusted."

More lanterns flared, and Jonmarc could see that both Rania and her guests had brought reinforcements with them. Two Eastmark soldiers waited along one wall, while an equal number of Nargi guardsmen stood along the other. The other men—plus the two holding Jonmarc and Maynard captive—were brawny ruffians.

Jonmarc's mind raced. He could probably slip the hold his captor had on him and escape the knife, take the man down along with one or two others. But he could not win his freedom fast enough to keep the man holding Maynard from slitting his friend's throat. And even with his experience in the Nargi fight games, he couldn't win bare-handed against eight armed men.

"So you sold me to both sides?" Jonmarc baited, playing for time. "One gets the body, the other gets my head? Sounds like a raw deal."

"You just delivered the goods," Rania replied. "Now, the bidding begins."

"There will be no bidding." The Eastmark emissary spoke with authority. "I come at the behest of General Alcion, brother to king Radomar. This man is wanted in my kingdom, and I will return him for justice."

"I thought we had a deal." The Nargi man to Rania's right made his anger clear. "I am prepared to pay you a generous bounty."

Rania laughed. "Boys, there's where we start, and where we end up. And right now, I'm open to offers."

"Let Maynard go." Rania looked surprised when Jonmarc spoke up. "He has nothing to do with this. You want me; you've got me. But let him go."

"Sorry, no. He's a witness, and he's likely to do something stupid, like try to get revenge," Rania replied. "Nothing personal," she said with a glance toward Maynard. "Just the cost of doing business."

A gasp from one of the Nargi guards turned their attention to an unlikely spectacle. Deep in the shadows of the warehouse, four tongues of flames appeared to float in mid-air, moving in a circle against the darkness.

Before anyone could move, one of the fireballs came

streaking toward them, dashing against the floor in front of the two Nargi guards and sending burning liquid all over them. The men screamed, and one began to flail as the flames caught on his uniform. The other fell to the ground shrieking, rolling back and forth to extinguish the fire.

Jonmarc seized the moment. He drove his elbow back into his captor's gut even as one hand thrust up and forward to move the knife from his throat. He felt a warm trickle of blood and knew he had not been entirely successful, but since he could still breathe, he counted it a win. He pivoted faster than the man behind him could catch his wind, and drove his fist into his attacker's face, flattening the man's nose and sending him sprawling.

Maynard grabbed his chance as well, stomping down hard on the instep of the man who pinned his arms, then ramming backward with his head, catching his captor full in the face with his head. That loosened the man's grip, and Maynard kicked back, hearing a satisfying crunch as his foot forced the other man's knee in a direction it did not naturally bend.

As they fought, Jonmarc heard two more explosions in short order, one of which set the Eastmark guards aflame and the other forced Rania's bodyguards away from the fight. The Eastmark emissary dove for Jonmarc and the two of them fell to the floor trading blows. The emissary might have been a decade older than Jonmarc, but he matched him in muscle and bulk, and skill as a fighter meant he was not an easy opponent to best.

One of Rania's bodyguards had worked his way around the burning section of floor to circle them, trying to get behind Jonmarc. Maynard launched himself at the man, grappling him before he could attack Jonmarc. The man twisted in Maynard's grip, landing several punches that made Maynard stagger. Maynard flipped them and pinned the bodyguard to the floor, swinging his fists.

"Watch out!"

Maynard glanced over his shoulder in time to see Rania running toward him, a knife raised in her hand. Just as she reached him, she stiffened, arching backward and crying out. She crumpled to the floor, with the hilt of a throwing knife between her shoulder blades.

Jonmarc faced off between the Eastmark emissary and the Nargi messenger, who eyed him with a wild-eyed intensity that said he was unwilling to leave without his prize.

Rania and two of her men were dead. The Eastmark guards were too badly burned to join the fight, and one of the Nargi guards looked equally injured. That left two more of Rania's men and a Nargi plus the emissaries, and all three guards advanced on Maynard.

Jonmarc's opponent's skill gave him little chance to watch what transpired around him, but he saw Rania fall and he knew Maynard was in trouble. Although he had a good guess where the fireballs had come from, he knew Petyr was no match in a fight for trained guards, and he had been extraordinarily lucky so far.

Maynard steeled himself for another attack, and Jonmarc cursed under his breath, wishing he could finish his own opponents in time to help. Despite the unexpected intervention, he could still end the night in chains on a boat crossing the river.

The doors to the warehouse slammed open, and a blur of movement sent a rush of wind through the space. Two of Maynard's would-be attackers flew across the room to hit the wall hard and fell, crumpling to the floor.

Before Jonmarc could register what was going on, impossibly strong hands tore the Eastmark and the Nargi opponents away from him, and Astir stood holding each man aloft by the neck. Maynard needed only a moment's distraction to end his last attacker.

"This transaction is over," Astir said, forcing first the Markian emissary and then the Nargi go-between to meet his gaze. Their expressions grew slack, eyes losing focus as they fell under Astir's *vayash moru* compulsion.

"You will return to your masters with a message," Astir said in a low, deadly voice. "Jonmarc Vahanian is protected. He has been of service to me and my kind, and he is blessed by Istra, the Dark Lady. You will not harm him. You will leave and not return. My brethren are in every kingdom. If you disobey, I will know."

With a shake of his wrist, Astir sent both men sprawling. Dignity no longer seemed to matter as the two men scrambled to their feet and went running from the warehouse.

Jonmarc turned to face Astir as Maynard dusted himself off and rose from his knees beside the body of his last opponent. "Thanks," Jonmarc said, eyeing Astir with a mixture of fear and surprise. "How did you—"

"I had a premonition," Astir replied. "On top of Maynard mentioning that my presence might be helpful."

"So what you said, about the Dark Lady—"

"Istra appeared to me in a dream," Astir said, fixing him with his gaze, to which Jonmarc had always curiously been immune. "She is the Aspect of the goddess that is the patron of *vayash moru*. She told me to lend my aid. I am sorry that I nearly arrived too late."

"No, you did just fine," Jonmarc said, chuckling with a hint of madness in his tone because it was all too much to take in at once. Rania's betrayal, the real threat of being returned to Eastmark for execution or to the death matches in Nargi, the fight, the flames, and Rania's death.

"You can come out now, Petyr!" Maynard turned toward the shadows as Petyr hesitantly stepped into the light of the lanterns.

"Don't be angry," Petyr coaxed. "I know I shouldn't have spied on you." He raised his head defiantly. "And that I had to kill that woman. But I'm not sorry that I came. I'm glad I could help."

Maynard shook his head. "What possessed you to follow us?"

"I heard you tell Jonmarc something about 'fattening the coffers.' I figured it had to be about starting the caravan back up, and I wanted to prove to you that I could be one of your star attractions." The stubborn jut of his jaw suggested that Petyr felt no remorse.

"I'd say you were the star of the show," Jonmarc said. He ached from the blows his attackers had landed, and he bled from his nose and a split and swollen lip. Rania's betrayal and death were a whole different kind of hurt, one he could not think about right now, maybe not for a long time. "Before you started lobbing those fireballs, our chances didn't look too good."

"Really?" Petyr grinned broadly. "So, I can have a job with the caravan?"

Maynard groaned. "Kid, if I ever start the caravan back up, you'll be the first one I come looking for—after Jonmarc. But that won't be for a while."

Petyr's face fell. "Oh."

Astir cleared his throat. "If you can put your skills to less destructive use, we are always happy to host good entertainers at Jolie's Place. I can arrange an interview with the owner," he added with a straight face.

"The whorehouse? I mean, everyone's heard of Jolie's

Place. Really?" Petyr's excitement gave him the look of a puppy with a fresh bone.

"Come tomorrow late afternoon. Mind you don't burn anything down," Astir cautioned. "Mistress Jolie will be expecting you."

"Thank you!" Petyr tugged his forelock and made an awkward, shallow bow, then took off running, too amazed by his good fortune to have the common sense to be the slightest bit awed by his *vayash moru* benefactor.

"Thank you," Jonmarc echoed. "For the assist and for helping out Petyr. For a while there, I thought our luck had run out." He tried not to let his gaze drift to Rania's body, blood-soaked and sprawled on the warehouse floor. The tangle of horror, grief, and betrayal made him feel cold and numb inside. *"Friends and family are just hostages to fate, waiting to be taken." I should have listened.*

"Visions are an unpredictable source of information, but I have existed long enough to have learned to heed them when they appear," Astir replied. "And now, I suggest we leave. Someone might come to investigate the lights."

Jonmarc moved to shake Astir's hand. "Tell Jolie I'll miss her," he said. "I don't think we'll be around for a while."

Astir shook his hand and accepted Maynard's as well. "I shall tell her. And she will say that you will always be welcome."

Jonmarc grinned. "Don't worry. I'll be back."

With that, Astir vanished in a blur, leaving Jonmarc and Maynard in a warehouse full of corpses. "Time to go, m'boy," Maynard said. "We don't want to have to answer questions."

Minutes later, their wagon creaked and jerked along the rutted road, heading inland, away from the river.

"We got more excitement than we expected," Jonmarc

said, leaning back as Maynard nudged the horses to pick up their pace.

"True. But we also got the money from both go-betweens, and we didn't die. So it's a good night."

"Think we'll have good luck in Ghorbal?"

Maynard thought for a moment before he replied. "I can't speak for luck, m'boy, but I suspect we're in for a *dimonn* of an adventure."

BONUS

INTRODUCTION TO THE LAST MILE

Sometimes an invitation comes to do a story for an anthology that is fun to write, but for whatever reason, doesn't lend itself to being released as a stand-alone.

This next story originally appeared in the Journeys anthology from Woodbridge Press, where the theme of every story was a tale from the road. If you've read my Chronicles of the Necromancer books, you'll remember that there's a point where Carina's twin brother, Cam, is given a difficult choice between fulfilling one urgent mission and protecting friends and family who are on another, equally essential, quest. Cam reluctantly completes his orders, and we don't see him again for a couple of books. Readers asked what happened on his return trip.

This is his journey.

THE LAST MILE

"Let me up! I have to go!" Cam struggled against the hand that gripped his shoulders and fought his efforts to rise.

"Easy there," a voice soothed. "You've had a bad go of it. Take it easy."

Cam looked around, wild-eyed, trying to figure out where he was and how he had gotten here. The featureless room provided no clues, and he did not recognize the thin-faced man whose grip on his shoulders kept him seated. "Where?" he panted, as his heart thudded.

"You're at the Goat and Marc tavern. Paid for a room and food for your horse before you passed out. Had enough left over to hire a healer, too."

"Healer?" Cam's mouth was dry, and his hair hung lank in his eyes. He glanced down to see himself dressed in a sweat-soaked nightshirt amid tangled covers on a sturdy wooden bed.

The thin man gave him a reassuring smile. "That's me. Beren. The innkeeper roused me and got me to tend you." His smile faded. "Good thing. You were pretty far gone."

"How long?" Cam croaked, feeling desperation rise in his chest.

"How long were you unconscious? Three days," Beren replied. He shook his head. "Took magic and then some to keep you in this world. You had the cough bad, in both lungs. Almost didn't make it."

Cam pulled away from Beren and swung his legs over the edge of the bed. "I've got to go." He tried to stand, only to waver and fall backward, caught by Beren before he could tumble to the floor.

"Wherever you're going, it's got to wait a bit longer," Beren said, easing Cam back into bed. "You're in no condition to go anywhere."

"You don't understand—"

Beren reached for a cloth in a basin on the bedside table and wiped the sweat from Cam's brow. "I understand that you've been very sick and almost died. And from what you said in your fever dreams, you're a young man with a vivid imagination."

Cam groaned. "What... what did I say?"

Beren chuckled. "Quite a tale," he replied. "You kept shouting for someone named Tris, about an ambush. Then you yelled for Carina as if you were looking for a lost child. Thrashed like you were fighting for your life. Took me and the innkeeper to keep you in bed at the worst of it. Thought we'd have to tie you down and gag you," he added, only partly in jest. "Oh, and you kept apologizing to Ban for leaving him," he said, raising an eyebrow.

"Sweet Lady and Childe," Cam muttered, closing his eyes.

"Are you a courier?" Beren asked. "I understand that you have urgent business, but you'll be too sick to travel within a few candlemarks if you leave now." He held up a hand to forestall Cam's protest. "Look, it's already dark outside, and bloody cold. Let me do another healing and get some warm soup into you, plus a good night's rest and a little whiskey. In the morning, you'll be fitter to travel, though I'd advise at least another day's rest. But at least you might not fall out of the saddle," he added.

Cam wanted to argue, but his body betrayed him. He outweighed Beren by at least a stone, maybe more, and hard work made for strong shoulders and arms. Years of soldiering meant he should have been able to easily throw Beren off him and get free. Maybe he could have done so, but he didn't try. He knew in his gut that Beren was correct, and the stakes were too high to risk another mistake.

"All right," Cam conceded. "I'll stay the night. But I have to leave in the morning. It's important."

"Where are you going?"

"Aberponte."

Beren canted his head as he regarded Cam. "The palace city?"

"How far?" Cam had no intention of disclosing his mission. Not now, with so much blood behind him and so much at stake awaiting his return.

"A day's ride, and that's at a good pace," Beren replied. "For the record, I also healed your horse. He'd been ridden hard." Cam heard the judgment in Beren's tone.

"Couldn't be helped," Cam murmured.

"Well, he's got a proper stable and food, and he'll not go lame on you."

"Thank you. For everything."

"I'll go see to getting you dinner," Beren answered. "The whiskey will help you sleep, and I'll mix some healing powders in with hot tea to help your lungs. It's still against my advice for you to leave so soon, but I don't think I'll be able to stop you."

The door shut behind Beren, and Cam let out his breath in a sigh that nearly set him coughing again. *Not Beren's fault. From his perspective, keeping me here makes sense.*

Beren didn't know the fate of the kingdom depended on a vial of elixir in Cam's saddlebags, hard-won from the witches of the Sisterhood hundreds of miles away.

Didn't know what Cam had sacrificed to get this far. That he'd abandoned his friends and his sister to slavers, left them to fend for themselves in the vague hope that Ban Soterius and Tov Harrtuck could get them free. One of those friends was Tris Drayke, the only hope neighboring Margolan had to unseat its Usurper King. For all Cam knew, he had damned Margolan to flames and chaos by his choice.

All to save another kingdom and another king. His home, Isencroft, and his monarch, King Donelan. Because the other thing Beren didn't know, that no one outside the palace's inner circle knew, was that Donelan was dying. Dark magic brought on a wasting disease and Donelan's strength faded daily. That's why Cam and his twin sister Carina had left on their desperate mission months ago, searching out the reclusive Sisterhood in search of a cure. They hadn't counted on getting tangled up in Margolan's bloody coup or having the caravan they traveled with be captured by slavers. Cam, Soterius, and Harrtuck had escaped by sheer luck, with Cam so badly injured his friends had taken him to one of the Sisterhood's citadels, and wasn't it just the way luck worked, those witches had the antidote Donelan needed.

Cam had to choose. His king or his sister.

Soterius and Harrtuck swore they would rescue Carina and the others. Cam knew they would try. But Carina was his twin, his responsibility. Tris Drayke and Jonmarc Vahanian and the other members of the caravan were his friends. And he had turned his back on them, gritted his teeth and done his duty, ridden in the opposite direction as hard as he could. Ridden through his tears, pushing himself and his horse to the breaking point, dodging the Usurper's soldiers during the long trek across Margolan, fighting his way through a roadblock at the Isencroft border that left him bloody.

He'd bound up his wounds, chased off the pain with whiskey and slept a few hours, then gotten back in the saddle. If he could reach Aberponte in time, get the antidote to Donelan, then at least some good would come out of the sacrifice. The king and the kingdom would endure. The next morning, against Beren's advice, Cam ignored the healer's protests and heaved himself up into the saddle. His gelding, a solid black massive horse, named "Dimonn," snorted in recognition, and if he resented how hard Cam rode him, his training forbade him from showing it.

"There's food and water and wine in your saddlebags, some bread, tea, and whiskey too, for the road," Beren said, making no attempt to hide his opinion of Cam's choice. Cam wondered if the healer would change his mind if he knew what lay at the heart of Cam's obsession, knew that the king's life hung in the balance. Then again, Cam was a patient defying orders. Maybe his opinion wouldn't change a bit, no matter what. Cam wouldn't get the chance to find out.

"Thank you. For everything." Cam put his heels to Dimonn's sides and took off at the fastest sustainable pace he could muster.

When Cam and Carina had gone looking for a cure, they both left behind clothing worthy of being the King's Healer and King's Champion for nondescript garb that would not attract attention on the road. Now, Cam knew from the sidelong glances he received that his torn, muddy, and blood-stained outfit gained him notice for all the wrong reasons. Onlookers might think he stole the horse, but the witches had given it to him along with the tack, though he had no way to prove it should anyone ask.

Other travelers got out of his way as Cam's horse thundered down the road, bent on making Aberponte in as little time as possible. Despite Beren's magic, Cam could feel the illness still lurking in his body, not completely vanquished, merely pushed back to await another chance. *I'm not important. I can be replaced. Isencroft can't afford to lose its king.*

Cam rode into the night until he knew his fever had returned and vertigo forced him to admit that he needed to rest or risk falling out of the saddle. Paying for the inn and healer plus the stable costs had taken almost all the coin Cam had. The food in his saddlebag might last him until Aberponte with luck. He found a quiet barn, saw to Dimonn's needs, and fell asleep on a pile of straw, with the precious saddlebags beneath him, his sword still on his belt and a knife clutched in one hand.

"What have we got here?"

Cam woke to see three men in a ring around him. He castigated himself for letting anyone sneak up on him. His training and experience should have had him awake and ready to fight long before they got so close, but he knew exhaustion and lingering illness were to blame.

"A broke traveler," Cam replied, shifting so that his cloak let the knife and sword remained hidden and glad he had buried the saddlebag with the elixir in the straw.

One of the ruffians glanced toward Dimonn. "Pretty nice horse for a beggar. Him and that saddle'll bring a coin or two, I reckon."

"Touch my horse, and I'll kill you." Cam rose to his feet slowly. The thieves took a step back, and Cam wondered if they had misjudged their mark. He stood a head taller than two of the young men, who barely looked to be out of their teens. Time in the king's army and before that, as a mercenary, had put muscle on Cam, broadened his shoulders and filled out his arms. He guessed that he might weigh more than two of his would-be attackers together.

"Three to one is pretty good odds, old man." The leader of the gang tried for flippant, but Cam heard the nervousness in his voice. Cam snorted in derision, guessing he might be five or six years their senior, though hardship made him feel much older.

"Last chance to walk away." Cam hoped the thieves took the bright glint in his eyes as madness instead of fever.

The man to Cam's right lunged forward, answering with his knife. Cam blocked with one arm, then brought his sword in an arc, slashing his attacker deep from hip to shoulder. His opponent fell back, gurgling blood but the other two pressed forward, too proud to back down.

The thief in the middle came at Cam with his knife gripped for an overhand strike. Cam's blade cut his belly open before the ruffian got close enough to strike and left him tripping on his own steaming entrails. A slash across the throat ended his suffering with more mercy than he deserved.

The third man had the good sense to run. Cam debated pegging him between the shoulder blades with a throwing knife but didn't want to go to the effort of retrieving his weapon.

"So much for a good night's rest," Cam said to Dimonn, grabbing his saddlebags from the straw. He smoothed his hand down the sleek, black neck, fished out a small, hard apple from his provisions for the horse, and dragged himself back up into the saddle.

Soldiering taught Cam to sleep in the saddle, to ride while

half dead. Cam slowed Dimonn's gait on a deserted stretch of road and took what rest he could, unwilling to risk stopping again. Long before dawn, he urged Dimonn on, picking up the pace until they thundered past farmers in the field and peddlers by the side of the road.

Cam's heart gladdened as he recognized landmarks. *Not too much farther. Almost there.* When they came to a crest in the road, and he glimpsed the castle's towers in the distance, Cam nearly wept. He ruffled Dimonn's mane affectionately. "We just might make it," he murmured, as much to encourage himself as the horse.

By midday, his hands shook enough that Cam stopped to make a small fire and brew some of the tea Beren sent with him. He felt the flush of returning fever, knowing it from the ache in his bones, different from the warmth of the sun on his skin. He felt worn thin, by travel and desperation, grief and guilt. *A good soldier lays down his life for his liege. All I have to do is live long enough to deliver the vial.*

Yet despite weariness, fever, and exquisitely sore muscles, Cam did not want to die. He trusted Soterius and Harrtuck with his life, had entrusted Carina's life to them as well, but it sat wrong with him to have turned and run, no matter what the stakes. Unfinished business lay behind him beyond the borders of his homeland, across the neighboring, war-torn kingdom of Margolan. *It's not just Carina. The crown of Margolan, the kingdom's fate, hangs in the balance with Tris's. I might have turned the odds if I had stayed. I should have been part of that fight, killing the slavers, freeing the captives.*

Despite recriminations, Cam knew he could only champion one cause at a time, and the witches of the Sisterhood had been clear about priorities. He hoped the witches' prophecies and foresight were true, though he generally believed only the proof of his own senses. Alone on his long ride, Cam had chanted two prayers to the Sacred Lady. *Please, let me reach Donelan in time. Please, let Carina and the others escape.*

No sign indicated that anyone heeded his supplications, but if he had to hold faith in anything, he clung to the hope that Istra, the Dark Lady, patron of outcasts and hopeless causes, might grant him favor. Cam drew in the reins and brought Dimonn to an abrupt halt as he stared at the ruined bridge in front of him. He could see the tallest spires of the palace city in the distance, but a wide, swift river flowed between him and Aberponte, and the stone bridge across lay in complete disrepair.

He cursed under his breath and wiped the sweat from his brow with his sleeve. The fever had returned, nearly as bad as before, so that his ears rang and his throat felt as if he had swallowed glass. The road from here to Aberponte would take him about half a day, depending on his speed. Cam looked upstream and downstream and saw no other bridges. He eyed the river, but it ran too swift and deep to attempt fording, even if he and his horse were not so exhausted.

Weariness settled in his bones as Cam considered his options. He would have to retrace his route to go back to the last main road that ran parallel to the river. Riding upstream from there would bring him closer to Aberponte, where the city's traffic might warrant more bridges. The farms downstream were unlikely to require as many crossings. The new route would cost him time Donelan didn't have.

"Come on, Dimonn," Cam said, patting the horse's neck. "We're going to have to go the long way 'round. I promise you a nice stall in the palace stable and the best horse food in the kingdom when we finally get there." Cam himself longed for a hot bath, a good healer, and a clean bed.

Clouds rolled in as they traveled up-river. The day, which had been sunny and temperate, grew dark and much colder. Cam pulled his tattered cloak close around himself and shivered. He knew fever as much as the weather set the chill in his bones, but it made him no less cold. Before long, rain pelted down, slowly at first, then falling fast and steady.

"Keeps getting better and better," Cam muttered as he hunched against the wind, pulling his hood out to shield his face. It didn't take long for him to be soaked through. Darkness kept him from seeing the spires of Aberponte, but he kept his attention fixed on the horizon where he knew the city awaited him.

He passed an inn, glowing brightly with its promise of shelter and food, but kept on going. They were too close to stop now, with luck they could be at the palace before the night was far spent, and he had no coin to pay for dinner or a room anyhow. Cam's hands gripped the reins white-knuckled, cramping from clenching tightly in the cold, and he wondered whether he would even be able to walk once they reached the city from so many candlemarks spent in the saddle. He'd ridden like this back when he fought with the mercenaries, but he was in his teens then, and quicker to heal. Now, he felt every knitted bone and old scar beneath aching muscles.

Dimonn's pace slowed. The road lay slick with mud, ruts hidden by pools of dark water. Every step splashed Cam with cold, filthy slush. Once they passed the inn, no other travelers ventured out on the road, leaving them alone. Cam managed to light a lantern, protected by the wind and rain by its glass sides, and with the moonlight that sometimes filtered between the clouds, it sufficed to show their path.

The next bridge arched across the river sturdy and whole, and Cam bit back a yelp of relief. "Let's go," he urged

Dimonn, sure that he recognized the crossroads and that the journey's end lay almost in sight.

He should have known better.

Just over the bridge, Dimonn faltered as one hoof sank into a hole hidden by standing water. The horse whinnied in pain, and the sudden shift tore the reins from Cam's faltering grip, pitching him into the mud.

"Easy there," Cam coaxed as the horse limped sideways, huge eyes staring at him. "Easy."

He moved to examine the damaged leg, relieved to find no broken bone, but certain the misstep lamed Dimonn nonetheless. Cam tore off a piece of his shirt to wind around the leg for stability, all that he could do until a dry barn and the king's farrier were within reach.

"Guess we both walk from here," Cam said with a sigh, knowing that Dimonn could no longer bear his weight. "Better get to it. Not like the palace is getting any closer on its own."

When the lights of Aberponte finally grew near enough to be more than pinpricks in the gloom, Cam groaned with relief. He felt almost as lame as his horse after finishing the last few miles on foot, sloshing through ankle deep water and mud, soaked to the skin. Cam leaned heavily on Dimonn for both support and warmth, shivering uncontrollably, sure his lips were blue.

The gates of the city had not closed for the night, but the guards looked askance at the ragged man and his injured horse as Cam and Dimonn made their way inside. He knew how he must look, especially since he had not bothered with a shave or a haircut since he left the Sisterhood weeks ago. Such things seemed unimportant in the midst of a quest to save a king, though now, Cam regretted not pausing at the inn to make himself presentable.

He realized the gravity of his mistake when he reached the palace gates.

"Be gone. There're no alms for you here," the guard said, regarding Cam with distaste.

Cam drew himself up and squared his shoulders, pushing back his hood. "I am Cam of Cairnrach, the King's Champion. I've returned from an urgent mission. I must see Major Wilym immediately."

The two guards exchanged a look and burst out laughing. "You want me to fetch the head of the Veigonn guards into the rain for you? Do you mean to beg him for ale money? Piss off."

Cam moved forward as if to go around the guards, but they closed ranks, blocking his way. "I am the King's Champion, and I must get through," Cam repeated through gritted teeth. Anger, fear, and frustration simmered just beneath the surface, straining what little control remained.

"No one told me to expect any 'King's Champion,'" the second guard sneered. "If it had been so goddess-damned important, they'd have made sure we knew when they did the roster."

Cam forced himself to take a deep breath, though his fists balled at his sides. "Let me through, or Crone take my soul, I'll see you're clamped in irons."

His threat won a barked laugh from the taller of the two guards. "Last warning. Be on your way, or you'll be the one behind bars."

Cam's patience reached its end, with so much at stake and finding himself blocked from his goal so close to completion. He reached to draw his sword, ready to fight his way through, when three more guards emerged from the darkness, their weapons already in hand.

"Don't." The command came from a thin, tall captain

whose expression made it clear that he intended to take out his unhappiness about being in the cold rain on Cam.

"I am Cam of Cairnrach, King's Champion. I must see Wilym!"

The captain's gaze flickered between Cam's sword, the good horse, and then back to take in his ragged appearance. "I don't know what you're playing at," he growled. "No one's seen the King's Champion in months or heard tell of where he's gone. I believe you might have stolen his sword and his horse, but if he'd been expected, I'd have heard."

Cam's jaw ached from being clenched hard enough to break a tooth. Cold rain made the torches by the gate waver and gutter, filling the night air with the smell of smoke. "They didn't know I'd come back today. Now let me through."

He knew that the average soldier had no idea what the "King's Champion" looked like, had never met him or expected to do so. Cam's usual place when at the court was at Donelan's side, or close at hand, far from the barracks of the common soldiers. On a better day, he might be grateful that the guards did their job so diligently, but tonight, sick and wounded and cold all the way to his marrow, he didn't feel thankful at all.

"Get out of my way!" he growled, trying to shoulder through, and found himself staring at three resolute swordsmen who would not be as easy to best as the ruffians in the barn. Under normal conditions, Cam knew he might fight his way clear, but not now, even if he were willing to draw blood from his own side's forces.

"Take him to the stockade," the captain ordered. "I've had enough of this foolishness for one night."

Cam held his hands up in a gesture of surrender but

sought the gaze of the captain for one last try. "Please," he begged. "The king is sick. I must get through."

"You're not going anywhere on your say-so alone," the captain snapped. "You can dry off in the jail while we figure out what to do with you."

Cam slumped in defeat, and the soldiers lowered their weapons. It was the only chance Cam would get, and he seized it, slamming his shoulder into the captain to send him staggering into one of the swordsmen. Cam drew his sword, lunging at the nearest guard, aiming to wound, not kill. He heard shouts as guards on the wall raised the alarm, and kept fighting, even as more soldiers came running. Only cold steel against his throat made him halt.

"Drop your sword, or I slit your throat," a voice hissed against his ear. Cam let his weapon fall, hoping that he had raised enough of a ruckus to attract the attention of a more senior officer, someone who might decide to check into the wild claims of a madman at the gate. He let himself be led toward the stockade, glancing over his shoulder to assure that one of the guards had hold of Dimonn's reins. Inside the small jail, rough hands shoved Cam into a cell and locked it behind him. He sank to the straw-covered floor, too cold and exhausted to argue, leaning back against the wall, and closed his eyes.

Cam might have slept, or he might have lost consciousness. Voices roused him, arguing.

"It could have been a trap." It sounded like the captain, a note of defensiveness in his voice.

"Exactly how often does someone show up claiming to be the King's Champion? Is it a common thing? Once a week? Oh, here comes another one? Is that it?" Cam recognized the voice and managed an exhausted smile.

"I haven't ever seen the King's Champion in person," the

captain retorted. "How am I supposed to know whether it's him or not? For all I know, he's a spy, and I wasn't letting a spy into the palace on my watch."

"Your stalwartness is commendable, but it needs to be tempered with intelligence," Wilym snapped. "I should have been notified immediately. You're relieved from duty until further notice." He paused. "Give me the damn keys." The key clanked in the lock and the cell door screeched open, and then Wilym knelt beside him, lifting him to his feet and getting under his shoulder to help him stand.

Cam looked up as a lantern lit up the small cell. "I figured… if I made enough noise… you'd find out."

"I'm sorry about this, Cam. I got here as soon as I heard. By the Whore! It's good to see you, even if you look like shit."

"The elixir. It's hidden in my saddlebag. Sisterhood swears it will work. Take it. Come back for me." He shifted to see Wilym's face. "Donelan—is he—?"

Wilym nodded. "He's alive, but he wouldn't have made it much longer. And no, I'm not leaving you here. Trygve can heal you once he's given the elixir."

"And my horse," Cam managed. "Lame."

"I'll have the farrier tend him. First things first. Come on; we've got a king to save."

The guards at the gate had the good graces to look abashed as the head of the elite Viegonn warriors half-carried their former prisoner beneath the archway. Two more of the Viegonn met them inside, and someone slipped a dry cloak around Cam's shivering form as they made their way into the palace. Cam never thought Aberponte had ever looked so beautiful.

"Take this to Trygve," Wilym ordered one of his men once they were inside the building, handing him the vial.

"Tell him the King's Champion brought what we sent him for. He'll know what to do with it. I'll join you in a few minutes."

"Go," Cam urged. "I remember the way."

Wilym fixed him with a glare. "Trygve doesn't need me to administer the antidote. I'll get you to your room before you fall down, and have a servant bring you dry clothing and draw a hot bath. I'd warrant you could use a good meal and some whiskey, too."

Cam lacked the energy to argue, leaning heavily on Wilym until they reached Cam's room and he sank into a chair. "I'll send someone up right away, and bring you news once we know something," Wilym promised. He paused in the doorway. "It's damn good to have you home. The kingdom's in your debt."

Cam slumped in his seat, barely registering the words. He completed his task, finished his mission. Donelan would live. But as exhaustion overtook him, all Cam could think about were the ones he left behind.

A few candlemarks later, Wilym returned. "A bath and some clean clothes do wonders for you," he said with a smile.

"Trygve patched up what he could," Cam said, taking advantage of being back in the palace by sipping at a goblet of the king's best brandy. "I'm mostly tired and saddle-sore. It'll heal with time."

"The farriers took care of Dimonn. His leg is fine. Thought you'd want to know."

Cam nodded. "Thank you." He was quiet for a moment. Wilym leaned back against the wall, arms crossed, waiting. "Have your spies heard anything out of Margolan? Any word?"

Wilym shook his head. "No. Nothing specific. The Usurper is still on the throne, and Tris Drayke has gone to ground. If he were dead or captured, we'd hear."

"They were heading for Principality," Cam said quietly. "Donelan's on good terms with King Staden, isn't he? If they make it, perhaps Staden will send word."

"He would." Wilym tilted his head, watching Cam closely. "I know you're worried about Carina. Perhaps one of the king's mages—"

"No," Cam said, a little more sharply than he intended. "Magic attracts attention, the wrong kind of notice. I'm just going to have to wait it out, and trust the Dark Lady's favor."

After a few minutes of silence, Wilym cleared his throat. "Donelan sent me to fetch you. He'd like to give you his thanks in person."

"Just doing my duty."

Wilym fixed him with a look. "I think we all know this went beyond that. Come on."

King Donelan lay propped up with pillows in his massive, four-poster bed. Cam saw the toll illness had taken in the king's thin face and tired gaze. Yet even after all he had suffered since Cam left Aberponte on his quest, Donelan looked much improved.

"My Liege." Cam sank to one knee.

"Rise, Cam. And come closer."

Cam did as he was bid. He had spent enough time in the king's presence that the circumstances were familiar, though they could never be entirely comfortable. "You look well, My King."

"You're a fine liar, Cam of Cairnrach. I look like shit. But I'm improving—thanks to you." Donelan met his gaze, and Cam read the understanding of what the journey had cost. "Tomorrow, we'll see what can be done, for Carina, and for your friends. Tonight, you've earned your rest and my gratitude. If there's one thing I've learned in all my years, it's to take your comfort where you can." He managed a smile. "That is an order from your king."

"As you wish, My Liege." It would be futile for Cam to ride back across a war-torn kingdom to find his friends. His place was here, in Isencroft, beside his king. But he looked out the window toward the rising sun, toward Margolan, and knew his loyalties were divided. *Be safe, my sister. And may the Dark Lady's hand be upon you, until I see you again, Carina.*

THE SUMMONER (EXCERPT)

BOOK ONE: THE CHRONICLES OF THE NECROMANCER

"Walk carefully, my prince," the ghost warned. "You are in great danger this night."

Outside the mullioned windows, Martris Drayke could hear the revelry of the feast day crowds. Torchlight glittered beyond the glass, and costumed figures danced, singing and catcalling, past the castle tower. Dressed in the four aspects of the One Goddess, Margolan's sacred Lady, the partygoers lurched behind an effigy of the Crone Mother, far more intent, this Feast of the Departed, on appeasing their appetite for ale than memorializing the dead.

"From whom?" Tris returned his attention to his spectral visitor. The ghosts of the palace Shekerishet were so numerous that he could not recall having ever seen this particular spirit before, a thin-faced man with heavy-lidded eyes, whose antiquated costume marked him as a member of the court one hundred years past.

The specter flickered and tried to say more, but no sound came. Tris leaned closer. Now of any time, the ghost should be the easiest to see, for on Haunts as the feast day was commonly known, spirits walk openly abroad and even skeptics cannot refuse to see. The palace ghosts had been Tris's friends since childhood, long before he came to understand that his insubstantial companions were not so easily seen by those around him. "Spirits… banished," the fading ghost managed. "Beware… the Soulcatcher." Tris had to strain for the last words as the revenant faded into nothing. Puzzled, he sat back on his heels, his sword clattering against the hard stone floor. The rap at the door nearly made him lose his footing.

"What are you doing in there, or aren't you alone?" teased Ban Soterius through the door. The latch lifted and the sturdy captain of the guards strode in. Nothing in the young man's manner corroborated the strong smell of ale on his breath, save for his mussed brown hair and the slight rumpling of his fine tunic.

"I'm alone now," Tris said, with a glance back to where the ghost had been. Soterius looked from Tris to the empty wall. "I keep telling you, Tris," the guardsman said, "you've got to get out more. Me, I don't care if I ever talk to a ghost… unless she's a good-looking lass with a pint of ale!"

Tris managed a smile. "Have you seen the spirits tonight?" Soterius thought for a moment. "Not as much as usual, now that you mention it, especially for Haunts." He brightened. "But you know how they love a good story. They're probably down listening to Carroway tell his tales." He pulled at Tris's sleeve. "Come on. There's no law that says princes can't have fun, too, and while I'm standing up here with you, I could be missing the love of my life down in the great room!"

Soterius's good humor made Tris chuckle. The captain of the guards was a favorite with the court's noble daughters.

Soterius's light brown hair was cut short, for a battle helm. He was of medium build, fit and tanned from training with the guards. Everything about his bearing and his manner bespoke his military background, but the mischievous twinkle in his dark eyes softened his features, and seemed to make the marriageable maidens flock to him.

Tris was just as happy to have those same young girls and their ambitious mothers distracted. He stood a head taller than Soterius, with a lean, rangy build. He had been told often that his angular features and high cheekbones took after the best of both his parents, but the white-blond hair that framed his face and fell to his shoulders was clearly from Queen Sarae's side, as were the green eyes that matched those of his grandmother, the famed sorceress Bava K'aa. It was a combination the ladies of the court found quite attractive.

"I promise I'll be down right behind you," Tris said, and Soterius raised an eyebrow skeptically. "Honest. I just want to light a candle and put a gift in grandmother's room before I go. Then you can take me on that tour of alehouses you've been promising."

Soterius grinned. "I'll hold you to that, Prince Drayke," he laughed. "Get moving. The way the festival's going tonight, they'll run out of ale, and you know that brandy doesn't agree with me."

Tris heard his friend's boot steps fade down the corridor as he made his way to the family rooms. The silent stares from a row of paintings and tapestries seemed to follow him, the long-dead kings of Margolan, King Bricen's forebears. Bricen's lineage was one of the longest unbroken monarchies in the Seven Kingdoms. Glancing at their solemn visages and knowing the stories of what they had endured to secure their thrones, Tris was glad the crown would not pass to him. He picked up a torch from the sconce on the wall and opened the door into his grandmother's room. The smell of incense and potions still clung to the sorceress's chamber, five years after her death. Tris shut the door behind him. It was an indication of the awe with which even her own family regarded her that, even now, no one disturbed the spirit mage's possessions, Tris thought. But the sorceress Bava K'aa earned that kind of awe, and though he remembered her most clearly as an indulgent grandmother, the legends of her power were enough to make him hesitate, just an instant, before stepping farther into the room.

"Grandmother?" Tris whispered. He set a candle on the table in the center of the room and lit it with a straw from the torch. Then, he set out a token gift of honey cakes and a small cup of ale, over which he made the sign of the Goddess in blessing. And then, with a glance to assure himself that the door was shut and he would not be discovered, he stepped onto the braided rug in the center of the room. Plaited from her sorceress's cords, the rug matched the warded circle of his grandmother's workspace, and Tris felt the familiar tingle of her magic, like the residue of old perfume. With his sword as his athame, Tris walked the perimeter of the rug as his grandmother taught him, feeling the circle of protection rise around him. Its blue-white light was clear in his mind, though invisible. Tris closed his eyes and stretched out his right hand.

"Grandmother, I call you," he murmured, stretching out his senses for her familiar presence. "I invite you to the feast. Join me within the Circle." Tris paused. But for the first time since her death, no response came. He tried once more.

"Bava K'aa, your kinsman invites you to the feast. I have brought you a gift. Walk with me." Nothing in the room stirred, and Tris opened his eyes, concerned.

And then, a glimmer of light caught his eye. It seemed far

beyond the circle, struggling and flickering as if trapped within gauze, but as he strained to make it out, he recognized the form of his grandmother, standing at a great distance obscured by fog.

"Grandmother!" he called, but the apparition came no farther. Her lips moved, but no sound reached him, yet a chill ran down his back. He did not need words to recognize a warning in his grandmother's manner. Though Tris could not hear Bava K'aa's voice, the indication of danger was clear enough.

Without warning, a cold wind howled through the shuttered chamber, guttering the torch and extinguishing the candle. It buffeted the circle Tris cast, and the image of his grandmother winked out. Two porcelain figures crashed to the floor, and the bed curtains fluttered as the gust tore scrolls from the desk and knocked a chair to the ground. Tris gritted his teeth and strained to keep his warding in place, but he felt the gooseflesh rise on his arms as the chill permeated even the area within the cord and circle. Like a glimpse of something there and gone, impressions formed in his mind. Something evil, something old and strong, lost, hunting, dangerous.

And then, as quickly as it came, the wind was gone and with it Tris's sense of foreboding. When he felt sure that nothing stirred in the room, Tris raised his shaking hand to silently thank the Four Faces of the Goddess, and then closed the circle, shivering as the magic light faded in his mind. He looked around the room. Only the torn parchments, shattered figurines, and overturned chair testified that anything was amiss. More troubled than before, Tris turned to leave.

From the corridor, a woman screamed. Tris bounded for the door, his sword already in hand. In the shadows of the hallway, Tris could make out a grappling pair, the dark figure of a man looming over one of the chambermaids who struggled to escape.

"Release her!" Tris raised his sword in challenge. Seizing the moment, the terrified woman sank her teeth into her attacker's arm and wrenched free, running down the corridor for her life. Tris felt his throat tighten as the assailant straightened and turned, recognizing the form even before the thin gold circlet on the man's brow glinted in the torchlight.

"Once again, you've spoiled my fun, brother," Jared Drayke glowered, his eyes narrowing. King Bricen's eldest son started down the hallway, and Tris could tell by his brother's gait that Jared was well into his cups this feast night. Tris stood his ground, though he felt his heart in his throat. Ale never compromised Jared's swing nor blunted his swordsmanship, and Tris had taken enough bruises at his brother's hand to know just what kind of a mood Jared was in tonight.

"You're drunk," Tris grated.

"Sober enough to whip your ass," Jared retorted, already beginning to turn up the sleeves of his tunic.

"You can try."

"You dare to raise steel against me?" Jared roared. "I could have you hanged. No one threatens the future king of Margolan!"

"While father rules, I doubt I'll hang," Tris replied, feeling his heart thud. "Why don't you bed one of the nobles' daughters, instead of raping the servants? Or would it be too expensive to pay off their families when they disappeared?"

"I'll teach you respect," Jared growled, close enough for Tris to smell the rancid brew on Jared's breath. And with a movement almost too quick to see, Jared drew his sword and charged forward.

Tris parried, needing both hands to deflect the thrust he had no doubt was meant to score. He fell back a step as Jared drove on, barely countering his brother's enraged attack. Jared pressed forward, and the anger that burned in his eyes was past reasoning. Tris fought for his life, knowing that he could not hold off Jared's press much longer as Jared forced him back into the glow of the torch sconce.

In the distance, boot steps sounded on the stone. "Prince Jared?" Zachar, the seneschal, called. "My prince, are you there? Your father desires your attendance."

With an oath, Jared freed his sword from Tris's parry and stepped back several paces. "Prince Jared?" Zachar called again, closer now and more insistent.

"I heard you," Jared shouted in return, watching Tris carefully. Warily, Tris lowered his sword but did not sheath it until Jared first replaced his own weapon.

"Don't think it's settled, brother," Jared snarled. "You'll pay. Before the dawn, you'll pay!" Jared promised. Zachar's footsteps were much closer now, and Jared turned to meet the seneschal before Zachar could happen upon them.

Tris stood where he was for a moment until his heart slowed and he caught his breath, shaking from the confrontation. When he regained his composure, he headed for the great room, slowing only when the sounds and smells of the festival reached him as he neared the doors to the banquet hall.

Soterius looked skeptically at him as Tris joined his friend. "What's your hurry?"

The armsman was far too observant to overlook the sweat that glistened on Tris's forehead on a chill autumn night, or the obvious flush of the fight. "Just a little conversation with Jared," Tris replied, knowing from long acquaintance that Soterius would fill in the rest.

"Can't your father—?" Soterius asked below his breath.

Tris shook his head. "Father can't... or won't... admit

what a monster he sired. Even good kings have their blind spots."

"Good feast to you, brother." A girl's laughing voice sounded behind them just then, and Tris turned. Behind him stood his sister, Kait, her prized falcon perched on her gauntlet. A dozen summers old, at an age when most princesses gloried in mincing steps and elaborate gowns, Kait was radiant in the costume of a falconer, its loose tunic and knickers hiding her budding curves. Her hair was dark, like Bricen's, plaited in a practical braid, which only accentuated how much she resembled both Tris and Jared. Dark-eyed like her father, with her mother's grace, Kait was likely to catch the eye of potential suitors before too long, Tris thought with a protective pang.

"Didn't anyone tell you you're supposed to get a costume for Haunts?" Tris teased, and even the events in the corridor could not keep a smile from his face as Kait favored him with a sour look.

"You know very well, brother dear, that this is the one night of the year I can wear sensible clothes without completely scandalizing mother and the good ladies of the court," she retorted. The falcon, one of the dozen that she tended like children, stepped nervously in its traces, restless at the noise of the boisterous crowd.

"Are you going to take that bird with you on your wedding day?" Tris bantered.

Kait wrinkled her nose as if she smelled spoiled meat. "Don't rush me. Maybe I'll take him with me on my wedding night, and not have to start birthing brats immediately!"

"Kaity, Kaity, what would mother say?" Tris clucked in mock astonishment, as Soterius laughed and Kait swung a lighthearted punch at Tris's shoulder.

"She'd say what she usually says," Kait returned unfazed.

"That she had better find me a suitor before I've scandalized the entire court." She shrugged. "The race is on."

"You know," Soterius said with a wink, "she might find you someone you actually like."

Kait raised an eyebrow. "Like you?" she replied with such a withering tone that both Tris and Soterius chuckled once more.

Soterius raised his hand in appeasement. "You know that's not what I mean."

Kait looked about to make another rejoinder when she glanced at Tris, who had fallen silent. "You're quiet, Tris."

Tris and Soterius exchanged glances. "Had a bit of a run-in with Jared," Tris said. "Stay out of his way tonight, Kaity. He's in an awful temper."

Kait's banter dropped, and Tris saw complete understanding in eyes that suddenly appeared much older than her dozen years. "I'd heard," she said with a grimace. "There's talk at the stables. He thrashed a stable hand down there half to death for not having his horse ready." She rolled her eyes. "At least I've managed to stay away from him for a few days."

Tris looked at her and frowned. "Where'd you get that bruise on your arm?"

Kait felt for it self-consciously. "It's not bad," she said, looking away.

"That isn't what I asked, Kaity," Tris pressed. He could feel his anger burning already, for this welt and all the others over the years.

Kait still did not meet his eyes. "I earned it," she sighed. "Jared was taking it out on one of the kitchen dogs, and I clipped a loaf of bread at his head to let the pup get away." She winced. "He wasn't very happy with me."

"Damn him!" Tris swore. "Don't worry, Kaity. I'll make

sure he stays away from you," he promised, though they both knew past attempts had only limited success.

Kait managed a wan smile. "After the party, think you could do up one of your poultices? It does smart a little."

Tris ruffled her hair, feeling such a mixture of anger for Jared and love for Kait that he thought his heart might break. "Sure thing, Kaity. I don't even have to sneak the herbs out of the kitchen anymore."

Long ago when they were children, Tris dared night runs to the kitchens to get the herbs he needed to bind up the bruises and cuts Jared inflicted. Though he was only eight years Kait's senior, he was her self-appointed guardian since the day she was born. Maybe he had been stirred by how small and lonely she had looked in the nursemaid's arms. Or perhaps it was Tris's fear that a baby would prove a more amusing target for Jared's cruel humor than the ill-fated cats and dogs that disappeared from the nursery with distressing regularity.

They stuck together, and he frequently took the brunt of Jared's tempers for her. Jared drove off one nursemaid after another with his outbursts. As Kait got older, she and Tris found safety in banding together against Jared, able to make him back off when they no longer made such an easy mark.

"Father's got to listen soon," Kait said wistfully, breaking into his thoughts.

Tris shook his head. "Not yet he won't," he said. "He won't hear a word I say, even though he and Jared argue more and more. Some days, I think they argue about saying 'good morning.'"

Kait sighed, and the bird on her gauntlet fidgeted. "Maybe mother—?"

Again, Tris indicated the negative. "Every time she tries to say something, father accuses her of favoring her children over Jared. I don't think he's ever quite gotten over Eldra's death," he added. Jared's mother died giving birth to Bricen's first-born, and it took the king nearly ten years to find the will to wed again, a decade in which young Prince Jared had little supervision and less correction as his father retreated into despair.

"Mother won't even bring it up anymore," Tris added. "She just tries to keep you out of his way."

"Uh oh," Kait whispered under her breath. "More trouble." Tris followed her gaze across the crowded great room, to the red-robed figure that stood in the hall's entrance. A hush fell over the room. Clad in the flowing blood-colored robes of a Fireclan mage, Foor Arontala, Jared's chief advisor, made his way through the crowd. The throng parted in front of him in a desperate haste to get out of his way, yet the fine-boned, porcelain-pale face that peered from beneath a heavy hood and long dark hair did not even acknowledge their presence.

"I hate him," Kait whispered in a voice that only Tris and Soterius could hear. "I wish grandmother were here. She'd squash him like a flea," she added, with a little stamping motion for good measure.

"Grandmother's gone," Tris replied tonelessly, thinking of his unsuccessful attempt to contact Bava K'aa's spirit earlier in the evening. He moved to tell Kait what happened, and then, out of long habit, stopped. Bava K'aa always kept his training such an elaborate secret that even now, he was unwilling to put it into words.

"I wish your father had been quicker to bring a new mage of his own to Shekerishet," Soterius added in a whisper. "Even a grannywitch would be better than that," he said with carefully shielded distaste.

Foor Arontala passed among the hushed partygoers as if

he did not notice their existence, gliding with preternatural smoothness through the crowd to exit on the other side of the hall, but it took several minutes before the revelry began again, and even longer before it began to sound wholehearted.

"Crone take him," Tris swore under his breath.

"He looks like She already has," Kait giggled.

Soterius took it upon himself to lighten the mood. "Do I have to remind both of you that there's a party going on?" he reprimanded with mock sternness. "Carroway's been telling tales for most of a candlemark over there," he said, gesturing, "and you've missed it."

"Is he still there?" Kait said with sudden interest. "Is there room?"

"Let's go find out," Tris said, hoping that the diversion would break his heavy mood.

Carroway, Margolan's master bard, sat in the center of a rapt audience. It was evident by the press of partygoers around him that the storyteller was building to the climax of his tale.

Carroway leaned forward, recounting the adventure from the time of Tris's great, great grandfather's rule in a hushed voice that forced his listeners to lean closer. "The Eastmark raiders pressed on, cutting their way toward the palace. Valiant men tried and failed to push them back, but still, the raiders came. The palace gates were in sight! Blood ran ankle deep on the stones and all around, the moans of the dying cried for justice." As Carroway spoke, he leaned to the side and casually lit two gray candles.

"King Hotten fought with all his might as all around him, swords clashed and the battle raged. Twice, assassins closed around him. Twice, hurled daggers nearly found their mark." With lazy grace, Carroway's arm snapped up, and *thunk, thunk*, two daggers appeared from nowhere, thudding into the woodwork behind the rearmost listener. The children screamed, then giggled at Carroway's sleight of hand.

"But the weary defenders had no more troops to spare," Carroway went on. "Now it was the eve of the Feast of the Departed—Haunts as we call it—when spirits walk most boldly among us. They say that on Haunts, the spirits can make themselves solid if they choose, and cast illusions so real that mortals cannot sense or feel the deception until—" he paused, and a well-timed small "poof" and a puff of smoke appeared by sleight of hand, "—everything so solid the night before vanishes with the morning. Knowing this, King Hotten begged his mage to do anything that would stop the invaders. The mage was nearly spent himself, and he knew that summoning a major spell would probably be his death, but he harnessed all the power he possessed and called out to the spirit of the land itself, to the Avenger Goddess, and to the souls of the dead. And with his dying breath, the fog began to change.

"From the blood-soaked stones, a mist began to rise. At first, it hovered above the street, swirling around the raiders' legs, but it grew higher and denser, until it reached the horses' bridles. Soon, it was a howling wind, and as the terrified raiders watched it took on faces and shapes, distorted by the tempest. And on that feast night so long ago, the spirits chose to take on form, to manifest themselves completely, to seem as real and solid as you or me." A thin fog was rising from Carroway's candles, swirling along the floor of the castle, sending its tendrils among the listeners who startled as they noticed it and stared at Carroway, eyes wide. As they watched, the thin veil of smoke formed itself into the figures of the story, phantom wisps in the shapes of rearing horses and fleeting ghosts.

"The spirits of Shekerishet rose to defend it from the

raiders, by the power of the dead and the will of every valiant fighter who ever died to defend king and kingdom. A howl rose above the wind, the shrieks and warning wails of the rising ghosts; and the fog was so thick that it separated the attackers from each other." Carroway's wrist flicked and two small pellets scattered from his hand, screeching and wailing as they hit the hard floor. His audience jumped out of their seats, wide-eyed with fright.

"Confounded and terrified, the attackers ran," Carroway went on. In his gray bard's robes, dimly lit by the flickering torches, he looked like something out of legend. "The wall of spirits drove them back, onto the waiting blades of the Margolan army. The ghostly guardians of the palace pushed back the enemy, pursuing the raiders until they scattered beyond the gates," he said, stretching out his hand. His audience shrieked in good-natured fright as the smoke rose at Carroway's command, shaping itself into a man-sized apparition of a skeletal fighter, poised to draw his sword from the scabbard that hung against his bony leg.

"They say that the ghosts still protect Shekerishet," Carroway said with a grin. "They say that the spirits of the castle defend it from intruders and will let no harm come to those within. They say that the curse of King Hotten's mage still carries power, and that every king's mage since then has added to it with his dying breath," Carroway continued. "And that," Carroway said, sitting back with satisfaction, "is the story of the Battle of Court Gate."

Tris chuckled as the wide-eyed children filed away, leaving their costumed storyteller to gather his belongings. Kait danced up to Carroway and blew him a teasing kiss. "I loved it!" She piped up enthusiastically. "But you've got to make it scarier." She winked at the bard. "If I hadn't already sworn never to get married, I'd pick you," she added. Tris suspected that Kait was only partly jesting, though she had known Tris's childhood friend for so long that Carroway was like a brother.

"You're going to give her nightmares," Tris joked, rescuing the blushing minstrel.

Carroway grinned. "I hope so. That's what Haunts is all about." He stood, shaking out the folds of his cloak. A group of costumed revelers passed them, arms entwined, singing loudly and badly off-key.

"Good Haunts to you, bard and all," one of them called out, tossing a golden coin to Carroway, which the storyteller caught in midair.

"Good Haunts to you, sir!" Carroway called in acknowledgment, holding up the coin and then, with a flourish, making it disappear to the delight of the partygoers. Carroway was as tall as Tris but thinner, moving with a dancer's grace. His long, blue-black hair framed features so handsome that they veered toward beauty. Light blue eyes, with long lashes, sparkled with intelligence and a keen wit.

Ban Soterius appeared at Carroway's side. "Don't let the priestesses hear you call it that," their friend warned in mock seriousness. "It's Feast of the Departed, young man." Soterius grinned and rubbed his knuckles. "I got reminded of that more than once when I was in school."

Carroway grinned. "Haunts is a lot easier to say," he replied archly. "Besides, what else are you supposed to call a holiday for dead people?"

"I suspect you're missing some deeper point on that," Tris laughed.

"I'll see you three later," Kait said, reaching up to calm her falcon as a noisy group of revelers passed by. "Good Feast to you," she called. "Don't get into too much trouble."

"Easy for you to say," Tris rejoined. He turned to

Carroway as Kait blended into the departing crowd. "Come on, or we'll be late for the feast." The three young men were easily Margolan's most eligible bachelors, not yet twenty summers old, and were the targets of the court's ambitious mothers. While Soterius relished the attention, and was rarely without a lady on his arm, Carroway was more likely to choose his partners from among the castle's entertainers, singers or musicians whose talent he respected, and who were less star-struck over his court position and friendship with Tris.

To the chagrin of many of the court mothers, and even, sometimes Tris suspected, his mother Sarae, Tris had successfully evaded the matchmakers. Jared's escapades made Tris wary, and he had yet to meet any of the local nobles' daughters with whom he could carry an interesting conversation more than once. His self-imposed solitude was in sharp contrast to Jared's wantonness, and Tris was well aware that some of the court wags invented their own, less flattering explanations for his unwillingness to choose and discard consorts with the same regularity as the rest of the court. Let them talk, he thought. He had no intention of bringing a bride into Shekerishet with Jared nearby, and even less desire to subject children of his own to Jared's cruelties.

Perhaps some day, he thought wistfully, watching as Soterius and Carroway bantered easily with the costumed girls who passed them. *Someday, when I'm safely out of Shekerishet, in permanent residence at father's country manor, far from court, far from parties, far from Jared.*

"Tell your fortunes?" a voice rasped from behind them. Tris turned, startled, to find a bent old woman in an alcove, gesturing with a gnarled finger. He knew at once that she was one of the palace's ghosts, although this night, the spirits walked openly, seemingly solid. "For you, Prince Drayke, and your friends, there is no charge."

"Where did she come from?" Soterius murmured.

Carroway shrugged. "Let's go see what our fortune holds."

"I'm not really sure I want to know," Soterius balked, but Carroway was already dragging Tris by the sleeve.

"Come on," Carroway teased. "I want to know how famous a bard I'm going to become."

"Speak for yourself," Soterius muttered under his breath. "Really, I'm not sure—"

"I'm with Ban," Tris murmured.

"No spirit of adventure. Come on," the bard insisted.

The crone looked up as they approached, and her jaw worked a wad of dreamweed. A bit of spit dribbled down her stubbly chin as she pushed back a lock of greasy hair and nodded, taking in everything with piercing green eyes that seemed to see through them. Her dress was made of faded silk, expensive once but now long past its glory; and she smelled of spice and musk.

The seer sat before a low, intricately carved table, its worn surface wrought with complicated runes. In the center of the table was a crystal globe, set atop a golden stand. Both the globe and its stand were of much greater quality than Tris anticipated, and he looked more closely at the crone.

She raised a bony finger and leveled it at the bard's chest. "You, first, minstrel," she rasped, and motioned for Carroway to kneel. She looked up at Tris and Soterius, and her eyes narrowed. "Wait in silence."

She hummed a raspy chant, ancient and strange, intoned just below Tris's ability to catch the words. Her gnarled hands caressed the crystal, brushing its surface, shaping themselves around it gently, hovering just above its smooth contours.

The globe began to glow, a cold, swirling blue that began at its nexus and gradually filled the whole crystal with a brilliant flare of blue. The crone closed her eyes, humming and swaying.

When she spoke, it was in the clear tones of a young girl, without a trace of the smoky rasp they heard before. "You are the maker of tales and the taker of lives," said the girl's voice, bell-like and preternatural. "Your tales will be the greatest Margolan has ever known, but sorrow, yes, great sorrow will teach you your songs. Take heed, dream spinner," the voice warned. "Your journey lies among the immortals. Guard well your soul."

Tris realized he was holding his breath. Soterius stared, unmoving. Carroway, eyes wide, watched the swaying seer with amazement. The seer's face relaxed, as if a curtain had fallen, and the voice went silent.

"Let's get out of here," Soterius said.

"Stay," the crone commanded, and while she did not raise her rasping voice, the grated command froze Soterius in place. "You will come, soldier," she said as Carroway, still dazed, scrambled to his feet. Ashen, Soterius obeyed.

From the voluminous pockets of her frayed robe, the hag withdrew a well-worn pack of cards. Jalbet cards. Tris recognized the stock-in-trade of roadside oracles and the parlor amusement of ladies at court. Deftly, the crone laid down four cards.

"The Ox," the crone grated, naming the cards. "The Black River. The Coin. The Dark Lady." The crone gave a harsh laugh. "These speak for the Goddess," she rasped. "Look with care."

"I don't understand—"

"Silence!" Her twisted finger stroked the first worn card.

"The Ox is the card of strength. Your health and strength will serve you well, soldier. Together with the Black River, the cards speak of war," she spoke as if to herself, her dry voice taking on a singsong quality. "You will prosper. That is the tale of the coin. But," she hissed, as one broken nail quivered above the last card, "beware. For your journey shall be taken along dark roads, in the company of the dead and the undead. You will be among the servants of the Dark Lady. Guard well your soul."

Soterius swallowed hard, staring at the cards. He gave a nervous glance at the globe, which remained clear and unremarkable. The crone looked up at Tris, and wordlessly beckoned. His heart thudding, Tris obeyed, settling nervously into his seat as Soterius hurried out of the way.

"Give me your hand," the crone commanded, reaching across the table. Slowly, Tris extended his hand, turning it palm up as the witch drew it toward her.

"A great quest will come to you, Son of the Lady," the crone whispered, tracing a barely visible line on Tris's palm with her nail. "Who can see its end?" she mumbled, her nail tracing the folds of Tris's palm. "Many souls hang in the balance. Your way lies in shadow." She caught her breath, her finger trembling.

"What is it?" Tris breathed, afraid to speak above a whisper.

"You are indeed the Lady's own," the crone rasped. "Your hand betrays no time of dying."

"Everyone dies."

"As the Lady sees fit. Your time is of her making. You are truly in the Lady's hands," she whispered. "Guard well your soul, or all is lost." Then, before their eyes, the crone's image wavered, and while her mouth moved, they could not hear her words. Tris could feel a strange power pulling at the spirit, a force he could not identify. The spirit seemed to disintegrate, fading first to haze and then to nothing.

Soterius tugged at Tris's shirt, nearly pulling him to his feet. "Come on!" the soldier urged, his voice just shy of panic. "Let's go."

The smell of roasting meat wafted from the banquet hall. A roaring fire crackled in the huge hearth and musicians played a lively tune as the guests hustled in. With a grin, Carroway joined his companion minstrels, eagerly accepting the lute that one of his friends pressed into his hands. Tris could see Jared at the front of the room near the king's table, angrily berating a servant. Tris saw the studied control in the seneschal's face as Zachar struggled to show neither his disapproval nor his embarrassment. Kait motioned Tris toward two seats next to her, and he and Soterius slipped through the crowd to take their places. Kait's falcon shifted, nervously, and Kait signaled to the falconer, who accepted her bird onto his gauntleted arm and whisked the predator away to quieter mews.

"Your father's never allowed falcons at the table in the manor," Soterius whispered to Kait. "I'll have to tell him how it's done at court."

Kait gave him a bantering look of disappointment. "Another fashion you can share with the rural nobility," she said with feigned ennui.

Tris glanced at Soterius, aware that the other tensed. "What's wrong," Tris asked, scanning the crowd which awaited King Bricen's arrival.

Soterius shook his head, and while his expression was neutral, his eyes showed their concern. "The guards assigned to the feast aren't the ones I ordered," he said barely above a whisper. "I'm going to have a word with the lieutenant over there," he said. But just as Soterius moved to leave the dais, a trumpet's herald announced the arrival of King Bricen of Margolan.

"Later," he murmured, frustrated at the delay. Tris watched Bricen and Queen Sarae process through the throng, stopping to greet the well-wishers who pressed around them. His father's ruddy exuberance told Tris that the king had enjoyed a few pints of ale in his private rooms before joining in the celebration. Sarae, always so coolly self-possessed, seemed to glide across the floor, graciously accepting the courtesies and bows of the ladies and nobles who formed an aisle among the tables. Bricen assisted Sarae onto the dais just as Jared concluded haranguing the servant, and Bricen glowered at his eldest son, whose mute glare in return made no pretense to shield the tensions between father and son from onlookers.

"Good Gentles," the king boomed. "Tonight, let both the living and the dead make merry! As we are now, so once were they. And by the Goddess, as they are now, so we shall someday be, so best we eat and drink while we may!"

The king took his seat and washed his hands in the proffered bowl. The cupbearers began their work, and a procession of kitchen staff followed the steward to the king's table, bearing steaming trenchers of roasted game. Carroway and his fellow musicians struck up a jolly tune, and the buzz of conversation, interrupted by the king's arrival, resumed its din. But despite the festive atmosphere, Tris felt a chill settle over him. The ghost's cryptic warning repeated in his mind. Glancing around the great room, Tris could see none of the palace spirits that were usually so evident, even to those without a trace of magical talent. Never could he recall the ghosts' absence from such a feast, especially on Haunts.

As dinner wore on, Tris could sense Soterius's increasing tension. At the first opportunity, Soterius excused himself and slipped over to speak with the ranking lieutenant. In a few moments, he returned looking no less concerned. "What's going on?" Tris murmured.

"I don't like it. The lieutenant said he was ordered to change the guards by Jared." Soterius gave a barely perceptible shake of his head. "Look around. They're all new guards, the younger ones who fancy Jared's talk of a bigger army. I'd ordered more of the seasoned men, whose loyalty to the king I don't doubt."

Tris looked out over the crowd. Soterius was correct. For months, Jared had been visiting the barracks. To "raise the spirits" of the guards, the prince replied in answer to his father's questions. Bricen, perhaps tired of the incessant arguments with his heir, let it go at that. Now, Tris felt his misgivings renewed about Jared's sudden interest. Of equal concern, he noted, scanning the guests, were the faces he saw—and did not see—among the partygoers. Few of the older nobles were in attendance, lords and barons whose loyalty to the crown was absolute. Those who figured among the guests looked ill at ease, a rarity at one of Bricen's legendary fetes. Instead, Tris saw many of the newer nobles, landowners whose first-generation status had been won on the field of combat or bestowed by recent favor. And like the guards, Tris knew that these newly titled men looked favorably on Jared's fiery rhetoric of expansion and conquest, finding it much more exciting that Bricen's stable statesmanship.

On pretext of returning a poor goblet of wine, Tris signaled to Zachar. A whispered question and confirmation gave Tris his answer, though it did nothing to allay his concern.

"Zachar says that many of the older nobles responded late to the invitation as if they hadn't received notice in time," Tris related to Soterius under his breath. "Very strange. And there seemed to be some pressing reason in each case why they couldn't attend."

"You think they know something we should?"

Tris stole a glance toward Jared's end of the table, where Foor Arontala sat next to Jared, toying with the food on his trencher but consuming nothing. "Maybe there was some 'help' creating those pressing reasons," Tris said, looking away as Arontala's unblinking gaze leveled in his direction.

"So what do we do about it?" Soterius asked, his words muffled by a bite of venison.

Tris paused. "I want to get a look at what's going on in Arontala's workshop."

Soterius choked on his meat, and the servant behind him had to pound on his back. "You want to do what?" he rasped after he took a sip of wine. "Are you crazy?"

Tris did not reply for a moment, mindful that Jared's eyes were on them. When Jared resumed his conversation with the red-robed mage, Tris glanced again at Soterius. "If Jared's up to something, you can bet Arontala's behind it. And we won't know what it is until we get a look in that workshop." Although he was not prepared to recount the ghost's warning, Tris already concluded that if such a thing as a "soulcatcher" posed a threat, then the first place to go looking for it was the library of the Fireclan mage.

"You know I'm not much for magic," Soterius retorted under his breath. "But I believe my guards when they tell me that the doors to Arontala's rooms are spelled tight. No one comes or goes without him."

Tris chewed thoughtfully on a leg of mutton. "Then let's try the window."

Soterius bit into his bread. "No. Uh huh. Not a good idea. Besides, I thought you hated heights."

"I do," Tris admitted. "But it's for a good cause. Come

on, you've been dying to get me back up in your climbing rig ever since last year. And you know you always like to try some stunt on Haunts, just to give Zachar a few more gray hairs." He chuckled. "One year you decided we should rappel from the tower and we nearly got shot by the guards. The next year you decided to try to swing from the sleeping rooms to the other side of the courtyard, but you landed in the stable instead."

"Thank the Mother and Childe it was hay and not manure," Soterius replied dryly. "You're serious about this, aren't you?"

Tris nodded. "Too many things aren't what they should be. We'll get our chance when dinner is over, and the festival moves down into the town."

The rest of the long feast went uneventfully, with a series of jugglers, acrobats, and magicians that even lifted Tris's mood. Carroway, the mastermind behind the evening's festivities, looked quite pleased with himself as he fussed over his actor friends, adjusting the elaborate costumes and makeup in the far corner of the feast hall and watching with pride as one group of performers after another strove to outdo themselves before the king. As Carroway finished a long, haunting ballad which was among Sarae's favorites, Bricen, showing the same gusto in his feasting for which he was legendary on the hunt, clapped and roared his approval, prompting even louder accolades from the guests. But Tris thought his mother looked distracted, as if she might be marking time until she could make her exit to the private rooms. That was unusual, he thought with concern, for his mother—though never as boisterous as Bricen—was known for her graciousness as a hostess and was usually quite partial to Carroway's ballads.

As the bells in the tower tolled midnight, the outer doors to the great room swung open. A black-robed figure, its face shrouded by a deep cowl, stood in the doorway bearing a glittering chalice. Soundlessly, the figure bowed in deference to Bricen, who stood playing his role in the drama.

"Greetings, Grandmother Spirit," the king intoned. "We are ready for the march." From behind the robed figure of the Crone emerged three costumed actors, each in one of the other faces of the quartern Goddess: Mother, Childe and Lover. Four faces of one goddess, the light aspects of a single deity. The king offered his arm to Sarae, and together they led the procession down the aisle toward the waiting players, the tables emptying as the other guests filed in behind them. Tris saw Soterius catch Carroway's eye and make a slight gesture; the minstrel nodded in acknowledgment as the procession left the feast hall.

Tris pulled Soterius into a side corridor, letting the rowdy supper guests push past. Carroway dodged into the hallway a few minutes later. "What's going on?" the bard asked as the last of the revelers passed. The three friends moved farther into the shadows, and Tris cast an anxious glance toward the torchlit main hall to make sure they were alone.

"Father and the rest of the family will take leave of the guests at the main gates," he hissed. "As late as it is, they should all head up to bed. Once it's quiet, we can head for the tower and climb down from there."

Soterius looked askance at Tris. "Let's be clear about royal prerogative here," he objected. "Tris has a hare-brained idea that's likely to get us all charred into bits or turned into frogs," the guard complained, his expression resigned as Tris explained the night's work to Carroway.

"I'm game," the minstrel chimed in when Tris was finished. "We bards are quite accepting of magic," he said with mock snootiness aimed at Soterius, who scowled.

"Unlike those plebeian military types who only believe in what they see. Count me in."

"What I see worries me enough," Soterius groused. "Wait here. I'll go get my gear."

END

Read the full adventure in *The Summoner*, Book One in the Chronicles of the Necromancer.

ABOUT THE AUTHOR

Gail Z. Martin is the author of *Vengeance*, the sequel to *Scourge* in her Darkhurst epic fantasy series, and *Assassin's Honor* in the new Assassins of Landria series. *Tangled Web* is the newest novel in the series that includes both *Deadly Curiosities* and *Vendetta* and two collections, *Trifles and Folly* and *Trifles and Folly 2*, the latest in her urban fantasy series set in Charleston, SC. *Shadow and Flame* is the fourth book in the Ascendant Kingdoms Saga and *The Shadowed Path* and *The Dark Road* are in the Jonmarc Vahanian Adventures series. Co-authored with Larry N. Martin are *Iron and Blood,* the first novel in the Jake Desmet Adventures series and the *Storm and Fury* collection; and the *Spells, Salt, & Steel: New Templars series (Mark Wojcik, monster hunter)*. Under her urban fantasy M/M paranormal romance pen name of Morgan Brice, *Witchbane* and *Badlands* are the newest releases.

She is also the author of *Ice Forged, Reign of Ash,* and *War of Shadows* in The Ascendant Kingdoms Saga, The Chronicles of The Necromancer series (*The Summoner, The Blood King, Dark Haven, Dark Lady's Chosen*) and The Fallen Kings Cycle (*The Sworn, The Dread*).

Gail's work has appeared in over 35 US/UK anthologies. Newest anthologies include: *The Big Bad 2, Athena's Daughters, Heroes, Space, Contact Light, With Great Power, The Weird Wild West, The Side of Good/The Side of Evil, Alien Artifacts, Cinched: Imagination Unbound, Realms of Imagi-*

nation, Clockwork Universe: Steampunk vs. Aliens, Gaslight and Grimm, Baker Street Irregulars, Journeys, Hath no Fury, and *Afterpunk: Steampunk Tales of the Afterlife.*

Find out more at www.GailZMartin.com, on facebook.com/WinterKingdoms, on twitter.com/GailZMartin, on Pinterest.com/gzmartin, and at DisquietingVisions.com.

OTHER BOOKS BY GAIL Z. MARTIN

Darkhurst

Scourge

Vengeance

Ascendant Kingdoms

Ice Forged

Reign of Ash

War of Shadows

Shadow and Flame

Chronicles of the Necromancer / Fallen Kings Cycle

The Summoner

The Blood King

Dark Haven

Dark Lady's Chosen

The Sworn

The Dread

The Shadowed Path

The Dark Road

Deadly Curiosities

Deadly Curiosities

Vendetta

Tangled Web

Trifles and Folly

Trifles and Folly 2

Other books by Gail Z. Martin and Larry N. Martin

Jake Desmet Adventures

Iron & Blood

Storm & Fury

Spells, Salt, & Steel: New Templars

Spells, Salt, & Steel

Open Season

Deep Trouble

Close Encounters

Printed in Great Britain
by Amazon